Michael MacMurdy

# CHANGES WROUGHT

## BOOK 1
### A BLACK ALBATROS

Changes Wrought Book 1
Copyright © 2025 by Michael MacMurdy. All rights reserved.
Second Edition

First edition originally published by Newman Springs.

No part of this book may be used or reproduced in any manner whatsoever without written permission, except in the case of brief quotations embodied in critical articles and reviews. For more information, e-mail all inquiries to info@seacoastpress.com

Cover artwork by Jim Laurier

**SEACOAST PRESS**

Published by SEACOAST PRESS
1 New Hampshire Ave | Suite 125 |
Portsmouth, NH 03801 | USA
603-546-2812 | www.seacoastpress.com
Printed in the United States of America
ISBN-13: 978-1-966799-25-2 (Paperback)
ISBN-13: 978-1-966799-26-9 (Hardcover)

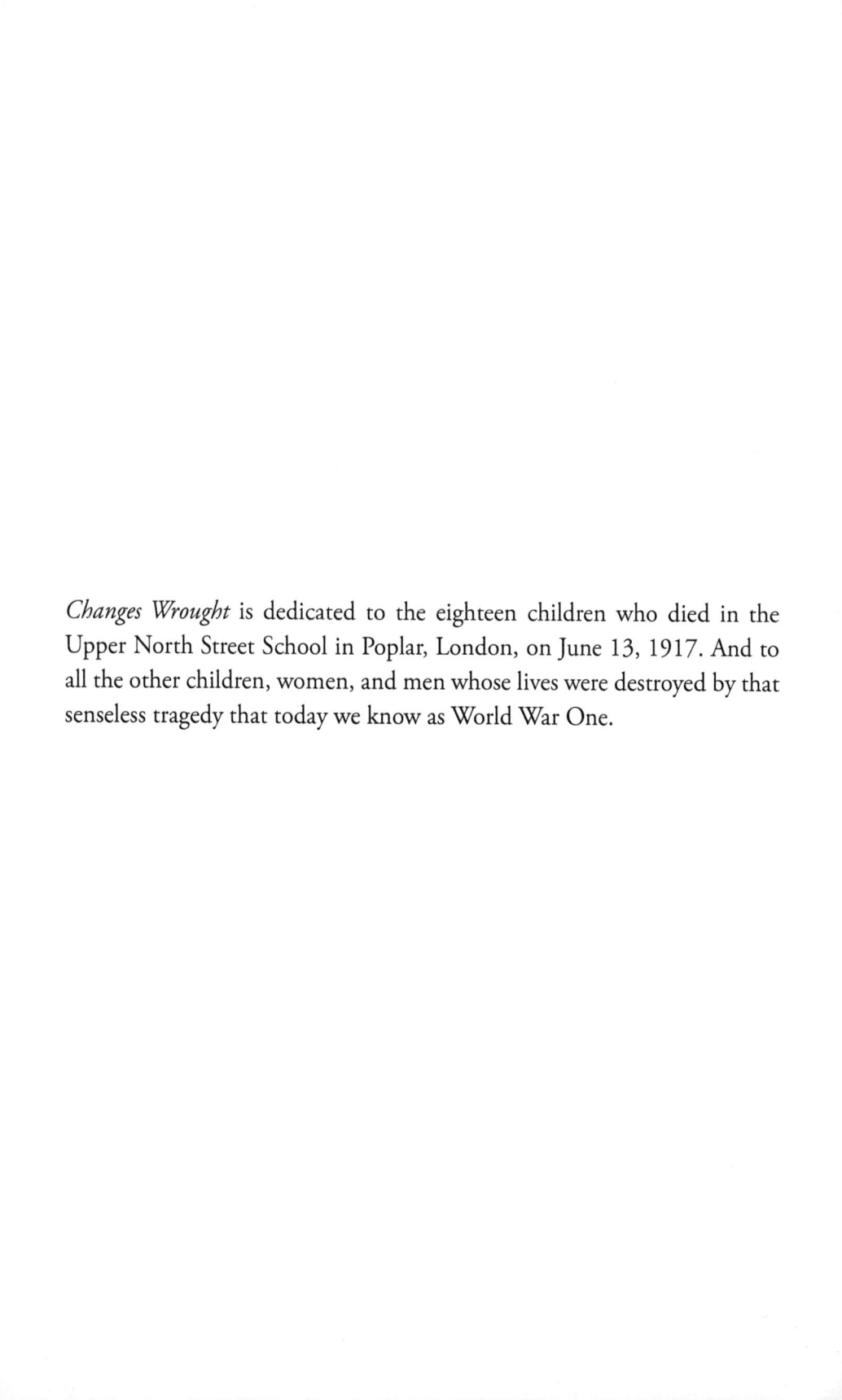

*Changes Wrought* is dedicated to the eighteen children who died in the Upper North Street School in Poplar, London, on June 13, 1917. And to all the other children, women, and men whose lives were destroyed by that senseless tragedy that today we know as World War One.

What passing-bells for these who die as cattle?
— Only the monstrous anger of the guns.
Only the stuttering rifles' rapid rattle
Can patter out their hasty orisons.
No mockeries now for them; no prayers nor bells;
Nor any voice of mourning save the choirs,—
The shrill, demented choirs of wailing shells;
And bugles calling for them from sad shires.

**Anthem for Doomed Youth**
Wilfred Owen

# Contents

All by Oneself ...................................................................1
Triplanes and the Department Senior Secretary ..................14
Messines Ridge ................................................................20
The Wildflowers Café .......................................................32
The Royal Navy in France ................................................49
A Welcome to Flanders ....................................................64
Jousting ..........................................................................80
Second Lieutenant Phillip Newin .....................................86
Trees .............................................................................110
A Dinner Party ..............................................................134
The Spartans .................................................................142
A Black Albatros ............................................................155
A Liberal Party MP? ......................................................161
The Menin Road ...........................................................168
Home Defense Duty ......................................................183
Mutiny ..........................................................................198
Horizontal Relaxation ...................................................211
A Story to Tell ...............................................................223
The Lady in Black .........................................................231

| | |
|---|---|
| Pete Catches a Break | 241 |
| The RE8 | 268 |
| Point-Blank Range | 280 |
| Lutz | 294 |
| England | 308 |
| | |
| Glossary | 325 |
| Author's Notes | 332 |
| About the Author | 337 |

# All by Oneself

*66 Squadron RFC, Sopwith Scout Fighter Aircraft*
*Liettres Aerodrome, Northern France*
*July 31, 1917, 0315 hours*

Pete Newin bit his lip as the clouds and rain closed in, reducing his world to the hum of the rotary engine, the dim flight instruments, and the water sliding across tight fabric as the Sopwith pushed through the wet darkness. A diffuse bubble of life in the dead gray of a Flanders morning. He looked down and to his left without moving his head—the little road he'd been tracking northeast from the aerodrome had disappeared. He checked the altimeter at 3000 feet and eased the control column forward, brought the throttle back a notch and tweaked the petrol lever for low-altitude cruise. Listened to the hum of the Le Rhône rotary engine for a few seconds—all good. He sat straight up and held his body still…the pressure on his backside, the wind across his face, the little bubble of the inclinometer centered. The airplane was in straight and level flight. He didn't bother to look at the airspeed indicator; the Sopwith was doing eighty mph, give or take two knots. His leather jacket swept the wind and rain aside, but the water, mixed with the constant spray of castor oil off the Le Rhône, had soaked through his scarf and was working its way down his back. At least he was awake, although he could use another cup of coffee. But he'd left his flight thermos back at the aerodrome—there wouldn't be time for coffee breaks today. Not on this mission.

The clouds thinned, the drumming of the rain on the taut fabric lessened, and the dark ground came into view again through the gray haze. He blinked and wiped his goggles, but there wasn't much to see. The sky was pitch-black to his left and only a little lighter to his right. He made out a road, and a few buildings here and there. At least with some ground contact, it was easier to keep the wings level. Scanned out in front, and his eyes picked out a break in the gray-black murk. A little silver-blue line, parallel to his course. A few seconds later he picked out two more lines, followed by a much larger one. The Dunkirk Canal.

He studied the ground to his left...no. To his right...there—the highway he was looking for. At least he hoped it was. He turned ten degrees right to parallel it and visualized his map. The highway should swing right, then come back left as it approached Hazebrouck. He leveled the wings and checked his magnetic compass, for whatever that was worth. It was bouncing around in the general direction of northeast. He ran through the sequence again, like an acolyte reciting his Sunday chant:

Hazebrouck.

Follow the railroad to Bailleul.

Five minutes east to Messines.

Fifteen degrees right to cross the front line. Pick up the river and Ypres Canal around Comines.

Follow the river to Menin.

Twenty degrees left to avoid the other aerodromes and hold that heading for three and a half minutes. And if he got that far, make a last right turn to east for the run in.

To attack heavily defended Heule aerodrome.

All by himself, in a single-gunned Sopwith Pup.

For the moment, he didn't have much more to do than hold the wings level. Took a drink of water from his bottle; spat out the first oily tasting one and swallowed the second. Shifted in his seat and rotated his shoulders. Settled into his seat as the uncomfortable numbers came back to him. He figured at least a sixty percent chance he'd be dead an hour from now. If he lived through the attack, fifty-fifty he'd end up as a prisoner of war. His chances of making it back to the British side without serious injury…pretty damn small. He supposed he should be thinking about the significance of life. Thinking about God, or his mother or late father. But all he could think about right then was how shitty he felt after three hours of sleep, soaked and sitting on a wooden seat in an eighty-mile-per-hour wind, his face and mouth coated with castor oil courtesy of his Le Rhône rotary. And this was nothing compared to what was waiting for him on the other side of the line.

He wiped his goggles and caught a glimpse of an airplane in front of him, before the mist swallowed it up. Five little Sopwith Pups spaced one minute apart, to avoid hitting each other in the darkness. Five little lemmings marching to the cliff. Five experienced pilots, but no flight commanders in the group. Orders from above. He couldn't imagine why.

He spotted the town four minutes after crossing the canal. It was still dark, but the small canal and the rail lines showed up and he'd seen them enough times before: Hazebrouck. He swung the Pup east and gently leveled the wings. Shifted back and forth in his seat, trying to ease the stress on his back. Fired a few rounds from his Vickers .303. Do something other than sit and wait and think. *Juliette? Would he ever look into those beautiful blue eyes again?*

The rotary engine hummed along, pulling the Pup through the wet darkness. It would be a perfect time for the engine to let go, but the chaps had it tuned to perfection. Too bad. He cocked his head to the side. Did

## ALL BY ONESELF

he really want that? Did he really want the engine to let go now, still on the British side? He supposed not—one must do one's duty. Bailleul Aerodrome was coming up on his left. There was lots of activity down there—busy day coming up for the reconnaissance chaps. He turned ten degrees left and looked for the road into Messines, although trying to pick out a particular dirt road on a dark and wet Flanders morning was a fool's errand. The sky out in front of him lightened as he came out of the rain showers, and he sensed Messiness Ridge, which passed for high ground in Flanders, rising above the ground fog. He picked the most likely looking road and tracked it east. If he missed the town by a mile or two, it shouldn't matter.

Some colonel from 9th Wing had come down to brief them on the operation. He'd taken the podium and swept the room with his eyes, paused, and began speaking slowly. "During the last two weeks, over *three thousand* British and French guns have fired over *three million* shells into the Hun positions in Flanders—a barrage *unprecedented* in the history of mankind." The colonel paused, presumably for effect.

"The day after tomorrow, the thirty-first of July, 1917, as directed by Field Marshal Douglas Haig, the British Expeditionary Force will launch a major offensive in Flanders. Spearheaded by our newest Mark IV tanks, the army will smash through the Hun defenses; recapture the Belgian ports of Zeebrugge and Ostende and the enemy's bomber bases at Ghent. This will deprive the Hun of his most important U-boat bases and the ability to hit London with his Gotha bombers." The colonel paused a second time before bringing his tempo up.

"The victory achieved by the British Expeditionary Force, with the untiring support of the Royal Flying Corps, will be the first real nail in the coffin of the German Army. With control of the Belgian ports and the Flanders high ground, and with the Americans on the way, there will be no stopping the British Army and the Royal Flying Corps. We will be in Berlin by October, and home in England for Christmas."

The colonel finished on that high note and looked out expectantly at them...and twenty-odd pilots had stared back. But the best news was yet to come—five lucky pilots were to make single-ship attacks on five German aerodromes. The silence from the pilots had been deafening as they took that bit in.

Messines—he was passing just south of the town. There was less than a mile to go to the line. He started the clock and turned right. The airplane mushed its way into and out of the turn, letting him know it wasn't happy about the extra hundred pounds of bombs and release mechanism on board. He grabbed a quick last drink of water, wincing as the word "last" passed through his consciousness. Glanced at his oil and fuel quantities and checked the time: 03:29. He looked down over the railing: he could just make out the darker lines of the forward British trenches. In twenty-one minutes the officers would blow their whistles and the chaps would go up the ladders. They'd push through the mud and the waterlogged shell holes and the barbed wire. Into the Hun machine-gun fire while the shrapnel shells burst a few feet above their heads, the lead balls sweeping across the ground like a broom through dust.

He eased the Pup up into the safety of the gray mist. Focused on holding the wings level and got his map out. Took a last look at the black line he'd plotted: about 8000 yards to the river on this heading. Call it three minutes, if the forecast winds were close. Twenty left at Menin for three and a half minutes, followed by a hard right turn for the run-in. He put his map away and tensed his abdomen—the butterflies were back, flapping about his stomach as he watched the second hand make its little circle. At 140 seconds he swallowed hard and eased the column forward. He felt the Pup descend, and a few seconds later the dark terrain came into view as she slid out of the clouds. It wasn't quite dawn, but there was enough light to see the shine of the river on his right. He motored ahead and picked up the silver line of the Ypres Canal. Swung left to parallel the river. He made out the outline of Comines just right of the Pup's nose; Wervicq would only be a few miles farther on. Still no ground fire from the Huns. Too dark. Too early. Just another lovely morning in Flanders for them—for another twenty minutes or so. Attack and disrupt. His orders were to attack and disrupt. Besides the single Vickers, the Pup was carrying four twenty-pound Coopers. He'd drop those in a string on the first pass. Get the extra weight off. He was abeam Comines now, still all quiet.

He eased the Pup up into the patchy bottoms of the clouds. Staring into gray nothingness was like closing his eyes at night when he wasn't sleepy—it was guaranteed to get the wheels turning. He came back to the dilemma that had been dogging him ever since Captain Fleming had told him he was one of the lucky five pilots. Could he get away with three passes? Cause plenty of disruption while having some chance of surviving? Stay above 200 feet? Hitting a target with a machine gun, and conversely being hit, was all about proper aim and bullet dispersion. The greater the range, the greater the dispersion. He drummed his gloved fingers on the throttle lever and sighed. The chaps on the ground didn't get to decide when to stop advancing. And if he did that, played it safe and lived, he'd live with it for the rest of his life. Live with knowing some chaps on the ground likely died because Pete Newin didn't want to. No, he'd press the attack as long as he could. Maybe the Huns would shoot the Pup to pieces; he'd crash-land and live through the war. That would be ironic—on this mission, the closest to an RFC suicide mission he'd ever heard of. But more likely, he would die this morning. By a Hun machine-gun bullet in the gut or the head. Or worse, by fire from the Pup's unprotected twenty-five-gallon fuel and oil tank, two feet in front of his knees. The Pup would spiral down and smash into the ground. The Huns would souvenir what they could from the airplane; throw some mud over his mangled body and go to breakfast.

He spotted Menin railway station through some breaks in the clouds. All quiet down there, but the bomber chaps would be along soon enough. He turned northeast and restarted the clock. Squirmed in his seat, mouth dry and stomach tight. Swallowed hard—it wouldn't be long now. He tapped the trigger button with his thumb; found the unfamiliar bomb release with his left hand. They'd rigged it for single release: four pulls, one after the other. He needed to find the aerodrome without overflying it, without letting the Huns know he was there. The second hand completed another circuit: 120 seconds.

150 seconds.

He slid the Pup down out of the clouds and wiped his goggles clear. Looked out front, to his left, to his right. The Courtrai highway and the canal were diverging off to the right. He didn't see an aerodrome or a large town in front of him, so he might be in the right place. He checked the second hand again. It was on the two…on the three. When it pointed straight down, he'd turn. Nice poetic touch—he hadn't picked up on that in his preflight planning. Last stop—straight down…*and…now*. He rolled hard right and pulled the Pup around to southeast. Leveled the wings and restarted the clock, his heart pounding. *Breathe, Pete. Breathe.*

He spotted a darker, indistinct area in front of him. Courtrai. He turned ten right to point at the center of it—that should take him straight to Heule. Just northeast of Heule was Ceurne Aerodrome, but today's target was the Albatros fighters of Von Richtofen's Jagdgeschwader 1, and Intel had them at Heule. He glanced at the clock: forty seconds. He should be able to see it now. He strained his eyes…fields, a little road, light rain.

Fifty seconds.

Sixty seconds.

The town was clearly visible—had he missed the aerodrome? If he had to fly around in circles looking for it—he rested his eyes for a couple of seconds and looked again… There. Just left of the nose…something was out of place. Three of them—big and boxy. Hangars. But nothing that looked like a landing field or airplanes, which meant he was on the back side. Lucky. But he needed some maneuvering room and he eased the Pup back into the clouds. He'd go past the aerodrome and come back around, to run down the line of airplanes. He tried a little prayer as the Pup motored along unconcerned, but his heart wasn't in it. Took a deep breath, and a second one. Pushed the Pup out of the clouds and sliced back into a left turn. The hardest part was over.

He picked up the hangars again as the Pup came around the turn. Pushed the nose down further and rolled out, pointed at the east edge of the field, and the overburdened Pup wobbled under its unaccustomed bomb load, like a farmer's wagon with hay bales stacked ten feet high. *Easy on the controls, Pete.* The armaments officer had told him to porpoise the airplane up and down if the bombs hung up—that he might be able to shake them off. *Great.* The Pup was picking up speed in the descent, the wind pushing harder past his face. He spotted a light-colored airplane, and a second one. Held his heading, judging height and distance…there were at least eight airplanes lined up. He pushed the nose down another notch and turned to run down the line of airplanes. Spotted some ground crew moving around like ants in the semi-darkness. Smiled for the first time that day. *It's wake-up time, fellows.*

The first little flash from the ground. Someone had seen him, but it was only rifle fire. He was drifting right of the line of airplanes and made a quick left turn to compensate. Held the release handle with his left hand. *Don't jerk it and break the damn thing, Pete.* He'd never dropped a bomb in his life but if he flew his backside over the target, the bombs would be on line. They said judging long-short was more difficult than left-right, especially without a bombsight, but he had a nice long line of airplanes to work with.

He focused on the middle airplane: a single-seat Albatros fighter. It looked like he'd found the right aerodrome. His gunsight tracked through the line of airplanes as the Pup rushed toward the ground. As the sight reached the Albatros he pulled the release handle. The Pup twitched as the bomb came off.

He pulled it twice more; felt each bomb come off. He was far too low for comfort, and with the feeling that every German on the aerodrome was watching him as they reached for their weapons. He came back hard with the column as he let the fourth bomb go; the Pup bottomed out and began to rise. He banked her forty-five degrees right, still climbing, looking over his shoulder. His eyes snapped shut as a yellow-white flash seared the semi-darkness, quickly followed by two more. He blinked his eyes open and looked. Nodded. The first bomb had hit short, but the next two blasted the tail sections of a pair of Albatros fighters. But he'd only seen three explosions—the fourth must have been a dud. He brought the nose down and rolled out of the turn as the Pup went into the clouds. At least the bombs were off and he had a normal Sopwith Pup to work with. He allowed himself to drone through the clouds for twenty seconds—breathing, hoping the pounding of his heart would ease. Hoping the Pup's wings were something close to level. He eased the column forward and she responded like a loyal hound—follow her master anywhere. He made a one-eighty back toward the aerodrome, and if the Huns hadn't been awake before, they sure would be now.

He was tight to the aerodrome and swung hard left to get some turning room. Winced as a searchlight caught him; looked away from it and found the line of airplanes. The two damaged ones stood out—knocked out of place in the otherwise straight and ordered line, smoke wafting above them. He focused on the nearest airplane. Walking bullets from a single Vickers down a line of airplanes would be a waste of time—time he didn't have. Better to put one more Albatros out of the fight. He rolled back right and steepened the dive as the first stream of tracers reached toward him.

A second stream rose through the haze. He came back left and pulled the gunsight to the parked Hun. Steadied to fire, sensing a third stream, and now a fourth—with much larger flashes. He glanced over before focusing on his target again. *Might be one of their new thirty-seven-millimeter cannons. Wonderful. Maybe Hindenburg was visiting Heule today. Or the kaiser.* Bullets were passing above him, below him, and out in front. Gunsight steady on the Albatros, he pushed the trigger button and got the familiar *pop, pop, pop* from his pathetically slow-firing Vickers eight-millimeter. But the bullets were on target and the Albatros twitched from the impacts.

Ting. Ting. Crack.

Sparks flew in front of him and a bullet cracked the windscreen a foot from his nose. His Vickers stopped firing, even though he was still pushing the trigger button. He hunkered down in the seat and pulled straight up as hard as he dared; sensed the wing spars groaning under the load. Winced at the telltale *tap tapping* of bullets punching through straining fabric as the Pup rose, followed by a metallic *twang* next to his right ear as a bullet cut a support wire.

His eyes went wide. He'd overdone the pull and the Pup's nose was almost in the vertical. He pushed over as he approached the clouds, tracers still crisscrossing in front of him, and kept the push going for another two seconds as the safety of the gray closed around the Pup. He neutralized the control column. Were the wings level? No—he felt a left-turning motion. He rolled right for two seconds and brought the column back to neutral. That felt better…no, he was light in the seat. The airplane was descending. He came aft with the column, nice and easy, for two seconds before going back to neutral. *Focus Pete. What is she doing?* He studied the turn bubble… forcing his brain to function…*it's saying you're banked left, Pete.* Panic hit— was he spiraling down toward the ground?

The Pup came out of the clouds, nose low, in a left turn directly over the aerodrome. So much for seat of the pants flying. Flashes came from the ground as he rolled and pulled for the clouds. The tracers wrapped around him again and he cringed as at least three bullets ricocheted off the front left side of the airplane. Engine or fuel tank, most likely. More bullets tore into the upper-wing fabric just to his right, and something whacked the side of his head as the Pup rose back into the gray wet.

*Nice and easy, Pete. Get the nose down and level the wings. Those were little bullets—the big fellow didn't get us.* He realized his head was throbbing. Did he just take a bullet and his body hadn't caught on? He'd heard stories of infantry chaps trying to carry on with half their brain shot away. He held the Pup at what felt like straight and level. Flexed his fingers. Counted out loud: one, two, three, four, five. It looked like his central nervous system was intact. He felt around his helmet with his left hand while holding the airplane steady with his right. The leather wasn't torn and his head was still in one piece. Either a ricochet or a splinter. He took a few seconds and looked over the Pup. Besides whacking him in the head, the Huns had broken his windscreen, hit the Vickers, and punched God only knew how many holes in the fabric. They'd gotten the engine, too—the Le Rhône was coughing every few seconds. Other than that, everything was just fine.

He eased the throttle back, but it barely moved before hanging up. He leaned down and looked at the throttle quadrant—there was no damage to the linkage that he could see. It must have been hit further forward. But he still had the petrol lever to…and before he finished that thought the Le Rhône coughed harder and shut down. Puzzled, he looked at the quadrant again. The throttle was at 70 percent and the petrol lever at 35. The engine should be running. But what *should* be obviously didn't much matter right about then.

He set the engine problem aside and focused on the airplane. On the wind going past his face, the pressure on his backside, the turn bubble… the airplane was banked to the right. He made a little, left-and-back-to-neutral motion with the control column. That felt better.

He checked the airspeed: seventy-five mph. He held back pressure on the column to maintain altitude. Once he got down to fifty, he'd let the Pup descend. With the airplane stable, he turned his attention back to the engine. Closed the petrol lever. The throttle didn't want to come back so he left it where it was and counted off ten long seconds. Plenty of time for the fuel to clear if the mixture was too lean. If it was too rich…well, that might be a different story.

He pushed the nose down to hold fifty mph and brought the petrol lever forward to 40 percent. The Le Rhône coughed. He had ignition. It coughed again and began to wind up…and died. There was a faint smell of fuel, although that could mean anything in an airplane full of holes. He closed the petrol lever again. If the mixture was too rich it would need about thirty seconds to clear…in an undamaged airplane…with the throttle closed.

He looked up. The sun was peeking through the mist and the Huns would start shooting as soon as he came into view. He held the airspeed at fifty; the only noise was the chugging of the windmilling propeller. Watched the altimeter slowly wind down. The gray thinned and he saw green below him. If the engine wouldn't start, he'd dive for the ground and get down before they shot him to pieces. With luck, the Huns who grabbed him wouldn't be the mates of the blokes he'd just blown up.

He set 90 percent throttle; the lever went forward without any problem. Pushed the petrol to 50 percent and the Le Rhône coughed. Coughed again. Making up its mind. He came out of the clouds in a gentle descent. A couple of flashes, but only rifle fire. The Le Rhône went quiet again as a stream of tracers reached toward him, fortunately from long range. He let out a sigh as he closed the petrol lever again. *Maybe it's not your day, Pete. But you're still breathing.*

There were trees in front of him and he swung right toward an open field. Be a bit silly to get killed by a tree at this point. He frowned as the gunner shifted his aim and the stream of tracers slid back toward him. He pushed the nose down to get under the tracers, and further down as the bullets passed two feet above his head. He'd get on the ground and shoot a flare into the fuel tank. Standing orders—don't let the Huns get their hands on RFC airplanes. Not even a battered Sopwith Pup.

The airplane picked up speed in the dive and the propeller turned faster. A group of Huns at the far end of the field were popping off with their rifles. Great sport, no doubt. But he wouldn't have time for flare shooting once he got down. He'd have to semi-crash the airplane, but that'd be easy enough.

Fifty feet. For lack of a better idea, he set the petrol lever at 15 percent and left the throttle at ninety. A rather nonstandard configuration for engine start, but it couldn't be any worse than the others he'd tried. More flashes out in front, and he flinched as a bullet glanced off the cowling in front of him. Hope they're enjoying themselves.

Twenty feet. He looked at the ignition switch. At five feet he'd come forward with the column for the controlled crash.

Ten feet. The Le Rhône gave a little cough, and he stopped his hand just short of the ignition switch. He held it there, afraid to move. The Le Rhône coughed again…and roared to life. He'd about given up on that, but it took him less than a second to react. To pull the Pup into a climb and turn to put the sun behind him. The Le Rhône was misfiring, but she was putting out something near full power. If he could get into the clouds before the Pup took too many more bullets, he might just make it.

# Triplanes and the Department Senior Secretary

*National Physical Laboratory*
*Southwest London*
*May 1917*

Ten weeks before his younger brother attacked Heule Aerodrome, Mark Newin was finishing off a second blueberry scone with clotted cream in his office at the National Physical Laboratory. He slid his hand across the desk to his cup, sipped his tea, and slid the cup back into its spill-prevention spot—the corner made by his wooden pencil box and an engineering reference book. As usual, he ate and drank without looking away from his reading. Or in this case, from a front quarter photo of a Sopwith Triplane. He pursed his lips as he studied it. Drummed his fingers on his desk. Three wings, fuselage interference, bracing wires, and a round nose to house its Clerget rotary engine. All that drag. Along with long, narrow wings which were bound to flex and twist under heavy loading. And those wings were only anchored by a single outboard wing strut—unlike the dual struts of most British biplanes. He sighed and set the photo aside. Went back to the MIT wind tunnel data, trying to make sense of it all. But it wasn't adding up. What was he missing?

"What's so interesting, Mark?"

He looked up at the director of the Lab's Engineering Department. He hadn't heard Professor Stanton come in. "Oh, it's the Sopwith Triplane report. I still don't get it."

"The Sopwith Triplane report? Little late for that, isn't it? Last I heard, the navy ordered a hundred and fifty of them."

"I suppose you're right. Would you like me to put it aside?"

"Before I answer that, why don't you tell me what's bothering you."

"The drag coefficient is high. It's in the data, and you can see it in the photos. Sure, we get more lift from three wings. But if two wings give us enough—"

The professor was looking at the triplane model on Mark's desk. Nodded for him to go ahead.

"With respect to stability, the test pilot reports imply high stability. But as you know, nothing is free in airplane design. The BE2 is wonderfully stable, but I haven't heard anyone say it gets in and out of turns quickly."

"And from what I gather, it takes some muscle to hold it in a dive, which rules myself out as a potential BE2 pilot. But the field reports on the triplane were generally positive."

Mark gave a little sigh. "I know. But can adding a third wing somehow improve both stability and maneuverability? Or at least improve stability without a corresponding loss of maneuverability? In other words, be some sort of aerodynamic elixir that we don't understand—that somehow compensates for the additional drag? I don't see why that would be so—how it could be so."

"Go on. You have my attention."

"Clearly, a third wing means more weight and drag. More structural issues to deal with, more wing-to-wing interference. Our own report is generally consistent with the MIT report. One can tinker with the wing intervals and the stagger, the shape of the airfoil, but there's no way to get around the inefficiency of the middle wing."

The professor was looking at Mark's bookcase. Scratched his beard. If Mark hadn't known him better, he would have thought the professor wasn't listening. "So why do the pilots like it?" the professor asked the bookcase. "Why do they like the triplane?"

"I've been asking myself that same question. I'm wondering if the answer is less about the number of wings, and more about power. The Pup has the eighty-horsepower Le Rhône. They started the triplane at one-ten, and now the Clerget one-thirty is standard. That's eighty to eighty-five horsepower per thousand pounds. The Pup is down around sixty to sixty-five. What if we put a bigger engine on the Pup—say a Le Rhône one-ten? Might we have a real fighting machine, even better than the triplane?" Mark gave a little smile. "Although my brother Pete would tell you the Pup is badly in need of a second Vickers."

"If we add weight to the nose of the airplane, like a bigger engine, we'd have to make some adjustments to the tail surface," the professor pointed out. "Maybe lengthen the fuselage. If we're doing that, we'd want to keep your brother happy and add a second Vickers. That starts to sound like a new airplane, Mark." The professor shifted some books from a chair and sat down. Adjusted his suspenders absently. There were little bits of his breakfast stuck in his thick black beard.

"I know. Nothing is simple."

"If it makes you feel better, I was at a meeting at the War Office last week and Tom Sopwith told us they're testing a one-hundred-horsepower Gnome on the Pup, but the initial pilot reports weren't favorable. They're also concerned about the structure…if it can handle the additional weight and torque."

The professor was looking at the wooden Pup that rested in a corner of the bookcase, and Mark had seen that glassy look before. The professor was running through the structural issues associated with putting a heavier engine on the lightly built Sopwith Pup. Mark waited, and the professor shook his head. "My guess is the Pup isn't up to it. The frame is too light." He turned back to Mark. "Regardless, we're past that point. The triplane is here and the Camel is on the way—if they really call it that. Seems an odd name for a fighter airplane. Either way, I can't see the War Office putting a lot of effort into improving the Pup."

The professor stopped talking and stared at the books on the desk. This time he picked up again after a few seconds. "For what it's worth, Mark, some people at the Admiralty and the War Office may share your concerns. One hundred and fifty is a small order these days, and the RFC hasn't ordered any. Rumor is they're looking at several thousand each of the SE5 and the new Sopwith biplane."

Mark didn't reply at first. He and the professor were both uneasy with the extreme maneuverability (and lack of stability) of the Sopwith Camel. "Dare I say it? I still wonder if we gave up on the monoplane too soon."

"Blasphemy." The professor took his glasses off, looked at them, and put them back on. "The accidents they had in testing…the structural issues are difficult."

"They are. But even allowing for additional bracing wires, a single wing appears best in terms of efficiency. It would save weight, too."

"The Bristol Monoplane prototypes are out there, but no orders yet. I know they're concerned about the high landing speed, and if I recall, the downward visibility from the cockpit is poor."

Mark kept the frown off his face. He'd only seen photos, not the airplane itself, but the Bristol's "fat cigar fuselage" had always struck him as a bit off. *Had Bristol tried an inline six cylinder?*

"Still, I wish we had time to take another look."

"Unfortunately, young man, we do not. That ship has sailed. As for your triplane report, I'll meet you halfway. Take the rest of today, but starting tomorrow I need you to put your ballistics hat on. The army is restructuring their anti-aircraft artillery training, and they need our inputs on their gunnery manual. There are some troublesome issues involved with targeting a moving airplane, and we need to get it right."

"Will do, Professor. I'll start first thing in the morning."

Mark buried himself in triplane aerodynamics. Sometime later—perhaps thirty minutes, perhaps two hours—he heard a familiar female voice. "Finally, from so little sleeping and so much reading, his brain dried up and he went completely out of his mind."

He chuckled and kept his eyes down. After a few seconds of pondering, he shook his head. "Literary. But I don't know it."

"Cervantes. *Don Quixote.*"

Mark looked up into the pleasant face of Rachel Brooks, the one person he was always happy to have interrupt him.

"I didn't know you went in for Spanish literature."

"I don't. But I've always liked that one, and it seems especially applicable around here."

Rachel gave him her standard office smile, and Mark regarded the department's senior secretary. Tall and thin, fair skin, black hair. Widowed, and likely a few years older than himself. "It took a little doing, but you were right. Here's the 'Additional Supplementary Data,' to use its official American name, to the MIT Triplane Report."

He admired her long fingers and nicely trimmed nails as she handed him a folder. He knew better than to check his own nails by way of comparison.

"Also, the professor asked me to reach out to the RFA for any additional data on their gunnery manual. I'll let you know what I dig up. Our RFA liaison is right here in London, so with luck, it won't take long. Is there anything else I can do for you?"

She had been her usual efficient self, and he shook his head. "No, thank you."

"Would you like me to straighten up your office?" There was a little twinkle in her brown eyes. Mark looked around the tiny office. The bookcase was jammed full. Books, reports, and papers were piled here and there. A trail of scone crumbs meandered across the desk.

"No, it's fine. Thank you."

She paused by the door. "By the way, Physicist Newin, don't forget you asked me to lunch tomorrow. I know you scientific types can be forgetful."

Hmm. He had forgotten about that, but recovered quickly. "Right. One o'clock." They'd been out to lunch twice and he'd enjoyed both, despite being conversationally outgunned by her. Of course, just about anyone who spoke English outgunned him, but the difference was particularly noticeable in her case.

He went back to the MIT study. There was no getting around the extra drag—a triplane would be slower than a biplane with the same weight and power characteristics. Nor, despite what some engineers and pilots seemed to think, did more wings naturally equate to better climb capability. A three-wing airplane had excellent performance near stall, but even he knew that pilots didn't normally fly around near stall speed. In a tight turning-circle fight the triplane should perform well, but how often did that happen?

He let out a sigh and drummed his fingers on his cheek. He needed to talk to Pete about this. His eyes wandered around the office and stopped on the little wooden triplane perched on the corner of his desk. He lowered his head and tilted it. Studied the lines of the triplane.

Increasing the separation of the wings would reduce interference and increase efficiency, but the structural issues would become more difficult. Structural issues can be dealt with, but with a weight, and likely drag, penalty. Shorter wings would make everything simpler, but how much wing area could they afford to give up? All of which brought him back to where he started—did three wings make sense in the first place? And if they didn't, how had everyone gotten so far down the triplane road?

# Messines Ridge

*6 Squadron RFC, BE2 Reconnaissance Aircraft*
*Abeele Aerodrome, Western Belgium*

Lieutenant Norman Frazier stepped outside his hut and took in the familiar flat and muddy scenery. Cupped his hands and lit a cigarette. The wind was already blowing, bringing the smell of fuel and lubricating oil as the mechanics got the airplanes ready for another day in Flanders. Sometimes his observer (and best friend) Bill Burns would join him for a morning smoke, but that wouldn't be happening today.

They'd been spotting for the British artillery southeast of Ypres and were under German anti-aircraft ("Archie") fire. The insistent black bursts. The invisible shrapnel—sometimes close enough to hear its wobbly whistle as it went past the cockpit. Somewhere north of them were three other 6 Squadron airplanes. He couldn't see the other BE2s, but no one could miss the impacts of the British artillery, flinging mud, equipment, and occasionally the body parts of some unlucky mammal thirty feet into the air.

He looked down to fix his position relative to what was left of Battle Wood and spotted something out of place in the shattered terrain…camouflage netting. He wiped his goggles clean with the little rag; squinted and focused…They were very faint, but he made out the telltale black lines of artillery barrels. The guns were a few hundred yards west of the railroad, maybe eight hundred yards north of the canal. He studied his map and worked out the coordinates. Pulled the power back to reduce the roar of the V-8 six feet in front of him, leaned forward and shouted to his friend.

"New target, Bill. Not firing. Coordinates: Ink, Thirty-Five, Don, Seven, Five. I say again: Ink, Thirty-Five, Don, Seven, Five."

That should be close enough. Bill gave him a thumbs-up and his head went down to tap the message out on the wireless. Norman made a few small turns to make sure no one was sneaking up on them. They didn't have any fighter cover today, and the German Albatrosses loved finding BE2s out all by themselves. Satisfied the airspace behind them was clear, he turned obliquely toward the battery. Picked up the muzzle flash, and about fifteen seconds later a single eighteen-pound high explosive shell erupted into the mud below them. He visualized an imaginary clock over the target, oriented north. The impact was northeast of the target at about four hundred yards. He pulled the throttle back and shouted the targeting correction. "Edward Two, Bill. Edward Two."

Norman winced as an Archie shell burst slightly above and in front of them, as if punctuating his shouted correction. The airplane shuddered as metal cut through wood and fabric; he bit his lip and listened to the engine. The BE2 steadied up and soldiered on, and he shrugged it off. It wasn't unusual to come home with some holes in the airplane. But they might have another problem: two airplanes well above them were approaching from the east. He rested his eyes for a couple of seconds; focused on them and frowned. They were orange and white.

He turned forward and shouted to his friend. "Did you copy Edward Two, Bill?" He put the BE2 into a turn, swinging her tail away from the Huns.

"Bill?" he tried again, as he gauged the distance to the approaching Germans, and to the nearest clouds he could hide out in.

No answer. Norman turned around. Bill had slid down in his seat, his head resting against the rail. Norman looked at his friend for a couple of seconds, sick to his stomach. He pulled the BE2 around to the west; went full throttle and pushed her into a dive. Held the column forward as the BE2 accelerated and pushed back, trying to pull her nose up, not wanting to go fast. He looked back at the two Huns, but they were holding their course and altitude. They hadn't seen him, or more likely, had something more important to do. But Archie was awake and watching, and Norman zigzagged through the black bursts, still holding the BE2 in her dive. Archie gave up as he got lower, but he'd gotten down into small arms range and there were little flashes here and there from the rifles of the Hun infantry, and a stream of tracers rose toward him as a machine gun opened up. He ignored the flashes, and ignored the shakes and groans from a BE2 flying over max design airspeed. Crossed no-man's-land at 500 feet, still descending and still chased by the tracers of the Hun machine guns. He crossed the maze of the British forward trenches and leveled at 200 feet, looking for his battery of eighteen-pounders.

He passed over the support trenches, along the communication trenches, to the reserve trenches. The Ypres Canal was on his left. His battery would be astride the highway, north of the canal. He turned north and ran along the highway…and spotted the guns. Swung the BE2 left—about two miles west was some sort of headquarters next to an open field. He'd seen it when they were checking in with the battery. Abeele was another ten miles west and if Bill was alive, he was bleeding out. He had to get him on the ground. He turned south and passed over the field at fifty feet, letting the airspeed bleed off. The field wasn't as smooth as he'd thought, and he was drifting left. Must be a good fifteen knots of wind out of the west. If he landed north-south, the BE2 would end up on its back. He didn't care about the airplane, but a crash-landing would complicate things. Could he land to the west? The field was comically narrow for that, but he'd be pointed into the wind and there were only a few bushes and stumps on the east edge to clear. He held the BE2 at fifty feet and made a 270-degree turn back to the west, his groundspeed slowing as the airplane turned into the wind. He eased the rpm back and the airplane slowed further.

*Lower, Norman.*

Airspeed forty-eight.

*Lower.* It didn't matter if he scraped the hedgerow with the undercarriage, but he couldn't afford to catch it hard and flip the airplane onto her back.

Airspeed forty-four. He brought the power up 200 rpm.

*Hold her down, Norman. Watch her speed…* he cut the power as the undercarriage scraped the bushes. The BE2 hit and bounced; he went right with the column as the right wing came up. She hit again, rocked left and right, and settled onto the ground. He pulled in his breath as the airplane headed straight at the command dugout—wide-eyed soldiers were shouting and scattering. He kicked the rudder bar and the airplane swung sideways, her wheels digging into the soft ground. The BE2 tipped right… and came to an abrupt stop with her right wingtip stuck in the mud. He unbuckled, straightened up, and shouted to the onlookers.

"Need the orderly!" He pointed at Bill. "He's hurt bad."

Norman looked at his friend as the soldiers shouted for the medical orderly. Bill wasn't moving. He let out a long sigh and climbed out of the cockpit. Took a few steps back and looked over the airplane. Her right wheel was half buried, so she wasn't going to roll away.

An orderly came running up to the cockpit. He felt Bill's wrist, then his neck. Felt his wrist again; turned to his lieutenant and shook his head. The lieutenant called to the small crowd that had gathered. "Wallace, Sobel, I need you to pull him out." Two large privates stepped forward.

"Grab a couple of those crates. You'll need something to stand on."

"Gently now, fellows." They manhandled Bill out and laid him by the airplane. The orderly knelt beside him for a few moments. Straightened up and walked over to Norman.

"Sorry, Lieutenant. He's dead. Shrapnel hit him in the chest." Norman looked at the young orderly. Swallowed some saliva, but his throat was closed. "There's a nice cemetery about three miles west of here, sir. By the lake. We'll put him there."

After the orderly left, Norman knelt next to Bill. Took his friend's gloves off and touched his hand. Looked at the face he'd grown to love over the last few months. A face he'd seen drunk and sober, laughing and crying. He stood up, brushing back a tear. Took his leather jacket off and set it next to a tree stump. Sat on the jacket and leaned back. The roughness of the bark against his back, the breeze across his face. Above him, blue sky and scattered white clouds. There was still a bit of nature left in the world. The lieutenant squatted down next to him.

"What squadron? We'll give them a heads-up that you're here." Norman stared into the youthful face. Had this fellow even started shaving? He tried to speak and nothing came out. Swallowed and tried again.

"Six Squadron. Abeele. Lieutenants Frazier and Burns."

The lieutenant disappeared into the dugout. Norman leaned against his stump and watched the comings and goings. Watched them take Bill away on a stretcher; listened as the phones rang almost nonstop. Calls to and from the batteries, the ammo column, division headquarters, and others he couldn't identify. Figured out that he'd found the 190th Artillery Brigade, the parent unit of his battery. He would have been fine sitting against the stump for another hour or two, but there was a war on. He stood up as a captain walked over to him.

"The colonel is asking if your airplane is flyable, Lieutenant. If it is, he needs you to go. Otherwise, we'll pull it under cover." The captain pointed northeast to a Hun observation balloon, bobbing in the wind. "The Huns can reach us with their heavy stuff here, and they may decide your airplane is worth the trouble."

Norman struggled to get his brain moving. "I think so, Captain. Let me take a look." He inspected the airplane: shrapnel had cut one of the support wires on the vertical tail, there were some holes in the fabric, a cracked wing rib, and a bit of wingtip damage from the landing. He pulled a few branches out of the undercarriage, lifted the wingtip out of the mud and brushed it off. Checked for free movement of the flight controls. He took a couple of steps back, looked her over and shrugged. She flew in. She would probably fly out. He nodded to the captain. "I should be able to get her out of here, sir. If we can pull her onto a drier spot and find someone who can crank the prop without killing himself, I'll get moving."

He decided to take off northwest, accepting some crosswind for more ground to work with. They pulled her out of the soft grass and her RAF 1a V-8 started up without a hitch. He taxied to the southeast end of the little field, scraping the bushes with the wingtip as he turned. Powered up and the BE2 started forward. Picked up speed—she was quicker without the weight of the observer. She rocked left and right as she negotiated the little bumps. Tapped a wingtip against the ground, then the other, but the column was coming alive as the weight came off her wheels. He got the tail up and she rolled easier, but he was already uncomfortably close to the end of the field. He came back with the column as soon as he dared, to get the old girl airborne.

She rose to five feet and hung there. He bit his lip as the bushes got bigger, but didn't dare pull back on the column. They scraped their way through and came out the other side, the BE2 wobbling left and right with her nose high, as if balanced on the head of a pin. He half expected her to settle onto the ground—that she was done for the day. But he held her level and ever so slowly, the airspeed crept up. At sixty knots he eased her into a gentle climb.

Back at Abeele, he washed up and sat in the orderly room. Stared at the two blank report forms in front of him. He hadn't said a word to anyone since landing. The squadron recording officer, Captain Tom Harvey, sat down across from him. Their eyes met.

"I took the call from the artillery chaps. It's a shame. He was a good man."

Norman cleared his throat before trying to speak. "He was. A good friend."

"I took you off your afternoon flight. Go into town. Take a walk. Get a woman. Anything."

That had been yesterday morning. Now he was sitting in the Officers' Mess, with a brand-new observer-on-probation sitting across from him.

Second Lieutenant Harry Booth's alarm went off at 07:30. He turned it off before it woke his roommates and gathered his things to go to the washroom. Paused by the door; Ethan was looking at him. "Sorry. Tried not to wake you fellows."

"You'd have to be quiet as the dark to slip past an RFC-trained killer like myself, young man. That, plus I have gas. Perhaps you noticed me flapping the sheets, spreading my man scent about for the enjoyment of all."

"Fortunately, I didn't," said Harry, opening the door and crinkling his nose at the acrid smell. The chaps were dumping ashes in the landing area and rolling them flat. From what he'd heard, the fight against the rain was nonstop in Flanders. But unlike some other RFC aerodromes, which weren't much more than tents pitched in an open field, Abeele had wood huts with floors and oil heaters. The only drawback was the frog pond—the little buggers made a hell of a racket at night. Ethan had told him some of the chaps had tried night frog shooting, but the CO put a stop to it when the fellows on the early schedule complained. Beyond the dust and mud was a line of brand-new 4 Squadron RE8s. They were finally replacing the BE2s, and rumor was 6 Squadron was next. There were also rumors the RE8 wasn't any better than the BE2, and maybe even worse, but at least the observer sat in the back seat, where he belonged. He washed up and went to the Mess; sat across from his pilot and ordered tea and toast.

Lieutenant Frazier was reading the paper and ignored him. Harry managed a few bites of toast as his stomach churned, feeling acutely self-conscious as he pretended to read the paper. He was making up his mind whether to go to the orderly room by himself when someone spoke.

"Well, Norm, looks like they gave you a hardened one."

Harry looked up. A tall pilot with an impressive mustache was standing next to their table. Norman put his paper down and looked at Harry. "My punishment, I suppose. Looks like he's out of nappies, but not by much."

Harry looked at the newcomer. Should he introduce himself—or would that be ridiculous after just being insulted? He could get up and walk away from these two bounders—but would that look childish? He could compromise—excuse himself and leave. Norman stood up and saved him from sitting there and looking stupid as he made up his mind. "Let's go, Liverpool. We've got work to do."

Harry followed Norman into the orderly room; sat down and scrunched up his nose. Something wet. Rotting. It reminded him of that day when he and Billy Simpson were nippers, and they'd found a dead rat in the road. Its fur was slick with rain, the bloodred guts shiny. Billy had picked it up by the tail and chased him around with it. He leaned over and looked in the waste can. Some of last night's fish, resting in its butter sauce. A glassy eye stared up at him and a fly was motionless in the butter. Licking its fly chops? Drowned in fly ecstasy?

Harry moved two tables over and the smell receded, to be replaced by the resident master: stale cigarette smoke. Dry and acrid. Nor was this master one to confine himself to a waste can. He wandered into every nook and cranny on the aerodrome and left a thin film behind. Captain Harvey was behind the counter, looking at the readiness board. He turned and nodded to Norman but didn't acknowledge Harry's presence, despite having formally introduced him to the Mess the night before. Thirty pairs of eyes had looked at Harry like he was some sort of insect that had crawled in under the door. "Morning, Norm. How's the golf course coming along?"

"All laid out. A par four and two par threes, behind Four Squadron. The major's on board. He's a good player. But that, of course, we cannot use RFC resources for this."

"You'll find a way. Just let him win once in a while, okay?" Harvey was thumbing through a pile of folders on the counter. "Here it is. Photoshoot. Messines Ridge. Fifty-Three's short airplanes, so you're on loan to Ninth Corps." Harvey puffed on his cigarette and gave Norman a side glance. "The major got a call from Wing about this one—to put one of his best pilots on it. So try not to muck it up and make us look bad." Harvey frowned as he glanced around the room: two NCOs were behind the counter and three tables were occupied by pilot-observer pairs going through their mission folders.

"Brooke and someone from photo should be here to brief you. I don't know where they got off to."

"I went over the shoot with them earlier," said Norman. He sat down across from Harry and opened the folder. Spoke to Harry without looking up. "Lieutenant Brooke is Tenth Corps Intel. Liaison for all reconnaissance and artillery spotting missions. In other words, pretty much everything we do. I ran into him on the way to breakfast."

Harry pursed his lips. He didn't like they hadn't included him in the briefing. When Norman didn't say anything else, he went to the counter and looked at the situation map: 6 Squadron was attached to X Corps, in the middle of the Wipers sector. To their south: IX Corps, opposite Messines Ridge where the front line bulged to the west. Someone had told him the Huns grabbed the high ground back in '14, and it looked like they were still on it three years later. The rumors were flying about a big attack, and it didn't take a general to see what was coming. Attack the flanks of the bulge or, what the hell, go straight through them. Tally-ho, here comes the charge of the Light Brigade, on their BE2s. He blew out his breath. Almost snorted. *Wipers.* Of all the places they could have sent him, this had to be the worst. He stared at the map for another minute, seeing nothing. Gave up and sat down.

"We'll rendezvous over Cassel at nine thousand feet with two Fees from Forty-One Squadron," said Norman, still not looking up.

"What's a Fee?" Harry regretted the question as soon as it was out. Highlighting his ignorance.

"FE8. Pusher-prop type."

Harry rolled his eyes. Figures. If you send outdated recce airplanes across the front line, you might as well send outdated fighters along as escort. Easier to collect the bodies. It took a bit of searching, but he found Cassel on his map.

"Cassel is west of us?" His voice quavered, but he got it out without stuttering.

"We need time to climb. We want to cross the line at our final altitude, and it'll take us about thirty minutes to get to nine thousand feet. So we'll head west out of here."

Well, one thing made sense around there. He studied the mission planning map on the table in front of Norman. The Huns held the ridge that ran from Messines north to Wytschaete and off to the northeast. Ridge being relative, as this was Flanders, but it must be high enough for the Huns to see onto the British side. That would draw the interest of the generals and even Harry knew the RFC was here to serve. There was a north-south highway about a mile on the German side, and their photo run was centered a mile and a half east of the highway, along the back side of the ridge. Right where the Huns liked to put their artillery. How many anti-aircraft guns had the Germans packed onto that ridgeline, that they were about to fly over in an underpowered relic? Harvey had said 53 Squadron was running short of airplanes. Maybe they were all getting shot down over Messines Ridge.

"E-Type camera, ten-inch lens. Nine thousand feet. South to north, make a one-eighty and run back south. That should do it."

Norman looked up when he didn't answer. Harry stared back. *Whatever you say, Norman. I'm only a wingless second lieutenant observer just out of nappies.* After a few seconds of mutual staring, Norman went back to his folder.

"The runs are usually longer than this. But the longer the run, the less likely we make it back with their precious plates. We caught a break with this one. I'll be focused on the ground once we cross the line. Keep your eyes open and call out any airplanes you see."

Harry heard the words but no meaning registered. He was seeing himself as a lifeless pile of flesh in some muddy field, draped over the BE2's V-8. Blood pooled inside him, his body cold and hardened. With his eyes still open? Only the whites showing? He'd read somewhere people shit their pants when they were hanged. Would it be the same being shot down and killed? Or would his feces stay inside him, to rot with the rest of him? Even if he shit them out, it wasn't like someone was going to clean him up nicely. Wipe his cold green ass.

"You with me?"

Norman was staring at him again. He nodded and forced himself back to business.

"We'll draw Archie fire, and the booms may shake you up. But we can't change altitude during the shoot. The scale of the photos wouldn't be the same. Questions?"

Harry shook his head, teeth clenched as his breakfast heaved in his stomach. His armpits were moist and he pulled his elbows in closer. Norman looked at his watch and stood up. "Right on time. I'll see you in ten minutes to get suited up." Norman started to walk away, then stopped. "Oh yeah, we'll use hand signals as much as we can. It's not a problem so much on the photoshoots, but if I need to talk to you, I'll pull the power back, tap you on the shoulder and yell. Otherwise, you'll never hear me."

The corporal at the counter was on the phone, motioning for them to wait. "Just a second, Norman," Harry managed.

The corporal hung up the phone and looked at Norman. "That was Wing, sir. Forty-One Squadron canceled. They're trying to find you another escort."

Harry stared, processing what he'd heard. They might go across the Wipers front in a BE2 with no escort? Shouldn't they cancel the mission? How would getting shot down and killed help the war effort?

He looked at Norman, eyes wide, but Norman only nodded.

# The Wildflowers Café

*66 Squadron RFC, Sopwith Scout Fighter Aircraft*
*Vert Galand Aerodrome, Northern France*

"The major wants to talk to you," said Captain Hugh Fleming, 66 Squadron recording officer.

"Can I get cleaned up first?" Pete asked. He'd just walked into the building after the worst flight he'd ever had: a short-notice mission babysitting a BE2 on unfamiliar ground up in Flanders, and a dead wingman.

"No."

Pete followed Fleming down the hall. His flight commander, Captain Roger Browne, was standing outside the major's office. "Wait here," Fleming said to the two of them. Roger looked at Pete and gave a shrug with his eyebrows. In the office, Fleming and the major spoke in low voices.

"Come in, gentlemen."

They sat down. His squadron commander looked at Pete. "Verbal report," said Major Thomas Pritchett flatly.

Pete looked at the major, who could have been a poster boy for the RFC. Silver hair and mustache. Tanned skin, athletic build. Whereas Pete was filthy and smelled like castor oil. Maybe this was some sort of secret CO strategy, to put blokes on the defensive. He picked up the mission after they'd crossed back onto the British side. His brand-new wingman had crept in too close again; they did that when they got scared. Pete gave him the push-away signal for the third time that day. Beyond the plodding BE2 in front of them were patches of green in the sea of brown-gray mud; the waterlogged devastation was fading as they flew west. He wiped the oil from his goggles and checked the time. In three minutes, he could drop the BE2 off and go home. In three minutes his life would become simpler.

His eyes caught movement off his right wing…a gray or silver airplane was paralleling them about two miles away; it must have been hidden behind the clouds. This fellow was almost certainly a Hun—the British didn't go in for gray and there weren't many French airplanes in Flanders. He made a quick check behind them before focusing on his new friend…as he would have guessed, it was a two-seater. But something else was moving out there, and it took his brain a few seconds to sort out what his eyes were seeing. There was another airplane, no, two airplanes, beyond the German. Farther away and lower, also headed west. They were dark colored, with the same basic shape as his Pup. British 1 1/2 Strutters. His airplane back in 45 Squadron.

He glanced at his fuel quantity before coming back to the German. Should he go after him once he dropped off the BE2? He might or might not be faster, depending on its type, and he had a brand-new wingman to keep an eye on. It'd be worth a try, but he'd need to keep the Hun in sight while not losing track of the BE2. His mind made up, he mechanically turned to look behind him; jumped as adrenaline hit him like a brick in the face. He snatched the column back and right as he kicked right rudder. Two Albatrosses were sweeping toward his tail, the leader almost in machine-gun range, with two more in trail.

The Pup was shaking, protesting at the max-speed dive, but Pete was smiling for the first time that day. The Huns were running for home, and he had the angle to cut off the wingman. For some reason they'd only made one pass before giving it up. The wind rushed past him as the Pup raced downhill, closing the gap. He eased the column back to break the descent as he came into long range. Set the bead two ship-lengths in front of the Hun to get a feel for the deflection. He was still out of range, but closing steadily…and the Hun broke hard into him. He pulled up and left; he still had plenty of energy from the dive. Watched the spacing develop and stole a glance at the Hun leader: he hadn't turned back to help his wingman out. Pete rolled right and pulled down to stay inside the German's turn. Close quarters maneuvering was one thing the Pup was good at, and the Hun wingman was on his own. He stabilized a hundred yards behind the German, both airplanes in a shallow descent.

He didn't have time to waste; the Albatros would start pulling away any second. He pulled the gunsight in front of the Hun, judging the crossing angle…and pushed the trigger button. His single Vickers thumped and the tracers reached out. He let off the trigger after two seconds and shook his head. He'd punched a few bullets through the low wing, nothing more. God, what he wouldn't give for a second Vickers—a single eight-millimeter just didn't do it. The German reversed his turn and Pete slotted in directly behind him. *Thank you very much for that.*

He set the bead just in front of the Hun's nose as they turned, but as he pushed the trigger the Albatros dropped below the stream of tracers. The Hun had pushed over at the last second. Pete let off the trigger and pushed the column forward to stay with the German, rising in his seat against his lap belt. The bead was lowering onto the Hun, his thumb ready on the trigger button. He had him now. The Albatros dimmed, surrounded by a fuzzy white. It went dimmer still, and was gone. Pete cursed as he pushed the trigger for five long seconds, firing into the white nothingness, giving the rudder bar a little left-right kick. He looked out front and shook his head. The cloud layer was solid.

The major had listened to Pete without interrupting. "You spotted the wreckage of Lieutenant Cochrane's airplane on your return leg?"

"Yes, sir. The wreckage was scattered. I don't think there's much chance he survived."

"He didn't. We got the call." The major looked at his desk for a few seconds. "Sounds like he was late picking up the Huns. Did the photoshoot get done?"

"I think so, sir. The clouds were well scattered over the ridge. The thicker stuff was above us, and farther east."

"The BE2 made it home?"

"As far as I know, sir. He was well out in front, and the Huns were busy with the two of us."

"I imagine he did. At least I haven't had a call from Six Squadron looking for their airplane."

There was a break in the conversation and Pete glanced around the office. A relatively clean desk, a small bookshelf, filing cabinet, picture of smiling wife with two children. A typewriter was clacking from the outer office where the admin corporal sat.

"The Huns broke off the attack after one pass?"

"That's correct, sir. The leader may have had an engine problem…low on fuel maybe. But I really don't know."

"You pursued and attacked the wingman as they flew east, and he escaped into the clouds?"

"Yes, sir."

Major Pritchett looked at Pete, his eyes hard. "It's your job as a flight leader to bring your wingman back with you, Lieutenant. You went chasing after the Huns and left a brand-new wingman on his own."

Pete started to say Cochrane was likely already dead, before deciding against it. "Combat situation, sir. After I turned to cut off the Huns, I took a good look at where he should be. If Cochrane or the other two Huns were anywhere close, I would have seen them. I had the angle on the trailing Hun and figured I could catch him with my altitude advantage. It's our job to kill Germans, isn't it, sir?" Pete bit his lip as those last words came out. They were unlikely to help.

"You let me worry about the squadron's job, Lieutenant." The major let out a noticeable sigh, without overdoing it. Practiced.

"I expect better from my flight leaders. You let a distant airplane distract you, then went chasing after two other airplanes that were out of the fight. And Lieutenant Cochrane's dead. Because of you."

The major was silent for a few moments. Turning something over in his head, or letting that last word hang in the air for effect.

"That's all for now. Make sure we have your report today. There's another busy day coming up tomorrow."

Pete gave an invisible shrug. Unless the weather grounded them, almost every day was a busy day for 66 Squadron. He followed a limping Roger Browne down the hall to what passed for their club. Roger ordered beer and they sat down at one of the little tables. The corporal working behind the counter brought two mugs of beer and a damp towel for Pete. He wiped the grime off his hands and face. "Thank you, Corporal."

"Welcome, sir."

Neither of them spoke at first; Roger wasn't much more talkative than he was. Pete eyed the beer in front of him. Beer before lunch wasn't his thing, but he managed a couple of sips. Looked across the table at his flight commander. Muscular fellow. Looked like an out-of-shape boxer, minus the battered face. Even-keel type. If Roger had the kind of inner turmoil Pete struggled with, it didn't show. Pete liked Roger, although he wasn't sure he'd call them friends. Pete wasn't sure he had any friends.

"Shame. He hadn't been here long, but he seemed like a decent enough fellow. First wingman you've lost?"

Pete nodded.

"I bet he picked them up late and panicked—to not even give you a warning burst. He wouldn't have been the first bloke to put the Pup in a screaming dive and rip the upper wing off." Roger glanced behind him and lowered his voice. "I taught advanced flight with Pritchett at Joyce for a few months. He'd flown RE7s, towing targets, taking generals for rides. He's not a bad pilot, but he's never been in a situation like that. Hell, if you hadn't turned around when you did, you'd be dead too."

At the time, Pete thought he'd done the right thing. Once he'd saved his own backside, he'd looked for Cochrane. He didn't see him and went after the Huns. Sitting in the club, sipping a beer, now he wasn't so sure. Cochrane might have been alive and fighting somewhere behind the clouds. Well, he could struggle with the moral issues later—he had lots of practice with that. And whether he admitted it or not, he'd wanted that kill. He'd wanted a third Iron Cross next to his name on the readiness board.

"I'm surprised the Hun leader didn't turn back to lend a hand. Sounds like you almost had his wingman."

"I did almost have him. When the wingman broke into me, I figured the leader would be right behind, and it'd be two against one. Who knows? Problem with his airplane, or maybe he had diarrhea and didn't want to unload in his pants."

Roger took a large slug of beer and moved on. Cochrane was hardly the first pilot they'd lost, and a newbie at that. "Mark Henderson's back in hospital. Stomach problems again. A new bloke, Duncan, got in last night. Birmingham sort. I guess we'll get another one tomorrow. You know they don't like empty seats in the Mess. Suppose they're afraid we might notice some of the chaps are getting killed. That we might feel bad and want to go home."

Roger looked at his beer and gave a little shake of the head. "The mind of an RFC general, Pete. It must be a strange and alien place. You'll have to do some of the checkout flights, since I don't have Mark."

"Does this mean I'm an old hand now?"

"Two Huns down and still alive after…three months here?" Pete nodded. It would be three months next week, with two Huns to his credit. The first a lone AEG two-seater. Unescorted on the British side of the line, leaving a trail of steam from his overheating six-cylinder Mercedes. A week later he put two bullets into the pilot's leg and forced down an Albatros two-seater, but not before the Hun observer had hit him back. They counted twelve bullet holes in the Pup after he landed, and he'd swallowed hard when he saw how close some of them had come to the cockpit.

"Training seems to think the blokes they send us are ready to go." Roger set his beer down and gave his opinion of that with a small belch. "The first couple of flights we show them the local area, so they can find Vert all by themselves. Let them shoot up the practice range. Do some basic formation work. If they're not too dangerous to the rest of us, throw in some basic combat maneuvering. That is, assuming Pritchett, Wing, and the Huns don't interfere with A-Flight scheduling."

Pete pushed his chair back and crossed his legs. Thought about his path from maths teacher in Dorset to Vert Galand Aerodrome. He'd had it easy coming out of flight training: Home Defense in the BE2. Those days of trying to claw their way high enough to get at the Zeppelins. Roger waved to the corporal for another beer; Pete's was still three-quarters full. He took another sip and looked around the familiar surroundings. Besides the bar and some tables and chairs, the club comprised a dartboard, a couple of decks of cards, and a chess set. A gramophone and piano for the musical types, a group which did not include Pete Newin. The decor consisted of a single war poster, this one in the popular, "Remember Belgium" category. In the foreground a British soldier stands ramrod straight with rifle and bayonet, while a mother and child flee their burning village in the background. In case there was any doubt about the point being made, "Enlist Today" was printed in bold white letters at the bottom. Roger stretched out a leg and grimaced.

"Are you hurt?"

"Hun artillery at second Wipers. The doc said he thought he got all the shrapnel out. But it acts up once in a while."

"Thought. Meaning he didn't commit himself. Infantry?"

"Yep. Vickers machine-gun crew. I think they picked me because I was big enough to lug the damn thing around." Most of the former army chaps didn't want to talk about what they'd gone through, but it didn't seem to bother Roger.

"For how long?"

"A little over a year. Twenty-Eighth Division. Mostly regular army fellows, but they added some of us machine-gun types before they shipped out. It was good being one of the chaps, everyone in it together. But I got tired of the mud and the rats. Blokes getting their faces or their bollocks ripped off. It's better here."

Pete was watching Roger as he spoke. Life in the trenches. Something he'd never known. Never would. But there was no chance he was going to say what was going through his mind. That to the outside world Pete Newin was a (fill in the blank: brave, heroic, etc.) Sopwith Pup combat pilot. And maybe he was. But he thanked God he'd never have to go face to face with a Hun on the ground. Trying to bayonet each other. Gouging an eye out or slamming a knee into the other bloke's balls. He simply could not visualize that. But presumably he would have gone up the ladders with the others when the whistle blew, as the army had an incentive program in place to deal with this exact issue. They shot the ones who stayed behind. He sipped his beer again and his mind circled back to the present. "How's the family?"

"Cheryl's good. And the baby. Little fellow will be two next month. Granddad died back in April. Black lung. Dad's got it, too. They go on strike every few years. Try to make things better. But the government always sides with the money, even when there isn't a war on."

"At least the war got you out of the mines."

"Yeah, it did that. Oh, I almost forgot." Roger lowered his voice. "Pritchett says we're moving. Top secret, of course."

Pete's eyebrows went up. "Kent? Devon?"

"Nice try. We're headed north."

"Flanders is north of here. It's lovely up there, if you like mud and bombed-out cities."

Roger downed the rest of his second beer and stood up. Tried unsuccessfully for another belch. "Defensive patrol tomorrow, Pete. Midmorning and afternoon. I'll see you at lunch."

Pete washed up and checked the schedule in the orderly room. They'd tagged him for a late afternoon training flight with a brand-new C-Flight pilot. Well, that was fine with Pete Newin, not that his preferences counted for much around Vert. He stepped outside to get some air. The sun was out, scattered clouds and gusty winds. Six well-worn Sopwith Pups were parked in front of their hangars. Further down the field sat the SPAD VIIs of 19 Squadron, and behind him, on the other side of the road that cut through the aerodrome, the SE5s of 56 Squadron. All under the direct control of Major General Boom Trenchard, Commander, Royal Flying Corps in France. Meaning wherever there was trouble, that's where they went. Like today. The throaty roar of Hispano V-8s reached his ears, most unlike the refined buzz of Le Rhône rotaries. That would be 56 Squadron taking off in their SE5s. Lucky sots. He walked down to the end of the 66 Squadron flight-line and stopped in front of an old barn that was now the squadron machine and rigging shop. Beyond that was the tennis court. Originally grass, now mostly dirt. Four mechanics were fitting a Le Rhône to a Pup. Some good-natured swearing as they coaxed and shoved the engine into position, the wooden A-frame groaning under the load of the nine-cylinder rotary. At least the chains looked secure enough, and the fellows should have time to get out of the way if the whole thing came crashing down.

He retraced his steps, sat on a bench and took it in. Blue sky, green grass. Trees moving with the wind. No roses, but Shakespeare had it right about natural beauty. His eyes stopped on a familiar white object in the trees on the far side of the field: the remains of a BE2 wing panel. He considered the mangled white rectangle surrounded by swaying branches and green leaves—yet another example of mankind's ever-expanding ability to cock up God's creation.

He worked on his combat report for a few minutes before setting it aside. Closed his eyes… A familiar humming woke him—a humming that grew into the buzzing roar of Le Rhône rotaries. C-Flight was coming home, and it looked like they were all in one piece. The four Pups maneuvered to land and the flight leader bounced onto the ground. Pete gave a little nod—the gusty winds were making things interesting.

He frowned as the second Pup came in. The pilot was overcontrolling and the airplane was rocking back and forth in the wind. It dropped the last three feet; hit the ground square on the main wheels and bounced into the air, its nose too high for anything resembling a landing. The Pup started back down, rocking left and right as the engine wound up in a too late attempt by the pilot to go around and try it again. Pete bit his lip as he waited for the impact. The left wingtip and wheel hit together with an unhealthy *crunch*, followed by a *snap* as the propeller cracked. The right wingtip stayed up and the Pup marched around on its left wingtip, jolting up and down as the broken propeller plowed through the field, flinging chunks of dirt and grass fifteen feet into the air. Pete caught a whiff of fuel as the pilot finally thought to cut the engine power, and the battered Pup came to a stop.

The third and fourth airplanes slid over to land next to the beached Sopwith. Like most aerodromes in that part of France, the landing ground at Vert was nothing more than a grass field. The last two Pups landed uneventfully, and Pete eyed the wrecked airplane. The impact had separated the lower left wing at the root and broken the undercarriage, along with the propeller and maybe a cracked longeron or two. She wouldn't be flying again anytime soon. If ever. Another Army Form W3347, Report on Casualties to Personnel and Machines, was in the works. The squadron lost an airplane or two every week for noncombat reasons. What was that little word the RFC Brass like to use…? Wastage—that was it. His uncle Charlie had told him once the army used the same term, although their number was bigger. Five thousand. As in five thousand men expected to be killed or wounded. Every day.

"Can't even get a cup of coffee in this place," the old man at the next table grumbled in English while the waitress took their order. Outside, it was a beautiful day: low clouds and rain, with the wind blowing hard out of the northwest. The third day in a row of all flying canceled, and Pete and John Wilcox had braved the weather to have lunch in the Wildflowers Café in "downtown" Blessy. Roger had been right; along with 19 and 56 Squadrons they'd moved to Liettres Aerodrome, about forty miles north of Vert Galand. That much closer to the charming Flanders countryside.

The waitress turned around and chastised the old man in French, ending in "Grand-père." She turned back to Pete and John with a little smile. "My grand-père talks tough, but he's really quite nice," she said in French-accented English. Grandfather scowled as he waited for his coffee, but Pete saw the fondness in his eyes as the old man looked at his granddaughter.

"Flyboys," he said, looking at them now. Pete guessed he was about sixty-five years old—short and thin with gray-black hair and a beard cut short. "I was a *real* soldier. Infantry. Fought the Prussians back in seventy. Under Napoleon the Third. Captured he was. Too bad the Huns didn't do us a favor and keep him. We should have put the empress in charge anyway. She was more of a man than he was."

Pete listened, warming up to the old fellow.

"The Chassepot. That was a weapon. About the only thing our government ever did right. Damn thing was bigger than I was, and accurate to a thousand meters. Kicked like a mule, too. Paper cartridges. We had to keep them dry; not let them get torn up. Not like those fancy brass cartridges you fellows have. The first time I fired it for real, at Froeschwiller under Marshal MacMahon, I got a Hun at six hundred meters. Officer. I know because he was carrying a sword. His head blew up like a melon. I bet the fellow next to him was all put out. Got blood and muck all over his uniform."

"That's enough, Grand-père," came a female voice from behind the counter. "You're not the only one who speaks English here. No more talk about exploding heads."

The old man glanced toward his granddaughter and lowered his voice. "We held them off most of the day. Until they brought up their artillery. Modern steel breech-loaders. Not like ours. We made it back to Châlons and they tried to reform the army." The old man shook his head. "They were teaching the new recruits how to load the Chassepot on the march to Sedan. To fight the German Army. Vive le France," he snorted.

Pete asked him where he had learned his English.

"My father was English, and my wife taught French and English. She made me learn it proper when we were first married. She said it would make me more…rounded."

The waitress, Juliette, overheard this last bit as she brought his coffee. "I doubt Grand-père was a good student," she said to Pete and John. "But Grand-mère knew how to handle him."

"That's right—pretty much beat me every day, she did. Miracle I survived so long."

Juliette gave her grandfather a side glance as she headed back to the counter. "Angel she was, to put up with you all those years."

The old man took a sip of his coffee. "About time. I thought they were growing the damn beans out back."

Pete chuckled, pulling his eyes away from Juliette. Twenty-three, he guessed. Pretty in a plain sort of way. Small girl. Blonde hair to her shoulders, blue eyes. A war widow with two young boys. This was Pete's third visit to the café, and he was looking for a chance to ask her to lunch, or to tea, or to whatever it was that constituted a first date in wartime France. She disappeared into the kitchen and he looked across the table at his fellow A-Flight pilot. Second Lieutenant John Wilcox, Royal Military College, Sandhurst. Whereas Pete was a product of the far more pedestrian Officer Training Corps—a semi-proud member of Kitchener's New Army. Despite their trip through the rain, John's uniform was clean and pressed.

Rumor was John came out of the cockpit with a neatly pressed uniform. How did he do it, and why would anyone bother? Good-looking chap, too. Fortunately, he was only twenty and had a pretty sweetheart back home. Pete looked at the old man again, who was stirring his coffee absently. Thinking about something.

"In '14, the Huns showed up with machine guns and heavy artillery," he said, looking at his coffee. "What did our boys have? Red trousers and antiques for weapons. Oh yes, we had élan, too. Can't forget that. Our secret weapon." The old man snorted again. "Generals or politicians. I don't know which is worse." He sipped his coffee and looked across the café at his granddaughter. His expression changed. When he spoke again, his voice was quieter. More somber.

"Her husband was with the Fourth Army. Artillery. Paul was a good boy. Respectful. Hard worker. It happened near Bouillon, in August of '14. Marshal Joseph Jacques Joffre." The bitterness was back, although he kept his voice down. "Goddamn fool. Attacking in Alsace while the whole German army moved around his flank. At least Briand fired him before he could completely lose the war."

Pete's eyes widened. This wasn't the kind of talk one normally heard in public, as the French government severely frowned upon anything considered defeatist. He glanced around the café: no gendarmes today. Juliette was back from the kitchen, and he looked at her while he considered what the old man had said. He decided not to respond. Joffre had certainly been slow to react to the threat on his left, absurdly blaming the initial failures on a lack of offensive spirit. What the French called élan. But when Joffre finally saw the danger, he created the French Sixth Army. That army, together with the BEF, broke the advance of the Germans at the Marne—the battle that turned the German advance on Paris into a full-scale retreat. What they called the "Race to the Sea," although it was more of a series of pitched battles, before the armies settled into their trenches. That had been over thirty months ago, with almost no progress made since. He frowned as he thought back to that summer of '14—the newspapers had been full of stories of a quick victory and the boys being home by Christmas. Well, this wasn't the first war that hadn't quite gone as planned, although the level of miscalculation this time around was remarkable. Nor, at least from where Pete Newin sat, did the British high command yet seem to understand the nature of the war they were fighting. That massive artillery bombardments followed by headlong attacks into the enemy's triple defensive lines did nothing more than gain a few thousand yards of ground, at best, at a horrendous cost in lives.

Lunch arrived. A small portion of beef with lots of vegetables. Red wine. This part of France still had enough food, for the people with money to pay for it. The old man accepted a second cup of coffee from his granddaughter and waited until she left.

"Of course, the government tells us nothing. The telegram comes: 'Dear Madame so and so, most regretfully your husband has been such and such. Please accept our most sincere so and so.' But Paul's friend André was in the same battery and told me what happened. They were exchanging fire with the Huns, and a caisson of shells was next to the gun. The Huns had the high ground and could see the fall of their shots. They scored a direct hit on the gun and the ammo. Sixteen soldiers were killed; more wounded. André said Paul died quickly. I hope so."

He looked across the café at his granddaughter. "She doesn't know that part. There's no need to."

As Pete was deciding how to respond, the front door clattered open and four children burst in, followed by a middle-aged lady and some rain.

"Grand-père! Grand-père!" Two boys, about three and five, swarmed onto their great-grandfather. Pete almost laughed at the change in the old man's face. He looked like the sweetest bloke in the world as he took their raincoats off and gave each of them a kiss. He set one on each knee, although the younger boy slid off and ran to his mother. The older boy began explaining the parts of a tree to his grandfather. Apparently, they'd had science class that day. The old man listened and asked several questions.

The two girls who had followed the boys into the café had crowded around Juliette. Both were talking about some adventure at school.

"Bon après-midi, Madame Lambert," Juliette cried over the noise of the children.

"Bon après-midi, Juliette," called the lady.

Pete helped madame out of her wet raincoat and she sat down with Juliette's grandfather. "Isn't it terrible how this war is dragging on?" she began. "And that explosion in the factory at Toulouse. All those women killed. Terrible."

"Yes, Madame. It is a tragedy."

"The papers say General Nivelle is to be replaced. How is this possible—the Hero of Verdun? Perhaps it is a trick to fool the Germans." Pete gave a little nod. Another disastrous Allied offensive, another general losing his job.

"The Germans are bad men," said the little boy.

"Quiet now," the old man told the boy. "Madame and I are talking."

"Perhaps it is a trick, Madame. Certainly, our government cannot tell us everything."

"But surely, we must win soon. The many victories we have won."

"Yes, Madame, that seems most likely. France has the finest men and equipment in all the world. I'm sure we will win soon."

"I see why you like to come here," said John as they finished up lunch. "It's a nice break from the aerodrome." If he'd noticed Pete's interest in Juliette, he was polite enough not to mention it. As they paid their bill, Pete told Juliette in his best French that she had lovely children. She thanked him, and for the first time he saw a trace of sadness in her blue eyes. They said goodbye to her grandfather and Madame Lambert and pedaled back to the aerodrome, battling wind and rain.

Pete went to his room and changed into dry clothes. The aerodrome was full to overflowing after the big move, and they'd needed volunteers to stay at some nearby farmhouses. Pete had raised his hand. He figured it would let him practice his French, although as it turned out, neither his elderly landlord nor his wife was the communicative sort. But it was quiet there, and he had his own side door and a small bathroom. On his little table were some books and his combat notebook. Two similar notebooks, labeled "BE2" and "1 1/2 Strutter," were back home in Devon. He tried to write down everything he learned along the way. He figured it might save his life someday.

An orderly had left a letter from his mom on his bed, and his eyes widened as he read. His little brother Phillip was in training to be an RFC pilot. This the kid who had spent most of his waking hours after the age of eight poring over a chessboard. First in his class in almost everything, and last in Officer Training Corps. Pete had always assumed Phillip would be a doctor, or a scientist. And now, knowing nothing about war or life or staying alive in France, Phillip could be tussling with Hun Albatrosses in a few weeks. How come the brainy kid couldn't find a nice staff job somewhere if he wanted to play army? He threw the letter on the table.

Juliette? How to go about the next step? He thought about it for a couple of minutes without coming up with much of a plan, other than to just ask her. So be it. As some sage person once opined, every omelet demands the breaking of the eggs. He ran his eyes over his reading collection and picked up his combat notebook. Flipped back to the day he'd lost Cochrane. First page: flight composition, airplane issues, weather, mission. Second page: a diagram of the dogfight. The Huns had broken off the engagement when they had the upper hand. He'd had the angle to cut off the wingman and a temporary speed advantage as he traded off altitude. He'd gone up and back down nicely when the German turned into him, working to get on his tail. The two airplanes were established in the same plane of motion and in range, although he was a bit outside his seventy-five-yard sweet spot. The deflection looked good: the German was about midway from the ring to the bead, with a relatively low crossing angle. Or had he been closer to the ring? He'd missed low and right, hitting the inside wing with a couple of bullets. A small downward vector relative to the Hun when he fired could explain that. Maybe a mis-rigged Vickers—he still banged in his landings now and then. He'd have the armament fellows check it out.

He frowned and closed the notebook. There was no way to be sure. If not for the clouds, his next shot would have been from dead astern and no more than seventy-five yards, and he would have gotten his third kill. Which, of course, was neither here nor there.

# The Royal Navy in France

*66 Squadron RFC, Sopwith Scout Fighter Aircraft*
*Liettres Aerodrome, Northern France*
*June 1917*

Pete opened his eyes, listened, and pursed his lips. Some wind was blowing, but nothing like the buffeting of the last three days. He checked the time, got up, and peeked out the window. Shook his head. Good visibility and scattered clouds, which meant game on. He went into his little bathroom, shaved mechanically and regarded the face in the mirror. Average looks, although the pointy nose and mustache added character. Blue-gray eyes, which Emily both loved and disapproved of. They'd bicycled down to the coast that day for a picnic lunch, and he was looking out over the water. The sea was almost calm, the waves bumping on the rocks, not smashing against them. She was looking at him.

"They say God is perfect. But I've always wondered if he didn't make a mistake with you."

He gave her his best level look. *Maybe more than one.*

"Your eyes are too hard. They're like steel. You should have baby blues. Like your brothers and your cousins have."

He didn't know what color eyes his cousins had, but he'd take her word for it.

"I shall pass your critique on to God when I see him."

"I think it's part of your protective shell. To hide what's inside."

Oh boy, were they going to talk about his internal self? He could hardly wait. What *was* inside? Like his three brothers, yet different. Mark: physics. Charles: math, statistics, and later British Army Intel. Phillip: chess. But what drove Pete Newin to be the best at everything he did? The countless hours poring over a chessboard trying to keep up with his little brother. Being a better tennis player than the three of them. And so on. He shrugged and finished dressing. Headed down the little dirt road that ran behind the flight-line and was in the Mess eight minutes later. Ordered toast and coffee and picked up yesterday's *Globe*. He had two rules for reading the newspaper.

Rule Number One: Any good news was something between an exaggeration and an outright lie.

Rule Number Two: If the news was bad enough to have made it into the paper, the truth must be really bad.

The front page was all about the German bombing of Folkestone. Seventy-six killed, mostly women and children. Large twin-engine bombers. The navy claimed three Huns shot down, but there were no pictures to prove it, and the newspapers were asking lots of questions about the defense of London. Would they be ready when the Germans came back? Pete's answer was—probably not. Not when the RFC was still flying BE2s and pusher-props in France, the theater which presumably was their highest priority. Other than the bombing, it was the same non-news as always. The war was going well. The navy had (once again?) invented a foolproof electronic device for defeating the U-boats. An explosion in a French munitions factory in Toulouse—the *Globe* delicately described the result as "a number of workmen and workwomen were unable to escape from the building." An article titled "Russian Morale Improving." Uh-huh. Could it go any lower? Napoleon once said an army's morale was more important than any other factor. If so, the Russians had lost their war months ago.

He set the newspaper down and drank his coffee as the rest of A-Flight filtered in. Roger, Ian Crosse, and Pete were flight leaders. Wilcox, Duncan, and Harris were wingmen, the last two squeaky new. Pete glanced at Harris and did a double take. He was wearing a cavalryman's badge and tunic, and sporting a mustache well beyond regulation limits. Bit bold for a new chap. As usual, Crosse was reading the *Times*.

"Big news, gents. 'The War's Swiftest and Completest Victory. Great Numbers of German Dead. Our Losses Light.' And so on." Pete looked at Crosse.

"Messines Ridge?"

"Yeah. Says we took over six thousand prisoners. They planted nineteen mines under the ridge. That's what we felt Thursday morning. Hope the Huns didn't spill their coffee." Crosse turned the page. "And for you artistic sorts, or if you simply need a bit of relaxation, I have good news. *A Little Bit of Fluff* continues its run at the Criterion. So if you haven't caught it yet, you'll certainly want to the next time you're home. And if I'm not mistaken, the Criterion is entirely underground. So the fluff will go on fluffing, Huns or no Huns."

Duncan and Wilcox got into a discussion as to how much longer the Germans could hold on. Pete tuned them out, remembering the headlines of last July. The advance on the Somme was going well. The high ground taken. Etcetera. And that line that still stuck with him: "We've elected to give the Germans all the battle they want, and there is every reason to be most sanguine as to the result." Right. He'd talked to some of the fellows who were there, and they all called the Battle of the Somme "The Great Fuckup." That we'd taken horrendous casualties to gain almost nothing, and had kept at it long after everyone there knew it was hopeless. And somewhere on those endless casualty lists were the names of his cousins: Martin and Ritchie Burkhard, 9th Devonshires. Even if this latest news was true, Messines Ridge was only one piece of the high ground the Huns held in Flanders. There'd be plenty more chances for Haig to muck things up.

Roger sat down with his standard double breakfast. "Fellows, Mark Henderson is still in hospital," he said between bites, "and Jimmy Musgrave is on loan to Forty-Six. Fleming doesn't know when they'll be back. Which means, at least for now, A-Flight is the six of us."

"What's Forty-Six fly?" asked John Wilcox.

"Nieuport two-seaters," said Roger.

"Jimmy knows how to fly those crates?"

"They haven't sent him back, so I suppose he does now."

There was a lull in the conversation as the chaps ate, and Ian Crosse made a point of checking the time on his Swiss wristwatch. He noticed Billy Duncan admiring it. "If you want to know what time it is," Crosse told Billy, "ask the Swiss. It's better not to ask the Germans, and definitely do not ask the British. Just look at the airplanes we build."

Roger read from the ops order. "Four-ship offensive patrol. Myself, Wilcox, Crosse, Harris. Twelve thousand feet. Working area is the triangle made by Dough-Eye, Sec-Lynn, Deny. We're taking a break from the Wipers sector today. What a shame."

Pete visualized his map, projecting Roger's Yorkshire French onto it. It was their old working area, northeast of Arras.

"Destroy any enemy airplanes in the area. Have a nice day. Love, General T." Roger paused long enough to swallow a mouthful of eggs and sausage.

"You chaps each take five seconds spacing on takeoff. I'll circle over the aerodrome so you can join up, then head southeast to pick up the highway down to Arras. Gun check at three thousand feet. Standard signals for June. Red from you chaps means help. From me, rally and continue. White for washout. Green for engine or gun problem. If you new fellows can't remember that, write it down." Roger paused for a large shot of coffee. "We'll pass north of the city. Cross the line at—" he pulled the small map out of the mission folder "—Fam-Pooh. Third Army country." Roger looked at Harris. "Lieutenant, stick with Lieutenant Crosse. Protect his backside. Don't wander off."

"Yes, sir," replied Harris, followed by something resembling a sigh of condescension.

Roger looked at Harris with raised eyebrows, and there were an uncomfortable few seconds before he continued. "Pete, take Duncan up for basic fighter maneuvers. Beat him up good but stick near the aerodrome."

Pete nodded. It didn't bother him to stay back and play instructor.

After breakfast he gave Billy an overview of the flight, and they stepped outside into a cool French summer morning. A Le Rhône powered up, and he stopped to watch Roger's Pup bump its way forward. Once all four airplanes were airborne, Pete squished his way to a dull green-brown airplane, with a white horizontal stripe indicating it belonged to 66 Squadron, and the letter D on the fuselage identifying an A-Flight airplane. The airplane officially known as the Sopwith Scout, which the pilots had christened the Pup, considering it the offspring of the larger Sopwith 1 1/2 Strutter. In this case, his Pup. B1719.

"Is she ready to go, Paul?" asked Pete, returning the salute from Air Mechanic First Paul Fletcher.

"All ready, Lieutenant. She's had some rest, and we're caught up." After a quick walk-around, Fletcher helped him strap in and Pete ran through his cockpit routine. Always first: verify the ignition switch off. Next the gun. He shouldn't need it, but if he did, two pulls on the handle and it would be ready to fire. On his left side, the hammer was in its pocket. He'd thought the armament chaps were kidding when they told him to whack the Vickers with a hammer when it hung up. It turned out they weren't kidding. Pyrene chemical fire extinguisher. Very gun with six flares, two of each color. His maps. All the accoutrements of twentieth century air warfare. He checked fuel and oil quantities and normal movement of the flight controls. Pumped the fuel pressure to 2.5 psi, set the throttle and mixture levers for engine start.

"Switch off," called Pete.

Fletcher swung the prop a few times so Pete could adjust the mixture. When they were ready, he looked across to the next airplane and got a thumbs-up from Billy Duncan. He nodded to Fletcher.

"Switch on," called Fletcher.

Pete flipped the ignition on. "Contact."

Fletcher swung the propeller. The Le Rhône coughed and fired up. Pete brought the throttle back; adjusted the mixture and listened. Tweaked the mixture lever back and the engine settled at idle. The smell of burnt castor oil hit him, but he hardly noticed anymore. The whole aerodrome stunk of castor oil. And cigarettes.

He let the rotary warm up for thirty seconds, gave the throttle-up signal and went to full power. The Le Rhône roared and the Pup strained forward, held back by two mechanics at the tail. He let the tachometer settle at full power: 1300 rpm. Not bad. He throttled down, checked that Billy was ready and gave Fletcher the chocks-out signal. They had about three minutes to get airborne before the engines overheated. He nudged the throttle and mixture forward as Fletcher held the wingtip, and the Pup swung toward the end of the field. He did a double take as he taxied past Billy—smoke was pouring from the nose of the other Pup.

Pete leveled the Pup at 16,000 feet. Tweaked the throttle and mixture and listened...the Le Rhône seemed content. He'd be safer at 18,000, but he hadn't dressed for a high-altitude patrol and was already freezing. But at 16,000 feet the Pup should (just) be able to hold her own against the heavier Hun fighters. He flexed his stiff fingers and moved his toes inside his flying boots. Chuckled again, despite the cold biting at him. Duncan's engine had caught on fire during start and Billy had neglected to cut the ignition before he jumped out. The burning Pup slipped its wheel chocks and commenced taxiing about the aerodrome, drawing a crowd.

Pete sat back, to the extent possible in the Pup's cramped cockpit, and took in the blue sky and the scattered clouds. The ground far below. The buzz of the Le Rhône, the faint hum of the wind through the wires. He was alone in the sky in his Sopwith. But that solitude came with a price—there was no wingman to look after his backside. He rolled the Pup sixty degrees right and checked the airspace below and behind him. Repeated the roll and scan to the left. Leveled the wings and fired a one-second burst. The Vickers didn't like getting cold, and it was damn cold 16,000 feet above France that June morning. He picked up the St. Pol–Arras highway and turned left to pass north of the city. Toward his old stomping grounds. But he'd stay on the British side of the line. Sun Tzu himself said a wise soldier balances risks versus gains, and who was Pete Newin to argue with the master? On his next scan he spotted a pair of westbound RE8s following the road off to his right. Those chaps had been up early that morning.

Arras came into view. Battered to hell, and too close to the front line for the French to think about fixing up, even if they had the money. He motored past the city and turned north toward First Army sector. There was still a fair amount of green down there despite April's big attack; zig-zagging white lines in the chalky soil marking the trenches. So different from Flanders, where the waterlogged terrain reminded him of some horrible skin disease: cracked, scabrous, and slimy. The decomposing body parts of the men and the horses and the trench rats. The urine and the feces. All pooling with the water, to stew into the Flanders sludge of war.

The clouds were thicker as he headed north, but the visibility was excellent and he picked out Vimy Ridge between the clouds. That would be the Canadian Corps down there, proud new owners of the high ground north of the city. The generals prized the high ground for the same reasons generals had always prized it, but to the infantry blokes it meant more. It meant not living in knee-deep mud day after day, month after month. It meant not eating food that tasted like mud. He gave it another minute and swung back south, visualizing the map in the orderly room. Canadian, then VII, VI, and VIII Corps as he went south.

He was about to turn back north when he picked up a black speck low and left of the nose. He rested his eyes and looked again…the speck became two specks, then three, then more. All of them making little circles in the sky. Whoever they were, they were well below him and just about over no-man's-land. He focused on the nearest airplane...*well, what do you know? If it wasn't the Royal Navy.* It was the first time he'd seen one, but there was no mistaking a Sopwith Triplane. His eyes picked out the brightly colored Huns, a mix of Albatros and Halberstadt single-seaters. He allowed himself a closed-lips smile—he could use his height advantage to drop onto them, and as busy as they were, it was unlikely they'd be looking up. But as was so often the case with Pete Newin, it wasn't that simple. The butterflies flapping about his stomach were having their say—to not plunge into that swirl of airplanes and machine guns, in a wood and fabric tube two feet from an unprotected fuel tank. Without a wingman, and at low altitude where the Huns would have the advantage. To just fly away. Who would know?

He let out a long breath and fired another short burst from the Vickers. Regardless of what his body wanted (and he had more sympathy for its point of view than he'd ever admit) he couldn't stomach looking in the mirror tomorrow and seeing the face of a coward. As much as he didn't want to die today, the alternative had to be worse. Semi-convinced, he eased the Pup's nose down. The wind pushed back as the airspeed increased in the dive, the Pup becoming more responsive to the control column. Jumpier—as if she knew what was coming. As the speed continued to build he banked her into a wide spiral and nudged the mixture lever forward for the lower altitude. Brought the nose up a notch to control her speed, to let her come down at her own pace. As always during the last quiet moments, his mouth was dry and his stomach twisted. After two more wide spirals he spotted an opening. Took a deep breath, said a quick prayer, and rolled her into a dive.

An hour later Pete was sitting in the squadron office, where Hugh Fleming and the equipment, transport, and armaments officers made their homes. Pete ran through the engagement for Fleming. He'd nailed a

Halberstadt that was chasing a triplane, and a few seconds later a triplane got the Albatros that was shooting his Pup to pieces.

"It was a Halberstadt," Fleming said into the phone. "Blue. No, it wasn't burning. May have broken up on the way down." Fleming looked at Pete, who nodded that he had it correct.

Pete liked Hugh Fleming—they'd flown 1 1/2 Strutters in 45 Squadron until Fleming had lost a hand in a landing accident. Now he was a penguin: an RFC officer who wore pilot wings but didn't fly. Pete looked over as the transport officer, Lieutenant Lewis Norris, hung up his phone. "All good in transport, Lewis?"

"Things are never all good in transport, Pete. Breakdowns, traffic jams, mud. Not enough lorries. Fuel shortages. Should I go on?"

"No, thanks. I get the idea."

Fleming hung up the phone and looked at him. "I think you're out of luck on this one, Pete. The forward spotters saw four come down—two in flames and two out of control. But they were too far away to see details, and the two flamers went down on the German side. Naval One lost one of theirs, and the other three pilots claimed six Huns down. But none of their pilots can confirm your blue Halberstadt."

Pete managed not to snort. He'd risked his backside and put at least five bullets into the Hun's critical area. Saw the sparks fly and the Halberstadt spiral into the clouds. Yet it didn't count. Rules. One thing the RFC had plenty of.

"Oh yes," said Fleming, reaching for his ringing phone. "They thanked you for your help."

Pete gave a raised eyebrows shrug. As he stood up, a familiar voice came from behind him. "Saved by the navy. Christ, Newin, why don't you go back to teaching maths?" The speaker made a sound between a laugh and a heavy sigh, and Pete shook his head. Mr. Congeniality himself, Ian Crosse, who had come in to chew on Lieutenant Wall about the Vickers on his Pup. It kept jamming at altitude. Besides berating the staff, Crosse liked to opine on the money and women he'd have after the war (he had political connections of some sort). He was also known to expound at length on the shortcomings of certain senior RFC officers. On at least one occasion, Crosse had attributed these shortcomings to careless selection of sexual partners by a parent of the officer in question, and the ease by which certain diseases are transmitted by sexual contact.

"Ian," said Pete, trying to be civil, "all the Vickers have problems at altitude. The lubricant gums up. Fire it once in a while, or fly lower. There's nothing Wall can do about it."

"What the hell would you know about machine guns, Newin?" Crosse snorted. "A maths teacher thinks he's Mr. Vickers."

Pete shook his head as he headed out the door. He should have known better.

Hugh Fleming finished his pipe and eyed his inbox: combat reports, supply issues, personnel changes, and all the other sundries that made up the administrative life of an RFC squadron. He'd done his duty as a reconnaissance pilot and lived through it, minus his left hand, and was content as a squadron recording officer. Content, but frustrated with the RFC, who continued to send them pilots who weren't ready for combat. Pilots who might have two or three flights in the Pup before tangling with experienced German pilots flying better airplanes. Major Pritchett signed the condolence letters, but Fleming wrote them. He decided to "make his rounds" and deal with the paperwork later. As the major had explained it, anything that wasn't the CO's job was Fleming's job. In other words, if the armaments officer or the equipment officer or anyone else fouled up, it was Fleming's fault—and Hugh Fleming had been around the army long enough not to think such an arrangement was unfair.

As he stood up to leave, their chief of maintenance poked his head in the door. "Do you have a minute, Captain?"

"Sure, Matt." Fleming sat back down.

The sergeant major offered Fleming a cigarette. He shook his head. "Oh, that's right. You're a pipe man." He lit up and took a couple of puffs, blowing the smoke away from Fleming. "B1499 came in from depot yesterday, sir. Rebuild job. The pilot who brought it in said it 'flew poorly.' I saw him land and was surprised he didn't break something. I asked a couple of questions and didn't get much in the way of answers. He was a young fellow, maybe fresh out of training back in England. Anyway, I had the chaps take a look. Two of the rods were out of tolerance on the Le Rhône, and the aileron rigging was sloppy. Like whoever did it had a few too many whiskies the night before."

"Can you fix it?"

"Be done today, sir. But it's a bit arse-backward, us fixing airplanes come from depot. It's not the first time we've had problems like this."

"Understood, Matt. What was the airplane number?"

"B1499."

Fleming pulled the depot folder out of his filing cabinet and wrote himself a note. "I'll speak with the major. I'm sure he'll make a call."

"Thanks, Captain, but a kick in someone's butt might be better. Nice day, sir."

After one more glance at his inbox, Fleming walked down the hall and peeked into the orderly room. The readiness board showed all six A-Flight airplanes in the air, four C-Flight pilots were briefing to head out, and the B-Flight mission folders were in place. Intel had updated the situation map: they'd finally got to move the black line when Second Army took Messines Ridge. Although it might be Messines Valley now; the mines they'd exploded had shaken everyone in the squadron awake. Rumor was they even woke old Lloyd George up back in England. But the Germans still held most of the high ground, protecting their hold on the Belgian coast. He didn't get many calls from Field Marshal Haig, but one only had to look at the map. If they could break through the northern portion of the ridge, they could roll across the flats. Take the massive Hun rail depot at Roulers and push north to the sea, cutting off the U-Boat bases at Ostend and Zeebrugge. Take the Hun's U-boats away and he might as well give it up. But it all hinged on that little word: "if."

He stepped outside to a beautiful summer morning. A little yellow bird in a bush by the squadron building chirped at him as artillery rumbled in the distance. At first he'd been struck by the contrast between the beauty of nature and the horror of war, but now it all blended in. His first stop was the squadron's supply tent. Everything from bullets to soap to lorry parts was logged and stored there. In theory, supply came under the control of their equipment officer—one of those chaps who tried hard and consistently came up short. Which meant that Quartermaster Sergeant Roger Gray, with twenty-three years of service to king and country, effectively ran supply for 66 Squadron. In Fleming's opinion, to say Sergeant Gray was "past his prime" would be most generous. Gray had two browbeaten corporals and six privates who did the work. He spent most of his time reading the paper and smoking cigarettes.

"All good, Sergeant?"

Gray took another puff on his cigarette and set it down. Stood more or less erect, holding on to his back as he did so.

"All good, sir." The words were correct, but the body language asked, "Why are you bothering me?"

"No problems?"

"Nothing big, sir. They keep shorting us machine-gun rounds. Must be a holdup somewhere. Some broken whisky bottles in yesterday's shipment for the officers' club."

"That happened last week, too, didn't it?"

"Yes, sir. Those fellows up at the warehouse should be more careful. Take proper care of government property."

Not for the first time, Fleming wondered if government property was making its way onto the local black market. If he could prove that he might be able to get rid of Gray, although Major Pritchett didn't like to make waves. But as things stood, they were stuck with Gray until he was due to rotate. Four months and counting. "You're a bit of a whisky man yourself, aren't you, Sergeant?"

"Oh, just the occasional, sir. Takes the edge off. Fighting a war and all that. You understand, sir."

Hugh Fleming thought he understood perfectly. "Looks like you're holding up fairly well, Sergeant."

"I try, sir. Gets harder, of course, as we get older. But I do my best. We can't fly airplanes and fight the Hun without supplies."

A corporal and two privates were stacking crates and logging them in. They had greeted Fleming properly when he'd come in and had not looked in his direction since. "You don't want to give them a hand, Sergeant?"

"I do when I can, sir. But the truth is, that sniper got me bad at Colenso. I'm not the complaining type, sir. You know that. But it flares up bad some days."

Fleming had seen the medical report—a bullet had glanced off a rib. Odd it still bothered Gray so much eighteen years later. But as usual, there was nothing to be done.

"Of course, Sergeant. Carry on." He walked toward the rigging shop, stopping to watch two Pups come in. Should be Newin and Harris. Pete Newin had shaped up nicely. Good pilot, didn't take crazy chances. He'd be a good instructor for the new fellows someday, if he lived. As for Harris… he seemed all right, if a bit eccentric. But no one paid much attention to the new chaps—not until they made it past the first month or so.

Pete cringed as the Pup's tail hit and came back up; for a horrible second he thought she might flip over. Not that he would have been killed, probably not even hurt, but it would have been monumentally embarrassing. But the Pup settled back onto the grass with no more than the usual bouncing about, and he made it to his parking spot without further ado. He was waiting for Harris when a Vickers .303 banged from behind him. He wandered over and found Michael Wall and two of his armament mechanics on the firing range. Nodded a greeting as they put the Vickers back together. The corporal tested the action a couple of times; wiped the oil off his hands with a rag. Satisfied, he looked up at Wall. "We're ready, Lieutenant."

Wall scanned the firing range. "Go ahead."

The corporal fed the belt in place and pulled the charging handle twice. Fired a one-second burst and paused for a few seconds. Fired a second burst, followed by another pause, then a third burst. Unlike the army's water-cooled Vickers, the RFC's air-cooled version didn't like being fired from a stationary platform. "Works fine, Lieutenant. It was just gummed up."

"Okay, nice work, fellows. Let's pack it up."

Pete nodded toward the Vickers as the corporal unloaded it. "How are they holding up?"

Wall shrugged. "It's built solid, but it's still a gun, and guns jam. From the cold, or all the muck that gets thrown off the engine. They hang up and you fellows whack them with the hammer. Maybe that fixes it, but sooner or later something gets bent."

"What's the fix?"

Wall gave Pete a wry smile. "That you fellows stop flying so high. That the RFC puts an engine on the Pup that doesn't throw castor oil everywhere. That the factories work to design tolerances. But realistically…I suppose we could put a cowling over it. Keep it warmer. Keep the oil off. But you fellows wouldn't have access to it inflight. Not sure the pilots would go for that."

"I doubt we would."

Michael squatted down and lifted the ammo belt. "The fabric belt's another problem. It gets wet and rots, sitting in the box. Freezes at altitude and stiffens up. Big problem for you Pup fellows. Not so much now, but in wintertime. The word is they're testing a metal belt."

"The Huns use metal, don't they?"

"They do, yes. That might be where we got the idea."

Pete mused on the difference between the sound of a Vickers on the firing range and the same gun mounted on a Pup. The infantry Vickers fired about nine rounds a second; but on the Pup, the Vickers was paired with the Kauper interrupter gear. Necessary to avoid shooting holes in one's own propeller, but the interrupter reduced the rate of fire. Since the Pup only carried a single gun, the rate of fire was crucial. "Any idea how much the Kauper reduces the rate of fire?"

Wall gave him a side glance. "The manual says it causes a *slight* reduction to the effective rate of fire."

"Slight. Not the word I would have used." Unlike the gun he'd just heard, when he fired the Vickers in the air he could hear the individual *pops* as each bullet fired. "One would think the RFC armaments branch could be a little more precise."

"Yes, one would think."

"Did they give up on trying to synchronize the Lewis?"

"I think so. Open bolt operation, so the rate of fire isn't constant. At least not at first. If I had to guess, it'll be the Vickers for shooting forward. At least if we're shooting through the propeller arc."

"I don't suppose you could figure out how to mount a second gun on the Pup?"

The question brought a smile from the normally serious Lieutenant Michael Wall. "I imagine we could mount a Lewis on the upper wing, to shoot above the propeller. It works on the SE5. You're welcome to speak to the major about it."

Pete frowned. He'd heard stories about chaps trying to change a Lewis drum in the middle of a dogfight, with fingers stiff from the cold. The additional weight of the gun and the ammo drums. And no doubt the RFC had regulations governing airplane modifications—they had them for everything else. No, the Pup just wasn't the airplane for 1917. The little girl had seen her day.

# A Welcome to Flanders

*6 Squadron RFC, BE2 Reconnaissance Aircraft*
*Abeele Aerodrome, Western Belgium*

Harry walked into the orderly room, feeling like hell. A Hun bomber had harassed the aerodrome during the night; he'd spent over an hour in the dugout at two in the morning and barely slept after that. He sat down near four other observers: three sergeants and a second lieutenant. Their uniforms were dirty and smelled of fuel and oil, a sure sign they'd flown the early go. He exchanged good morning nods with the lieutenant. The three sergeants ignored him. He didn't drink coffee but poured himself one from the pot anyway. Added some cream and a spoonful of sugar.

"Spencer and White didn't make it back yesterday," he heard from behind him. "Went down in a field over by Kemmel. They're both in hospital."

"Good show for them."

"Not for White. I heard he's missing half his face."

"Let's hope it was his bad half."

Laughs all around. The conversation paused while cigarettes were lit. Picked up again. "There's a rumor we'll get the Bristol. We might have a chance in that."

The lieutenant shook his head. "Sorry, fellows. I talked with the RO yesterday. It'll be the RE8."

Groans greeted the news, and the lieutenant raised his eyebrows. "I'm surprised and, to be honest, a little disappointed in you gents. The RE8 is the latest in airplane technology. Brought to you by the Royal Aircraft Factory—the finest builder of airplanes in the world. Just ask them."

"Why not the Bristol? We're in the thick of it here."

"Policy from above, chaps. Word is we're moving to all officers as observers. As soon as you gents are all dead, we can have the Bristol."

That brought smiles from the three sergeants, and they thanked the lieutenant for the good news. The group broke up, and the lieutenant stopped by and put out his hand.

"Blake Webb, East-Ender." Harry shook hands. Firm handshake.

"Harry Booth. Liverpool."

"When did you get in, Harry?"

"Feels like a year ago."

"I've been on leave. Who are you paired with?"

"Norman Frazier."

"C-Flight. Well, welcome to Wipers." Blake smiled at the look on Harry's face. "Cheer up, mate. You're not dead yet. Beer's on me tonight." Blake gave him a slap on the shoulder and Harry watched him go. East Ender maybe, but there wasn't a trace of Cockney in his voice. He must have gotten out of there as a youngster.

Harry got out his wireless codes and tried to study. The quicker he could send messages, the less time they'd spend getting shot at. G for Fire. O for Over, S for Short. *What do you know—someone in the army knows how to spell.* NF for Guns Now Firing (meaning move your arses, fellows). SW for Switch. Something warm pushed against his leg, and he looked down into the face of the squadron's yellow Labrador. "Hey, morning, Heathcliff." He gave the Lab a rub on the head. "Good boy." Harry enjoyed the moment. It brought a sense of normalcy to the place, and Heathcliff was happy to put his head on Harry's leg and soak up the attention.

"Morning, Harry. Found a friend?" Thomas, one of his roommates, had come in.

"I have, yes. Heathcliff. Funny name."

"It's from a novel. *Wuthering Heights.*"

"What's a Wuthering?"

"I don't know. It's the name of a house, I think. In the book."

Harry shook his head. "I've never heard of it. Any good sex scenes?"

The normally serious Thomas chuckled at that. "Not that I recall."

Harry liked Thomas, and according to the board they were on the same four-ship mission today. He went back to his wireless codes, but Heathcliff had wandered off and that familiar feeling of dread was back. Was he going to die today—with no one to give it a second thought? *That new observer kid, Booth, bought it this morning. Shame. Yeah. Hope it's not that fish for dinner again; I spent an hour in the loo last night.* He blew out a sigh and went back to his codes. Walked down the list with his finger and said them almost aloud. Anything to keep his mind from wandering. Norman came in, picked up their mission folder and sat down across from him.

"The Hun bombers come often?"

"Sometimes. You'll get used to it."

*Great.* Get used to no sleep and feeling like hell.

"We're back with Tenth Corps. Counter-battery work with the Forty-First Division," said Norman, looking at the folder. "It's been mostly trench bombardment the last few weeks. It's our turn to have some fun."

Harry looked at Norman. Obviously, they didn't have the same idea of fun. Norman didn't say anything else, so he turned to the 1:40,000 scale map of Flanders posted on the wall. X Corps sat midway between Y-chat and Wipers. Further south were IX Corps and II ANZAC. By some miracle, the army had taken Messines Ridge and straightened the line out.

He'd watched the intel chaps redraw the black line the other day—he'd never seen grown men so excited. Norman set the 1:10,000 targeting map on the table and pointed with his finger.

"The Forty-First is northeast of Saint-Éloi. By the canal. We'll be working Johnny Twenty-Five and Thirty-One. Around Shrewsbury Forest." Harry went back and forth between the targeting map and his 1:40,000 big-picture map, pushing his brain to get moving. The large blocks on his map were identified by a letter, and the thousand-yard squares within each block were numbered one to thirty-six. The Johnny that Norman referred to, RFC speak for the letter J, identified the large block east of Wipers. Norman pushed the map aside and picked up the ops order.

"There'll be four of us working the back side of the ridge, with four pusher-props from Forty-One for cover."

Harry picked up the resignation in Norman's voice when he mentioned pusher-props. Still, the more British airplanes flying around, the better his chances. Norman nodded toward a pilot who had just come in. Harry recognized his flight commander, with whom he'd exchanged about twenty-five words since arriving at 6 Squadron. "Captain Gallow will lead today. You up on your wireless and targeting procedures?"

"Yeah. But in training, they told us the pilots handle the wireless."

"You observer chaps do it in the BE2. Once we switch to the RE8, I'll handle it so you can keep lookout. I haven't heard much good about the Harry Tate, but at least you'll have a proper field of fire for the Lewis."

Harry sighed. Harry Tate. The comedian whose name rhymed with RE8—the implication being the airplane was a joke. Still, it would have to be better than the BE2, wouldn't it? Norman pushed the ops order across the table. About thirty codes for communication with the battery, paired with two frequencies and three tone settings. With only four airplanes in the flight, the radio operator for each battery should recognize his assigned airplane. At least that was the idea. Standard two-letter clock code for targeting corrections: the first (letter) for miss distance in yards, the second (number) for bearing from target to impact point. They'd check in with

Battery B of the 190th Royal Field Artillery Brigade on the way in, and the battery would signal back via louvre panel if they were receiving the wireless. No point in going across the line if the wireless wasn't working. Be a shame if that happened.

Light rain was falling as they walked to their airplane, along with the familiar smells of mud, oil, and fuel. The mechanics pulled the tarp off and he climbed into the front seat of the BE2. Not much there: Lewis gun with three extra ammo drums, and a leather pouch for his papers. No straps or belts. If he needed to fire the Lewis, he'd put one foot on the floor and a knee on the seat, with a seventy-mile-per-hour wind beating on him. Hopefully, Norman wouldn't make any sudden moves while he was trying to shoot. More than one BE2 observer had been tossed overboard during combat maneuvering, and the RFC didn't bother with luxuries like parachutes. When he finished settling in, the AM1 who was standing by handed him the folder he'd left on the wing.

"Thank you, airman."

"Welcome, sir. New here?"

"Sort of," he said, discouraging further conversation.

He checked the Lewis gun—it swiveled normally on its pillar. With three extra ammo drums he had almost two hundred rounds on board. He looked around the still unfamiliar surroundings, gauging his field of fire. Even if he could somehow contort himself behind the gun without falling overboard, the engine, propeller, and wings would block firing forward. Nor could he shoot to their blind spot—Norman and the tail would be in the way. Which meant his field of fire was about fifteen degrees off the tail, forward to about fifteen degrees behind the wing-line. In theory, the pilot could fire the gun to the front-quarter area. Just how well that would work in practice… He rechecked the ops order and set the tone and antenna length on the wireless. Sat back and waited for Norman, butterflies flapping about his stomach.

They plodded along at 3000 feet, bouncing about as they went in and out of the clouds. His stomach was churning, sweat was running down his face, and he was surprised he hadn't vomited—yet. But thank God for small miracles, the FE8s had shown up and were trailing them a half mile back. There were breaks in the clouds below and he could see the ground through the haze. Gray mud pockmarked with shell holes. The occasional little road. Some busted-up trees. Norman had told him to leave his map in its pocket and keep his eyes outside the cockpit, but it all looked the same to him anyway. He knew they were headed east by the yellow spot in the haze that marked the sun, but that was about all he knew.

Captain Gallow yawed the nose of his airplane left and right, the signal for friendly airplanes in sight. Harry looked up and saw the upper wing of the BE2. The Royal Aircraft Factory had given the pilot a cutout in the wing to improve upward visibility, but the observer didn't rate such consideration. Their BE2 yawed left and right in response, so whoever they were, Norman had them in sight. A few seconds later six SE5s sped past them. He pulled the ops order out of its pocket and reviewed the check-in. Norman throttled the engine back.

"Let out the antenna, Harry," he shouted, and pushed the power up.

*Yeah, that might help.* He released the catch on the drum and felt it spin. Saw bits of green below them in the sea of mud. Camouflage netting? But exactly where their battery was down there... He shrugged; it wasn't his problem if they weren't in the right place. In fact, he hoped they weren't. They droned around in circles for a few minutes, a steady rain falling. A few miles north of them an observation balloon bobbed in the wind like a bloated sausage.

"They're ready, Harry. Send it."

Harry looked at his piece of paper, holding it low to keep it out of the wind and wet. Took a deep breath, began typing, and made a mistake on the second letter. He sent the reject code and started over. Got halfway through before cocking it up. Cursed and started to send the reject code again. The airplane rolled back and forth, and he looked up. Norman pointed toward the battery and gave him a thumbs-up.

*Well, fine.* He put the wireless codes back in their pocket and looked around. Rain, clouds, haze. No doubt typical Flanders weather, and this was the nice time of year. He took the dirty rag out of its pocket and wiped his goggles dry for the third time. Norman closed on Gallow and the two airplanes made four more wide circles, still bouncing about. The smell of oil and fuel, along with the bouncing, were getting to him. Should he take his glove off and put his finger down his throat—do a quick honk and be done with it? He hadn't made up his mind when he spotted the other two airplanes closing on them. Both pilots gave Gallow a thumbs-up, so all four airplanes were a go. Unusual. From the chatter he'd heard in the squadron, normally at least one airplane dropped out. Gallow rolled out headed east; Norman spread wider and throttled up. Damn it. They were going across the line.

Harry watched the sky above, below, and behind them as best he could from his front seat. Kept both hands on the Lewis, telling himself he was ready.

No-man's-land. It was the only mud around that didn't have trench lines in it.

He jerked as a shell burst in front of them. Archie had seen them. A second burst. A third, closer. Black and ugly. He started to swing his Lewis gun around before realizing he wouldn't have the slightest idea where to aim. He settled for cursing at the gunners instead. That the bastards had eaten rotten sausage that morning and squiggly little bugs were chewing holes in their intestines. That in a few minutes they'd all bleed to death from their assholes. A fourth burst, further away, then quiet as the four BE2s droned eastward. But it seemed like they were barely moving, and his stomach churned as he waited. Knowing what was coming. He cringed as four black bursts mushroomed in front of them. Held his breath… and let it out. There was plenty of empty sky between the bursts. If there were only four guns, this wouldn't be bad. But the black bursts doubled.

Doubled again a few seconds later. His eyes widened as they doubled a third time—every single burst throwing invisible shrapnel. Were they going to fly through *that?*

One went off directly in front of them. He let go of the Lewis and put both hands on the railing, sick to his stomach. Another burst, just below and to the right. Close enough to hear the explosion over the roar of the engine. To smell the cordite. The BE2 wobbled, steadied, and soldiered on. A few seconds of quiet, other than his heart pounding and his lungs sucking air…an explosion next to them— the closest one yet. The BE2 reared up and right; she seemed to hang motionless. Her nose sliced down and Harry stared at the mud of Flanders through the spinning propeller. Bit his lip as he waited for the spiral. For the impact that would impale him on the engine and break his spine—the rest of the BE2 spearing through his mashed body a split second later.

Norman pulled the airplane back to level flight. Still holding on to the railing, Harry looked at the right wing and counted three holes. Not little eight-millimeter bullet holes, but big tears in the fabric, exposing a broken wing rib. His breakfast came up—that bitter taste of vomit at the back of his throat. He swallowed hard and pushed it back down.

A shout came from behind him. "Watch for Huns, Harry."

Oh yeah, he'd forgotten about that. He'd been too busy watching the nice black bursts, and the lovely scenery below them. He searched the gray sky as best he could from his front seat, gripping the Lewis tight. The cold steel through his gloves gave a bit of reassurance—a link to staying alive. The BE2s had split up so they must be approaching their assigned area. He loosened his death grip on the gun and flexed his fingers, the pounding of his heart easing as the fire from Archie slackened. He spotted a north-south highway behind a small ridgeline. Not exactly towering peaks, but it must pass for high ground in Flanders. He looked for the FE8s and didn't see them. Hopefully, they were around somewhere.

Norman pushed the nose down and rolled into a turn. To confuse Archie, or he needed to take a closer look at something. Harry could see the ground well enough, but there were still lots of clouds and haze around—maybe they'd call the whole thing off and go home. As he finished that thought a rush of wind knocked his head back. He looked to his left, confused. A big tear in the fabric and a wing rib sticking straight up, close enough to touch. *Jesus.* The shell must have passed right through, set to explode at higher altitude.

Norman was giving him a hammering-down motion. He stared… and remembered. The signal to open fire. He gave Norman a thumbs-up, looked at the wireless, and…nothing. Took the codes out from their pocket, and praise the Lord, just held on as the wind grabbed them. Pressed the paper flat against his leg. The letters were fuzzy, and he wiped his goggles again. Target number followed by G. He gave a little shake of the head— *what was so hard about that, idiot?* He started tapping and cocked up the target number. Sent the reject code. Started again and fouled up the G. He couldn't get his fingers to stop twitching.

"You okay, Harry?"

Not trusting himself to speak, he gave a thumbs-up without turning around. *Take your time, Booth.* There. Done. "Sent," he yelled over his shoulder and sat back, feeling mildly proud of himself. Remembered his other job a few seconds later and went back to his visual lookout. There was only the occasional Archie burst now as the BE2 came and went from the shelter of the clouds.

Norman gave him the signal for five, followed by three hundred. Harry looked at him. "The shell landed at five o'clock and three hundred yards, you bloody idiot," shouted Norman. "Send the correction."

*Let's see…code 5 for five o'clock. And three hundred yards? Hell. Freddie was for five hundred, Edward for four hundred, so three hundred must be Don.* He tapped it out.

"Nothing," shouted Norman after a couple of minutes of circling. "Did you send it?"

Had he flipped the order, or did he just muck it up? "I'll send it again."

He looked down at the wireless and heard the boom. Felt the airplane rise. The black smoke engulfed them, along with the sickening sound of metal tearing across metal. The acrid smell of the cordite. *Was the engine hit? If they couldn't make it back to the British side, they'd be taken prisoner and he'd live through the war.* He listened, holding his breath… The engine was misfiring, maybe down a cylinder, but the damn thing was still running. He sent Don Five and gave Norman a thumbs-up. Listened to the engine again. Maybe shrapnel had cut a fuel or water line.

Archie had gone quiet. Long may it last.

Norman gave him the Fire for Effect signal. He sent the two-letter code and sat back with something resembling a smile, and lost it as Norman rolled them hard left. Further left, and he grabbed the railings with both hands. They rolled past ninety degrees of bank and the ground pulled at him, his butt sliding forward on the wet wooden seat. He squeezed the railings as hard as he could, jerked as his forward panel exploded in his face. He came out of his seat, his heart pounding like it was going to explode.

*Squeeze harder, Harry*! His arms burned as his gloves slipped on the wet wood of the railings.

*Harder*! His butt was up against the railing; the BE2 still on her back and turning. He bumped over the railing, and his heart skipped a beat as he lost his grip with his left hand. He reached out and grabbed one of the struts; tried to do the same with his right hand as he came out of the cockpit. But his fingers wouldn't close on the strut, and he was losing his balance. He started to fall out of the airplane, lunged and got his arm around one of the support wires. Bent one knee and hooked a foot around something to brace himself as he teetered in the wind—a warm, wet rush in his crotch as he peed himself. He hung there, more out of the airplane than in, as the wind buffeted him and the ground pulled at him, to fall to the mud 3000 feet below. He clenched his teeth as the wire cut into his right arm, his grunts of pain swept away by the wind. His right arm was going numb and he was losing strength in his left hand, but finally they were rolling back upright, and the ground stopped trying to pull him out of the airplane.

His breath exploded out—he must have been holding it. He slowly unhooked his right arm and eased the death grip of the fingers on his left hand. Sank back into his seat and sat motionless, pulling air in and pushing it out. Trying to refill his empty lungs. *How close had he just come to dying? And he was still in a BE2 on the German side of the line.*

He tried to get hold of the Lewis gun, but his arms were shaking and the fingers on his left hand were still locked. He massaged them with his right hand—got them to move a little, then a little more. Watched a green-and-white airplane roll over them, moving from inside their turn to outside. Stared at the black Iron Crosses. God, it was a Hun fighter. And close enough to see the pilot. He swung the Lewis in the general direction of the German; Norman ducked—he must have almost hit him with the barrel. He tried to track the Hun with the Lewis, but he dropped behind their tail before Harry could get the gunsight anywhere near him. His heart was still pounding and he was sweating under his lightweight jacket. Norman rolled back right; the Hun was below them, moving inside their turn. Harry squeezed the Lewis gun to steady his hands, pointed it somewhere in front of the German and pulled the trigger. The Lewis kicked and the ammo drum rattled. *Yes! He was doing something. Harry Booth was fighting back!*

He let off the trigger; went to fire again and Norman waved him off. He looked from Norman to the Hun…and understood. The Hun was out of range—not even close. He clenched and unclenched one fist, then the other. Stared at the German as he closed the gap, the black machine guns stark against its white nose. His stomach twisted; eight-millimeter rounds could punch through his body in the next few seconds, and he'd bleed to death in a shabby BE2. Or burn, if the Hun got the gas tank. The twin machine guns were pointed directly at him. He held his breath, aimed, and fired a long burst. Watched the beautiful tracers reach out…and pass behind the German.

*Damn it!* He shifted his aim forward, grimacing at the twin flashes from the Hun's nose. At the tearing of fabric in the BE2's tail section. He fired another long burst; let off the trigger and stared at the Hun as he passed underneath them. Beautiful and deadly—like a brightly colored poisonous snake. He caught himself after a few seconds and looked behind them. Christ, another one was rolling in. He got the Lewis on it and Norman waved him off. He stared at the approaching silhouette; it was one of the FE8s, chasing the German. As he went past Norman gave him the signal for Next Target.

Oh, that's right, they were spotting for the artillery. He'd been having so much fun, he'd forgotten. He bent to the wireless. Anything to ignore the world swirling around him, where his life was nothing more than some barroom conversation in German. Nothing more than a little blue, white, and red circle on some asshole's scorecard.

He took a few seconds to review the message and managed to get it right. Looked up to see an airplane spinning past them, trailing smoke. It was one of the FE8s, the pilot leaning out of the cockpit as it spun around. He spotted another airplane above and behind them.

It was a little larger now, but still just a dark silhouette in the haze.

Larger still; he swung the Lewis and pointed it up. There wasn't much relative motion; he aimed at its upper wing to compensate for the gravity drop. Was it a Hun, or one of theirs?

The airplane came into the clear: rounded nose and fuselage. Light colored. He squeezed the trigger, but the Hun's nose had already lit up with dual flashes. The Lewis began thumping, and stopped. It hadn't kicked back at him—it just stopped firing. He stared down at it. Hell, the ammo drum must be empty. He pulled the hammer back and clawed at the drum, the BE2 twitching as it absorbed more German bullets. He glanced at the German as he swept past them: silver with a green stripe along the fuselage and a mottled camouflage pattern on the wings. At least they were going to be killed by sharp-looking airplanes.

He got the drum off and into the rack; grabbed a new one and it slipped out of his hands. He fumbled with it through his stiff leather gloves; it squirted away and rolled out of reach, tearing up the floor of the BE2. The hell with it—he grabbed another one with both hands, set it on the Lewis and pushed it into place. Let go and grabbed the railings as they rolled past ninety degrees and into a dive. *Christ, not again.* He braced himself in tight with his legs, noticing his shattered front panel for the first time. Those bullets had come within inches of him.

"Twelve o'clock, four hundred yards," Norman yelled as they rolled back upright.

Harry settled into his seat and turned to the wireless. *Let's see. That would be…Edward Twelve.* His fingers had stopped twitching; he took his time and got it right. When he looked up Archie was shooting again, which should mean the Hun fighters had gone. Well, it didn't much matter. He was going to be killed either way. Norman gave him a second targeting correction, followed by Fire for Effect. Elation flowed across him a couple of minutes later as he realized they had turned west, replaced by that same sick feeling in his stomach as they turned back.

"New target, Harry," shouted Norman. "I think it's an Archie battery."

*An Archie battery?* Harry smiled under his scarf. *It's payback time.* He wrote the coordinates down as Norman signaled them. *All right, Booth, get it right for once. Esses William for Switch, Nuts Freddie for Now Firing, plus the coordinates.* He bent to the wireless, paused, and tapped out the message. Norman had him send Switch to New Target and Fire, as some battery commanders didn't trust reports about targets their own intel hadn't reported.

The first shell landed about three minutes later; they sent two targeting corrections followed by Fire for Effect. Harry couldn't see the Archie battery but fervently hoped it was under those explosions. They were only eighteen-pounders, not the real heavy stuff. But eighteen-pounders were plenty big enough if they were on target.

And so it went, for what seemed like an eternity. But finally, they crossed back onto the British side and Archie went quiet. His fear faded as they plodded toward home. He was exhausted—completely wiped out. And pissed off. How could the RFC send them on a mission like this? In an airplane that was nothing more than a flying target, with some old pusher-props for escort? An airplane appeared in front of them, and it took him a few seconds to recognize another BE2. Flight commander streamers flew from the uprights, so Captain Gallow had made it back. The two airplanes went into a circle, and halfway around Harry jumped when he saw two airplanes above them, but a second later he recognized what was left of their escort. A third BE2 joined them; both right outboard uprights were broken and the upper wing was sagging at the wingtip. The observer waved to him; he recognized Thomas and gave a half-hearted wave back. They did three more circles, presumably waiting for the fourth airplane, before Gallow's airplane steadied up west and the other two BE2s moved into a V formation. They were headed home. Somehow, he had lived through it.

Harry sat in the orderly room and waited for Norman. He'd managed not to throw up and his stomach was settling down, but he'd looked in the mirror and he was as white as a sheet of paper. Fortunately, his pissed trousers had dried and no one had noticed. Norman came in talking with the other two pilots. They weren't joking around, but nor did they appear upset about losing one of their mates. For the first time, Harry noticed Norman had an athletic build. Golfer type, someone had told him. Blond-haired, blue-eyed, decent-looking chap.

Norman sat down and started working on his report. Spoke without looking up. "You were slow on the wireless. Very slow." He was speaking softly, hoarse from shouting. "The more time we waste on the Hun side, the more likely we end up dead. We lost one of ours today, and two of the Fees." He looked up from his report. "This isn't some game we're playing, Liverpool. Some of those fellows are dead. Maybe all four of them."

"I know it's not a game." Harry resented the implication.

"If you ever swing the Lewis through me like that again, I'll smash your face when we get back. Clear enough?"

Norman stared at him, and Harry stared back. *Up yours, Frazier.*

Norman went back to his report, and his tone was softer when he spoke again. "You need to know how many rounds are in the drum. If you've shot halfway through and you have time, change it. Don't wait until it's empty. Borrow a Lewis from the armaments officer. Fire a few bursts and guess how many rounds are left. Then take the drum off and count them. With luck, it will jam on you. You're going to deal with jams—best see them on the ground first."

"All right."

"Did you recognize the Huns?"

"Rounded noses. Albatrosses, I think."

"The three that hit us were D2s. You can recognize the newer ones, the D3s, by their wing struts. They're V shaped, like the French Nieuports. I only saw one of those today: orange with white trim. He was probably the jasta leader—they like to be recognizable to their mates."

*Three of them? Had he completely missed an attacking airplane?*

"Work on your wireless. It may save your life. And mine." Norman signed his report and looked up. "I had to remind you to rewind the antenna. Forty-Two Squadron killed one of their mechanics a few weeks back—the wire wrapped around him on landing and the weight hit him in the head. Let's not do that."

Norman got up and tossed his report in the inbox, and Harry semi-listened as he reviewed the mission with Captain Harvey. Harry couldn't think about the flight now. He'd tackle that later. Or maybe he'd just forget about it.

Halfway home, he'd started shaking. He might have fought off an attacking Zeppelin, but that was about it. After they'd landed and shut down, he struggled out of the cockpit and walked around the airplane. Like the real pilots and observers did. Besides the hits near his seat, there was damage to the propeller, the engine, both wings, and the tail. He figured that one was headed for the scrap heap, and good effing riddance, when he heard Norman speaking with the mechanic.

"What do you think?"

"At least one strut and the propeller, Lieutenant. The broken ribs… and the engine chaps will need to look at the V-8. We won't know more until we pull some fabric off. I'd guess we'll send her back to depot."

"Thank you, Sergeant." Norman turned toward the squadron building without looking in Harry's direction.

"You don't look well, my friend."

Harry looked up. Thomas appeared unruffled, if a bit grimy.

"I'm all right," Harry lied.

"I looked at your airplane. It's almost as bad as ours. I didn't know a BE2 could fly with a wing sagging like that. Lieutenant Wilson said he had full power and almost full rudder in all the way home. Did you hit any of the Huns? I hit one in the wing—I saw the fabric tear."

Harry shook his head. Thomas seemed a nice enough bloke—not like the rest of them around there. But he couldn't think of anything to say.

"Let's check the board," said Thomas after waiting a few seconds. "See what's on for tomorrow."

*Board? Tomorrow?* Harry's eyes went from Thomas to the readiness board and back to Thomas.

*He could be doing this again tomorrow?*

# Jousting

*Teddington, Southwest London*

"Anything else, Miss Rachel?" the elderly waiter asked.

"No, thank you, Pierre."

"Sir?" He looked at Mark.

"No, thank you."

They were finishing lunch and she'd been talking about her family. Her grandfather was a retired admiral, she had two cousins in the army, another who was a socialist, and a younger sister whom Rachel described as lively.

"Lively in what way?"

"Most ways. You'll understand if you meet her."

The door of the restaurant opened and for the third time since they had sat down, she waved hello to the new entrants. Unlike himself, she seemed to be acquainted with most of the people in the local area. She turned to the window as a bright-red motorcar went by, kicking up spray. The sun had come out, but the street was still damp from the rain earlier that morning. An overburdened lorry went by, crates stacked high, followed by a double-decker bus. One still saw horse-drawn carriages about London, but there was no doubt which way transport was headed. His eyes wandered around the restaurant: beige walls, white curtains. The restaurant must not be open at night, otherwise they'd have blackout curtains. Not that the little gas lights on the walls would put out enough light to attract the German bombers. Two posters adorned the walls, the subject matter wartime England standard:

Poster 1: Soldier extending hand.

Headline: "Have you a friend or relation serving?"

Relations, yes, with respect to Mark Newin. Three brothers, and two cousins killed at the Somme last year.

"Have you thought about giving him a hand by enlisting?"

He had thought of that.

Poster 2: Soldier in green kilt climbing hill, bearing the Union Jack.

Headline: "He carried the flag to victory."

And at the bottom: "Share his glory by buying national war bonds."

Mark had done that—done the buying of war bonds part. Somehow the sharing of the glory bit hadn't come through. Still, he was doing his part, wasn't he? Professor Stanton reminded them every so often of the importance of the work they were doing—how it was appreciated by the War Office. That the Lab helped save British lives every day. All of which was true. But it was also true that twenty-eight-year-old Mark Julian Newin had no notable physical deficiencies (other than an extra stone or two around the midsection) which would disqualify him from active military service. The navy had turned him down in '14 for an irregular heartbeat, but he'd had it checked twice in the last year. Both times the doctor had told him he was fine. Yet he sat in an office in London with an approved exemption. He realized he was frowning while at lunch with a lady friend and set those thoughts aside.

Rachel was still turned to the window, and Mark looked at her. Fine features, small nose. Lovely brown eyes that bespoke intelligence or a quick wit, both of which applied in her case. She was wearing a gray-and-white dress and a red scarf. As to her age…judging a woman's age wasn't his specialty. He'd go with twenty-eight to thirty-eight at a ninety percent confidence level. Some people might consider Rachel plain, but with the sun shining through the window onto her neck and shoulders, she was beautiful. He looked at the large black buttons on her dress. Turned to the window.

"I haven't spilled potato soup on my dress, have I, Mark?"

The restaurant's truncated menu consisted of potato soup and bread, or fish and bread. They'd both opted for the soup. He turned from the window—her eyes had a little twinkle in them. He inspected her dress for foreign matter. "No, you have not spilled potato soup on your dress."

"And no unsightly crumbs of bread?"

He shook his head. "No unsightly crumbs of bread."

"There must be some other problem with my appearance, the way you were looking. My unmentionables aren't showing, are they? Or a button not properly buttoned?"

She'd caught him looking, although he managed not to blush at the mention of a woman's unmentionables. "Your appearance is fine. Nor is anything improper showing." With that reasonably solid answer, he hoped the subject was closed. No such luck.

"You do know what unmentionables are, don't you, Mark?"

"Well, I'm not an expert on the subject," he said cautiously. "But at least on a conceptual level, I know what women's unmentionables are. There's even a fair chance I'd recognize them if I saw them."

"By the way, Mark, a woman always knows when a man is looking at her. You shall have to learn to be more discreet." He took a few seconds to formulate an answer.

"I was admiring your outfit."

She gave a small nod. "That is a reasonably good response given the situational disadvantage you have maneuvered yourself into, and understanding your limited aptitude with respect to mastering our English language. Although I wouldn't say you're on the conversational high ground quite yet."

He gave a bit-lip smile, uncertain how to respond, and knowing he'd be hopelessly outclassed by her if it came to verbal fencing. Well, it didn't matter; she was only toying with him. As he had his entire life, he sought refuge in his work and thought about the ballistics report sitting on his desk. Checked his watch for the third time in the last ten minutes.

"You are aware we're not on a precise hourly schedule at the Lab, aren't you, Mark?"

He looked up. "I am aware of that, yes."

"Nor do I believe you have an important meeting on your schedule this afternoon." She paused, with that ever-so-faint smile of hers. "Ergo, I must be boring you. A simple, middle-aged secretary like myself, having lunch with the brilliant young physicist. Talking about my books, my gardening, my family."

Mark frowned. "You are hardly simple. Nor am I brilliant. Therefore, your comment is incorrect on at least two counts." He sat back, pleased with his response. Had he gained an edge in the conversational jousting?

"Well done. But I notice you didn't critique the 'middle-aged' part."

Hmm. There was significant downside risk in this latest turn of the conversation, and he just stopped himself from drumming his fingers on the table as he considered his response. "I might be older than you think. In fact, I probably am." He'd come up with another solid answer and breathed an invisible sigh of relief.

"Nice dodge. For a scientific type. Of course, people have seen us together, and they will talk. To wit, Anne from Accounting has paid more attention to us than she has to her lunch companion since they came in." Rachel nodded toward a woman with short blonde hair wearing a red dress, sitting two tables from them.

The woman looked away as Mark looked over. He only vaguely recognized her. "I don't know Anne from Accounting."

## JOUSTING

"It appears she knows you. And if she doesn't know your name, she certainly will by the close of business today." He didn't reply, and she continued. "As I said, Mark, people will talk. Does it bother you they will talk about us? That they will make certain assumptions…the spidery widow casting her web and ensnaring her youthful victim. Allowing the poor soul no chance of escape."

"No." Which was true, he didn't care. And he was certain to be oblivious to any such office chitchat anyway. "Nor do I consider you spidery."

"Well, that's something, although we may need to work on your repertoire of compliments for us members of the fairer sex. Most women will expect something surpassing not being spiderlike."

There was a pause while he waited for her next broadside, and she didn't disappoint. "You do like girls, don't you, Mark?"

His eyes widened as he took in the question, his last spoonful of potato soup stopping midway to his mouth. He returned it to the bowl and stirred it around a bit. "Beg pardon?" he asked, looking at his soup.

"Perhaps you *are* older than I thought, if you are hard of hearing. I asked if you liked girls. I've worked with you for over two years and have never seen you with a girl. Or even heard you mention one."

"Are you asking me if I'm…if I'm a—"

She looked to be enjoying herself as he stumbled on the word. "A homosexual, I believe you were trying to say? To be accurate, Physicist Newin, I did not ask if you are a homosexual. Your lack of precision with our storied English language disappoints, although regretfully, does not surprise me. To clarify, I merely asked if you like girls. I imagine most homosexuals like girls just fine."

Mark took an invisible deep breath and tried to regain his composure. He had the impression Miss Anne from Accounting was listening in. "For the record, yes, I like girls. And although, as you correctly point out, you did not ask, I am not a homosexual."

"Actually, I didn't think you were. I mean, no one is going to mistake you for a lady's man. But I can, albeit with some difficulty, picture you in the company of a young lady. You're even reasonably attractive, in a frumpy sort of way."

Ouch. He was taking hits left and right today. What was coming next? Was she going to ask about his (nonexistent) experience level with women? He looked at her again. At the older couple at the next table. He breathed an invisible sigh of relief—she wouldn't ask that. Not today, not in a restaurant. He remembered her last comment and looked down at his clothes. White shirt, black tie, black trousers. His one pair of scuffed black shoes. Had he combed his hair that morning? "Frumpy? I've never thought of myself as frumpy."

"I'm sure you haven't. Let's say it's part of what makes you interesting."

He seized the opening. "Ah, so you concede I have one redeeming quality?"

"I am willing to concede that point, yes. Although that said, you are in dire need of assistance in certain areas. Do you wear the same shirt every day, or do you own five identical white shirts?"

He always wore white shirts to the office. He looked down again. Did he have three of this one, and three more of another? Or maybe they were all the same?

"Not to worry, Mark. We'll leave soon and your torment will end. Sunday next, I'm having some family over for dinner. The professor and his wife will be there. I'd like you to come."

"I would love to come," he said, somewhat less than one hundred percent truthfully. He liked being around her, but social mixing was hardly his strong point.

"Excellent answer, Physicist Newin. And as your reward, we may now return to the office."

# Second Lieutenant Phillip Newin

*Number 1 Aircraft Depot*
*Saint Omer Aerodrome, Northern France*

As he expected, Pete found his little brother reading a book in the expansive St. Omer officers' club. Phillip saw him coming, stood up and put out his hand. Pete ignored it and hugged his little brother. They sat down and Pete ran through his standard scan for war posters; he already had two in his collection that he'd found undefended. St. Omer was below average with only a single poster: a French advertisement for war bonds. To emphasize the critical need for funds, a forlorn-looking French soldier in a shabby uniform is stepping forward from his trench, weighed down by pack and rifle. Pete had seen advertisements for war bonds in the British and German papers as well. Modern war didn't come cheap, and all the governments were looking for money. The easiest place to look was one's own citizens, and Lloyd George and his finance blokes were likely skittish about being too deep in debt to the Americans.

Phillip was drinking soda water; Pete ordered the same. Looked at his little brother and forced a smile. "Good to see you, brother. I'm proud of you. But why the hell couldn't you get a nice staff job somewhere? There's all kinds of research going on for a brainy type like yourself."

"I could ask you the same thing, Pete."

"I'm not Mum's baby. She'd be—"

"I'm not either," Phillip retorted. "I'm twenty years old and a second lieutenant in the Royal Flying Corps." Pete suppressed a smile. The one surefire way to make Phillip mad was to call him the baby of the family. Pete's thoughts wandered back to that day at the river. He and his two cousins had been lying in the sun, drying off.

"You like her, Peter. I know you do." Eleven-year-old Ritchie never missed a chance to poke at Pete. "Peter's sweet on Suzie," Ritchie chanted, and his brother Martin picked up the refrain. "Peter's sweet on Suzie. Peter's sweet on Suzie."

"I am not!" Pete almost shouted. He didn't like them teasing him, and so what if he liked her? She was pretty, with her long golden hair and freckles. And she was smart, too. A lot smarter than his dumb cousins. She'd made the highest grade on the first three maths exams that year. But he'd studied every night and beat her on the fourth. He didn't look at her when the teacher handed back his exam first, but he knew she was looking at him. He rolled onto his side, away from his cousins, and his eyes went wide. His little brother was running for the ledge, as fast as his short legs would go. The ledge that was their diving board to the river twenty feet below.

"No!"

Phillip disappeared, arms flailing. Pete and his cousins ran to the edge. Nothing. Should he jump in? But he might land on top of the idiot as he came up. He ran down the side of the hill, slipping and sliding in the dirt. Banging his toes on the rocks. *Damn it!* He was going to strangle the little kid. He got down to the pool and spied Phillip bobbing along the slow current, his head going under now and again. Pete ran along the bank, hands out in front, pushing the branches away.

"Damn it!" A branch caught him just above the eye. He dove in and swam toward Phillip, who had gone under again. There, he spotted a head above the water. He took a few more strokes; reached out and grabbed hold of an arm. Felt for the bottom with his foot and stood up. The water was up to his chest. Phillip's feet must have been bouncing along the bottom—the only reason the little idiot didn't drown. He dragged Phillip to the bank, more or less keeping his head above the water. Handed him up to his cousins and climbed out. Glared down at his little brother. "Are you crazy? You could have drowned. Mum would have killed me!"

Phillip was coughing and spitting out river water. He looked up at his big brother triumphantly. "I did it. You fellows said I couldn't, but I did it."

"Yeah, and if you ever do it again, I'll kill you. Come on, we're going home." He'd had enough of his stupid little brother and his stupid cousins for one day.

Pete blocked the smile that had started to form. "When did you get in?"

"Been five days now."

"Keeping busy?"

Phillip snorted. "I flew a DH4 over to Boisdinghem yesterday. It's only ten minutes west of here, but I flew around for an hour. It flies nice, for a bomber type. Other than that, I've been mostly sitting right here."

Pete had heard good things about the DH4, not that he had any desire to fly it. "How's Mum?"

"Worried. About you. About me, now. But Deb and the girls being there keeps her busy. That helps."

Pete nodded toward Phillip's book. "What are you reading?"

Phillip held up a small book with a green cover. *Modern Chess Openings*.

"Second edition?"

"Third. Came out last year."

"Anything in particular?"

"Sicilian Defense isn't popular these days. But I've been running through some interesting lines."

"Tell me about training. It must have gone okay. You're here."

"Let's see. The first few flights weren't bad, and they turned me loose solo. After that…I smashed the undercarriage of a Shorthorn trying to land—the wind had got up a bit. Caught a wingtip landing an Avro the very next day. Got my butt chewed by the RO, along with a suggestion that I might be better suited for the infantry. What else? On my cross-country, I was trying to get down to see Mum from Bromwich. There was fog down south that afternoon and I ended up in a field near Bridgwater. Spent the night in the farmer's house. Somehow, I didn't bust the Avro up on landing, and flew back the next day. You should have seen the farmer's daughter. Big green eyes and long blonde hair. Beautiful—and she liked me."

"Interesting. How old?"

"Hmm, I'd say twelve. Maybe thirteen."

"Standard stuff. Have you seen Mark or Charles?"

"I saw both of them last week. Mark's the same as always—the bumbling scientist. I think he's happy, but it's hard to be sure with Mark. He may have found his niche at the Lab. Charles is tucked away at headquarters in London. He didn't say much, but I think it's cryptography stuff."

"Physics, cryptography, and you. I must be the dummy of the family."

"I doubt many people consider you dumb, Pete. But I am a much better chess player than you."

"I seem to recall beating you twice in tournament play. Once with black."

Phillip gave a pained smile. "I remember that one. Ruy Lopez gone bad. My defense caved when I moved my rook pawn. The time pressure was brutal. I was under a minute with four moves to time control. But as soon as I took my hand off that pawn, I knew I was done for."

"If that's your excuse for losing, I've heard better ones."

"Okay, you won twice and drew three, out of eleven tournament matches, if memory serves. I'm getting married, by the way."

"What? To who?"

"Alice, of course. Who else?"

Alice Caldwell. Nice enough girl, but not the cerebral type.

"You're looking serious, Pete. Do you not like Alice?"

"Of course, I like her. She's a very nice girl. If the two of you are happy, that's what matters." Pete was truly happy for his little brother. Phillip, like Charles, could be incredibly smart and content with life at the same time. Whereas Pete and Mark…

"I got my assignment an hour ago."

Pete sat up. "Yes?"

"Seven Squadron. BE2s."

Pete kept his face impassive. "Have you flown it?"

"A few times. It's not hard to fly."

"Yes, it does have that quality." Pete sat back and looked at the wall. At his little brother.

"Go ahead, Pete. Say what you need to say."

"It's that…we lose a lot of pilots, Phillip. The reality is either one of us could be killed any day. If it's me, tell Mum there are no regrets. This war had to be fought, and I did my duty. What do you have, fifty flight hours total?"

"Forty-five."

"You know I flew it with Home Defense. Bottom line, the design is about five years old and airplane development has moved on. I mean, the BE2 was outclassed by the Fokker Eindecker, and the new Albatrosses are a world away from the Eindecker. It's slow, you know that. Nor does it get in and out of turns quickly. Put it in a dive and it wants to come back to level flight. Archie must love it. Don't make his job any easier. Change altitude and course when you can, even a little bit will help. Every Hun fighter will be faster and more maneuverable than you, and your observer has a limited field of fire. If you're low and slow and they're shooting you full of holes, put it in a field. That's better than getting killed."

Phillip had been looking at the table, waiting for Pete to finish. "I know the score, Pete," he said quietly. "I'm not a kid anymore."

"I know you're not. But I've seen a lot of pilots killed, especially in their first month or two. So please, stay alive. For the sake of our mother and Alice, if nothing else." Pete sat back and sipped his soda water. He'd done what he could. "Where's Seven Squadron at?"

"Officially, at Proven. But the airplanes are attached to three other Second Army Corps squadrons. At Bailleul and Abeele."

"Ypres sector. My new home."

"They're sending most of the fellows that way. Sounds like Second Army took Messines without much problem. I hope I didn't miss the big one."

Pete grimaced. "You didn't miss anything, Phillip. There's plenty more fighting to be done in Flanders."

The words came back to Pete as he looked at his little brother—the "BE2 Pilot's Psalm."

*Thy joystick and thy prop discomfort me,*
*Thou prepare a crash for me in the presence of mine enemies,*
*Thy RAF anointed me with oil...*

He set his glass down. "Come on. I'll show you the Pup. She flies nice. Take her for a turn if you want."

Pete woke to that most wonderful of sounds: wind and rain. He rolled over and went back to sleep. Two and a half hours later he sat down in the Mess for a late breakfast of eggs, toast and coffee. Retired to the club and spent the rest of the morning reading Porter Alexander's *Military Memoirs of a Confederate*. Next to him, the wind pushed the water droplets about on the window, making little rivers on the dirty glass. Farther on, the flight-line was empty of airplanes, and the swaying canvas of the tents glistened in the rain. He eventually set Porter Alexander aside and read most of yesterday's *Western Daily Press*. Later, he ran into John Wilcox and Drew Harris at lunch.

"Heavy cavalry versus infantry squares in the Napoleonic era," Harris was saying as Pete sat down. "The Romans. All the way back to the Egyptians. Cavalry has been war's ultimate breakthrough weapon. Until now. Until this war."

Pete glanced at John, who looked to be more interested in his steak with Madeira sauce flanked by potatoes and onions than in the historical impact of cavalry on warfare. But Pete was happy to join the discussion. "The signs of change were there in the American Civil War, Drew. There weren't much in the way of cavalry charges against infantry or artillery. The weapons had become too accurate. Longer ranged, with higher rates of fire."

"And here we are." Drew's voice had turned bitter. "Three years of stalemate. Of slaughter. Don't we pay a general staff to plan for war? More specifically, for the next war, and not the last one? Were they not aware that Russia and Japan fought a war not long ago that demonstrated the effectiveness of machine guns against attacking troops? Perhaps they were too busy planning their next parade and missed it. Or maybe they were paying attention but drew the obvious conclusion—that the Russian and British Armies are very different. After all, what are a few machine guns against the esprit de corps of the British Army—the army that broke the advance of Napoleon's Imperial Guard at Waterloo?"

Pete was always happy to talk military history and thought back to what he'd read about the Russo-Japanese War. With hindsight, that war had clearly foreshadowed what they were seeing now: the incredible killing power of machine guns and modern artillery.

"When I went through Basic Horse," Drew was speaking again, "our manual still had some nonsense about the *thundering majesty of the cavalry charge*. How the *cold steel of the saber* would overpower mere rifle fire. I hope I still have my copy somewhere. I'll frame those pages after the war, on the off chance I live through this. Or maybe I'll send them to a newspaper." Drew blew out a long breath and shook his head. "I was with the Sixteenth

Queen's Lancers back in '14. Irish Command. The idiots sent us to France, *carrying lances*."

Drew looked at Pete, down at his half-eaten steak, then out the window. His voice was quiet, somber, when he spoke again. "I rode a beautiful gray charger. Hardly a scratch on her through two years of war. It was last October, somewhere north of Wipers. They'd told us we were out of range and we put fifty of them in a temporary pasture. The Hun artillery opened up on us. I was the first one into the pasture when they stopped shooting." Drew's normally inscrutable, dark-brown eyes were on the verge of tears. "I'll never forget that sight. Those screams. I shot six of them in the head before I had to get out of there. The next day I put in for the RFC."

John stood up. "I think I'll take a walk, fellows. Thanks for the history lesson. At least it wasn't maths."

"Generals and politicians." Drew said with the trace of a smile after John had gone, pushing his chair back and crossing his long legs. "The Romans had it right, Pete. If the leadership isn't performing, kill them off and put someone else in. I have this beautiful vision of the front page of the *Times*. Let's see what you think."

> David Lloyd George and General William Robertson have been arrested and executed for crimes against the state. Fellow conspirator Winston Churchill has been placed under house arrest and his cigars have been confiscated. Field Marshal Douglas Haig, the man who single-handedly saved the British Expeditionary Force and our entire war effort from our meddling politicians, has proclaimed himself lord protector and prime minister. Our LP/PM has affirmed that the glorious campaign in Flanders will continue to its heroic conclusion. God bless Field Marshal Lord Protector Prime Minister Haig!

Pete chuckled, while glancing around the Mess to be sure the major wasn't in earshot. "Then a month or two later," continued Drew, "a follow-up story."

Justice has been done! The usurper Haig, who seized power while viciously murdering our lawfully elected leaders, was placed under arrest yesterday. Latest reports are that he will be tried tomorrow and executed on Friday. Major General So-and-So has agreed to accept the role of PM in this time of crisis, and has announced an immediate halt to the senseless slaughter in Flanders. Our new PM has also mandated a twenty percent increase in wages for our soldiers, better food, and improved brothels. Hmm…maybe we should leave that last bit out.

Pete was enjoying himself. He'd never heard anything quite like Drew's diatribe and waited for its conclusion.

Regretfully, we must report that German sympathizing factory workers attempted to undercut our war effort yesterday, staging demonstrations in…let's say…Manchester and Bristol, in support of the formation of a new…Socialist-Labour government. The cowardly workers blocked the flow of critical wartime supplies to the ports, resulting in numerous deaths of our soldiers in Flanders as they had to fight off German attacks armed only with forks and spoons. The demonstrators also blocked the distribution of food to cute and hungry little children across Great Britain. Fortunately, the enemy-inspired demonstrations were stopped before they could seriously damage our war economy. Special thanks to our brave RFC pilots, who risked their lives flying low altitude bombing and strafing runs against these enemies of our great British state.

Pete eyed Drew. "You certainly have a gift for journalism. Although going back to the Roman method of selecting the political leadership might be a reach."

Drew was looking out the window again, fingering his mustache. "Yes, as well-meaning as they were, they may have taken things too far.

Besides dispatching the underperforming leaders, brothers and sons would be done away with. Sometimes even mothers and sisters. It's a bit difficult to visualize reading about that in the *Times*."

A few hours later Pete sat down in the Wildflowers Café and greeted Juliette politely, not wanting his interest to be too obvious. He ordered tea and biscuits and plodded his way through *Le Matin*. According to the paper, the war was (still) going well. They'd replaced Nivelle with Pétain, although nothing negative was said about the outgoing general, of course. Not permitted. Pete didn't know much about Pétain, but the general would have his work cut out for him. The rumors coming from the French lines were ugly—that half their soldiers were ready to lay down their rifles and go home. Two gendarmes came in and one of them put his arm around Juliette as she took their order; to Pete's relief she stiffened a bit. The gendarmes were talking and laughing, pleased with themselves. They'd caught a deserter outside of town: a young Frenchman trying to go home. He'd been in civilian clothes, but the army boots always gave them away. Another one for the firing squad, they joked. That made two this week. If they tied them together, they might only need one bullet.

Pete waited until the gendarmes drank their tea and left. He paid his bill and asked Juliette when the café closed—a question to which he already knew the answer.

"Oh, in just a few minutes, Lieutenant."

"Would you permit me to walk you home?" he asked in his most polite French.

She looked at him noncommittally before answering. "Of course. Thank you."

Pete walked his bike beside her with only a light mist falling. She talked about who lived where; who had husbands, sons, or grandsons away at the war. They arrived at a little brick house that had been painted white some years before. The mortar was cracked in places; a side wall leaned outward and had been braced with boards. A pile of bricks and some building materials were by the house, so it looked like a repair job was in the works.

There was a vegetable garden around back. For the first time, he noticed her small hands were roughened from working outside.

"Bonne après-midi, Alicia," Juliette called to a woman who was digging in her garden across the street.

"Bonne après-midi, Juliette," replied the woman. She looked at Pete and waved.

"Her husband was a flier," Juliette whispered. "He was killed last year. But he wasn't a pilot. He fired the machine gun."

"The observer. I used to fly those airplanes." He heard the boys running around behind the house.

"Won't you come in for tea, Lieutenant?"

It might have been better style to decline, but he accepted and followed her into a fair-sized room: kitchen, dining, and den. Plain wood furniture, two oil lamps, and a wood-burning stove for cooking and heating. Her grandfather was reading the newspaper at the small dining table. He looked at Pete without surprise and gestured to the seat across from him. "Evening, Lieutenant. Have a seat."

Juliette asked her grandfather to fix tea and went to check on the boys.

"Evening, sir," said Pete, sitting down.

"Name's Arthur."

"Arthur." Pete looked at the photos on a side table while Arthur boiled water. Two sets of grandparents, and he recognized Arthur with his attractive wife. An older photo of a French captain with his wife—presumably Juliette's mother and father. Several photos of Juliette and her husband and the boys.

"Where's her father now?"

Arthur looked at him from the stove. At the pictures. "Don't really know. He doesn't write much. Last I heard, he was up near the British sector."

"Your son?"

"No. Juliette's mother was my oldest daughter. She died four years ago. Consumption." Arthur brought the tea to the table and sat down. "Sugar?"

"No, thank you." Pete took a sip of the lukewarm, watery tea. "What did you do after the Prussian War, Arthur?"

"Got married and moved to Arras. I'd known my wife since we were children. Did clerk stuff with our foreign service. Paid regular but bored me to death. My wife didn't like the big city, so we came home after a few years. I did some metal working. Some farming. Whatever it took to put food on the table."

He stirred his tea absently, and Pete sensed a change of subject.

"This war is dragging on, Lieutenant. First, the papers said the boys would be home by Christmas. Then it was home by Christmas of '15. Then '16. The front line isn't moving. If we were really making progress, it would be all over the papers. All those young men killed. Young women without their husbands, children without their fathers. I keep asking myself why."

"The Yanks will be here soon. That should make the difference." That was the best Pete could do.

"I hope France has some young men left when it's over. Paul would be twenty-six now, two years older than Juliette." He looked out the little window. "My friend Hugo has four grandsons in the war. Well, three now. Gaspard is back home, badly wounded. The oldest boy was home on leave last week." Arthur's expression became more serious and he lowered his voice, even though they were alone in the house. "Some units are refusing to go back to their place in the line."

Pete's eyebrows went up. He'd heard rumors, but nothing definite. Of course, it wasn't something you'd read about in the papers—if anything was contagious in a dispirited army, it was mutiny. Three years of slaughter. Three years of living in the mud with the rats and the lice, and nothing to show for it. More than one army chap had told him the French use their dead as sandbags. So it wouldn't surprise him the soldiers in the trenches might have had enough. Still…mutiny?

Arthur spoke again, his voice sad. "I understand the frustration. The anger. I saw it back in seventy, and what we went through was nothing like this. War is becoming deadlier, Lieutenant. Like a giant killing machine. Sucking in people and money. Grinding them down and spitting them out. Still, I suppose one must do one's duty." Arthur's tone was conflicted, as was Pete.

Juliette came in. The evening had turned cool and she added a log to the stove. Sat down and smiled at Pete. "I hope my grandfather is behaving himself."

"Oh yes. I enjoy talking with him." He could think about war and a soldier's duty later.

"He can be quite nice, *when* he's on his good behavior."

Her grandfather smiled at her, excused himself and moved to a chair by the window. Pete ran through his preplanned topics, asking about the café, the boys, how they were getting along. Kept the conversation going while they drank their tea; stood up to leave. "If you will excuse me, I need to get back. Evening, Arthur, I enjoyed our chat."

"Anytime, Lieutenant."

Juliette walked him outside and called to the boys. "Say hello to Lieutenant—"

"Newin," Pete told her.

"Lieutenant Newin. He's English and flies one of those little airplanes we see."

The two boys shook hands. Paul proudly told him, "England is an island. In the ocean."

"You are correct, young man. Perhaps you can visit me someday."

Pete turned back to Juliette as the boys ran off. "Thank you for letting me get away from the war for a bit. I like your grandfather."

She nodded and lowered her voice. "Almost everyone does. He tries to appear tough, but he isn't like that. The war has been hard for him. Sitting, reading, waiting for news. Every so often, someone's son or grandson is killed or wounded."

"One day it will end. Perhaps soon. I hope to see you again, if you don't mind."

"Of course, Lieutenant," she replied, a little mechanically.

Pete went by the farmhouse to change out of his damp clothes. His landlady was in the kitchen, and he tried (without much success) to engage her in conversation. He was still unclear if they didn't like him, or they didn't like the British, or they just didn't like to talk. Well, no matter. He went outside and walked down the road to the armaments hangar. Crates of Vickers .303 ammo were stacked above his head. Bins containing machine-gun parts, cases of lubricating oil. A disassembled Vickers was spread out on a table. A corporal and an AM2 were tidying up. "Evening, Lieutenant," said the corporal, nodding toward some wooden boxes on a workbench. "I checked those. They're ready for you."

"Thanks, Randy."

Pete sorted through a box of fabric ammo belts until he found one with no obvious flaws; spent the next hour looking at .303 rounds. He discarded three for scratches and two because they felt light. As each round passed inspection, he slid it into the belt. When he'd finished, he laid the belt out and adjusted several rounds, making sure each of the 250 rounds was seated identically in its little jacket. It was time-consuming work, but he figured it was worth it. Good chance a jammed gun had cost more than one RFC pilot his life.

Harry weaved his way back to the hut after one too many whiskies. Well, maybe two too many. As always, after dinner they'd toasted the king's health, plus that of a couple of generals. There was no getting around that in an RFC Officers' Mess. They'd lit the smoking lamp once the toasts were done—everyone seeming to agree that death by suffocation was better than life in the RFC.

Their cigarettes lit, Blake and his buddies had gotten down to some serious drinking, pounding them down one after the other. Lots of singing once the major had left, the lyrics ranging from negative on the war to flat out unprintable.

He paused by the door, sweating, his hand against the wall. Took a few breaths of the cool night air. Should he go to the loo and throw up? Or maybe right there—who would care? He jumped as two loud bangs came from inside the hut. Christ, he'd heard stories about RFC suicides, or blokes shooting themselves in the foot to get to hospital. Ignoring his heaving stomach, he pushed the door open. His three roommates were playing cards, and there was a smoking pistol on the table. Ethan glanced at him.

"I got the little bastard," he said, nodding toward Harry's cot. Something dark was under his side table. Harry blinked twice, trying to focus. Steadied himself on the door frame and looked again. It was a rat, and blood was oozing onto the floor. He blinked again…the rat looked to be missing its head.

"Are you going to get rid of him? He's by my cot."

"The orderly will get him in the morning," said Ethan. "It's cool in here; won't smell much tonight. This is war, you know. We all must make sacrifices for the cause. Lord Nelson himself said so. Maybe."

"Right."

Harry wobbled his way across the hut and kicked the rat into a corner. Made a point not to check his boot or the floor for rat brains. Sat on his cot and regarded his roommates. Thomas was about his age, George and Ethan were a few years older. George was nice enough but a bit of a stuffed shirt. Ethan reminded Harry of himself. They even sort of looked alike, although Ethan carried an extra stone or so around his midsection. There was a folded piece of paper on his little side table. He picked it up. It was some sort of meal listing.

"Beef Wellington. Mushroom barley soup. Chicken with rice and asparagus… What's this? Is someone monitoring my diet? They're worried about my health?"

George looked over. "That's your Mess bill for last month, mate."

Harry looked at the bottom of the page: £3–1s–4d. For a little over a week. At that rate, along with his bar bill, he'd hardly have anything left. "This can't be right. Doesn't the army have to feed us? Isn't that part of the deal?"

"Sure," answered George. "If you don't mind eating bully beef and tinned peaches every day. Serving that to the generals when they come to visit."

Harry snorted. Damn cheap army. But the generals could eat dead rats for all he cared.

"Before Ethan started shooting, we were talking about how this mess started," said George, perhaps sensing a change of subject might help. "My uncle's Royal Navy, some sort of foreign service liaison. He told me Serbia's response to Austria-Hungary after the assassination was to bugger off, and they wouldn't have said that without Russia backing them up."

"If that's true, I bet the tsar would like to have another crack at it," said Thomas.

"I'd like another crack at Mary Anne Cooper," said Ethan, with a little shake of the head. "She was ready, willing, and no doubt able, and I let her slip away. That said, perhaps the young lady might wish to renew our acquaintance. Myself a decorated war hero and all."

"Aren't you happily betrothed?" asked Harry.

"It's not official yet, but my mother thinks so. It was her idea, actually. Yes, the widow Mayhew. Charming woman, and quite well-endowed. Financially, and in other ways. The poor thing is heartbroken, of course, as we all are, at the tragic and unexpected passing of Lord Mayhew. While His Lordship left her well provided for, mere material wealth cannot compensate for the loss of a loved one. And I, the humble and simple soul that I am, can only try to ease her pain."

Harry laughed. Ethan was in good form tonight. Deciding he was unlikely to vomit on their card game, he got up and joined them. Put a penny in the pot.

"Maybe you fellows remember," said George. "Back in '14, our newspapers were predicting a quick victory. That the boys would be home by Christmas. My uncle said the French, Russian, and German papers were all saying the same thing."

"I read Kitchener pushed the government to get ready for a long war," said Thomas.

"And the other generals laughed at him," said George. "I suppose by Christmas, they'd stopped laughing."

"He's a sodomite," said Ethan. "Or was."

"That's not fair, Ethan," said Thomas. "I read a long article on him back in school. His intended died when she was eighteen, and the word is he never got over it. That he always wore a locket with a strand of her hair in it."

"Really, Thomas," said Ethan, rolling his eyes. "Here we are trying to speak disrespectfully and irreverently of the dead, and you have to spoil it."

"There's more," said Thomas, undaunted. "His father was a hard-hearted sort. Beat him all the time when he was little. Made improvements to the family farm in Ireland and charged higher rents to the tenants. When they couldn't pay, he set the dogs on them. Turned them out into the street."

"Another in the long line of fine British disciplinarians. Certainly, the traits of the parents pass to the offspring," noted Ethan. "One need only look at myself. Both my parents are attractive and intelligent. Eloquent, and with a natural command of the social graces."

"So what went wrong?" asked Harry.

"I shall attribute your question to base, yet perhaps understandable jealousy, and decline to respond."

"Regardless of how the war started, I'd like it to stop," said Thomas, returning the conversation to its more serious roots. "I read the German

Socialist Party wants to end the war. No annexations. No reparations. Just stop fighting and we all go home. That sounds good to me."

Ethan and Harry nodded agreement.

"My uncle mentioned that, too," said George. "As you say, the German Left is in favor of peace. No winners or losers. But Hindenburg and Ludendorff want to keep the ninety-odd percent of Belgium they have now, and not give an inch of Alsace-Lorraine back to France. That in Germany, there's no civilian war cabinet like we have. The military calls the shots."

"So what's the good news?" Harry asked.

"Let me think—" George gave him a wry smile "—there's a rumor Brazil's coming into the war on our side."

"Wow. How many squadrons do they have?"

"I don't know. Probably not very many."

Harry thought for a moment. "Then have them send women…the Brazilian Morale Booster Corps. The BMBC. Sounds like some sort of secret weapon—the Huns will be terrified. I'll even volunteer to be liaison officer. Design their summertime uniform. See to their accommodations, and any special needs they might have. Day or night."

"I'll be sure to tell Lloyd George next time I see him." George paused long enough to deal the cards. "Here's another cheery thought for you chaps. My uncle told me there are some powerful business interests, and even some workers, who wouldn't mind if the war drags on for a few more years. That they've never had it so good."

"Then let the bastards bloody well come and fight it," said Harry, and winced as Ethan blasted twice at a rat in the far corner, the pistol less than a foot from Harry's ear.

"Wily little bastard. I'll get him next time."

"Stop that goddamn shooting, you bloody arsehole," came a muffled yell from the next hut. B-Flight. They had the early go in the morning.

"Can't hear you," Ethan shouted back. "Too much shooting. Must be the Hun. You fellows had better head to the dugout."

Harry laughed, although the B-Flight blokes would pay them back sooner or later. Ethan pushed the whisky bottle to him, and Harry surprised himself by pushing it away. He drank water instead, knowing he'd feel like hell in the morning. He noticed Ethan was reading the *Globe* between hands. "Anything interesting?"

"Absolutely. It says here that for those of you, and I quote, with bad breath, coated tongue…with a sallow complexion, acid stomach, or subject to bilious attacks of constipation…which I dare say describes most of the fellows around here rather well, should drink warm water with limestone phosphate every day. That it washes the bad stuff out of the liver, kidneys, and bowels."

"Not sure I've seen limestone phosphate on the Mess menu," said Thomas.

"No doubt that will soon change, young man. As said limestone phosphate—" Ethan paused and cleared his throat "—cleanses and purifies the entire alimentary canal. Without it, your ten yards of bowels absorb dangerous impurities."

"Maybe we should make you bowels cleanliness officer, Ethan," said Harry. "You know, inspect the chaps. Check on their impurity levels and proper supply of limestone phosphate to the Mess. I'll speak to the major if you like."

His suggestion only elicited raised eyebrows from Ethan, and the game broke up. Harry undressed and got into bed, still wide awake. Christ, he'd love this place if only they didn't have to go across the line and get killed. He even had an orderly to pick up after him and shine his shoes. Harry Booth, the Liverpool fabric shop kid, had a servant.

He needed to get away from the line. But how does a lowly lieutenant observer get a staff job, or get transferred back to England? Or even to Mesopotamia, which had to be the biggest shithole in the world. But not so many chaps were getting killed over there. Could he get engaged to some field marshal's granddaughter? He didn't exactly run in that circle, and who knows, some of those blokes might be proud to see their granddaughter's true love get killed—it'd be their way of paying the same price as the common soldier. He drummed his fingers on the wood frame of his cot. But there might be a way…maybe he'd do some poking around London when his leave came up.

Lieutenant Ian Crosse ran through his scan, beginning about ten degrees to his left. Closing steadily was a nicely built, but not overstated, fair-skinned girl with long, dark brown hair. Pointy features. Could she be Russian? She was wearing a black dress with white trim, black fishnet stockings, and (he estimated) three-inch heels. Not only did Miss Black Dress look fully capable of handling close quarters maneuvering, he awarded her additional points for style. He monitored her approach for a few seconds and frowned. She wasn't on an intercept course to their table. Rather, her course would take her to a table of four drunk army chaps directly behind Ian and Larry. He continued scanning right, to a pair of standard-issue, petite French brunettes sitting at the bar. Further right, a thin blonde was chatting with a not-as-thin blonde. At the far end of the bar, a flight of four was in close formation. Dark hair and fair skin, but beyond that, their precise characteristics could not be ascertained due to the dim lighting.

He checked behind them: Miss Black Dress had her arms around the remaining unattached army bloke. She was whispering into his ear and that seemed to do the trick, as a few seconds later she was sitting on his lap. The black and white clad waiter was watching the action from his spot at the end of the bar.

"Ninety seconds, plus or minus thirty," Ian said to Larry.

Lieutenant Larry Pitman reluctantly broke visual contact with his preferred petite demoiselle française and looked at Ian. "Until what? The end of the war?"

"Afraid not," answered Ian. "Until the waiter is at the table behind us, taking Miss Black Dress's drink order."

"Not that she'll be paying for it," noted Larry.

"Of course not." Ian was keeping an eye on his watch. "Shame about Albert Ball. He was one of the good ones. Played violin."

"Shame about anyone getting killed."

"If it happened to him, it could happen to me or you," said Ian. He nodded to his right—the waiter was approaching the table behind them. "One minute fifty-five. I win."

"I missed what the bet was," said Larry, focusing on his French friend again.

"A thousand pounds. But you can pay me tomorrow, no problem." Ian waved to the waiter as he went by and motioned for two more whiskies.

"Right. Speaking of pilots getting killed, I just got here two weeks ago, and I've already decided this pilot on the continent stuff is far too dangerous for a young man who's going places."

"Agreed," said Ian. "It's just not clear to me what to do about it."

"Wedded bliss, my friend. Wedded bliss is the answer. Here, let me show you a picture of my beloved." Ian waited as his new friend Larry searched through his wallet. He'd found a nice, out of the way place in downtown Aire, and this was the second time he'd run into Larry—a stocky SE5 pilot just over from England who shared his fondness for both Irish whisky and attractive young ladies. Larry slid the photo in front of him and two things jumped out at Ian. The house in the background was huge, and if he wasn't mistaken, that was a Rolls-Royce Silver Ghost parked in front of it. His eyes went to the smartly dressed young lady in the foreground. She was overweight and, at best, might reach Plain on the Crosse Scale. In poor visibility.

"She's...lovely."

"She's rich, my friend. But even better, Daddy is an Earl. Unfortunately, my darling Edith and I only met last month, and I thought a measured pace would be best. The wedding is set for my next leave, but clearly Edith and I cannot wait *that* long. The poor thing is dying of anticipation. Me too, of course."

"Right."

"She's terribly worried about my safety, too. She's already spoken with Daddy about a staff job for me in London—not that I encouraged her. That would hardly be proper." Ian's only answer was to flick his eyes in Larry's direction, before returning to his scan of the female terrain.

"She has two sisters, one of whom is still available. I might be able to help you out there, once I'm part of the family. Daddy has a heart problem. It's a shame the title won't pass via marriage when he goes. It's an unjust world we live in."

"Indeed. Is Daddy a Conservative?"

"Of course. Although the Liberals aren't *all* bad. Just most of them."

"My uncle is the MP for Bristol East. William Bannerman."

Larry's eyes met his, serious for a moment. "Really?" He drummed his fingers on the table, regarding Ian. "You're a well-spoken sort, for a pilot. Good-looking chap, not that you're my type. Might you be thinking along political lines, once this damn war is over?"

"Perhaps. But I don't know anyone other than my uncle. Nor do I have any money."

"But you have RFC pilot wings, my friend. You have combat experience. Let me think…your best bet would be to get wounded. But not badly, of course. Just a bit of shrapnel here and there. A nice scar across your cheek. Recover back in England. Be just the thing."

"I'll speak to the German Archie chaps next chance I get. See if we can manage it."

"In the meantime," said Larry, waving his little French friend over, "we must enjoy the life we have to the fullest."

Petite Brunette 1 reacted quickly, leaving her assigned station and heading directly for them. Petite Brunette 2, clearly a competent wingperson as prostitutes go, stationed herself slightly back and offset from her flight leader. She held that position as they closed on their target. PB1 settled gently into Larry's lap. PB2, aware she was uninvited to the gathering, paused and looked at Crosse. He glanced at her, non-committal, and she sat in the chair next to him. Slid it closer and put her hand on his leg. Said something in French which he ignored.

"Money helps, of course." Larry was looking at him again as PB1 kissed his neck. "Or having a daddy in the House of Lords. Your problem is combat veterans will be a penny a dozen after the war. You'll need more than that."

PB1 continued her measured advance by kissing Larry's ear. So far, his defenses were holding steady.

"You're from Bristol?" Ian nodded.

"Let me think…are there four constituencies there?" Ian was impressed. Larry had been doing his homework.

"North, South, East, and West."

"None of them are Labour held, are they?"

"No, but I'm sure you've heard the talk about suffrage. That women will get the vote, and a lot of them will vote Labour."

Larry snorted. "With luck, Parliament will put some reasonable restrictions on the ladies. Monied class only, between the ages of forty and forty-two. Something like that." Ian nodded. He and Larry looked to be in full agreement on the issue.

"Circling back to Bristol," said Ian, "Liberals hold three of the four seats. Bristol West is Conservative: George Gibbs. I heard him speak once before the war. He isn't a bad sort. Fought in the Boer War, I think."

"Where's your home?"

"Bristol South. Roger Clarke's held it for the last hundred years. With luck, he'll move on soon."

PB1 had paused in her assault on Larry. Reassessing the battlefield. Meanwhile PB2 was looking mildly put out and had scooted her chair back a few inches.

"But not too soon," said Larry. "You don't want some young healthy chap to get in there before you're ready. It's all about timing, my friend. And knowing people."

PB1 had changed tactics and was working on Larry's chest with her fingernails. Ian sensed the defenses beginning to give. One of her hands slid lower, out of Ian's line of sight.

Larry polished off his whisky and stood up, holding PB1's hand. She maintained her pleasant countenance. She'd won, but there was nothing to be gained by gloating.

PB2 leaned over to him. Switched to French-accented English.

"You and I go upstairs, General? We have a good time. Like your friend and Jeanne do."

Crosse frowned as Black Dress went by their table, headed upstairs with her drunk army friend. He'd have to cross her off the target list. Shame. He looked at PB2 and motioned for her to stand up. She complied.

Motioned for her to turn around. She did so.

Not a bad derriere. Really not bad at all. But she just wasn't in Miss Black Dress's category. Crosse patted his lap and she slid into position. He smiled at her. "Yes, I'd like that. Ten francs, yes?"

Her blue eyes went wide. "Ten francs." She'd almost spat it out. "Twenty-five, General. And that's a bargain. Only for you. We have a good time for twenty-five."

"Very well. Twelve francs. No more."

He smiled as PB2 stalked off, muttering in French, and went back to his whisky. Larry was right about one thing. Being a combat pilot wouldn't be enough to get him into Parliament, and it came with a damned uncomfortable chance of getting killed one of these days. He needed to find *his* Edith, like Larry had, and the sooner the better. *Bristol or London, which would be best?*

Bristol would keep him close to the voters…and the Bristol Aeroplane Company was there. What was the name…Sir Robert Cawthorne. That was it—Chairman of the Bristol Aeroplane Company. And Sir Robert was likely on good terms with the War Office, given the good reviews the Bristol Fighter was getting.

Perhaps Sir Robert had a daughter named Edith.

# Trees

*66 Squadron RFC, Sopwith Scout Fighter Aircraft*
*Liettres Aerodrome, Northern France*

Pete was sound asleep when the first bomb hit, and wide awake to hear the second, third, and fourth. Then came the whine of the air-raid siren.

Typical. The alarm sounds when the attack is over. He pulled on his clothes and trotted down the little road. Joined the crowd heading for the dugout, wincing at the booms from the squadron's three-inchers and the bright white of the exploding shells against the dark sky. But unless the searchlights found the bomber, Pete figured the Huns were safer than the people on the ground. Fortunately, A-Flight had the afternoon go the next day, and once back in bed he slept until eight. Breakfast in the Mess: eggs, toast with marmalade, coffee. Yesterday's newspaper. Life was good again—as good as it could be in wartime Flanders. He stopped by the office and chatted with Hugh Fleming about the navy's triplanes and the new Sopwith Camel. Word was the Camel was faster and more maneuverable than the Pup. And best of all, armed with dual Vickers. About damn time.

"What engine?" asked Pete.

"From what I gather, they're looking at some different options. But best guess is the Clerget one-thirty."

"That will help. Do you have any idea where they'll go first?"

Hugh Fleming gave him a wry smile. "Word is the navy."

"I think the Royal Navy rates higher in certain quarters than does the RFC, Captain."

"Could be, Lieutenant. But we'll get it, or at least something to replace the Pup. You just need to stay alive in the interim."

"Thank you for the sage advice, sir. I shall certainly consider it." Late that afternoon, Pete took off with Billy Duncan on a defensive patrol. Third Army sector, down near Arras. He followed the highway southeast easily enough; the sun was behind them and high enough to highlight the ground. But the low cirrus clouds became a solid undercast as they reached the higher terrain near Bruay, blotting out the ground.

He started his clock and pulled out his "big picture–south of Liettres" 1:100,000 map. Eyeballed the distance to their working area…about nine inches. About nine minutes flying time, per his "big picture map rule of thumb for flying with the wind." Nine minutes later he swung the two Pups into an orbit at 8000 feet. He would have preferred higher, but once again, Wing had not asked his opinion. Fifteen minutes into their orbit he spotted six round noses headed their way from the west, about 2000 feet above. He squinted against the sun. Albatrosses going home? Six against two Pups, medium altitude, and Billy Duncan as wingman? He weighed his options as they closed in. Most RFC pilots would take on the Huns regardless of numbers, but Pete preferred to fight when he had the advantage. The same as the Huns did. He studied the approaching airplanes as the first butterfly flapped about his stomach…and let out a sigh of relief. No decision would be required today—the butterfly could return to base. They were SPAD VIIs. Another Allied airplane that put the Pup to shame.

They made a few more circuits, hopefully somewhere close to their assigned area. With the cloud layer solid below them, he could only guess at what the winds were doing to them. He turned a little further west, better to err in that direction. As he rolled wings level, his Le Rhône missed a beat, and missed another a few seconds later. He nudged the petrol lever back, making the fuel mixture less rich. Listened…something was off, and he winced as the tachometer flinched at a third miss, this time with a metallic *kink* sound. He nudged the petrol lever forward, past the original setting. He didn't have a good feeling about this, but the Le Rhônes went out of trim all the time. Maybe she just wanted a little more fuel with her air.

He sighed as she kicked again, along with that unhealthy *kink* sound. He ran through his options. There were some breaks in the cloud layer to the east. If the engine quit and he went that way, he'd have a good chance of surviving, with one caveat. He'd be a prisoner of war for at least a year.

To the west, the clouds were almost solid…call it fifteen miles to the clearing line. He'd never calculated the glide ratio of a Sopwith Pup, but it was unlikely to be good enough. Not fifteen miles into the wind from 8000 feet. He gave it another two seconds, made up his mind and swung the Pup into the setting sun. Toward home. Throttled back and lowered the nose. With luck, he could milk the engine long enough…the Le Rhône kicked harder, followed by a metallic rattling. He eased the throttle and petrol further back, grimacing as the rattling got louder…followed by a metallic ripping sound as his Le Rhône self-destructed and shot pieces of itself through the cowling, shaking the airframe. He shrugged—in other circumstances it would have been impressive. As it was…he killed the ignition and shut off the fuel. Let the airspeed roll back to fifty-five and pushed the nose down. Looked across at Billy Duncan and pointed at his engine; gave the "cut" signal. He pointed at Billy, then toward home. There was nothing Billy could do.

The Pup drifted downward, the only noise the gentle chugging of the windmilling propeller. He spotted a small break in the clouds to his right and swung over to take a look…and shook his head. It was solid forest below. There was another opening to his left…more trees. Out of options for the moment, he leveled the Pup's wings and glided west. He could fire off all his bullets—the lighter the airplane, the better his chances. But who or what was below him? He decided against it. It was unlikely to make a difference. He tightened his lap belt. The less he bounced around during whatever was coming, the better.

The air was perfectly smooth and the Pup floated down without complaint. The quiet struck him. The propeller turning slowly with the wind, the cylinders of the Le Rhône pumping up and down. Like nine little sailors on a sinking ship, cranking the pumps as the water gets deeper and deeper. Or at least the cylinders that weren't on the ground somewhere behind him were still pumping. The cloud layer was becoming more distinct, its darker swirls overlaying the gray-white background. His airplane silhouetted on the clouds, a beautiful orange ring around it. He thought about his mother and father. How he'd loved Christmastime when he was little. Juliette. Those blue eyes. Being in the presence of the Lord.

He cleared his thoughts as the gray of the clouds swallowed the Pup. *Keep her on an even keel, Pete.* Any bank angle would increase his descent rate and reduce his chances. RFC airplanes weren't equipped to fly in clouds, so he'd have to do it by feel. By the wind against his face and the pressure on his backside. By the better than nothing, but not by much, turn bubble.

*How low did the clouds go? Would he come out over trees, or open fields?*

He kept perfectly still. Any weight shift would affect the Pup's flightpath. Each breath the same. Was he holding the wings level? His body told him yes. The airspeed started to roll back; he nudged the control column a half inch forward and held it there.

Fifty-three miles per hour. He flicked his eyes down and left: solid gray. Same to the right. He went to wipe his goggles and stopped. *No extra movement, Pete.*

*How far down did it go?* If the clouds were down to 200 or 300 feet above the ground, he'd damn well better come out over a field. He held the column steady, afraid to move it again. Not unless he had to. Saw a bit of green from the corner of his eye. Pulled in a deep breath and let it out. This would be over soon, one way or the other. He got a glimpse of green in front of him through the haze. Trees?

*Focus, Pete. Keep the wings level.* There was green in front of him again… fading to a hazy green gray…and the Pup came out of the clouds.

He was in a slight left bank, airspeed fifty-two. He sat upright and leveled the wings.

Looked out in front: trees.

To his left and right: more trees.

He checked further back. There were some openings behind him to his left.

He banked hard left; he had about five hundred feet of altitude to work with. The Pup descended more quickly with the loss of lift, but he had no choice. He had to get turned around. He rolled her out pointed at the clearing.

She was about three hundred feet above the trees. Fifty-one miles per hour. He gauged the distance to the clearing and the Pup's descent rate… he was too low.

He swung further left, looking at a much smaller opening in the trees.

Two hundred feet. Fifty miles per hour. He made a small right turn to avoid a large tree on the edge of the clearing.

One hundred feet. Forty-eight miles per hour. He could make out the small branches at the tops of the trees; sick to his stomach as the realization sank in.

He wasn't going to make the clearing. Would fifty feet of altitude be the difference between life and death?

He could see the individual leaves.

He checked the airspeed: it was holding at forty-eight. He raised the Pup's nose the tiniest bit. He could go a little slower, but he had to *fly* the Pup through the trees. If he stalled and dropped it in, he'd be killed.

He bit his lip as a small branch slapped the bottom of the Pup. Braced himself with his left arm and kept his right hand on the control column, to hold the Pup's nose steady. More slapping. Louder. He increased back pressure on the column to keep her nose up. The slapping was much louder and he cringed at the noise. A hundred hands clapping in his ears. The branches flicked past him like a motion picture running slow, and he flinched as one slapped him across the face.

A tree trunk loomed in front of him. He pushed left rudder and the Pup nosed left. He let go of the column and braced himself with both hands. There was a snap as the propeller cracked, followed by a scraping thud as the engine hit the tree. He bounced back and forth against the cockpit railing, straining forward against his belt. The instrument panel was pushing in on him as the Pup fought her way through the trees. One wing spar cracked, then the other, and he sensed the wings folding in on him…but it wasn't so loud now. The Pup was slowing down. He was leaning against the instrument panel, looking at the ground over the Pup's nose. She was barely moving. It was almost quiet and there was one last little bump as her nose hit the ground.

He was looking straight down, what was left of the airplane held upright by the trees. He fumbled with his belt and got it undone, wincing at the pain from his left side. He smelled fuel and sensed children running about. A boy shouting in French that an English airplane had crashed. Impressive. The kid must know British roundels from the French. He lifted his eyes without moving his head. His neck was hurting, too.

There was a small house in front of him, in the center of the clearing he'd almost made. He grabbed the railing with both hands and tried to pull himself out…and sat back down. There was no strength in his left arm. A Frenchwoman and three children were looking up at him. He took a couple of deep breaths. *Let's go Pete, we need to get out of here.*

He straightened up and braced his knee on the battered instrument panel. Held onto the railing with his right hand. Right leg over, left leg over. Paused to balance himself…and slid down. He grunted, eyes wide and watering, as something ripped into his right leg.

He hit the ground and lost his balance, but the Frenchwoman and the older boy grabbed him. They steadied him up and tried to move him, but his body didn't want to move.

"Le carburant, le carburant," said the woman, pulling him.

"The fuel, the fuel," said the boy, in case he didn't understand, also pulling.

They staggered toward the little house, pain jolting his left side at every step. They got him inside and seated at the table. It was almost dark in the house and the woman told the boy to light the lamps. Pete settled in the chair and looked himself over, as the mechanics might inspect a battle-damaged airplane before going to work on it. His left side hurt like hell and he already knew not to move it. But his left arm was intact—all the fingers were present and moveable. There wasn't any blood on his left side, but his right leg was a different story. Something had ripped along the boot and into his leg. Lots of blood. Like all boys he'd taken his lumps over the years, but he'd never felt a searing and throbbing like that. It was bad enough to make his eyes water. Shame it wasn't wintertime—he would have been wearing his fleece-lined thigh boots. He asked for a mirror and inspected his face: there were two nasty scratches but away from his eyes. He remembered pulling his goggles off; they'd stayed in place for the ride through the trees.

He looked around the house. The two smaller children were looking at him. A boy and a girl, five or six years old. He gave them a little wave. The woman came over and looked at his leg, straightened up and went to the cupboard. She was older than Juliette. Thirty-five maybe. Not thin, but not fat. She came back with scissors, some cotton, and a small bottle. Pete knew what was coming before she said it. Alcohol. He nodded. She cut the torn fabric of his trousers away, wet the cotton, and he grunted as alcohol met the open wound. There was a minute or so of discomfort while she worked on him, but the burning subsided once she finished.

"Water," he asked. "Water, please."

He downed the glass of water and she brought another; told the older boy to make tea. He smiled at that—the English have arrived, so there must be tea. He leaned back and closed his eyes; allowed the relief to wash over him. He'd lived through it.

B1719 was done for, and she'd taken him through some tough times. But ultimately, she was a collection of wood, fabric, and metal. An entry on Table of Available Airplanes—66 Squadron. The squadron would ring up 9th Wing and get a new airplane from depot. The squadron? They'd be wondering where he came down, and if he was alive. Which begged the question—where was he?

He opened his eyes and looked at the woman. "Où som-mes-nous? Telephone?"

The woman responded with a name he didn't recognize. The older boy, who looked to be about twelve, took a tattered piece of paper from the cupboard and spread it in front of Pete. It was an old military-style map. The woman pointed to the western edge of a wooded area where someone had drawn a red X.

"Nous sommes ici." She slid her finger to the town of Hermin. "Telephone."

Pete checked the scale of the map. The town was about three miles away.

She moved her finger further east, to Souchez. "Canadians."

Pete thought of his duty to this woman. He told her it was important to keep the children away from the airplane. Very dangerous. She nodded that she understood. He asked if the boy could take a message for him. The boy answered, resulting in a brief back-and-forth with his mother, after which he left scowling. Pete asked for pencil and paper and wrote that his Sopwith had crashed three miles south of Hermin. He requested a guard for the airplane and transport to an aid station. Also that they notify 66 Squadron of his whereabouts. That done, he leaned back and asked the two children their names.

"Je suis Gabriel," said the boy. "Elle est Caroline."

Pete told them they had lovely names, to which the boy scrunched up his nose. Pete admonished them to stay away from the airplane. They both nodded. Caroline, gravely; Gabriel, less so.

There were photos on a side table, including one of a soldier in a French infantry uniform standing next to a train. Blue tunic, bright-red trousers and hat. Rifle, but no helmet. Pete guessed it was from 1914, before the armies had learned how flashy colors interacted with modern sniper rifles. "Your husband?" he asked the woman.

She nodded. He would be home on leave next month. She had Gabriel bring him a cup of tea and Caroline a piece of bread with cheese. He didn't want to eat but got it down with the help of the tea. There was chocolate in the Pup's cockpit. He'd like to give it to the woman, but retrieving it was out of the question.

Her son returned with an older boy. Pete gave them the note and told them to take it to the Canadians. He had them take the map. They would need to show the soldiers where the plane crashed.

Once the boys were gone, the woman helped him move to a rocking chair by the window. He chatted with her for a couple of minutes before closing his eyes and rocking gently in the chair. She was nice enough, but talking took too much effort. His left side and right leg were still hurting, but the pain was nothing compared to the incredible feeling of being alive.

At some point, he realized an older couple had shown up. He must have dozed off. He managed some polite French conversation and closed his eyes again.

A motorcar engine woke him. Doors opening and closing. Voices. A second lieutenant, a sergeant, and three privates came in. All Canadian. They'd brought the two boys with them. One of the privates was wearing the white armband of a medical orderly. He bent over Pete.

"How are you feeling?" asked the lieutenant. Like most infantry second lieutenants Pete had met, he looked to be about eighteen years old.

"I'm still in one piece."

"You came out of it better than your airplane. Might even be due for a spot of leave." Pete hadn't thought of that.

"I'll need to clean the wound, sir," said the orderly.

Pete started to say the woman already had, before realizing it would be pointless. He nodded and once again experienced alcohol applied to an open wound, although the orderly was more liberal in its use. He cleaned a cut on Pete's neck that neither he nor the woman had noticed and bandaged him up.

"I rang your squadron and spoke with a Captain Fleming," said the lieutenant as the orderly worked on Pete. "They know you're alive, although I couldn't tell them anything about your condition."

"I think he'll do for now, sir," said the orderly. "But the doctors will need to look at him. I don't know that he'll be flying about in the morning."

"Is there anything you wish to get from the airplane?" the lieutenant asked.

Pete didn't carry a pistol. He'd hate to lose his maps, but someone poking around a crashed airplane in the dark, with half a tank of fuel splashed about…

"No. The squadron blokes should collect everything tomorrow."

The lieutenant explained to the woman in excellent French that the soldier would be outside all night to guard the airplane. That other soldiers would come tomorrow to take it away. She could bring the soldier something to eat in the morning if she wished, but he was not to enter the house. She nodded and thanked him. The lieutenant turned to the private who had guard duty, and who looked even younger than the lieutenant. "Any questions, Fortin?"

"No, sir. Perfectly clear."

Pete thanked the four children for their help and shook hands with each of them. Shook hands with the woman, thanked her, and wished her and her husband all the best. The orderly and another soldier helped him to the car and guided him into the backseat.

Once they were underway, Pete asked the lieutenant where they were headed. "Bit north of here. Barlin. There's a proper British hospital. With real nurses, I'm told. Of course, you're welcome to stay with us."

"Another time, perhaps. It's my duty to the crown to get proper medical care." They were silent for a few minutes, the driver proceeding at an unusually reasonable pace. "Were you at Vimy Ridge?" Pete asked.

"Yes. Things went well for once. We're out of the mud now."

"Let's hope they keep it up, and we can all go home one of these days."

The Germans had stopped the French advance in the south, and the Arras sector had settled back into stalemate. As far as Pete was concerned, the generals could come up with all the grandiose plans they wanted, but a lot of the chaps who went over the top were going to get slaughtered. If the incredible loss of life they engendered bothered the senior Allied generals, Pete hadn't seen any sign of it. Someone once told him they sanded the road before Haig's daily horseback ride, so the general's horse wouldn't slip. Hopefully, that was just another rumor.

They stopped in front of a large wood-framed tent, the sign out front welcoming them to Casualty Clearing Station 6. An orderly guided him to a cot and helped him undress. Pete looked around the tent. There were about sixty cots, maybe a third of them occupied. "The doctor will be around a bit later, sir," said the orderly. "But you caught us at a quiet moment."

"Is this the whole station?" Pete asked.

"Oh no, sir. This is just one of the marquees for the walking cases. The CCS can handle about six hundred patients."

He lay back and watched a nurse tidy up. She smiled at him mechanically as she went by. She was about fifty years old, her uniform dirty and her face lined with fatigue. She wasn't at all like the girls in the posters. He put his head back and closed his eyes against the bright white of the overhead electric lights. He stayed still; he couldn't change position without a jolt from his left side.

A young doctor with a brisk manner showed up about an hour later, breaking his uncomfortable state of limbo. The doctor had him stand and pressed firmly on his left side, and Pete readied himself as the doctor worked his way down his rib cage. He gasped at the fifth press, but the rest of the exam was uneventful. "Sixth left rib broken," announced the doctor.

The orderly made a note in Pete's file. The doctor had Pete sit and unwrapped the bandages on his leg. To Pete's dismay, he pulled the cut apart. "Midthigh to midcalf. About half an inch deep. Wash it out, numb him up, and I'll be back in a few minutes."

The orderly finished his notes and wheeled a cart over. Swabbed the wound clean with an alcohol solution, digging deeper than Pete would have preferred. When he was done, he gave Pete four little shots in the leg. "That should take care of you in a few minutes, sir. You're lucky. Last week, we about ran out of Novocain. Only the bad cases got some."

The doctor came back and went to work. There were no more than five minutes from first stitch to last. When he'd finished, he pulled up a chair while the orderly bandaged Pete up. For the first time, the doctor didn't seem to be in a hurry.

"Your leg will be stiff for a week or two, Lieutenant. The strength should be there, but it will be uncomfortable to walk on."

"Understand, Doctor."

"You fly a fighter airplane, is that correct?"

"That's correct. Yes."

"Which means you have to twist around and look behind you?"

"If you want to stay alive, you do."

"That's going to be a problem for a few weeks. Broken ribs are difficult. It will hurt, and you won't have full range of motion. The more twisting around you do, the longer it will take to heal. I'll write a note recommending no flying for two weeks." The doctor scribbled a note. Pete thanked him and asked if they were finished.

"We are. Good luck, Lieutenant." The doctor glanced at the clock. "You might as well sleep here tonight. They'll turn the lights down in a few minutes, and be around with breakfast at eight."

"Thanks, Doctor. I'll take you up on that."

After the doctor left, Pete looked himself over and realized how filthy he was. He asked for some water to clean up. The orderly brought him a basin of warm water and a clean cloth, admonishing him not to get the bandages wet. He cleaned himself up as best he could and lay down, and his mind went back to the accident sequence. He could have been a couple of knots slower into the trees; but he'd lived through it, with no permanent injuries and maybe some leave coming up. England. To sit by the sea. His mom would push him to visit Emily, her best friend's daughter. She was a nice enough girl, and likely she'd say yes if he asked. That said, their letter writing had gotten a little perfunctory. He drummed his fingers on the wooden frame of his cot, watching a little bird strut about the beam above his head.

He closed his eyes. Those last few seconds before the Pup went into the clouds. He'd thought about his mother and father. And he'd thought about Juliette. But he hadn't thought about Emily.

He sniffed. Sniffed again. Coffee. He opened an eye and looked at the clock. It was almost eight. He must have fallen back asleep. He'd woken up every hour or so during the night. The Novocain had worn off and his leg was hurting. Bad. He put both hands on the railings of the cot and gingerly pushed himself upright. No surprise, his left side was stiff and hurt to move. He spotted a nurse in his forward right quadrant, closing. This one was in the young and cute category. She chatted while she tidied up, ignored his attempts at being friendly, and was off.

A few minutes later they came around with breakfast. Eggs, toast, and fruit. He ate his breakfast and sat back with his coffee, seeing no reason to be in a hurry. He eventually finished nursing a second cup of coffee, which unfortunately meant it was time to return to the RFC. He stood up carefully. His left side and arm, right leg, and even his neck hurt to move. He dressed slowly and made his way over to a little sink. Splashed some water on his face and combed his hair with his fingers. Regarded himself in the mirror. He needed a shave, and his uniform was torn and dirty. Well, it would have to do. It wasn't as if he had a spare handy.

"You're welcome to stay here for a few hours, Lieutenant," said the senior orderly, handing him a cup of something. "It's an alcohol-based mouthwash."

Pete gargled and spat it into the sink. Again, and then with water. His mouth no longer tasted like a castor oil/coffee combo. "Thank you."

"As I was saying, we have enough beds if you need to rest a bit more."

"I appreciate that, but I need to get back. Is there a phone I can use?"

"The phones went down last night and they're still not back up. You might try Division, in Souchez. Go left on the main road out front. There should be plenty of traffic headed that way."

Pete thanked him and eased his way outside. Two lorries followed by a car were headed his way. The lorries motored past; he spat out grainy dust and wiped his eyes. Put out his hand. The car skidded to a stop in the dirt. "Hop in, sir. Or do you need a hand?" The driver was a young Canadian corporal.

"I can manage." Pete carefully slid into the seat next to the corporal, as the car sat in its little dust cloud. "Division is down this way, isn't it? I need to find a phone."

"About five miles down the road, sir. If you're looking for Fourth Division, that is." The engine roared and the rear wheels spun as the corporal stepped on the gas. "That's where I'm headed," he was almost shouting over the engine noise. The car edged forward, wheels spinning in the dirt. He upshifted and backed off the accelerator. "You get tangled up with the Huns, sir?"

"Not exactly. See them from time to time, though."

The car was speeding up and already closing the gap to the lorries. Pete braced himself to keep his torso from moving as the corporal negotiated the first turn, the car sliding sideways in the dirt.

"I don't see them, being attached to division staff," the corporal said as they came out of the corner. "But I like driving, and it keeps me out of the mud. It was different before I got hurt. Ammo train. Bringing the shells up each night, through the mud. The Hun artillery was horrible. Killed two of my best mates. And me, I almost lost my leg. Shrapnel. I didn't know anything in the world could hurt like that. I spent three months in hospital back near London. I'm on restricted duty now, drive the general here and there. A mate of mine is an observer. Flies about and shoots the machine gun."

"Are you going to apply? I bet you could do it even with your leg."

The corporal gave Pete a side glance. "No, sir. My mate told me that, well, begging your pardon, sir, that most of the fellows don't last more than a month or two. The Huns shoot them down, or the airplanes crash. He says it's safer down here, and I'm not really the hero type. There's a girl back home I want to see again."

The engine roared as they passed one of the lorries, and Pete grimaced as the car negotiated the bumps. He pushed himself out of the seat as the shock waves pounded through his torso. Fortunately, they got stuck behind the first lorry and the corporal had to slow down.

"I don't blame you, Corporal. Near as I can tell, most heroes in this war end up as dead heroes."

They were coming into Souchez now, a curious blend of piles of rubble juxtaposed with buildings untouched by the war. The corporal stopped in front of a large building with a Canadian Maple Leaf flag out front, flanked by two guards with rifles. Once the Durand Hotel, and now the home of the Canadian Fourth Division. He thanked the corporal, slid out and brushed the dust off his uniform. Worked his way up the stairs, one at a time, holding his left side. The duty officer raised his eyebrows at Pete's ragged appearance, but lent him a phone without comment. He rang up the squadron and Major Pritchett came on the line. Pete gave him a rundown of the accident and his condition.

"Forty Squadron is at Bruay. Captain Fleming told me they're going to gather up the airplane for us. I'll send a car for you. It doesn't sound like we need you bumping about in the back of some lorry."

"I appreciate that, sir."

"Where exactly are you again?"

"Canadian Fourth Division, sir. Souchez."

"Okay. I'll have the driver look for you there. Don't wander too far." Pete rang off and looked around the lobby. There was the usual assortment of officers coming and going, French hotel staff, and ringing phones. Pretty much like every other headquarters he'd ever seen. He made his way outside and paused at the top of the steps. Scattered clouds, blue sky. A nice summer morning in France. Lady Luck had picked a rare low overcast evening in June for his Le Rhône to self-destruct. Well, it had worked out. He eased his way down the street and sat outside a café. Greeted the elderly waiter with a smile; said he hoped the gentleman and his family were well. Of course, the old fellow looked at him like he was a complete idiot. Pete kept smiling, ordered tea, and picked up *Le Figaro*. His smile disappeared and his eyes narrowed as he read: the Gothas had hit London again. At least fifteen school children dead, most of them five years old. Those Hun bastards—bombing little kids. They had to be squashed, like cockroaches. There was no other way. The greater economic power of the Allies, the population advantage, would make the difference. But could Britain and France hold on for another year or two, until the Yanks arrived in strength? There were grumblings now and then about a negotiated settlement. About our boys "dying for Belgium." He set his geopolitical calculus aside and finished his tea. Paid his bill, bought yesterday's *Times* from a little store and found a bench near Division. He watched the trees move with the breeze; trees with leaves, unlike the few that were still standing up in Flanders. Once again, there was that wonderful feeling of being alive, mixed with fury at a vision of the crushed bodies of little school kids. He'd just finished up with the *Times* when Corporal Foster pulled up in the squadron's twenty-five-horsepower Vauxhall. He'd be traveling in style.

"How are you feeling, sir? You look a mite tattered."

"Not bad. I think all the big pieces are intact."

"Let's stow you in the back, sir. More room. All right if we leave the top down?"

"That's fine. We'll enjoy the nice weather."

They'd only been on the road fifteen minutes or so when steam began pouring from the radiator. Corporal Foster pulled over and raised the bonnet. Pete waited. The corporal peeked around the bonnet a minute or two later. "The radiator line is broken, sir. I can't fix that."

Pete nodded and looked around. Another Vauxhall was coming down the road, and it stopped next to them. An RFC Major was in the front seat. "What's the problem, fellows?" asked the major, returning their salutes.

"Broken radiator line, sir."

"Very well. The squadron's just down the road. I'll send some of the fellows over. We'll get it taken care of for you."

Pete sat in the Vauxhall wishing he had held onto his *Times*, as it turned out either the major's idea of "just down the road" differed from Pete's, or the major's chaps were moving slowly that day. Two hours and two naps later they were underway, only to be held up by a military convoy using both sides of the road. Pete took the opportunity to treat Corporal Foster to a leisurely café lunch, ignoring the sacred officer-ranker divide. Fortunately, no senior officers were around to spot his transgression. It was early evening by the time he walked into the squadron office, to the sound of singing coming from down the hall. Hugh Fleming and Michael Wall were at their desks. Pete waved hello to Michael and sat down in front of Hugh Fleming, who was filling his pipe with tobacco. This was a delicate procedure since Fleming only had one hand, although maintenance had fashioned him a pipe holder out of a Vickers mounting bracket, including a secondary horizontal bracket for a match and a permanent striker strip.

"Cigarettes would be simpler, sir."

"English gentlemen such as I smoke a pipe, Lieutenant. You wouldn't understand such things."

"Of course not, sir."

Fleming looked at him for a few seconds before going back to his pipe-filling procedure. "I've seen you look better, Pete."

"I've felt better, Captain. But it could have been worse."

"Walk me through it."

Pete recounted the flight and his trip to the hospital. "Here's the doctor's note, sir. He's recommending two weeks without flying. Turning to look behind me is going to be difficult for a while."

"I took you off the schedule tomorrow and the next," said Fleming as he read the note. "I'll talk to the major and see what he wants to do. Maybe you can pull duty officer for a week or two." Pete caught the lack of conviction in his voice. "The chaps are picking your engine up from Forty Squadron. They'll dig into it—see what went wrong." Fleming placed an extralong match in the horizontal bracket and lit it with a second match. Picked up his pipe and puffed until the tobacco caught. Returned the pipe to its bracket and opened a folder; examined what looked to be a list of airplanes.

"They'll fly a new Pup in tomorrow morning. B5305. Factory fresh."

"Sopwith built?" asked Pete. The pilots preferred airplanes built by the original manufacturer, rather than by one of the many subcontractors who had popped up. That, and French-built Le Rhônes were much preferred over their British cousins.

"Let me see…" Fleming flipped the page and studied it for a few seconds. "Afraid not. Looks like Clayton and Shuttleworth. But they've been around a while. I think they built steam engines." Fleming picked up his pipe and clouds of blue-gray smoke wafted Pete's way. He didn't like the smoke but waited to see if any more information was forthcoming.

"The major went to a conference at 9th Wing yesterday. There's talk of a big increase in the size of the RFC."

"How big is big, sir?"

"Almost double."

Pete's eyebrows went up—that would be big. British industry had finally woken up and was turning out real airplanes, but double the size of the RFC? "Last I looked, sir, the RFC was short pilots. And training was topped out."

"That's about how I see it, Lieutenant."

"This is unlikely to alleviate the situation."

"Agree once again." Fleming puffed on his pipe and looked at him. Serious. "Have you met General Trenchard, Pete? Or General Henderson?"

"No."

"General Trenchard spoke at a recording officer conference a couple of months back. General Henderson visited Forty-Five Squadron last year. It must have been before you got there." Fleming lowered his voice. "As far as I'm concerned, every military organization in the world has its share of senior officers who are arrogant buffoons. And that includes the British Army. But not those two. I have no idea if they agree with this decision or not. As you astutely note, training all those new pilots and observers will be difficult at best. But if that's the decision, they will make it happen."

"They'll need lots more instructors," remarked Pete. "I would be a logical choice for that Captain, having a rib injury and all."

Hugh Fleming ignored him. "Get some rest, Pete. Of course, I'll need your report tonight."

"I'll do it right now, sir." Pete moved to the extra desk in the office. Michael Wall was looking at him.

"Welcome home, Pete. Glad you made it back."

Pete picked up a trace of concern in Wall's voice. That was unusual. Pilots came and went—most of the headquarters chaps didn't seem to give it much thought.

"Thanks, Michael. It's good to be home. But I don't know that your Vickers survived the ride through the trees."

"If not, His Majesty can afford a new one."

Pete finished his report and wandered down to the bar. The singing was still going strong, led by C-Flight. Roger Browne and John Wilcox were sitting at a table, along with Lieutenant James (Jimmy) Musgrave, who'd been out on loan for the last month or so. Pete ordered a beer and joined them. He would have preferred orange juice, but if he tried that someone would be pouring whisky into it.

All three pilots stood up to greet him, and Pete just stopped Roger from giving him a welcome home slap on the back. "Glad you made it," Roger half shouted over the din. "Where'd you come down? Duncan's estimate ruled out England and Bavaria, and that was about it."

"About five miles south of Bruay. There's a hospital a few miles east of the aerodrome." Pete wasn't surprised Duncan didn't know where they had been. When he was a new wingman he'd stuck with his flight leader and tried not to get killed. Some flights he only knew where they were for takeoff and landing.

"Welcome home, Pete," said John. "But it looks like the trees got the better of it."

Pete shrugged, knowing he would hear similar comments for the next few days. "I'm alive, and in one piece." He turned to Jimmy Musgrave. Originally handsome, a training accident in the Avro had pushed his left cheekbone out of place, resulting in a permanent squint. Jimmy didn't seem to care. Women probably liked it, anyway. "How was Forty-Six, Jimmy?"

Jimmy tossed off his whisky and lined up the empty glass with its three predecessors. "I hated it at first. Two-seat Nieuports. They're dogs. But the Pups showed up two weeks back. Brand bloody new. I nailed an LVG east of Arras the day before yesterday. Got him in the fuel tank. The cockpit was on fire, and the pilot climbed out and flew it while standing on the wing. The observer wasn't moving, pretty sure he was already dead. Better for him that way, I suppose. The Hun held it steady for a good thirty seconds, standing on the wing. Great stuff. I would have given anything for a camera. Next, he's standing on a burning wing. Next, no more wing. Bye-bye. Funniest thing I ever saw."

Pete had watched Jimmy's face as he told the story. They were both RFC pilots at war, but the similarity stopped there. Unlike himself, Jimmy loved killing. At least the German pilot didn't burn alive. That would be the worst. But the long fall, the details of the ground coming into view. Would he close his eyes if it happened to him? Wasn't like he'd be enjoying those last few seconds of life. Waiting for the impact. He motioned toward the C-Flight group at the bar. "They get some Huns?"

"They got a couple this morning," Roger answered over the singing. "But that's not the reason for the party. Mac got flight commander at Twenty-Three. SPAD VIIs."

This was good news for Mac. Unlike medals and rousing speeches from visiting generals, flight commander meant something. He'd have the first shot, with at least one wingman looking out for his backside. The SPAD wouldn't dance around the sky like a Pup, but Pete would take one in a second if he had the chance. The singing got louder. A whisky glass flew past them and thudded into the wall two feet right of the stern visage of General, Earl, Secretary of State for War, Knight of the Order of…Horatio Herbert Kitchener. The late general appeared unruffled by the alcoholic near miss and continued pointing at them. Asking—almost demanding—that they join the army. God would save the king, but the implication was patriotic Britons could assist God in said worthy endeavor.

About eight feet to the general's right was a second poster. In the foreground, a somber-looking German soldier with rifle upright and bayonet fixed; apparently thinking about his wife and three children back home, who appear angelically in soft white tones in the background. Nothing being sacred around Liettres (and to Pete's chagrin as he'd planned to abscond with the poster when he rotated out) the lovely young wife now sported a thick black beard and matching eyebrows.

A second glass followed the first, close enough to splatter the late general with whisky. But the third and fourth missiles were well off target, drawing boos and catcalls from the crowd. It appeared excessive alcohol consumption was affecting C-Flight's aim. Pete was worried about taking a glass to the head as their table wasn't far off the line of fire, but the others didn't look concerned.

"The doctor recommended no flying for two weeks," Pete was almost shouting, holding on to his left side. "Broken rib. But if you think three weeks would be better, I'll understand."

"Ha ha," said Roger. "I'll see what the boss wants to do. Be a shame to throw you back in just to get killed."

"This will give you a chance to visit the café again, Pete," said John, with the slightest knowing look.

"Yes, I enjoy getting away once in a while," Pete replied matter-of-factly.

"Maybe even England," said Roger. "Although I wouldn't get my hopes up quite yet, mate. Too bad you didn't break a few more—I don't know that one rib will do it. I could slug you in the side if you want. I bet I can still break ribs."

"Thanks for the offer, but I'll pass."

To Pete's relief, the singing subsided and there were a few moments of relative calm. But Jimmy took advantage of the lull. He grabbed a full whisky glass and jumped up on his seat. "Silence. Silence, you ruffians," he shouted.

Most of the crowd turned to look at him. "Silence. I'll show you boys how a real pilot shoots."

Jimmy turned to look behind him, balanced himself, and launched the glass over his shoulder. A roar went up as the glass nailed the German soldier, and Jimmy raised his arms in the victory salute.

"That's a load of bollocks," shouted a C-Flight pilot from the bar. "Kitchener was the target."

"Nonsense," asserted Jimmy. "The Hun's the enemy. Everyone knows that."

A large and obviously drunk C-Flighter rushed over, yelling that C-Flight bloody well knew their target and A-Flight could go to the devil. Pete recognized him but had forgotten his name. Irish type—he'd been around a few weeks. Normally the new blokes were more restrained. Good chance fear and alcohol were at work.

Pete sensed the new arrival planned to stop short and go eye to eye with Jimmy. However, he failed to control his overtake and smashed into Jimmy, who went flying backward off his chair. He came up swinging and the two of them ended up on the floor. Lots of punches were thrown as the crowd cheered on their respective favorite, but few hits were scored. Fortunately, enough sense prevailed not to widen the struggle into a full-scale brawl. Major Pritchett came in looking for the source of the excitement, prompting Roger to wade in and separate them. "That's enough for now, fellows. We'll call it a draw."

The two combatants went to their respective corners, accepting congratulations on a well-fought struggle. The noise level dropped as the major made his rounds, stopping to speak with each of his flight commanders. The three conversations ran along the same lines. "Any problems, Captain?"

"No, sir. All good. Congratulations on your promotion, sir."

"Thank you, Captain."

When he got to their table, the major looked at Pete and asked how he was feeling. "Good, sir. Just a little stiff."

"I read the note from the doctor." The major looked at Roger. "He can pull duty officer for a week. Do any depot runs that come up. He shouldn't have to worry about Huns jumping him going that way."

"Understood, sir."

Once the major had left, Roger looked at Pete. "A week. Not bad. And maybe we can squeeze out an extra day or two. A working leave now, and you'll still be due your regular leave."

"I heard a rumor Ninth Wing wasn't going to cancel all leaves this time around."

"You should know better than to listen to rumors, Pete. Don't you know the big attack is coming."

Pete blocked a snort. The big attack was always coming. He motioned toward the major. "He's getting promoted?"

Roger nodded. "He made lieutenant colonel. He's getting Twelfth Corps Wing. At…Beef Villas, I think it is. We're getting a chap from Second Brigade staff."

The singing started up again, and before long they'd be pushing beers or whiskies at him. Fortunately, he had a good excuse handy. "I'll leave you gents to it. I need to get some rest."

# A Dinner Party

*Teddington, Southwest London*

Mark knocked on the door of Rachel's flat ten minutes after the appointed time—his standard social event procedure on the rare occasions it was needed. She opened the door with a smile. Her small flat was almost full. "I'm busy in the kitchen, Mark. There are drinks on the counter. I'll let you make your own introductions."

She disappeared into the kitchen as Mark stepped inside. He poured himself a soda water and turned to a couple a little older than himself: Rachel's cousin Susan and her husband Andrew. Susan was tall and thin like Rachel. Andrew had a thick black beard and was a little shorter than his wife. "You're the physicist?" asked Andrew, shaking hands.

"One of them." Mark motioned toward the professor, who along with his wife, was speaking with an older gentleman. "Professor Stanton is a very distinguished physicist and is Director of the Engineering Department."

"Rachel's told us lots about you," said Susan. Her features were like Rachel's, but plainer. She didn't look to be wearing any makeup.

"That shouldn't have taken long."

"You have two brothers in France, don't you?" Andrew asked.

"Yes. Both Pete and Phillip are pilots. Charles is in the army, too. He served in France, but he's back in London now."

"Three brothers in the army," mused Susan. "Your family must be in favor of the war."

"Dear, Rachel made us promise..." Andrew looked at his wife, who glared back at him.

Mark gave a little shrug. "I can only speak for myself. I'm never in favor of war, which seems an incredibly primitive and barbaric way to resolve international disagreements. And on a personal level, two of my younger cousins were killed in France last year. But this is the world we live in. If Germany were to control France and Belgium, if an aggressive war that costs thousands or millions of lives goes unpunished, where does that lead to?"

"I'll tell you where it leads—" began Susan as Rachel poked her head out of the kitchen.

"Susan dear, can you help me in the kitchen, please?"

After his wife reluctantly departed, Andrew turned back to Mark. "Susan is a member of the ILP. She thinks Britain should be improving conditions for its workers. Not off fighting the Germans in France."

*The ILP?* Mark didn't pay much attention to politics. Independent Labour Party, perhaps?

"And yourself?"

"I'm an active Labour Party member and absolutely support making life better for our workers. But I agree with you, we have to win this war first. That said, the big industrialists shouldn't be getting rich off it. The workers and soldiers aren't getting rich."

*What was it he'd read in the paper?* "Parliament passed an excess profits tax," he began. "I don't recall the details—"

"Mark, the workers still pay a higher percentage of their wages in taxes than the owners do," said Susan from the doorway of the kitchen. "Someone please explain to me why that's fair. I'm a simple woman who doesn't understand these things."

## A DINNER PARTY

The conversations died down, but no one answered and Susan pressed ahead. "Mark, you're right they passed an excess profits tax. But it's only fifty percent of the excess. There's talk of raising it to eighty, but why not one hundred? Sir This and Lord That would still have their normal profits, and they were hardly suffering before the war."

Mark suppressed a grimace. Susan's tone was on edge, and she wasn't done.

"And how does the government taking in more tax money help the workers, anyway? Strikes are what's needed. That's the only time the government notices we have workers in this country. Oh, but silly me, I forgot. Parliament outlawed strikes in munitions-related industries, and I'm still looking for an industry that isn't munitions related. Perhaps ice cream. Yes, I shall look into that."

Mark could point out that labor stoppages in Britain would mean fewer airplanes and munitions going to France, which had to mean more British dead. As he debated on prolonging the conversation, Rachel intervened again. "Susan, help me with this, please. It's very hot."

Susan glared at her cousin, but relented.

"My wife gets worked up about these things," Andrew said quietly. "She's a dyed in the wool Socialist, which makes us very unpopular with some of our neighbors. Funny though, there's a young Marxist couple three doors down. They don't like us either."

Mark started to ask Andrew about his work. Anything to stay away from politics, but another voice spoke first.

"Have they convinced you yet?" A small man who looked to be in his seventies was looking up at him. "Convinced you we need to sue for peace now, before it's too late to save the working class?"

"Mark, allow me to introduce Rachel's grandfather," said Andrew. "Admiral Ashton Ross. The admiral is basically a good person despite a propensity to exaggerate, and an unwillingness to see more than one side of an issue."

Mark looked down at the admiral and chose his words carefully. This was supposed to be an enjoyable social occasion. "I agree the lives of our working class need to be improved. But we have to win this war first."

"Right you are, young man, and the Royal Navy—"

"Then someone needs to stop these horrible bombers." An attractive, twenty-something blonde from across the room interrupted the admiral's nascent speech. "I don't care if it's the army, the not-so-Royal-Navy, or bloody Manchester United. Dropping bombs on London and killing women and little children. Why is it so hard to shoot down a bloody bomber in broad, bloody, daylight?"

The voice was high-pitched and the blue eyes blazed from across the room. This must be Charlotte, Rachel's younger sister. Mark had heard the guns Wednesday morning and felt the tremors when the bombs hit. The newspapers were full of conflicting information, but the bombers hit a primary school in Poplar and killed young children. The pictures left no doubt about that. What he hadn't seen were any pictures of shot-down German bombers. If they'd got one and it fell on land, there'd be pictures. But changes had to be on the way. Lloyd George wasn't going to sit still while the Germans bombed London and killed civilians. Likely the generals in France wanted their airplanes and guns near the front line and not back protecting London. But if so, that was an argument they were going to lose.

Mark sensed the admiral bristling beside him and spoke to cut him off. He kept his tone level, trying to ratchet the tension down. "I imagine it comes down to wartime priorities." He looked at Charlotte. Her eyes were the brightest blue he'd ever seen. "Now that the Germans have shown they can bomb London and kill civilians, the government will make Home Defense a priority. My brother's a pilot and we talked about this last year during the Zeppelin raids. Pete told me the units in France get the newest airplanes, and Home Defense gets the leftovers."

The admiral looked up at him and nodded. "Good military leaders anticipate how advances in technology will force changes in strategy and tactics. If you have fools and politicians in charge, they spend their time making smooth-sounding speeches. Handing out money that isn't theirs. The generals and admirals focus on their next promotion instead of planning for the next war. And that's what we have: fools. In the government. At the Admiralty. At army GHQ. Look at our own Grand Fleet. We take a lout like Beatty, make him a vice admiral and give him the Battlecruiser Fleet. Not because he's a sailor—everyone knows he isn't. But because he's a handsome chap married to an heiress."

"Uh-oh," said Andrew. "I think we're going to refight the battle of Jutland again."

The admiral ignored him and looked at Mark. "I ran capital ship design and procurement for two years. Battlecruisers were lightly armored. They had to be, to give them the necessary speed. They were never intended to slug it out with an enemy battle fleet." Some bitterness came into the old man's voice. "That's why Beatty had the Fifth Battle Squadron with him. Four of our fastest and best battleships, and they hardly engaged the enemy. Meanwhile, Beatty lost three of our battlecruisers and damn near lost *Lion* as well. *Queen Mary, Indefatigable, and Invincible* carried over a thousand men each. There were *thirteen* survivors." The admiral was turning red.

"But we won the battle, didn't we?" asked Mark, hoping to calm him down.

"Yes, in that we drove the Germans back to base and the blockade remained intact. In the long run, that's what matters. But the cost in ships and lives was high—much higher than it should have been. If there's one thing the Lords of the Admiralty need to do, it's to put real sailors in charge of ships at sea, and let the others push papers around some office in London. They didn't do that, and thousands of our sailors died for their mistake."

The admiral took a sip of his drink and Mark was relieved to see the red fading from his face. When he spoke again, his tone was more level. "I never understood what the Germans were hoping to accomplish with their High Seas Fleet. They must have known we would never let them gain parity in capital ships. It would have made more sense to build fast cruisers and submarines, and use the rest of the money on the army. But like our own, their system is far from perfect. Politics. Interservice rivalries. Egos. One of my fellow admirals once likened the German military to a top-tier football team, but with some grammar schoolboys as manager."

"Sounds like you're getting a history lesson, Mark." Professor Stanton had joined them.

"Current events too. What the admiral is saying isn't quite what I read in the newspapers. But it makes sense."

The admiral smiled for the first time. "Even if the papers knew the truth, Mark, I'm not sure they'd print it. Even if the government let them."

"All right, everyone, we're ready," called Rachel from the table. She'd managed an excellent prime rib with biscuits and vegetables, and announced that political discussions were off-limits at the table.

It was mostly small talk during dinner, although at one point the admiral asked Mark about military service. The professor intervened before he could answer. "Admiral, the Lab works in direct support of the army, the Royal Flying Corps, and the Naval Air Service. Mark works aerodynamic and ballistic related issues. He qualifies for an exemption and we're lucky to have him. Very few people can do what he does."

"Actually, I spoke with the navy back in '14," said Mark, enjoying the look of surprise on the professor's face, and on Rachel's. "I had rheumatic fever when I was a child, and the doctor didn't like the way my heart sounded. He told me to go away." He'd also told Mark he needed to lose at least a stone, but Mark didn't mention that.

"I didn't know about this," said Rachel, looking at him. He smiled at her. "Not everything is in my file at the Lab." She frowned but didn't reply.

After dinner, they adjourned for tea and more small talk. Rachel asked Mark if he had heard from his brothers.

"I haven't heard from Pete lately, but I think he's still flying the Sopwith Pup. Phillip, the youngest, is a flier now too. Charles is back in London. He's married and has two little girls."

Charlotte was sitting next to him, and her blue eyes perked up as he spoke. "Is your brother Pete married, Mark?"

"Not that I know of."

"I'm single. My husband was killed at the Marne. We'd only been married three months."

No one said anything, and Charlotte continued. She wasn't one to put a damper on the evening. "Has your brother shot down any of those horrible bombers? Or maybe a Zeppelin?"

Mark shook his head. "He flew Home Defense last year. I know he chased some Zeppelins and shot at them, but I don't think he brought one down. Now he's stationed in France. Or maybe Belgium."

"I hope he kills lots of Germans. I hate them." Charlotte paused and looked to be mentally shifting gears. "Pete must be younger than you?"

Mark smiled at that. "Yes, he is. Pete would be about twenty-five now."

"I'm only twenty-three. Perhaps your brother would like to meet me?" Charlotte had leaned toward him, and Mark couldn't help noticing her dress stretching across a nice figure underneath. Knowing everyone was watching them, he was careful not to look away from her face.

"I'd guess Pete would be happy to meet you. I think he's due home on leave before long."

Charlotte sat back and looked at her sister. "Rachel, surely we can have a war hero pilot over for dinner when he's home on leave?"

"I imagine so. Depending on the war hero's schedule, of course."

"He'll spend most of his time in Devon," said Mark. "But he should be in London for a day or two."

Mark enjoyed the evening, and had even gotten in a dig at Rachel when the professor's wife complimented him on his appearance. He'd looked down at his new light blue shirt and red tie. "Thank you. It's a little thing, but I always try to present a nice appearance."

Once everyone else had gone, he offered to help Rachel and Charlotte clean up. "How gallant," said Rachel.

Mark washed dishes while the two ladies dried and put them away.

When they'd finished, Rachel made tea and asked him to stay for a bit. Charlotte asked about Pete again—what he liked to do. Mark told her Pete played chess and read history.

"Oh. Chess and history." Charlotte appeared let down, but Rachel came to Pete's rescue.

"Mark, didn't you tell me once Pete likes to dance?"

"Yes, that's right. What is that dance he does? Castle something. Castle Walk, I think. He's quite good. He was in some competitions."

Charlotte brightened up at the mention of dancing. "I like to dance. And I like to have fun. Does Pete like to have fun?"

"All of us boys are on the quiet side. But, yes, I would say Pete likes to have fun." He looked at Rachel. "Perhaps even more so than myself."

Rachel smiled at him but let it pass. Charlotte appeared to be thinking something over. She turned to him again. "And you, Mark. Are you courting my sister?"

The question hit him like a football in the face, although he swallowed his tea without gagging. "No. We're just friends."

Charlotte frowned. "I don't see why not. She's intelligent and reasonably attractive. And not too terribly old. Let me think. She must be—"

Rachel cleared her throat, and Charlotte turned back to Mark. "You like my sister. I can tell."

"Of course I like your sister. She has several admirable qualities." It was Rachel's turn to frown.

"That sounds like one of your technical reports. Are you going to enumerate my admirable qualities? With subcategories and footnotes?"

Mark's only reply was to raise his eyebrows, and Rachel turned to her little sister. "I think we can let Mark be. If we abuse him too much, he may not want to come back and see us."

Mark managed some more small talk, thanked the ladies and said good night. Paused outside the door and breathed in the night air. It had been a successful evening.

# The Spartans

*66 Squadron RFC, Sopwith Scout Fighter Aircraft*
*Liettres Aerodrome, Northern France*

Pete pulled duty officer until noon, splitting the shift with a brand-new C-Flight pilot. He didn't mind the primary function of a duty officer: to sit around the orderly room and look knowledgeable. But he hated the other part of the job: censoring the men's outgoing letters. He made it a point not to look at the writer's name and skimmed the personal parts as best he could. The duty officer also had to inspect the aerodrome, which Pete interpreted as taking a stroll to enjoy the nice weather they were having that day. After teatime, he grabbed a burlap sack from behind the Mess and bicycled into town at minimum speed. Stopped at a general store and bought as much coal as the owner's son could pack into the sack. Tied it off with a bit of red string he'd found in the office and admired the little bow. It would do.

He balanced the sack in the bike's small basket, wiped his hands as best he could and set off. He arrived at the almost empty café a few minutes before five and saw her inside. Sat on the bike and smoked a cigarette.

Frowned at the stink from the piles of trash flanking the café. Either the French didn't believe in garbage cans, or the cans had been requisitioned by the army. But the piles were only up to his knees, so someone must pick up the trash every so often.

She saw him and came outside. "Evening, Lieutenant. Are you coming in?"

"No, I'll wait for you here."

She smiled and went back inside, and he let out a sigh of relief. Her smile hadn't been a quizzical, "why would you be waiting for me," sort of smile.

She came outside a few minutes later, and he was pleased to see the concern in her eyes as she looked at him. "Are you all right, Lieutenant?"

"A little bruised, that's all. I thought I would walk you home again." Pete motioned toward the sack, which was leaning dangerously in its basket. "I brought you a present."

She regarded the filthy burlap sack covered in coal dust. "It's lovely, Lieutenant. Did you crash your airplane fighting the Germans?"

Pete shook his head. "I crashed into a tree."

"Lieutenant, if you wish to impress French girls, fighting the Germans might be better."

He nodded his agreement and they started walking, Pete pushing his bike alongside of her. When they arrived at her house, she held the door open. "Please come in."

He followed her inside and said hello to Arthur. Picked up the almost empty coal bin and carried it outside, mindful of his left side. Arthur had followed him outside and was looking at his bandages. He went to fill the bin, and Arthur stopped him.

"I'll get it, Peter." Arthur filled the bin, trying to keep the dust down. He wiped his hands on the grass but didn't go inside. Their eyes met and Arthur spoke in a low voice.

"I'm glad you're here, Peter. A real friend would be good for Juliette. She's glad, too, although I don't imagine she has said so. Of course, you're not the first young man to come around. Paul's been gone almost three years now, and she's an attractive woman."

Pete wasn't sure how to respond, so he didn't. But the silence wasn't uncomfortable.

"She works hard, doesn't complain," Arthur continued. "Likely she was a little embarrassed you brought her something. She tries not to show it, but she's very sad the boys are growing up without their father. She cried every night for a year after Paul died." Pete winced at that but still didn't reply, and Arthur motioned him inside. Juliette was boiling water for tea. "I think I'll walk down and talk with Hugo," said Arthur.

"Okay, Grand-père. See you in a little while."

Pete washed his hands in the basin. Standing next to her, he risked it and gave her a little side-to-side hug. She smiled up at him, but her body language was only neutral. He sat down at the table and listened. The house was quiet. "The boys?"

"They're down the road playing with Eva's little boy. She'll send them home soon."

Juliette brought the tea and sat down. Being a better talker than he was, she kept the conversation moving. Spoke of her two sisters. One down the road in Auchel, the other in Paris. Both married, no children. "Why don't you tell me about your family?"

Pete ran through his standard litany. His mother was in Devon, his deceased father had been American. His half-Russian stepfather was with the foreign service in London. He had three brothers: two older, one younger.

"You must have an English girl back home."

The change of subject caught him off guard, and he took a moment to answer. "There's a girl," he said slowly. "Emily. She's nice. I suppose everyone expects us to get married someday."

"Do you love her? This Mademoiselle Emily?"

Pete gave a little shrug. Met her eyes and looked away.

"Perhaps not enough. Have you ever had a French girl, Lieutenant?"

The question startled him. This little blue-eyed French girl could be very direct. He considered the question and came up with two possible meanings for "had," but in either case the answer would be the same. Nor did he have to decide if prostitutes counted, having thus far avoided the French brothels. "No."

"Your English girls are very proper, yes? This is our second date, so you may hold my hand. But you may not kiss me until the fourth date, and you must ask my mother's permission first. Like that, yes?" He smiled at her characterization of English girls.

"Something like that."

"We French girls are not like that. It's not that we are bad girls, no. We are, perhaps you English would say, we feel things strongly. Or that we don't hide our feelings."

Pete didn't answer. Talking about feelings with a woman wasn't his strong suit. But being alone with her, sitting close to her, it struck him how much he wanted to take her into his arms. To kiss her on the lips.

"I am making you uncomfortable, and you are a guest. What should we talk about, Lieutenant?"

Pete took the opening. "You don't work in the café on the weekends, right?"

She looked at him but didn't reply.

"Why don't we take the boys down to the river? We can have lunch and go swimming."

The stretch of the river near the aerodrome wouldn't do; it was too popular with the pilots. But he'd scouted out another section near the town.

"Yes, they would like that. Myself as well, of course. I don't think Jules will go in the water, but Paul will. He won't be afraid."

"Done, then. Let me look at my schedule, and we'll set a date."

He stood up, deciding he had stayed long enough. Outside, he put his hand on her shoulder to steady himself and gave her a kiss on the cheek.

Back at the aerodrome, he went by the orderly room to check the schedule. "St. Omer" had replaced his duty officer stint for the next day.

"I need you to bring a Pup back from depot tomorrow, Pete," said Hugh Fleming from behind the counter. "You fellows keep crashing them."

"Any particular time, sir?"

"No, but I need you back sometime tomorrow. There's lots of rumors going about." Fleming lowered his voice. "Including that we might be going to Calais."

Pete raised his eyebrows. "Why Calais?"

"Gothas."

Pete nodded. It made sense—get between the bombers and London. Get some payback from the bastards. He'd be in the cockpit for that, broken rib be damned. "When?"

"Soon, if it happens. Gothas dropping bombs on little kids in London must be front and center for the War Cabinet. How are you feeling?"

"Not bad. Just stiff."

"Well, you shouldn't run into many Huns between here and St. Omer."

"Hope not." Pete nodded toward the board. "Captain, I'm off the schedule on Saturday. Any chance we can keep it that way?"

Hugh Fleming's eyes flicked to the board and back to Pete. "I'll see what I can do, Lieutenant."

"Hey, Pete." A familiar voice came from behind him.

He turned around and smiled: Mark Henderson. They shook hands and he motioned for Mark to sit down. If they went to the club, they'd be shouting at each other. "How's the stomach?" Pete asked.

"Better now."

"That's too bad."

"I asked the nurses for something to make it worse. They wouldn't go along."

"I thought you might turn it into a holiday. Recuperate back in England."

"No such luck."

Pete was happy to see his friend again. But Mark had a family, and flying Pups in Flanders was hardly the safest way in the world to make a living. "How old's your son now, Mark?"

"He's five, and a bundle of energy. My brother came back from America last year with pictures of baseball, and the little fellow is hooked. We built a diamond in the field across the way and I pitch a kid's football to him and his friends. He's already talking about moving to America to play baseball."

"Good for him. Beats the army." Pete checked the board. Mark had five kills to his credit. "Flight commander should come through for you soon. As fast as things change around here."

"Hope so. I'd miss you and Roger, but you understand. The SE5 would be nice. Fly high and fast. Stay away from the machine guns."

"That would be my first choice. Lots of Camels are headed our way too, but the rumor is she's a dog at altitude. If so, those blokes will be down in the mud."

They were quiet for a moment. The noise level from the club was steady—alcohol and fatigue hadn't kicked in yet. "How's the wife?"

"She's fine. Visited me in hospital and filled me in on the goings-on back home. It's not in the papers, but there are lots of rumors about a big strike at Vickers. That there will be delays in ammunition production."

Pete snorted. "Just what we need in the middle of a major European war."

"The club not good enough for you two?" Drew Harris sat down with them.

"It's too noisy down there," said Pete. "Do you know Mark Henderson?"

"I do now," said Harris, shaking hands. "Strike at Vickers, huh?" Harris had overheard them. He sat down and crossed his long legs; scanned the readiness board. "Do you fellows know that much can be learned from the study of ancient civilizations? As one example, the Spartans discovered the perfect way of dealing with industrial disputes over two thousand years ago."

Pete gave Harris a side glance. He could guess the nature of what was coming next.

"They were far outnumbered by their subjects, so each new year they'd declare war on them. That way, if there were problems the troublemakers could be dispatched without any…shall we say, legal complications."

"So you think Britain should declare war on its factory workers each January?" ventured Pete. "And then execute any troublemakers?"

"Exactly. I retain a modicum of hope for you yet, Newin. Unlike most of the walking braindead that inhabit the RFC uniform. Granted our legal framework is somewhat different from that of five hundred BC Sparta. Presumably, we would need to make some adjustments. Check to see if the Magna Carta speaks to industrial disputes."

"Even so, it might be a tough sell. Especially to Liberal and Labour."

"Perhaps. Our modern progressive society. Rights of the common man and all that claptrap. But the chaps in the trenches, living in the mud with the rats and the lice. Getting ripped apart by artillery or catching a sniper's bullet in the eye. Don't they have rights, too? For example, the right to adequate ammunition to fight with?"

"Fair enough, Drew. We need to find a balance."

"We already have, Pete. The government outlawed strikes in critical industries. Any sort of work stoppage or slowdown is effectively the same thing. You break the law in the middle of a major war—that's treason and you pay the price. Case closed. Soldiers are dying by the thousands. What's a few workers going in front of the firing squad?"

Pete and Mark glanced at each other as Pete tried to gauge the seriousness of the discussion. He looked at Drew, but his expression didn't give anything away.

"Of course, the entire Spartan culture was geared to war," continued Drew. "Including the support of their women. 'Going off to war, darling? Have a nice time, but come back with your shield, or on it.' Meaning win or die. There was no middle ground. The absolute worst was for the husband or son to come back alive after a defeat, even if they were missing some body parts. It shamed the whole family. The women also ran about naked before they married, which is an interesting idea."

"Bit cool for that in England, isn't it," said Mark.

"Perhaps, although no reason it couldn't be instituted on a seasonal basis. Of course, the entire institution of marriage could be dispensed with. Quite a dated concept, and one with a direct impact on the production of little Britons. Any fool who picks up a newspaper can see the pressing need to breed more soldiers for the defense of the realm. Once again, we could look to antiquity for guidance. The more fertile Spartan wives were shared across several husbands, to keep the production line going. None of this silly modern and counterproductive fixation on monogamy."

"Aren't they the ones who threw babies over the cliff?" asked Mark. He wasn't smiling.

"The same. And in case you're wondering, while it might make sense from an economic standpoint, I don't advocate that. Human life is precious, and I hate to see it thrown away."

Drew paused, watching the AM2 update the next day's schedule. There was the noise of chalk scratching on the board, a voice coming from the earpiece of the phone that Hugh Fleming was holding a few inches from his ear, and somewhere down the hall a typewriter was clacking. Pete waited, guessing that Drew wasn't done. He was right.

"Speaking of throwing lives away, if the hereafter is indeed as described in our Christian Bible, certain European leaders are going to have some difficult questions to answer when their time comes. The kaiser for one, who I believe spent most of the July crisis sailing about on his yacht. Our erstwhile ally Tsar Nicholas, may his soul rest in peace if the Reds take over.

"And dare I say it, even the leaders of our most staunch ally, the vaunted Third Republic of France. Those Frenchmen who chose to risk millions of lives for a chance to wash away the stain on their honor—the loss of Alsace-Lorraine to the Prussians. They all have blood on their hands.

"And don't tell me this war couldn't have been prevented. We had two crises in those wondrous lands we know as the Balkans, and they found a way out short of world war. Did millions of people really have to die or lose body parts because a few Serbian lunatics assassinated an archduke of the ramshackle Austro-Hungarian Empire?"

"I have to admit," said Pete, "that I'm enjoying your vision of the kaiser in front of his Maker, trying to explain himself while he squirms and fiddles with his mustache. Maybe he'll try to hide behind his medals."

"It is a pleasing picture, isn't it? Perhaps the good Lord will allow spectators. All the dead soldiers? No, I have an even better idea: the soldiers to serve as jurors. The black water of the Styx flowing by in the background. The ferry boat tied to the wharf, waiting for the condemned souls. Or maybe it's tied to a cloud? The ferryman…a mangled soldier? The victim of a gas attack? Yes, that's better. Eyes and tongue hanging out, dripping goo. 'Welcome aboard, Your Excellency,' he slurs. 'Please make yourself comfortable. I have your lunch ready: a lovely blend of pig entrails and feces. Oh, why the long face? We prepared it especially for you just yesterday. But you needn't worry—we're headed quite a ways downriver, so you'll have plenty of time to enjoy it. That said, I most strongly recommend that every drop go down the hatch, as the headmaster is quite particular on this point. I'm told he sees a lack of compliance on the part of the new arrivals as, let us say, a failure to fully appreciate the gravity of their situation. And while he's never been anything other than perfectly pleasant to me, and by the way is quite a handsome fellow, it's probably best you don't start out on his bad side. The arrangements for your stay may not be finalized, and I'm told the upper floors are much nicer.'"

Harris gave a dark chuckle as Pete and Mark exchanged glances again. "Such a lovely picture, don't you fellows agree? Perhaps I'll commission a painting and have copies made. Offer them to the War Office as recruiting posters."

Pete was struggling to remember. *The river Styx? Dante's road to the underworld?* He suppressed a smile at the look on Mark's face. His friend had met Drew when the latter was in fine form.

"But it's difficult for us mere humans to judge how such things might play out," Drew continued. "If basic incompetency is a valid defense in said proceeding, most of our leaders may do just fine."

"You didn't include Britain in the group," Mark pointed out. "Whose leaders have something to answer for."

"No. As near as I can tell, our civilian leadership behaved reasonably at the time. But not so on the military side of our house. We Brits have proven, if there had ever been any doubt, that if one puts fools in positions of authority when fighting the German Army, human life will be wasted. In particular, the lives of our soldiers. Although that said, *fools* may be a bit strong. As Pete would tell you, I'm quite well-balanced in my viewpoints. Let's just say…I believe our illustrious field marshal would have been perfectly fine in his role if this war had been fought forty or fifty years ago. But today, in a war unlike any other in history, when judgment and adaptability are called for—"

"That's enough, fellows." Hugh Fleming had hung up the phone and caught the last bit of their conversation. He gave Harris a long look. "Why don't you continue your discussion somewhere other than the orderly room."

Pete's depot trip came off uneventfully, although he'd had his doubts after speaking with the mechanic at St. Omer. "She ready to go?" he'd asked the corporal who looked to be in charge as the Le Rhône wound down. Pete was surrounded by rows of airplanes, maintenance hangars of all sorts, and somewhere nearby was the army's hydrogen generation plant for their observation balloons. Hopefully they didn't allow smoking over there.

"Yes, sir. They finished up the rigging last night and she's been sitting a week, so I wanted to be sure the engine would start up."

"I appreciate that. What happened to her?"

The corporal looked at his notes. "Hard landing, sir. Broke the undercarriage and both main spars. Cracked a longeron. The propeller, of course. The squadron blokes took the wings off, put her on a lorry and drove her up here. We put new wings on. Patched her up good. She's ready to go now, sir."

"Undercarriage, spars, longeron, propeller," mused Pete. "Nothing else?"

The corporal thought for a moment. "Broke the seat, too, sir."

"I don't suppose anyone took her for a test flight?"

The corporal looked at him with a faint smile. "I think that's you, sir."

Despite what she had been through the patchwork Pup flew like any other Pup, and he descended to 300 feet as he passed Blessy. Circled Juliette's house and saw the boys out back. He dropped to thirty feet and gave them a wave and a wing rock—to an enthusiastic response.

The river trip had been a success. He'd swam with Paul and carried Jules around the pool. That was followed by lunch, checkers, and tag. The boys had run ahead and disappeared into the house. Juliette put her hand in his and rather than go in the house, she turned back toward the river. Led him down a side road and, a few minutes later, into a field of waist-high grass. She spread the blanket out and sat down. Pulled her knees to her chin. He sat next to her and put his arm around her. Neither of them said anything.

He watched the wind push little waves through the tall grass. Looked at her again. Her dress had shifted and he saw the little mole on her shoulder for the first time. How her blonde hair curved around her ear. Was it her? Could this beautiful, down-to-earth French girl fill whatever it was that had always been missing? Fill that empty space in the center of his being that he could never come to grips with? That nagging sensation of watching life pass by, and not living it?

He laid her back and looked into her blue eyes. Kissed the top of her head and around her eyes. Propped himself on an elbow and ran his fingers along the inside of her arm. Along her shoulder. Drew the back of his fingernails across her face. She had one knee bent and both thighs were showing. It would have been easy to caress the inside of her thighs. He didn't, and he wasn't sure why. He leaned over and ran the tip of his tongue over her lips. Kissed her closed eyes again. He rolled onto his side, so that their bodies were no longer touching. Watched her face.

She opened her eyes and looked at him. Pushed herself up on an elbow. "We must be careful, you and I."

He wasn't sure what she meant.

She spoke slowly. "Hugo's grandson Leo fixes airplanes. He says our French pilots are brave but careful. That they do not attack when there are too many Germans. But that English pilots are different. That they always attack, even when there are many more German planes. God willing, Peter, you will live through this war to marry one of your English girls. But I can't do it again. I can't go through what I went through with Paul."

Pete had been trading stares with a green-and-yellow grasshopper as she spoke. The words sounded like a brush-off, but that wasn't what he saw when he turned and looked into those blue eyes—brimming with the tears she couldn't hold back. He wasn't going to talk about love, he wouldn't know what to say. But he could talk about the war. "I'm the leader when I fly, and I don't attack if there are too many Germans."

She smiled faintly, likely seeing through his attempt at reassurance. He leaned over and kissed her neck, her cheek. Her eyes, knowing she would close them again. He sat up and ran his fingertips around her ankles. Up to her knees. Again. The next time higher, to midthigh. Again, giving her dress and chemise a little push upward. Her white drawers were showing.

He undid the top button of her dress, watching her face. Her eyes were still closed. Undid the next button, and the next. Ran his fingernails along the thin chemise as he worked his way down the line of buttons. Opened her dress a few inches. He ran his fingers across her mouth and down her neck. Around her small breasts, barely making contact through the cotton chemise. Down to her stomach. He lifted the chemise and ran his fingers along the top of her drawers. Slid his fingers inside the elastic and began to pull…she opened her eyes as the elastic stretched. Sat up and forced a smile before looking away.

He let out an invisible sigh. But if the timing wasn't right, so be it. "Jul—"

She turned back to him and put her hand on his mouth. Wiped away her tears, put her arms around his neck, and lay back.

# A Black Albatros

*66 Squadron RFC, Sopwith Scout Fighter Aircraft*
*Liettres Aerodrome, Northern France*

The two 7 Squadron BE2s slid in below and in front of them, and Pete swung wide to allow for the Pup's higher speed. He stabilized behind his charges and studied them—another in a long line of artillery spotter escort missions was coming up. The leader had flight commander streamers on his uprights, and the wingman…was that, or was that not, a familiar blue-and-white scarf wrapped around the pilot's head? Pete signaled Harris and Wilcox to hold altitude, closed his throttle and petrol and pushed the Pup's nose down as the Le Rhône died. He let the airspeed bleed back to seventy, leveled with the BE2s and fired up the rotary. Stared at the BE2 pilot from twenty yards. It was the familiar blue-and-white scarf, and the pilot underneath it was Phillip, now waving madly as he recognized his brother's Pup. Pete waved back and powered up, offering an invisible apology to the BE2 flight leader, who was no doubt baffled by the curious behavior of his escort.

They made their way onto the German side with only the occasional shot from Archie. Maybe the Huns were about out of ammo. Between the blockade, the RFC, and the British long-range artillery, their supply situation had to be difficult at best. The three Pups orbited above the BE2s as the British artillery began pounding the already shattered Flanders terrain below them. It was the same as always. South to north, scan the sky. North to south, scan again. Check on wingmen. Check on BE2s. Repeat.

Coming out of their turn back to the north, on maybe their sixth orbit, he spotted two airplane silhouettes to the east, about 2000 feet above the three Pups. He looked down and visualized a line from the impacts to the battery and found one of the BE2s; the other one shouldn't be far away. He gave the throttle-up signal to his wingmen. If it came to a fight the Pups would bleed energy quickly and extra airspeed could only help. He studied the approaching airplanes: small, flipper-like horizontal tail. Halberstadts. They shouldn't be difficult to handle, although the word from intel was the newer ones carried dual Spandaus. But his confidence faded a few seconds later. There were four more airplanes out there, higher than the first two, about a mile in trail. Rounded nose and tail. Albatrosses. He let out a long sigh. Beaters followed by the hunters.

The Halberstadts overflew them and rolled into a dive, working to get behind the Pups. His eyes flicked back to the Albatrosses: they'd split into two pairs. He watched the Halberstadts close on them, judging the angle. Higher up, the Albatrosses had begun to circle. Looking for an opening?

The Halberstadts were coming down quickly...*and...now!* Pete pulled up and left, enough to jam the diving Germans while keeping some speed on the airplane. One of the Huns fired as they crossed—a high-deflection front quarter shot. Dual flashes came from the German's nose, so intel was right for once. But the Albatrosses were the bigger problem, and as he'd expected, two of them were already slicing down toward him. He pushed right rudder and aileron to reverse the turn, pulling up into the new threat. He ignored the flashes from the leader's twin Spandaus, waited, and kicked the rudder bar and came back with the control column as the lead Albatros approached his wing-line. The Pup came around in a tight turn and he pulled her nose below the horizon to gain speed. The Huns were in a descending right turn. He cut across the circle to get behind the wingman and ended up too far forward on the German's wing-line with too much closure. Up and left to get some turning room; quickly back right and down. Use the vertical. Work to get on their tail.

As he dropped behind the wingman, the Hun rolled onto his back and pulled. Pete reacted instantly, staying inside the turn of the heavier Albatros, moving directly behind the German. It was a black V-Strutter with light-blue stripes on the wings and fuselage. An unusual black-and-white striped tail. He set two ship-lengths of lead and pushed the trigger as the faster Albatros pulled away, both airplanes on their backs in a steep dive. He let off the trigger after two seconds and watched the tracers tear into the Hun's tail. Shook his head; there was no chance that would bring him down. The Hun pulled through to level flight and made a couple of quick turns to spoil Pete's aim. Rolled out and continued straight ahead, using his speed advantage. Pete tinkered with his mixture lever to keep the Le Rhône running smoothly, but it wasn't going to matter. The speed differential wasn't great, but it was enough.

*Come on, turn and fight...* No such luck. The German was flying smart, and once he was clear, good chance he'd be back. Pete pulled up and right, twisting around to check behind him. An Albatros was closing on him, but was out of range and being chased by a Pup. A second Pup was farther away, wrapped up with the two Halberstadts. Which left two Albatrosses unaccounted for. He pulled into the pursuing Hun hard enough to keep him off the Pup's tail; looked below him as the airplane turned. The artillery had stopped firing, so the BE2s must be running for home.

He rolled out west and pushed the nose down, searching the sky in front and below...there! A BE2 at low altitude in a right turn, being chased by an Albatros. He rolled the Pup into a steep dive and shut the Le Rhône down. Held the Pup's nose as low as he dared, the wind racing past his face, an odd humming coming from the wires. A few hundred feet above the turning airplanes he brought the nose up and cut across the Hun's turn, who had stopped firing and was repositioning for another shot on the BE2. The German wasn't watching behind him as Pete leveled off one hundred yards back and brought his throttle and petrol up to restart the rotary. The speed bled off and he stabilized almost directly behind the Hun, no more than sixty yards back. He took an extra second or two to be sure of his aim—the bead just in front of the Hun's nose, gravity drop negligible. Held his breath and pushed the trigger button.

The tracers punched into the cockpit and a second later the Albatros was burning. Its nose fell toward the ground and the pilot tumbled from the airplane. Either he had a parachute or had decided anything was better than burning. Pete pulled his eyes from the falling pilot and focused on the BE2; saw the flight commander streamers. Phillip was in the other airplane. But where?

He ignored the wave from the BE2 pilot and turned northwest. Shallow dive, full throttle, ease the petrol lever forward. He listened to the hum of the rotary and tweaked the petrol back, still listening. He wanted every ounce of power he could get. Strained his eyes looking.

Nothing. He closed them for a couple of seconds and started over… something was moving against the mud, on the British side. He blinked twice. It was an Albatros at low altitude, swinging to the right, and then he saw the BE2. It was even lower than the Albatros. He cringed as the Hun rolled out and fired a long burst, and a few seconds later the BE2 plowed into the mud. But it wasn't a high-speed impact. It wasn't burning. Phillip might be okay.

Pete held the nose down, urging the Pup forward. Narrowed his eyes and studied the wrecked airplane, looking for signs of life. *Please, God…* It was too far away to be sure, but were Phillip and the observer moving? Starting to climb out? Somewhat reassured, his eyes went back to the Hun…and he sucked in his breath, eyes wide. The Albatros was rolling out of a turn, pointed directly at the downed BE2.

*No!*

He judged the range and deflection as the Albatros closed on Phillip. Fired from impossibly long range—anything to distract the German. The Hun closed to point-blank range and fired a long burst. The flashing of the twin Spandaus, the BE2 twitching from the impacts, seemed to last an eternity. Pete's eyes bore into the Albatros as it swept over the shattered BE2 and turned east, locking every detail in his memory:

Albatros V-Strutter. Black fuselage.

Silver propeller spinner.

Black-and-white striped horizontal tail. Standard green-purple mottling on the wings. Some sort of symbol, a star maybe, behind the cockpit.

He slid the Pup in behind the Hun, but the Albatros was out of range and pulling away. He guessed twenty feet of gravity drop and fired, holding the button down until the Vickers quit. Shook his head in disgust. At best he got a couple of bullets home.

He cursed the Pup for being slow as the German pulled away. Stared at the Albatros, praying that one of his bullets had gotten a fuel line. That fuel was leaking onto the engine and the airplane would burst into flames. That the bastard would burn alive. But that hope slowly faded as the Hun climbed away from him. He gave it one last, long stare; swung the Pup around to the west. Wilcox rejoined on him and Harris was holding above them. Pete made two circles around the stranded BE2. Neither Phillip nor the observer was moving.

He found a fair-sized road less than a mile away. Waved to Wilcox that he was okay. For them to go home. He lined up on the road and held the Pup at thirty feet to clear some lorries. Killed the engine and fought the crosswind to touchdown. The Pup hit, skipped, and came back down. The tail slewed around and she slid off the road backward, slowing as she plowed through the mud. She came to a stop as the tail crunched up against something. He doubled-checked the ignition and fuel off and jumped out, ignoring the wondering looks from the bystanders.

They had pulled Phillip and his observer out of the airplane and laid them on the ground. He looked down at the observer. The leather helmet was torn and bloody, the head misshapen. As if someone had hit it with a hammer.

He knelt by his little brother. The mud was cool against his knee. He felt Phillip's neck, his wrist, for any sign of life. Eased his goggles and helmet off. His little brother's face was peaceful. He saw the rips in the flying jacket; lifted Phillip up and put a hand on his back. There were two small holes in the leather. Entrance wounds. He felt the tears—unable to rise to his eyes.

*Oh God. His mother.*

A little cough came from behind him. "Sorry, sir. We need to take them. Dangerous out here, sir."

Pete looked at his brother's face for a few more seconds. Carefully laid him back and removed the plain silver cross Phillip always wore around his neck. Put his hand on Phillip's, gently kissed his brother on the forehead, and stood up.

# A Liberal Party MP?

*Westminster, London*

"Good to see you again, Uncle," said Ian Crosse as he shook hands with William Bannerman, Liberal MP, Bristol East.

"Welcome to Parliament, Ian. This is Martin Lucas, Cardiganshire. Besides being a good friend and an MP, Martin is… oh, how would I describe what he does. Let say, if an election doesn't go well, he's the one who gets to explain why to the leadership."

"It's a pleasure to meet you, minister," said Ian, shaking hands.

"Always a pleasure to meet one of our fighting men," replied MP Lucas. "As for what I do for the party, I'm more of an adviser these days. And if the leadership doesn't care for my advice, well, I don't worry about such things so much anymore."

MP Lucas was a small man with white hair, who Ian knew was a barrister and came from a wealthy family. Ian glanced at his uncle as they sat down; he was looking fit as always. William Bannerman had grown up working on the shop floor at Bristol Tramways in the early days of the trade unions. He'd moved on to middle management and later into Liberal politics.

Ian looked around the dining room as a waiter took their drinks order. White wine for MP Lucas, soda water for Ian and his uncle. The room was well adorned with absurdly ornate wood carvings and the chandelier above their table reached down like some sort of electrified weeping tree. The lace-trimmed white linen tablecloth was spotless. The room was crowded, but not a single woman was present. He turned back to his uncle, who was admiring his uniform.

"You're looking well, nephew." As instructed, Ian was wearing his service dress, neatly pressed and every detail correct. He'd even been watching his diet the last few weeks, and doing some press-ups in his room. "Tell us how goes the war. Without the details, of course."

Ian was ready for the question. "The Royal Flying Corps is all about the offensive. Find the Hun and shoot him down. That approach, along with the new pilots showing up with limited training, means our losses are high. We have the Germans outnumbered, but they're good pilots flying better airplanes. We're finally closing the gap with our newer models, but not many of those are in the field yet. Getting a new airplane type into the field in significant numbers isn't something that can be done quickly. Plus, most of the fights are on the German side of the line. That's a big advantage for them."

"I hope our own British and Colonial is responsible for some of these better airplanes that you say are on the way?"

"I haven't flown the Bristol Fighter, Uncle, but I've only heard good things about it."

"Good. Sir Robert will be happy to hear that. But enough about airplanes. How do you see the war playing out on a…strategic level?"

"Understanding I'm only a lieutenant who reads the papers—" Ian had decided that until he found his footing in this new political world, a bit of self-deprecation would be a good idea "—Germany is powerful, and Russia is crumbling. In our favor, of course, the Americans are on the way.

But everyone is sick of war. I wonder if a negotiated solution is possible. Germany keeps part of Belgium. France gets Alsace back and we keep our gains in the Middle East. Each government has something to point to for the folks back home…except Belgium, I suppose. But I don't know that they really matter. And the slaughter stops."

"Our people are certainly sick of war," said Martin, scanning the room while barely moving his head. "Although the Belgian question would be difficult. Ostensibly, the violation of Belgian neutrality was the reason we came into the war."

His scan complete, he looked at Ian again. Lowered his voice. "William tells me you may stand for Parliament at some point."

"I would like to, minister. If events play out as I hope." He said the second sentence a bit more softly, a bit more somber. He hoped it came across as, being a combat pilot who routinely risks his life for the Crown, it may be God's will that he not survive the war.

"Good. The party needs capable young men to step up, and I shall pray events turn out well for you. Allow me to give you some background on the political landscape as I see it, and please keep everything I say in confidence."

Martin paused while the waiter took their order. It was illegal to consume more than a two-course meal in public, but looking at the menu, some liberties had been taken as to what constituted a course. Lunch orders in place, Martin continued speaking in a low voice, and Ian moved his chair closer to hear over the noise. "General Robertson spoke to a group of us last week. I'm not a military man, but to the extent I understood him, he agrees with General Haig that the only way to defeat Germany is on the Western Front. That ultimately we will win, but the cost will continue to be very high. Also, that the Americans will not be much help for at least another year.

"Assuming the general is correct and we win the war, Lloyd George will be seen by much of the electorate as the one who led us to victory. If I had to guess, he would run in the next election under the current Unionist

## A LIBERAL PARTY MP?

Coalition. Although Minister Asquith has refrained from open opposition, the split in the backbenchers is significant. I won't go into the events of last December; I'm sure your uncle will discuss that with you if you wish. I'll only say I don't believe Lloyd George wanted to be prime minister, but accepted it when enough people viewed him as the best person for the job."

Martin paused while the waiter refilled their nearly full water glasses. "The political crosscurrents are strong. Lloyd George relies on Unionist support to hold the Coalition together but, to be honest, he does not have the level of party support outside of London that a PM would typically enjoy. It's no secret he has disagreements with the general staff, but the generals have strong support among the Unionist backbenchers. There is even talk General Haig communicates privately with His Majesty. Home Rule for Ireland has passed but will require amendment after the war. The Easter Rising and the growth of the Ulster Volunteers tell us that, unfortunately, this will not be a peaceful process.

"What else? Suffrage has gone quiet but will certainly come back after the war. Conscription has been a troublesome issue for the party, as it strikes directly at the rights of the individual versus the need to prosecute the war against a powerful and aggressive enemy. And there is still the Irish exemption to deal with."

Ian gave a wry smile. "I see what you mean, minister, when you say crosscurrents."

Martin sipped his wine and resumed his measured tone. "If we keep the current coalition, how well will party goals align with those of the Unionists once the war is over? What will our relationship be with the Labour Party and the trade unions? Labour is in a difficult position now, as some of the electorate see them as not supporting the war effort, and as your uncle would likely tell you, politics is ninety percent perception."

"Ninety-five," said William.

"That said, I would not write them off. The electorate will expand significantly at some point. When that happens, it is likely to benefit Labour."

Lunch arrived, and William spoke to Martin between small bites. "British and Colonial opened a second factory at Brislington. Most of the workers are in Bristol South and my Bristol East. Roger Clarke has Bristol South, but he is over sixty now. A decorated RFC pilot might be just the ticket a few years down the road."

"Minister Clarke is close to Edward Goodman. Their wives are sisters or cousins, I believe. Lloyd George has been impressed by Edward, and it is likely he will be in the government before long." Martin was speaking slowly, thinking it through. "But as you say, Roger is getting up in years. We've had MPs in the armed services, Winston being the obvious example, although I don't believe any of them were first elected while in the military. I'm not sure how that could be managed—some sort of long-term military leave, perhaps. Assuming an election in '19, the next one would be around '24. What are you thinking?"

"I think the second. Give him time to get on the local council. Get a job with British—I can make that happen. And most importantly, find his beloved and get married." William smiled at Ian. "Urchins, too, nephew. Children project stability. The more, the better."

Ian gave a pained smile. Marriage he could handle. Keep the wife in Bristol and the mistress in London. But he didn't need sniveling children crawling on him.

"British would be a good fit, especially if one had the support of both management and the unions, although as you know, that is not an easy line to walk." Martin turned to Ian. "You're not married, I take it?" Ian shook his head.

"As your uncle intimates, you may wish to marry before you stand for Parliament. The traditional route is to marry a girl from a wealthy family—a family with political connections. A local working-class girl is also an option, but choose carefully if you go that route. You'd want a woman of substance, who can connect with working people. Motivate them. But also one who understands your career comes first."

## A LIBERAL PARTY MP?

Martin glanced around the room again before coming back to Ian. "Being well-connected in London is important if one wishes to rise within the party. But nothing is as important as solid support in your constituency. The leadership pays more attention to MPs who they believe will be back after the next election. Going back to the subject of marriage, and please tell me if I'm getting too personal, there is a third option. Marry someone you are in love with. That is the route I went, and I never regretted it."

Martin took one more small bite of his oversized lunch and set it aside. "You fly a fighter airplane, is that correct?"

Crosse nodded. "Sopwith Pups."

"How many, victories? Is that the correct word?"

"It is. I have three Huns to my credit." More precisely, he had two and two thirds—four shared with one other pilot and two more shared between three pilots. But three was close enough.

"I'm not familiar with military decorations. About how many to get some sort of medal?"

"Perhaps five, minister. For the Military Cross. Depends."

"Something like that would bolster one's CV."

"I should be able to manage five—" Crosse looked at his uncle "—especially if the flight commander slot comes through. It's easier to go for a kill if you know someone is looking out for your backside."

His uncle looked at Martin. "I reached out to William West. His brother is a party member on the staff in London. We should be able to make this happen." William looked back at Ian. "You haven't heard anything yet?"

Ian shook his head.

"I can nudge again, but let's wait a bit."

Martin waved for his bill and looked at William. "This seems reasonable. I can envision a future Liberal Party MP sitting here with us. You gentlemen will have to excuse me. I have an appointment."

Once Martin had gone, William sat back and looked at Ian. "That went well. Martin's been around Parliament a long time. I don't know that he will stand for the next election. His wife's been ill. As he said, treat everything we've discussed in the strictest confidence. That's always the safest route to take."

"Of course, Uncle."

"One needs to tread carefully in this world. One wrong step at the wrong time and you're done for. There will always be someone who wants what you have. Cultivate relationships with senior officers, but be seen as a regular pilot. One just doing his job. Try not to make enemies. It's unavoidable in politics, but let's keep it to a minimum. Get your five kills and reach out to me, and we'll get you a staff job here in London. Or better still, some sort of liaison to B&C in Bristol. You can start getting to know people over there—the people who matter."

William checked the time and waved to the waiter. "Speaking of Bristol, Sir Robert Cawthorne's daughters are hosting a sixtieth birthday party for him sometime in October. Do you know the name?"

Ian knew the name—he'd been reading the *Western Daily Press* almost every day since his talk with Larry that night in the bar. And speaking of which, he still owed himself some private time with Miss Black Dress.

"Sir Robert is the chairman of Bristol and Colonial Aeroplane, if I'm not mistaken," said Ian slowly. He didn't add that he also knew the names and marital status of both daughters: Cheryl (married) and Judith (single).

"You're not, and he's an important fellow to know. I'll make a call and get you invited. That will be easy enough. But we'll have to convince the RFC to cut you loose for a few days." William drummed his fingers on the table. "General Henderson owes me a favor or two. I should be able to call one in."

William checked his watch. "We need to head over to the Strangers' Bar. I told Frank Allen we'd meet him. He's Swansea Town. As I said, at this stage it's all about getting to know people." Ian looked around the room again as they stood up. Well-dressed men in private conversation. Impeccable waiters standing by. French cuisine on fine china. He smiled an invisible smile. This place was all about money. About power. And he loved the feel of it.

# The Menin Road

*6 Squadron RFC, BE2 Reconnaissance Aircraft*
*Abeele Aerodrome, Western Belgium*

Harry blinked his eyes awake and looked around the hut. Thomas was up and gone, and Ethan and George were snoring in unison. He sat up on his cot and yawned. Picked up his logbook and flipped through it. Sixteen flights across the line. He'd survived sixteen flights. Archie. Those bastards. He still couldn't shake the thought that any second a piece of shrapnel could rip across his face or tear a chunk out of his leg, and he would sit there and bleed to death. But during the last couple of flights, an almost-manageable fear had replaced the sickening terror of the earlier flights. Maybe, just maybe, he could live through this.

He ate a proper breakfast with two A-Flight observers: Blake and Charlie. Turned out it was Charlie's second day in the squadron, which meant, to Harry's immense delight, he was no longer 6 Squadron's newest observer. Blake finished his eggs and sausage and looked at them.

"We'll need to break you gents in properly as soon as there's a lull. Margarite's Place, downtown Hazebrouck. After all, the RFC needs to be sure you two are of suitable moral character to serve as aircrew."

This elicited several comments from the chaps at the next table. "Yes, we need to see how they conduct themselves under combat conditions."

"One involving multiple enemy threats."

"Don't forget to file a full written report. And remember, the RFC wants details."

Harry could guess the nature of Margarite's Place and was already looking forward to a visit. He finished breakfast and went down to the orderly room. Nodded good morning to Captain Harvey, who, as usual, didn't acknowledge his existence. He leaned on the counter and studied the situation map while he waited for Norman. Miracle of miracles, all the artillery fire and the chaps on the ground running about and getting killed had accomplished something. They'd pushed the sacred black line a few miles east. But the Huns still held most of the high ground, and rumor was that was next up on Haig's list of things to do.

Ethan came in with an observer from another flight and greeted Harry with his usual banter. "Lieutenant Booth, need I remind you that the eyes of all England are on us today? God and the RFC must save the queen. No, I take that back. I suppose it would be the king who requires saving."

"Thanks, Ethan. I can die content now, knowing I helped saved the king."

Harry liked all his roommates, but especially Ethan, who didn't take things too seriously. Norman came in a few minutes later. He wasn't friendly, but at least he no longer treated Harry like a complete idiot. He sat down and opened the folder. Looked over the map and operations order. Frowned, which was a major show of emotion for him. "We're going deep onto the German side today." He was still looking at the map. "Army-level reconnaissance mission."

Harry looked at the mission map in front of them. Corps-attached squadrons typically stayed within three or four miles of the front line, but they were going way past that. Second Army headquarters was throwing their weight around—who the hell asked them to butt in? Norman went to speak with Captain Harvey, who was huddled with their intel officer. Harry picked up the map. Someone had laid out a large rectangle over the G-Velt–Menin Highway, divided into six rows of squares, which must correspond to the inbound and outbound legs of the three lucky BE2s tagged for the job. The eastern edge of the rectangle reached almost to Menin, about ten miles on the Hun side. Wonderful.

"All right, fellows, let's get started," said Norman. "As you can see, Second Army wants photos of the Menin Highway, and we've been selected for this honor." He nodded to Lieutenant Brooke, who stepped to the podium.

"Good morning, gents. The Menin Highway is the Hun's single most important supply route into Flanders. Road traffic will be light—as you know, the Hun mostly travels at night. But there should be reserve formations, supply depots, and some headquarters units hidden near the road. That's what we need a look at. Sergeant Connor will brief you on the mechanics of the shoot."

A tall young sergeant took the podium and spoke with a familiar Liverpool accent. "Good morning, gentlemen. Your airplanes are equipped with the standard E-Type camera. Ten-inch focal length and two eighteen-plate magazines. At nine thousand feet, this will give you a one point three by…"

Harry was looking at the sergeant but thinking about Margarite's Place. Blake must be a regular…how many girls would be there? Most would be French, but maybe a colonist or two from Africa or the West Indies? A tall, blue-eyed representative of their Russian ally? Speaking of girls, there'd bound to be some around when he went home on leave. Girls happy to meet a, home from the war (and not bad-looking) RFC observer. But he still had almost five months to go until his leave came up. Too bad his uncle wasn't a big-shot general—he could pull some strings and get

Harry a cushy staff job somewhere. He gave a little snort. Fat chance of that, even if shorty was a general.

"Going this deep, they're giving us a proper escort." Norman was speaking again. "Four navy triplanes and four Pups from Sixty-Six. We'll rendezvous north of Dickybush Lake, where the canal makes the ninety-degree turn. Three-ship V formation, ten second spacing for takeoff, form up over the aerodrome. Bill, you're on my right." Norman looked at a pilot Harry didn't recognize. "You'll be on my left. Is it, Max?"

The second lieutenant nodded. Swallowed hard. He had a nasty cut on his neck. He'd cut himself shaving, or maybe he'd already tried to slit his own throat. Harry blocked a smile. Had his own fear been so obvious those first few days? Probably so.

"If I drop out, Bill, you'll lead. Max, if neither myself nor Bill make it, you do the shoot for the number one airplane. The signal to…"

Harry tuned out again, looking at the map. That far on the Hun side, if the engine let go there was no way they'd make it back to the British side. A year or two as a prisoner of war wouldn't be much fun, but it would beat the hell out of getting killed. Norman finished his briefing and Harry stood up, with only a single butterfly flitting about his stomach.

As they squished through the soft ground on their way to the airplane, he noticed something out of place in the line of patched and mud splattered BE2s. Norman looked from the new arrival to Harry. "It's an RE8. A-Flight's switching over. We should get it in another week or so." Norman gave him a side glance. "There are controls in the backseat, so if I get shot, you can land it. At least that's the idea."

For the first time, he saw a trace of a smile on Norman's face. He'd started walking again, but Harry paused to look the RE8 over. It was bigger than the BE2. Sturdier. With a big V-12 on the front end, it had to be faster. Best of all, the observer sat behind the pilot, meaning he'd have a proper field of fire. He followed Norman and settled into their BE2. He still hated it—as far as he was concerned it wasn't much more than a flying target. But it wasn't the alien place it once had been. Norman ran through the preflight checks, and as always, engine start and taxi-out were noisy and rough. Norman powered up for takeoff and the roar of the Royal Aircraft Factory V-8 three feet in front of Harry rattled his guts and blasted his eardrums. RAF designers made some attempt to keep poisonous fumes away from the crew, but they didn't bother with niceties like mufflers.

They were in a slow climbing turn over the aerodrome and bored with admiring the Flanders scenery, Harry checked on the other two airplanes. Bill and Ethan's airplane was climbing normally, turning to close on them, but the third airplane was much lower and her propeller was barely turning. The BE2 rolled into a right turn. Further right, and Harry bit his lip. Even Harry Booth knew the rule for engine failure on takeoff: land straight ahead. The turning airplane shuddered as her nose came up. She hung there for a moment…and her nose dropped like a rock. She rolled onto her back and hit the ground like a dart coming down after being thrown straight up. Both wings bent forward from their roots and the fuselage crumpled. The wrecked BE2 settled onto her upper wing, her undamaged undercarriage skyward.

Harry shrugged. There was a good chance they'd lived through it—they weren't very high when the airplane stalled. On the bright side, unlike himself, they wouldn't have to go across the line and get shot at.

Other than losing an airplane, the initial portion of the flight was loud, bouncy, and uncomfortable. In other words, normal. He spotted the lake and the canal through the haze, and a couple of minutes later picked up four airplanes above and to their left: Sopwith Triplanes. The navy was on time. He pointed them out to Norman, thinking he had seen them first, but Norman only nodded. The BE2s circled and a few minutes later four more airplanes appeared above the triplanes. Must be the Pups—funny name for a combat airplane. But he supposed it was better than Kitten.

Harry took an occasional peek at the ground as they motored east. The desolate ocean of mud and waterlogged shell holes looked the same as every other time he'd seen it—the crisscrossing trench lines becoming more closely packed as they approached the line. But the haze wouldn't hide them from Archie, and the first ranging shot came about a minute after they'd crossed no-man's-land. The initial burst was well above them, but the Huns would correct soon enough. They always did. A second shot followed the first, then a third, all three well above the BE2s. Curious.

A cascade of black bursts went off above them—like corn kernels popping off in a red-hot skillet. Archie was firing for effect, and the shells were exploding well above the BE2s. Were they shooting at the triplanes? If so, that was fine with Harry Booth.

Twenty-one-year-old Leutnant Eddy Becker sat on the top step of his command bunker. Stretched his arms above his head as the rays of the rising sun reached through the morning haze. Life wasn't bad there, seven kilometers behind the front line where the British artillery couldn't reach them. His empty stomach growled.

*Breakfast? Let's see. I believe I'll have sausage and eggs this morning. Toasted rye bread with Tilsiter cheese.*

*And fried onions, Leutnant?*

*Of course, fried onions. What would breakfast be without fried onions?*

He snorted. Yesterday's breakfast had been bread fried in pork fat. The same the day before. He pushed away thoughts of frying onions and looked down into his bunker. Wooden floor, electric lights. A yellow stuffed armchair requisitioned from a local farmhouse. A hot plate to heat a barley and acorn mixture they called coffee—which wasn't bad when they had sugar for it. All under three meters of dirt and sandbags.

He turned his head at a familiar squeaking. Wagons, pulled by weary, muddy horses. They were running late today. Becker made himself look at the piled-up bodies. At the heads and feet turned to impossible angles. He pursed his lips. Artillery. The British artillery fire was heavier and more accurate every day. Aided by his enemy—their spotter airplanes.

Artillery and mud. If anyone was foolish enough to ask him what the war was like, that's what he'd tell them. Artillery and mud. And dead soldiers and dead horses. Food that tasted like mud. He frowned, thinking back to the heady days of August 1914. The cheering crowds at the train stations. Kisses from the girls; people handing out food. Paris in September, home by Christmas. It didn't quite work out that way, did it, Your Imperial Majesty?

He rubbed his left leg above the knee. He'd gotten careless the week before checking an ammo limber and a horse had kicked him. Unfortunately, the kick was at extreme range and didn't put him in hospital. He had three weeks to go until his leave. Please, God, that they don't cancel it. His wife had talked of rationing in her last two letters. That even bread was getting scarce, and some weeks it was turnips instead of potatoes.

The train ride home. Green countryside, not mud and shell holes. Real coffee served by young girls? Seeing his wife. Her smile. Taking her into his arms…and his lovely, ready to be kissed Luise disappeared with the harsh ringing of a phone. He trotted down the steps and picked it up. Listened and acknowledged. Turned to his chief gunner, who was parked in the armchair reading the paper. "Let's move, Sergeant. We have visitors. Triplanes."

Sergeant Pols looked up at him. Took another drink of his acorn coffee and folded his newspaper before following him up the stairs. Becker took the cover off his Zeiss 1.5-meter rangefinder as he searched the sky with his binoculars. The spotters had reported two reconnaissance airplanes and four triplanes crossing the line southwest of his position. Sergeant Pols grabbed the megaphone and alerted the gun crews while Leutnant Konrad, three days out of training and so excited he could hardly stand still, manned the angle of elevation meter. Becker found the Britishers in his binoculars: two BE2s with four triplanes above and behind them…and there were four more airplanes above and behind the triplanes. Most likely Sopwith Pups, up that high. The normal procedure would be to shoot at the BE2s. However, last week orders had come down to shoot at any triplane on the German side of the line. Of course they didn't say why, but it wasn't hard to figure out. The Luftstreitkräfte wanted to get their hands on one of the new British triplanes.

He lowered his binoculars and looked around. Four seventy-five-millimeter guns formed a large square around his command position. All four gun commanders were looking at him. He pointed the rangefinder at the lead triplane and adjusted the elevation. Rubbed his eyes, checked that the lens was set to low magnification and looked through the eyepiece. Adjusted the elevation again. Went back to his binoculars and found the Britishers; tweaked the rangefinder around and got a glimpse of a triplane. He centered the lens on the lead triplane and switched to the high magnification setting. Adjusted the vertical and lateral controls to recenter the lens on the Britisher. The dual-lens system displayed two overlapping images of the airplane. He tweaked the dial until the two images merged into a close-up view of a British triplane in flight. Close enough to see the number 1 on the side of the airplane, and two small, white vertical bars on the fuselage. This Tommy would be from one of their Royal Navy squadrons, according to army intel.

"Target, lead triplane. Range: five thousand two hundred and seventy meters. Estimated target speed one hundred twenty-five." Their fancy new targeting system had broken again, so he stepped back from the rangefinder and made a quick estimate of the triplane's course with his pencil and protractor. "Approach angle twenty-seven right."

Konrad read off the angle of elevation to the target. "Forty-two point six, Herr Leutnant."

Sergeant Pols checked the table for fuse time and deflection; raised his megaphone and relayed the targeting information to the number-one gun commander. The crew set the shell timer and sight deflection and loaded the gun while tracking the triplane in their sights.

"Ready, Leutnant," said Sergeant Pols.

"Fire."

"Fire," his chief gunner shouted through the megaphone. The number-one gun fired a single shot, which exploded low and right about ten seconds later.

"Add half a degree of deflection, Sergeant, and point two of elevation." Once the first shot was fired, Becker preferred to eyeball the correction rather than waste time fiddling around with the instruments. "Fire when ready."

The gun boomed again a few seconds later. Closer, but the shell had exploded too soon. "Add point one to the fuse time. Fire when ready."

The shell exploded just in front of the Britisher, and Becker smiled. *Good morning, Tommy. I hope you didn't spill your coffee.*

"Fire for effect, Sergeant."

All four guns opened fire and the ground under his boots trembled from the crashing recoils. The noise would have been deafening to a normal person, but Becker was long past that point. The gun crews took over—tracking the target and firing as fast as they could, the shells timed to explode as they crossed paths with the Britishers. He turned his head and spat—the air around him was already gray with the grit thrown from the guns. He'd let them fire until the bursts began diverging from the target, then call cease-fire as he judged the next correction. But today, the bursts were almost on top of the Britisher.

Harry squirmed down in his seat, trying to get comfortable. Archie was firing at the triplanes, and while they were shooting there shouldn't be any Hun fighters around. Of course, a shell could go right up his arse on its way to higher altitude, but for once the odds were on his side. But photoshoots were the worst—flying straight and level for the eternity it took to get the shoot done.

He scanned behind them, to the left and right. Bill and Ethan were paralleling them about a mile away. As he turned to check behind them again, an Archie shell burst next to a triplane, pushing her sideways and down. The triplane wobbled...and slowly rolled right, her nose dropping. The pilot leveled the wings and looked to have her under control—the airplane was descending out of formation, but at least the nose wasn't dropping further. But instead of looking almost straight on at her, he was seeing some of the side of the fuselage. He saw more of the fuselage and shook his head—the nose was going sideways and the pilot couldn't stop it.

The triplane shuddered and flipped onto her back, her nose plummeting. Harry watched, fascinated, as the nose fought its way back up toward the horizon. Was the pilot dead? Or was he wounded and fighting to keep the airplane upright? He told himself to focus on his visual lookout, but a few seconds later his eyes went back to the triplane. She was coming down in a "falling leaf" motion—the explosion had ripped away part of the upper wing.

Eddy Becker smiled as cheers replaced the crashing of the guns. Later, they'd argue about who got the Britisher. That didn't matter to Becker—his battery got him. "Cease fire, Sergeant. We'll target the reconnaissance airplanes on the exit if they pass in range."

He guessed the BE2s were on a photo-recce mission, and if so, they'd still have to make it home with the plates. Make it past him. He watched the triplane spiral down and hit the ground. It was unlikely the pilot survived, but there should be enough left of the airplane for headquarters to make use of. He estimated its position and ran to the phone; they'd need to gather it up before the British artillery ranged on it. He made his call and walked back up the stairs. Scanned the line of enemy observation balloons. The nearest one was four to five kilometers on the British side, altitude about one thousand meters. Meaning they could see it.

He examined the wrecked triplane through his binoculars. The pilot hadn't moved. Leutnant Konrad stood next to him, smiling like a schoolboy who'd just gotten away with something. They exchanged glances, and Becker waited for the show. There was activity in the reserve trenches in front of them, and a couple of minutes later a car and two lorries were heading toward the wrecked airplane. The first British shell landed as the three vehicles stopped at the crash site, the faint boom reaching his ears a few seconds later. Eighteen-pounder. Not their biggest, but big enough. Especially for troops in the open. The second shell was only a little closer as the crew scrambled to get the broken triplane onto the lorries.

Becker chuckled. He'd never seen soldiers move so fast. The British were firing high explosive rounds, not shrapnel, but that probably wasn't much consolation for the fellows out there. They'd manhandled the fuselage onto the first lorry when the third shell hit. It was much closer and some of the soldiers staggered from the shock wave as mud rained down on them. The fourth shell landed a little short and was immediately followed by a cascade of explosions. The British were firing for effect. It looked like only a six-gun battery was in action, but there'd be others soon enough.

The first lorry got underway amid flying dirt and smoke. Paralleled the line looking for a gap in the explosions before turning for home. It had to be at full throttle, the way it was bouncing. The rest of the crew finished throwing triplane parts into the second lorry and jumped aboard. Becker shook his head as he watched. Smoke was pouring from the exhaust and mud was flying from the rear tires, but the only movement was the rear end of the lorry sinking deeper into the mud.

The car, presumably carrying the lucky officer in charge, sped past the stranded lorry. It turned for home and disappeared in a cloud of smoke and dirt. A metallic boom reached Becker's ears as a tire bounced toward him before curving off to the right. He looked at the lorry again. The crew had piled out and was pushing. The lorry crawled forward…and rolled back. Again. A third time, smoke pouring from under the bonnet as well as from the exhaust. The lorry shook as artillery rounds bracketed it…and inched out of its rut, still spraying mud from the rear tires. Its former occupants chased it down and jumped aboard as it gathered speed and turned toward a gap in the artillery fire. Becker chuckled again. The way it was bouncing, it might still have a few triplane parts on board when they made it back. No matter. They could retrieve the rest after dark.

They were back on the British side. Of course, Archie had rattled them around on the way out and fabric was flapping on Bill and Ethan's airplane. Harry inspected their own BE2 and counted three holes in the lower-left wing, and the engine felt down on power. He sat back in his seat and closed his eyes; took a deep breath and let it out. He'd lived through another one. He opened his eyes and went back to his scan, but there wasn't much to worry about. Not on the British side with a seven-airplane escort. He took a swig of water and spat the oily taste out; swallowed the second one. Abeam Dickybush Lake the three triplanes rocked wings goodbye and turned south, and a minute later the four Pups turned southwest. He watched them go, thinking about lunch.

Harry shifted in his seat, staring at the cloud bank on their right, trying to pierce the swirls of light and dark gray. Twice he thought he saw an airplane keeping station with them in the clouds. *Relax, Harry. German fighters don't come this far onto the British side. Think about something important, like Margarite's Place. Maybe a nice, tall blonde. Give her a kiss on the neck; nudge her short black skirt up. Run your fingers along her thigh. But take your time. No need to rush things.*

He spotted an airplane right of the nose. Maybe 300 feet below them; closing quickly. It wasn't a BE2, and the nose wasn't right for a Pup. He wasn't exactly an expert on airplane recognition. He straightened up and gritted his teeth as the wind hit him. Focused his eyes on the top wing of the approaching airplane and squinted…and his heart skipped a beat. A black cross on a white background. He snapped around, halfway out of his seat. Looked at Norman and pumped his arm forward and right.

As Norman sat up, Harry fired his Lewis gun. Bill looked across and Harry pointed toward the Hun. Norman pushed the nose down, looking for whatever it was Harry was so excited about. He let go of the Lewis and grabbed both railings to keep from floating overboard. The Hun was close now—flashes coming from his nose. He was shooting at Bill, and Harry looked across in time to see splinters fly from the left side of the other airplane. The German passed below them, close enough for the wind to jolt the BE2, and to hear the roar of his engine. The Hun pulled up into the vertical; pivoted on his wingtip and came out in a dive directly behind them. Harry shook his head. It was a two-seater, but it handled like a fighter. Against a pair of beat-up BE2s.

The German dropped below them and closed in. No surprise, he was faster than they were. The BE2s went into a shallow left turn. They couldn't outrun the Hun, so Norman must be trying to give him a clear shot. The German swung to the right, moving outside Bill's turning circle, but still closing. Harry pointed the Lewis in front of the Hun and fired two short bursts from extreme range, more to distract him than anything else. There should be about thirty-five rounds left in the drum. Bill rolled back right and Ethan opened fire, but the German darted behind the tail of the BE2. The Hun was too close to get his forward gun on them, but the observer was hammering at them, his gun pointed forward and up.

Norman turned away from the German, giving him a shot. Harry held his breath, aimed, and fired a three-second burst from long range. The tracers reached out… and…*hell*. Not enough lead—he may have put a few bullets through the tail. Plus, the bullet dispersion was huge at that range.

He popped the drum off and stowed it. Got the next one on and pulled the handle back, slotting the first round into the chamber. He was ready with a full drum. If things got desperate there should be about ten rounds left in the first one. He bit his lip as he looked up—the Hun observer was firing again. Bullets tore into the other BE2 as Bill rolled further right and into a dive. The German pulled up and left; quickly came back right and sliced down inside Bill's turn. The bastard was moving in for the kill. The Hun was in range and Harry tracked him with the Lewis, but their wing struts blocked his shot. Damn BE2.

Norman turned away and the Hun moved aft in Harry's field of view. He judged the crossing angle, set two ship-lengths lead, and waited. More flashes came from the observer's gun—but this time the Hun was shooting at them. Harry ignored the flashes and focused on the relative motion of the German, who was tearing into Bill and Ethan again with his forward gun. *Maybe a bit more lead, Harry…* Their rear-wing strut passed through his sight and he squeezed the trigger. The Lewis thumped and the tracers curved back toward the Hun. He forced himself to let off after two seconds and watch. *Damn it!* The lead was good, but he'd shot low and hit the

Hun's frigging undercarriage. He raised the sight, reset his lead and pulled the trigger. This time sparks flew as bullets glanced off metal in front of the pilot. *Yes! Finally!* He fired again as the Hun pulled off, moving out of range. The second Lewis drum was empty; he popped it off and stowed it. Set another one in place and grabbed a drink of water. He searched for Bill and Ethan...and spotted their BE2 in a field. Narrowed his eyes and focused...and let out a sigh of relief. Ethan was climbing out of the airplane. His eyes went back to the Hun as he grabbed another drink of water. He stowed the bottle, watching the German's nose swing around toward them again.

He let out a deep breath as the Hun pulled off. Loaded his last Lewis drum. He was down to forty-seven rounds, plus about ten in the first drum. The German had made three identical attacks. He'd swoop down on them and Norman would turn into him. Harry and the Hun observer would shoot at each other as they crossed. The Hun would reposition and Norman would just get their nose around to face the attack.

As Harry watched and waited, the roof of a barn passed ten feet under his backside. He looked down, and understood the German's game. The BE2 didn't have enough power to make hard turns and hold altitude. The Hun was driving them into the ground.

"Get ready, Harry," shouted Norman. "This is it."

Harry gave him a thumbs-up as the German dove on them again. Between the intense activity and the low altitude, he was exhausted and burning up under his leather flying jacket. But there wasn't time to take it off now. Norman went into a shallow turn. He couldn't do any more than that—they were only forty feet off the ground.

The Hun was closing in. He bobbed up and came back down twice, working toward their tail. But he couldn't get below them so Harry would have a shot. Both airplanes were turning right; he set his lead and waited. The Hun closed in, his nose tracking a little in front of them. He'd open fire any second. Harry set one-ship-length lead on the German, maybe a foot of gravity drop. Held his breath—he had to get it right. He squeezed the trigger. The Lewis gave a single thump and blew a puff of blue smoke in his face. *No! Not now!* He sensed the German firing as he struggled with the Lewis; felt the *tap-tapping* of bullets punching through fabric. Something whacked his helmet as it tumbled by. He felt the leather with his left hand—his head was still in one piece. Big splinter, maybe. He wanted to scream at Norman to force-land. At least they'd live through this. But the German had stopped shooting, and he took a deep breath.

*It's a jam, Harry. You know how to handle this.* He pulled the charging handle back from mid-position, pried the ammo drum off and looked at the chamber. It was a double feed. A round had misfired and a second shell rammed into it. He struggled with the shells; pulled off his gloves and threw them on the floor. Pried the first bullet out, then the second, vaguely aware the German had rolled over them and Norman had reversed back to the left. He got the ammo drum back on and banged it into place. Pulled the charging handle back; the drum rotated and the round slotted into the chamber with a reassuring *click*.

The German had rolled out parallel with them, level and slightly ahead, and their observer was firing again. Harry sensed bullets passing a few feet behind him, punching through the aft fuselage of the battered BE2. He stood up and leaned outward, holding on to the Lewis to keep from falling overboard, and set his lead. His shot was blocked, but he squeezed the trigger anyway and held it down. Splinters flew from his own wing struts, but also from the Hun's cockpit area as the bullets hammered home.

Their observer gave a little jump and let go of his machine gun. *Yes! He'd finally gotten it right. But don't run off just yet, fellows. Here comes another one.* He set his aim to shoot again as the Hun pulled up and away from them. Harry tracked him with the Lewis, waiting for him to swing back around. But this time the German rolled out headed east, climbing for home.

They'd done it.

# Home Defense Duty

*66 Squadron RFC, Sopwith Scout Fighter Aircraft*
*Les Baraques Aerodrome, Calais*

"Gentlemen, your attention." Their new squadron commander, Major Paul Stockard, reminded Pete of a bulldog, and he'd spoken even more abruptly than usual that day. Despite the nice weather outside, every 66 Squadron pilot was seated in the Mess. "We've all heard the rumors. Lieutenant Colonel Barker from Headquarters Home Forces is here to give us the straight story." The major nodded to the short and somewhat overweight officer standing next to him. "Colonel."

The colonel thanked the major and took the podium. "Gentlemen, this Home Forces briefing is top secret and is not to be discussed with unauthorized persons. Our improved anti-aircraft defenses around London have negated the Zeppelin threat, but the appearance of Germany's Gotha bomber has changed the situation. The Gotha is a twin-engine bomber armed with three machine guns. We estimate its ceiling—" the colonel

# HOME DEFENSE DUTY

looked down at his notes, trying to find his place "—at eighteen thousand feet and its bomb load at five thousand pounds."

Pete and Roger traded quizzical looks at that last bit. "Five hundred pounds?" Roger mouthed to him, and Pete nodded. A Zeppelin might carry five thousand pounds of bombs, but no way a twin-engine bomber could. Not unless he was planning on taxiing to the target.

"Eighteen Gothas attacked southeast England on the afternoon of May twenty-fifth. Most of the bombs fell around Shorncliffe and Folkestone. Very few of the airplanes we put in the air reached the Gothas, but we believe we destroyed two of the enemy on their return leg. Seventeen Canadian soldiers and ninety-five civilians were killed by bombs." The pilots waited patiently as the colonel had a drink of water. They all knew what the Gothas had done on June thirteenth.

"We've identified two shortcomings in the London defenses. Firstly, the flow of information. Secondly, the type of airplane employed against the bombers. As a result, the army is transferring trained observers to the coastal areas near London, and communication procedures have been streamlined." The colonel looked down again and shuffled through his notes. Fiddled with his glasses, and got moving again after some throat clearing and another drink of water.

"Our three-inchers brought down a Gotha off Sheerness on June fifth. Two crew members survived and were taken prisoner, and the navy is raising the airplane to allow for a close examination. Finally, and what has brought me here today, were the tragic events of June thirteenth. Approximately twenty Gothas attacked London around twelve noon. Most of the bombs fell near Liverpool Street Station. One hundred and sixty-two killed and over four hundred injured, including eighteen young children killed at the North Street School in Poplar. Once again, very few of our airplanes were able to intercept the enemy.

"In response to this latest attack, the War Cabinet has directed two frontline fighter squadrons be transferred to home defense duties. Fifty-Six Squadron will go to Bekesbourne and Sixty-Six Squadron to Calais.

As much as we would like you to intercept the Gothas on their way to England, that will not be possible from Calais. Your mission will be to shoot them down as they return to their bases in Belgium. We estimate the bombers will pass within twenty-five miles of Calais, and one flight of six Sopwiths is to be kept on five-minute alert."

The colonel set his notes aside and finished with an obviously rehearsed attempt at inspiration. "The War Cabinet. The Royal Flying Corps. The people of Great Britain. All are counting on you, gentlemen. Do not let us down. Are there any questions?"

"Isn't killing school children against the laws of war, Colonel?" asked a C-Flight pilot. "Any chance we stand those two Gotha pilots up against a wall?"

"As much as I'd like to say yes, Lieutenant, I don't know the answer to that. Likely the War Cabinet would deal with such a question, due to the possibility of reprisals."

Pete stood up. "Sir, you mentioned communication issues. What about putting wireless receivers in the airplanes? Extra weight, but the ability to direct airborne airplanes toward the enemy—"

"It's been discussed, Lieutenant. I know the navy is concerned about frequency congestion. Most likely, it will continue to be panel signals." The colonel looked out over the pilot group again.

"Thank you, gentlemen. Good hunting."

Pete leaned back, his elbows sinking in the warm sand. Squinted into the setting sun and made out the Dover cliffs. Breathed in the salty ocean air, mixed with the smell of burnt wood and pork chops. Watched Duncan and Wilcox battle two B-Flight pilots in two-versus-two sand football. He thought about German bombs hitting London. About how bored he was after sitting around Calais for ten days doing nothing. About the Black Albatros—the picture of it as clear in his mind as it was that day. He'd gone up to Wing and done some digging; found a picture of a downed Hun Albatros with a black-and-white striped horizontal tail. Jasta 37. Wing kept the Berlin daily on file, too. He'd start digging through those as soon as they got back and see what he could turn up.

"Maybe tomorrow will be the day, Pete," said Roger, lying in the sand a few feet away and appearing to read his mind.

Twenty-three hours later it looked like Roger might have been right. Pete had the rotary cranking before he finished strapping in. They were already at the end of the field; he gave the chocks-out signal and pushed the throttle and petrol forward for takeoff. A-Flight had the alert and Roger and the rest of the fellows wouldn't be far behind, but Pete and Drew Harris had a head start and they were going to get the bastard.

The call had come in from the navy. A single Gotha headed east at medium altitude, twenty miles northwest of Calais. Pete turned north-northeast as he climbed, figuring the Hun was headed home to Gaunt. Test-fired the Vickers. Tweaked the mixture and listened to the hum of the Le Rhône; he wanted every ounce of power he could get. The Pup climbed steadily with only half a tank of fuel on board. Any more than that would be dead weight.

They passed through one cloud layer, then a second. Through a rain shower that soaked him despite his leather jacket and scarf. The spotters had reported the Gotha at medium altitude. Maybe he had an engine problem, or maybe navy spotters didn't judge altitude well. Pete leveled at 9000 feet between two cloud layers. The visibility was poor to the east in the haze, but it was even worse to the west, looking back into the setting sun. He checked behind him: Harris was about 200 yards back. Pete's B5305 was almost new and Harris's Pup couldn't keep up. *Well, that was just too bad.*

*Which way to go?* He turned southeast, nice and easy, since he didn't have a horizon line to work with. He'd hold that heading for five minutes and swing back northeast. That'd be as good as anything. He rolled out of the turn and drummed his fingers on the throttle lever… A solitary Gotha. Curious. Likely a recce mission of some sort. Or maybe the kaiser wanted to see London again. Visit his cousin Georgie. Drew had used the angle to rejoin on him and was signaling for Pete to throttle back a notch. To let him hang onto his wing. Pete shrugged and went back to his scan.

He was heading northeast when a dark spot appeared in the haze low and right of his nose. The spot disappeared a few seconds later. Was something out there, or was his mind getting ahead of his eyes? He banked right, turned thirty degrees and rolled out. If it was the Hun, he'd be closing on him. He rested his eyes for a few seconds and looked again…nothing but gray. Wiped his goggles dry and held them away from his face to clear the condensation. Put them on and looked again. Blinked twice, struggling to make his eyes pierce the dark gray haze.

He pulled in his breath, eyes wide: an airplane silhouette low and to his right. The silhouette faded into the gray…and disappeared.

He turned to cut the German off and eased the nose down. The Pup picked up speed and his heart beat faster. His mouth was dry and he swallowed some spit. *Don't lose him, Pete.* He got another glimpse a few seconds later. *Yes!* Big airplane, two engines. It was him.

The Hun was gone again; the gray clouds darkening as they flew east. He pushed the nose down further to close the gap, and to get below the German. To get him in sight before he lost him for good. He nudged the petrol lever forward for the lower altitude; he didn't need the Le Rhône acting up now.

Forty-five eternal seconds went by…of nothing but dark-gray clouds and rain. He kept the wings level by the seat of his pants, by the wind and rain across his face. But if the German had turned…

There. He'd cleared the heavy rain and had him again. Dead ahead, maybe five hundred yards. But it was tough to judge the distance through the dark gray mist, and the Gotha was much bigger than any two-seater he'd ever dealt with. He watched and waited…the Pup was a few knots faster and was closing the gap. He had hold of him now, but how to bring this big bastard down with a single, slow-firing, eight-millimeter Vickers? Fuel tank or pilot, that was his best chance. According to intel, he'd have three machine guns to deal with, one of them in a tunnel to cover their blind spot below the tail. Meaning no matter what he did, they'd be shooting back. But the usual twisting of his stomach just before action was gone. It was payback time.

He was close enough to see detail on the German—it had the same boxy tail as the British Handley Page. The Pup would be almost impossible to see head-on in the dark-gray sky. He'd get in close and give it everything he had; only reposition if the bullets went off target.

He saw the outline of the rear gunner's head and slid lower, hiding behind the tail section.

Closer. The Hun was wings level, in a shallow descent.

Closer. The Hun was huge now. The gray of the mist deeper, thicker, as they flew east.

Pete guessed sixty yards and set the bead just behind the Hun's nose, where the pilot would be. He moved his thumb onto the firing button… and tapped it three times as he studied the German. Paused. Tapped it twice more and slid his eyes outboard along the right wing. Made out a red-white-and-blue roundel in the gray darkness.

A pissed-off Pete Newin was drinking beer with Hugh Fleming and Roger Browne. "It's one of those things that happens in war, Pete," said Fleming. "Everyone is Gotha crazy after the Poplar school. A spotter gets a glimpse of a large airplane in the haze and he wants it to be a Gotha. So that's what he sees."

"I came within a whisker of shooting. The visibility was almost zero by the time I caught up with them. I don't suppose I would have gotten credit for a kill?"

"Somehow, I doubt it, Pete," said Roger. "A roundel would look a bit odd next to all the Iron Crosses on the board. I wonder where he was going."

"Lost, probably," said Fleming. "He wouldn't have been the first HP to land on the Hun side."

Pete almost smiled, remembering how four heads had turned toward him when he'd pulled alongside, shocked to find out they weren't alone in the dark sky. They'd followed him back to Calais and landed at a nearby aerodrome. "How much longer does our little vacation here last, Captain?" asked Pete.

Fleming shook his head. "Recording officers don't know much more than pilots, Pete. We just get chewed out more. But the major thinks we'll go home soon. There's too much going on in Flanders for us to be sitting here waiting on Gothas."

"Too bad." Pete didn't know if he meant it or not. It was boring sitting at Calais, nor was he going to find the Black Albatros around there. But that vision of little kids being pulled from the wreckage of their school hadn't gone away.

Harry cocked his head and frowned as boots squished through the mud outside their hut—the orderly was due to call him at six—and let out a sigh of relief as the squishing passed by. He looked at the clock: 08:05. *Yes! Saved by the weather.* He closed his eyes, but his brain was awake and thinking about yesterday's fight. Somehow, they'd fought off that Hun two-seater. Norman had told him afterward it was a DFW, which didn't mean much more to him than XYZ.

He reluctantly opened his eyes again and checked the other three cots. George was asleep and Thomas was reading the Bible. Ethan's cot was empty. Harvey had told them Bill and Ethan were in hospital; he didn't know any more than that. Harry sat up and waved good morning to Thomas. Checked himself over, remembering that something had slapped against his helmet. He couldn't find a scratch. "Breakfast, Thomas?" he asked, standing up. "After I get cleaned up?"

"A bit later. Thanks."

He gathered up his uniform and stepped outside. Light rain and fog. He counted three hangars—the fourth was invisible in the mist. Some voices and the clinking of tools—the mechanics never got a day off. He took a deep breath; tried and failed to blow a mist ring. Smiled. It was a beautiful morning. The only problem was the summertime sun would usually burn this stuff off by midday. He got cleaned up and went by the orderly room, which was empty except for a sergeant behind the counter. As always, it smelled of stale cigarette smoke. "Good morning, Sergeant. Quiet around here."

"That it is, Lieutenant. Nice for a change."

"The RO isn't up and about yet?"

"He was here earlier, sir. Checking on the weather. The fog's not supposed to burn off anytime soon. I think he went back to bed."

Harry checked the board: takeoff at 07:30 and 13:00. With luck the weather blokes would be right for once, and he'd have the day off. He moved down the counter to the situation map. Nothing much had happened since they took Messines Ridge. But it couldn't be much longer for the next big one. Not the way the army was going through artillery shells.

He wandered down to the Mess and nodded good morning to a couple of observers from another flight. Looked at the decent breakfast fare and decided he wasn't hungry. Sat by a dirty window and drank tea. A DFW, Norman had said. He'd go by intel later and look it up. Odd-looking thing—the wings looked too big for the fuselage. Handled well enough, though. Observers, and pilots for that matter, were generous in crediting themselves with Huns shot down. But for sure, he'd hit the German twice. He'd seen the sparks fly and the observer give a little jump. Shame the bounder didn't crash on the British side—he visualized an Iron Cross by his name on the board. That would look good—be worth a picture. But for the first time since he'd been in France, he felt a sense of accomplishment. Norman came in, put his hand on Harry's shoulder and said good morning. Sat down and, like Harry, opted for tea. Harry tried not to look surprised, but something had changed. "Did you get some rest?" Harry asked.

Norman held up his left hand. "Hard to sleep with this. The doc dug it out and stitched it up. But no Novocain. He said they were running short. I've had more fun in my life."

A splinter had gone through his flying glove. Harry hadn't known until after they landed. It had looked nasty, sticking out like that, with blood running out from under the glove.

"You didn't get a scratch, did you?"

"No. A splinter whacked my helmet, but no harm done."

"I spoke with Harvey last night when I got back. Bill and Ethan are going to be okay. They got Bill in the leg; he's still in hospital. Ethan got hit in the head, but it sounds like it was a ricochet. Harvey thinks he'll be back today." Norman was looking out the window, at the huts and hangars shrouded in the mist. He had the trace of a smile when he turned back to Harry. "Good shooting yesterday. But I would have sworn our wing struts blocked that last shot of yours."

Harry half smiled, half shrugged. Firing between the struts of a BE2 wasn't taught in training. But the Hun was shooting them to pieces, and he couldn't wait. When he checked after landing, he found two hits on the left struts from "outbound bullets." Most likely British .303 rounds. Compared to what the Hun was doing to them, that was nothing.

"The Lewis jammed on you, didn't it?"

"Double feed. But I'd seen it once before. On the range."

"The Hun pilot was good. He damn near shot both airplanes to pieces, and didn't want to take no for an answer. We were lucky, too. While you were struggling with the Lewis, the Hun set his observer up perfectly, less than a hundred yards, and he shot behind us. I talked to the fitter last night. They patched fourteen bullet holes in the aft fuselage and vertical tail."

They drank their tea, and Harry counted eight stitches on Norman's hand. "Can you fly with that?"

"Afraid so. It's my throttle hand. It's not going to do much for my grip though, not that I've been playing much golf lately. If you're done with your tea, why don't we take a walk down to photo? See if what we went through yesterday was worth it."

The odor of chemicals hit Harry as he opened the door of the tent. He counted eight people at work, and no doubt there were more in the dark rooms. Another of those forever-expanding RFC departments. A corporal looked up from his desk. "Morning, gentlemen. What can we do for you?"

"We photo-shot the Menin Highway yesterday. Can we see what we turned up?" asked Norman.

"Happy to, sir. I did those myself." The corporal pulled an envelope out of a large filing cabinet. He sorted through the photos, placed six of them on the desk, and handed Norman and Harry each a magnifying glass.

"These went to Wing and Second Army yesterday. This is the extreme northeast corner of the shoot. Notice this area that looks different from the surrounding terrain?" The corporal pointed with his pencil, being careful not to touch the photo. "That's rectangular shaped?"

Harry studied the photo through the glass and made out what the corporal was pointing to, but had no idea what he was looking at.

"If you look closely, you can see the straight lines and right angles. Here, and here, and again here. This is a vehicle park under triple camouflage netting. See how the shading pattern repeats in a line from here to here. And again from here to here. These are rows of vehicles."

Harry squinted. *Vehicle park? If you say so.*

"Here's another one, gentlemen, from the number two photo. They're very faint, but can you see these three light-colored lines? How they converge to this spot? There is no building visible, but notice how the ground is a different color and texture compared to the surrounding area. The lines are buried cable, and foot traffic has worn down the ground near the entrance. We can also make out the corner of a car underneath this copse of trees. This is almost certainly an underground headquarters or communication center of some sort. The plan was to hit both targets this morning. I suppose the bombers will go when the fog lifts. With luck, we'll get to see the postattack pictures here at the squadron." The corporal gathered up the photos and put them back in the folder. "Nice work, gentlemen."

They thanked him and walked back to the squadron building. The corporal may want to see more photos, but Harry had no desire to take another ride along the Menin Road. Norman picked up the newspaper. Harry started to; stopped and looked out the window. The mechanics were pushing a BE2 back into a hangar, to keep the water off it. *The BE2. We did something that matters yesterday…in a slow and outdated BE2. If they really hit those targets, some British soldiers will live because of what Norman and I did. Me. Harry Booth. The Liverpool fabric store kid who'd cocked up everything he'd ever done.*

The mechanics came out of the hangar and disappeared into the mist. Harry picked up the newspaper and for once read most of it. Put it down when Ethan walked in, a bandage around his head. Norman and Harry greeted him with gentle hugs. "How do you feel?" asked Norman.

"Headache. No one's hit me in the head with a hammer before, but I guess this is what it feels like. The doc said it must have been a ricochet."

"He doesn't know how hard your head is," said Harry. "How's Bill?"

"I had to drag him out of the airplane—what was left of it. The Hun got him in the leg, and I was afraid he might bleed out. But some army chaps saw us go down. Their orderly got there quick and bandaged him up. They ran us over to hospital."

"I saw you headed for the field," said Norman. "How badly were you hit?"

"Bad. We lost most of our aileron control the second time he hit us. The engine was misfiring and the propeller was about to fall off. But Bill hung in there. He used the rudder and sort of kept the wings level until we hit. I wouldn't call it a landing, but we're alive."

"Your roommate here hit the Hun twice, although he shot our struts to pieces to do it."

Ethan shrugged. "I'd shoot myself down if I could do it without killing us. The sooner we get rid of these antiques, the better."

They ate a light lunch in the Mess; telling the story of yesterday's fight twice as chaps came and went. After lunch, Ethan surprised Harry by asking him to take a walk. They stepped outside and enjoyed the beautiful weather: the visibility was still less than a mile with no sign of the sun.

"It was tough yesterday."

Harry looked at Ethan. He'd never heard such a serious tone from his friend before. Ethan was looking across the field, the darker outline of the trees just visible in the mist. He had lines around his eyes that Harry hadn't seen before. "A bullet creased my flying jacket. Another one glanced off the Lewis drum while I was loading it. That will get your attention…and the ricochet that hit me." He let out a long sigh. "Do you know they're still making BE2s back in England, Harry?"

Harry's eyebrows went up. "That can't be right. The RE8s are on the way."

"Be that as it may, a cousin of mine works at Whitworth. As we speak, they're churning out brand-new, absolutely worthless, BE2s. And charging the government a pretty penny, I don't doubt. If I could find the dolt who ordered these airplanes, I'd strangle him. Or make him come fly with us."

Harry looked at his friend again. He'd sounded dead serious as he said that last bit. The mist had thickened, and it began to rain. Neither of them was wearing a jacket, although Ethan didn't seem to notice. "Let's go to the hut. Wouldn't hurt you to lie down for a bit." He got Ethan stashed in his cot and decided he'd lie down too.

He thought about home, his mom, and what he'd do on leave. Charlene Crawford wouldn't be an option. Her brother would be watching them, and there was still that bit about her being married. But there'd be other girls around, girls interested in an RFC lieutenant home from the war.

Voices woke him. Thomas, George, and Ethan were playing cards. He stood up and stretched, blinking his eyes awake. Looked down at the table; the biggest bet was three pence. He gathered up his coppers; sat down and played a few hands, still trying to wake up. The only noise was the clinking of coins, and somewhere in the mist the mechanics were running an engine.

"Belly dancers," said Ethan, looking at his cards.

George, Harry, and Thomas looked at each other. "Are you feeling all right, Ethan?" asked George.

"I've always had a fondness for belly dancers. Alas, only from afar. An unrequited appreciation for the beauty of the dance. And the dancers. I can only say it's a grave injustice I wasn't born an Ottoman sultan. Ethanman the Magnificent. Ah, the palace I could have built. The secret passageways. Perhaps we don't give the Turks enough credit. There's a fair chance the French are going to shoot one. Shoot a belly dancer."

"I don't believe that," said Harry.

"You should believe it, young man. It's front-page material in France. The young lady in question has been remanded by the government, accused of being a German spy. Nor do I imagine this is the most opportune point in French history to be accused of spying for the enemy. You chaps didn't know I spoke French, did you? It's that we aristocratic cosmopolitan types prefer not to flaunt our accomplishments before you commoners, as well-intentioned as you may be."

"She Egyptian?" asked Harry.

"No. One paper says she's from Java. Another one says she's Dutch."

"Has to be Java. The Dutch don't belly dance. Any pictures?"

"Not the kind you're thinking of."

They played a few more hands and Harry won big, his earnings topping a shilling. Thomas broke his usual silence. "I can guess how she convinced her boyfriends to supply information. There might be some French generals who are worried right about now."

"If they are, you won't read about it in the papers," said Ethan. "Nothing embarrassing to the republic may be printed."

"I wish some belly dancer would try to get information out of me," said Harry.

"I'll let you know if I see any around here, but I imagine they aim higher than lieutenants."

"If they decide to shoot her, does she get to do a final dance? You know, instead of final words to say? Or maybe they'll shoot her while she's dancing—some sort of moving target practice for the troops?"

"I don't know. Final words may be an English thing. But the trial hasn't started yet, and who knows, maybe the French will be lenient. The fairer sex and all. But I wouldn't count on it this time." Ethan paused while he dealt the cards. "And if I had to guess, Miss Belly Dancer's trial will last awhile. The French like nothing better than good, sordid copy. And from the government's point of view, it will take people's minds off the war. A war which, you may have noticed, is taking longer to win than was originally planned." They played a few more hands, and Harry's winnings began to shrink.

"I was speaking of good, sordid copy," said Ethan, "and that reminds me of something else courtesy of our most beloved ally. Can you fellows guess what was on the front page of the French newspapers in July of '14?"

"That a major European war was about to break out?" ventured Thomas.

"Wrong, my young friend. Remember—we're talking about the French. The correct answer is the trial of Henriette Caillaux. The devoted wife of Joseph Caillaux, who was minister of…minister of something at the time. Finance, I think it was. A newspaper critic had, most ungraciously, printed a letter the minister had written to a mistress several years earlier. A letter that was both intimate and politically inconvenient. Madame Caillaux called upon said newspaperman, was ushered into his office, and shot him dead. Four times in the chest, if I recall."

"Did they shoot her?" asked Harry. "Maybe four times in the chest? That would be justice."

"They didn't shoot her. Not even once. She was acquitted by the jury. A crime of passion."

"I didn't know passion was a legal defense," said Thomas.

"Looks like it is in France," said Ethan. "Don't know that I'd want to rely on it back in England."

As the three of them took that in, Blake Webb stuck his head in the door. "Thomas, Harry, good news. We're scheduled to visit Forty-First Division on Monday. Hang with the artillery blokes for the afternoon."

Harry and Thomas looked at each other. "That's good news?" asked Thomas.

"Absolutely. We'll have our own transport, and I think a diversion on the way back might be arranged."

"As in Margarite's Place?" asked Harry. He was way overdue for some fun.

"You remembered. You know the old saying, a little horizontal relaxation never hurt anyone."

"Careful, gents," said George. "They'll stop your pay if you end up in hospital with the clap. If you're going to indulge, arm yourselves with condoms. And use them."

Blake gave a dismissive wave. "They check the girls, George. The French are more practical about these things than us Brits. That said, one does want to take proper care of Johnny. Keep him in good working order for the next time."

"Who's going?" asked Harry.

"The three of us and a couple of B-Flight types. It should be a good time for all."

# Mutiny

*Town of Blessy, Northern France*
*July 1917*

Pete and Roger walked into a busy Wildflowers Café. Juliette saw him and teared up; gave him a hug and a kiss. He'd gone by her house that night to tell her about Phillip and hadn't seen her since. Drew Harris and another pilot were on their way out. "C-Flight borrowed Drew for balloon busting," Roger told Pete. "How did it go?"

"Good," said Drew. "The weather wasn't bad up near the coast. We tried the rockets first. God may know where they went, but I sure don't."

Roger nodded. "The airplane has to be one hundred percent stabilized and coordinated when you fire. The tiniest slip or skid or pull and the rockets can go anywhere. Except where you're aiming."

"No matter. We got it with the incendiaries and it burned up on the way down. Great fun, but Archie didn't care for it and shot the hell out of us. But I spotted one of the guns and laid into them good with the Vickers. The gunner blokes scattered every which way."

Pete looked from Drew to Roger, who wasn't smiling. "Did you carry the letter?" Roger asked, his tone flat.

Harris patted his breast pocket. "Still right here."

"If you had bothered to read it, you'd know you certified that your incendiary rounds would only be fired against balloons. Not against airplanes, infantry, or anything else. Including anti-aircraft artillery crews."

Harris tried to shrug it off. "War is hell, boss."

"It will be for you, Lieutenant, if you go down on the Hun side someday. I guarantee you the Huns have a description of your airplane. Likely pictures too, and they'll remember this day if they get their hands on you. They've been very clear about incendiaries. Violators will be shot, British officer or not."

Drew's permanent look of confidence disappeared as Roger's words sank in, as coming down on the Hun side was hardly unknown of in this war. For once, Drew had nothing to say. Roger stared at him for a couple of seconds before motioning toward the door with his thumb. Looked at the menu.

"I'm sorry about your brother, Pete."

Pete still couldn't talk about it. He'd called Charles as soon as he'd landed that day, and his brother had gotten down to Devon before the telegram came. He supposed that was something. After looking over the menu, which he knew by heart, he thought of something to talk about. "If my maths is correct, with Mark and Jimmy back, I count eight A-Flight pilots."

"Your maths is correct, Pete. I talked to the major and Fleming about it." Roger was puzzling over the menu, mouthing the French words. "Mark's getting flight commander at Eleven. Bristol Fighters. It should be official tomorrow, and we'll send one of the new blokes back to St. Omer. Or maybe we'll send Ian. They like having experienced pilots in the pool, and A-Flight is heavy on flight leaders."

Pete smiled at the last bit. To be rid of Ian Crosse would be a blessing. Maybe he'd end up flying the BE2. Roger looked at him over the menu and lowered his voice. "The major said to expect some distant offensive patrols, and maybe contact patrols, until more SE5s and Camels show up. I know they're always saying the 'big attack' is coming. But this time it might be true."

Pete winced at the mention of contact patrols; he'd done those back in his Strutter days. The problem was attacking troops would invariably lose phone contact with the rear areas and fall back on runners or carrier pigeons, with predictable results. The *solution* was for the RFC to fly over the battlefield and spot the position of the forwardmost troops, via pre-arranged panel signals or flares. The pilot would mark their position on a map, fly back to the appropriate headquarters and drop it. Another in a long line of military endeavors that worked better in theory than in practice, as troops in action near the front line aren't usually keen on running about trying to signal airplanes or shooting off flares to mark their position. Juliette's arrival to take their order interrupted his fond reminiscing. "The usual, Peter?"

He nodded, and she looked at Roger. "Whatever Pete's having is fine."

She scrunched up her nose at Roger's Yorkshire accent before turning to Pete. He translated and watched her as she went back to the kitchen. Remembered the other bit Roger had said.

"Distant offensive patrols...what exactly does *distant* mean?"

"Good question, Pete. Same one I asked. Fifteen, twenty miles beyond the line. Maybe more. Depends."

Pete's eyebrows went up. That was a long way onto the German side. Flying home into the wind, sometimes with battle damage. A simple engine failure would mean another airplane and pilot out of the war, while the Huns would be over friendly territory and their spotters would tell them where the British were. Pete refrained from saying what he was thinking. It wasn't Roger's idea. "At flight strength?"

Roger nodded. "Normally all six airplanes. Maybe one of the other flights as well. Maybe the whole squadron."

"With that many airplanes, at least a few of us will make it back," said Pete, and regretted it as soon as it was out. Pointless.

Roger shrugged it off, as he did most things. "At least I don't think we'll be making aerodrome attacks. Almost anything is better than the Pup for that."

"Well, that's something." Pete had done more than enough aerodrome attacks in the Strutter, and the German anti-aircraft artillery was only getting better. "When do we start?"

"I don't know. Maybe next week."

"Can't wait."

They ate lunch and were drinking tea when Arthur came in with another man about his age, and a young man wearing dark goggles with a black scarf pulled across the lower half of his face. Pete shook hands and introduced Roger. Arthur introduced his friend Hugo, and Hugo's grandson, Gaspard. Arthur and Hugo had the same tanned skin and silver-black hair, but Hugo was half a head taller. Juliette brought a bottle of wine and gave them each a kiss. Gaspard's scarf had loosened and Pete glanced at him. His nose was gone, and most of the upper lip. The skin was red around the injured area, going to white near his chin and about halfway up his forehead. Pete couldn't see past the goggles, but it was obvious he was blind. The other side of war—the side the papers didn't talk so much about.

"Gaspard fought with the Fourth Army and was wounded near Champagne," Hugo told them. "He is third of my four grandsons."

"Yes, I've even learned to wash and hang up clothes," said Gaspard. The tone was empty. Dead. To be unable to read. To see the ocean waves or the blue sky. Would it be better to be killed? It was easy to say yes, but…

Pete remembered his manners and translated, but Roger stood up at the first break in the conversation. "I need to get back, Pete. I'll see you at dinner. How much was lunch?"

"I'll get it. We can square it up later."

Once Roger had gone, Arthur told Hugo and Gaspard that Pete was an English flier who, as they could see, spoke excellent French. This was an exaggeration, but Pete thanked him. Pete didn't say, and they couldn't know, that he spoke German well and a fair amount of Russian. The former at the behest of his late father, who insisted they needed to learn German because, like it or not, events in Europe would center on a united Germany. He'd learned some Russian because his mother had insisted on it after she'd married his half-Russian stepfather.

"Do you English pilots suffer château breakdowns?" Gaspard asked, with what might pass for a smile. Pete looked a question at Hugo.

"My second grandson, Leo, works on airplane engines. He told us sometimes their pilots make forced landings because of an engine problem. There's a little hole in a fuel line, or something comes loose. Funny though, the landing is usually near a large château. The airplane is damaged and the pilot hurt. Not hurt badly, but bad enough that he needs to stay and rest for a few days. And of course, the airplane must be fixed. Sometimes the phones go down and the squadron can't get a hold of the pilot. Sometimes the repair crew gets lost." Hugo chuckled, exposing two missing front teeth—the gap partially filled by his remaining teeth having angled their way in. Pete had to smile at the creativity of the French. A pilot might get away with that in the RFC. Once.

"The newspapers are still all about Pétain," said Arthur. "For months they talked of nothing but Neville. The hero of Verdun come to lead the great offensive. To smash the Hun and end the war." He snorted. "Neville. The fool who replaced the other fool."

Hugo whispered something to Arthur, looking at Pete, and Arthur nodded. Hugo spoke in a low voice, and Pete leaned forward to listen. "Pierre, the oldest boy, got a letter to us last week. Past the censors. The attack on the Chemin des Dames was a disaster. Some divisions lost over half their men, to move the line a kilometer or so. He said hundreds of the dead and wounded were lined up by the side of the road as they marched in. Waiting for transport. For the burial teams."

The front door opened; both Hugo and Arthur turned to see who came in. It was an older couple. Hugo continued, keeping his voice low. "It started in the Fifth and Sixth Armies. The soldiers refused to attack. Now it has spread to most of the army. Pierre says the soldiers will defend, but not attack. They want regular leave and better food. But most of all, they want an end to the madness. An end to attacks that cannot possibly succeed."

"The rumor is Pétain has called off further attacks," said Arthur, "and that they've started arresting the leaders. There are more rumors about trials and firing squads, but no one knows anything. But not a word in the newspapers, of course."

Hugo sat back and sipped his wine. "Tell me, Peter, do you think we win this war?"

It was a question Pete had given a lot of thought to. "I don't think we lose, Hugo. America will be incredibly powerful once she gets moving. If I had to guess…not next year, but sometime in '19. An American offensive supported by the French and British. More tanks, airplanes, and artillery than ever before. At some point, Germany has to crack."

"At least it isn't like back in '70," said Arthur. "We had to go it alone against the Prussians."

Pete nodded. "Even if Russia drops out and the Germans breakthrough in the West, I look at how France hung tough in 1870. Civilian armies raised in the provinces to take on the German Army. Fighting on for months with no hope of victory. Today, knowing the Americans are on the way, France would hang on."

"I hope you're right, Peter," Hugo said simply.

"I hope so, too, Hugo," said Pete, standing up. He waved to Juliette and made a walking motion with his fingers. Mouthed "walk you home tonight?"

She responded with a knowing smile. It was time to start walking her home again, with their little diversion into the field. She'd lift her dress and chemise up to her waist; put her hand in his and sit down. He'd gently lay her back and slip her drawers off. Inside of her, he could forget about the war.

Pete had finished his eggs and sausage and was working on his second cup of coffee. He wasn't usually a sausage for breakfast type, but he'd been up at 03:30 for dawn patrol, which had turned out to be a cold, wet, and uneventful tour of the airspace southeast of Ypres. They were getting ready to go out again. Roger, Drew Harris, Billy Duncan, and himself. Roger read the ops order between slugs of coffee.

"Six Twenty-One Squadron RE8s spotting east of Zill-Beak. Juliet twenty, twenty-six, thirty-one and thirty-two." He paused to study his map. Went back to the ops order. "Nineteenth Corps. Patrol at ten thousand feet. Protect the spotters. Same formation as this morning, fellows. The sun should be getting up. Burn some of this stuff off."

Pete handed his plate to the AM2 and waved good morning as a couple of B-Flight pilots trickled into the Mess. Glanced at the clock; pushed his chair back and crossed his legs. Closed his eyes and sipped his coffee. Down in the French sector, on the Aisne, not much had happened since the April disaster. It wouldn't make much sense to attack while sorting out a mutiny of one's own troops. But the Germans still held most of the high ground in Flanders, and Pétain's problems weren't going to deter Haig, who seemed perfectly happy to incur thousands of casualties to move the line an eighth of an inch on his precious map.

Pete set his coffee cup down and pushed those thoughts away. It was still too early in the morning for bitterness. Besides, who knew what sorts of demons other people might be harboring. Perhaps even generals who appeared to care nothing for the lives of their men.

He spat out oil as it sprayed from under his smashed instrument panel and tried to catch his breath. Held the Pup in a level turn and twisted around to keep track of the Albatros behind him. There was an unusual vibration in the control column; he glanced at the wings of the Pup and immediately came back to the Hun. The upper left aileron was damaged—that must be causing the vibration. He made quick right-left-right motions with the column, and the Pup responded with little rolls. He had flight controls, and the Le Rhône should run for at least another few minutes. If he could get above 15,000 feet, he'd have the advantage over the heavier Albatros.

He set that idea aside. The German would run him down before he made it halfway up. He tensed, ready to pull back into the Hun…and let out a sigh of relief. The German was turning away from him. Pete waited a few more seconds to be sure…yes, the Hun had broken it off. He swung the Pup toward Roger and Drew. As the airplanes closed, he held the column with his legs to keep the wings level and pulled out the Very pistol. Loaded a white flare, held the pistol away from the oil drenched cockpit and fired the flare across Roger's nose. Waved and pointed to his engine. Roger waved back and turned southwest; Pete turned to follow. He checked on Billy Duncan, who was maneuvering back toward him, possibly with pooped pants. He scanned the sky around them—they weren't home yet.

Roger dove to 8000 feet; he had them at full throttle to recross the line. Archie had been shooting at the RE8s but had gone quiet. Gone to breakfast, or more likely, getting ready to greet the Pups. Pete squirmed in his seat. Oil was still spraying all over the cockpit and had soaked through his trousers. He spat again and tried to wipe the oil off his goggles. Nudged the mixture lever forward and listened. The rotary gave off its normal buzzing roar—it should last until he made it home. And if it didn't, there were lots of aerodromes and fields in Flanders. He just needed to get to the British side.

He flinched as a shell burst in front of him, maybe 100 feet high. Close for the first ranging shot. Roger turned ten degrees right and went back into a dive. One, two, three more bursts. Directly in front of them. Roger swung left and leveled off. The bursts were thicker now. Black and ugly. Roger turned back right and lowered the nose again. They dove for thirty seconds and leveled off. One more minute and they should be through it.

A burst went off below him, maybe ten yards to his right. The Pup wobbled from the shock wave and he got a momentary whiff of cordite. Acrid, over the steady smell of the oil. The Pup steadied and pushed through the smoke. They were coming up on the line now…a burst directly above Roger. No problem—he'd seen Pups survive far worse. He checked on Duncan, who'd gotten back into a normal wingman position. Looked at Roger, who was turning toward him. Pete began to reposition, and stopped. Roger's Pup wasn't turning. It was rolling toward him—but the Pup's nose was sliding away from Pete. Roger's Pup yawed further sideways…and Pete bit his lip as it flipped onto its back. The Pup completed the roll and came upright, its nose just below the horizon and pointing away from Pete. It paused there. Unnatural, as if trying to fly sideways, and Pete cringed as the Pup's lower-right wing shifted backward. It was just the tiniest movement, but he saw it. The wing shifted back a second time, further, and a wing rib poked up through the fabric as Roger fought to control the Pup. To keep her from yawing sideways and spinning out of control. He'd have near full left rudder and aileron in, and full throttle. A second wing rib popped up, and Pete watched with despair as a third rib, followed by a fourth, poked through the fabric. The Pup hung there for one last second…snapped to the right and into a downward spiral, her wing flapping against the fuselage like a bird's broken wing.

Pete ignored his engine oil and landed back at Liettres. He wasn't sad—he was furious. Furious with politicians who didn't have the maturity to solve problems short of world war. Furious with RFC generals and their idiotic ideas. Furious with British industry, who gave them shit to fly. He climbed out of the cockpit, skipping his postflight debrief with Fletcher.

Roger's mechanic was standing in the next spot. Their eyes met and Pete shook his head; turned away as the shock registered on the young corporal's face. He went to the squadron office and filled out his combat report, vaguely aware that Duncan and Harris were talking to the major and Hugh Fleming in the orderly room. He finished his report in record time, threw it in Fleming's inbox and went outside. Walked down to the farmhouse and sat on his bed, trying to get hold of himself. Dead pilot—no problem, we'll send another. They're no different than lorry wheels or throttle levers—we have plenty. He tried filling out his combat notebook. Gave up. Tried reading American Civil War history. He kept putting the book down and picking it up.

He lay down on his bed, still covered in castor oil. Closed his eyes, and his mind began racing. *Phillip. Now Roger. Why?* He got up and looked out his little window. Went outside and wandered to the far side of the landing ground. Sat under a tree, looking away from the aerodrome. Listened to the birds up in the branches. Waited for one of them to shit on him. His mouth was dry and tasted of oil and gritty dirt. He spat. Spat again. Behind him, some SPADs started up and took off. He watched the trees and the birds. The clouds. The anger slowly seeped out of him as fatigue set in, followed by the sense of loss. Roger, who'd held steady amid the turmoil of the RFC at war. The young wife in Yorkshire who would get the knock on the door—open it and see the delivery boy holding the telegram. If Pete had a friend in the RFC, it was Roger. And now he was dead.

He gave one last, heavy sigh, and stood up. Went back to his room; washed and changed into a clean uniform. Like it or not, he was still Lieutenant Pete Newin, Royal Flying Corps.

He managed to do a little reading. Tried and failed to get some sleep. He skipped lunch and walked down to the club, which was empty except for a corporal behind the counter and someone moving about in the back room.

"Afternoon, Lieutenant." The corporal's voice was flat. Bad news travelled fast in an RFC squadron. "What can I get you?"

"Whisky."

The corporal set a glass in front of him and Pete sat there, staring at nothing. For once, he didn't even want to look out the window. He was nursing the same whisky when Duncan and Harris came in, with John Wilcox in tow. Tired of the silence, which was reminding him of a funeral, he waved them over. Asked Drew about their side of the engagement.

"Two of them bothered us while the other two went after the RE8s. Roger did some shooting, and I remember seeing one of the RE8 observers firing. A Hun got behind me, but I slipped and skidded every which way and he finally gave it up. Oh yes, your Halberstadt fell right past us, so you'll get your kill."

At that moment, Pete couldn't have cared less about Hun kills. John Wilcox broke the lengthy silence that followed. "It's a shame. He was a good man. A good flight commander."

"I have cousins in Yorkshire," said Billy. "I'll visit his wife next time I'm home. Tell her what happened. How everyone liked him. Respected him." He looked at Pete. "Thanks for your help today. I thought they had me."

Pete nodded. The Halberstadt had been shooting Billy's airplane full of holes, and Pete had nailed it seconds before bullets from the Albatros had torn into his cockpit. "I'll visit his wife, Billy. He would have done the same for me if it was the other way around. He would have gone to see my mother."

Hugh Fleming had come in and ordered a beer. He came over to their table. "Fellows, I need to speak with Pete."

The three lieutenants moved to a different table. Fleming sat down and took a sip of his beer. Like Pete, he wasn't a big drinker. Their eyes met. "This is war, Pete. Good people die. We've both seen it before."

Pete looked at the stained and chipped tabletop in front of him. Spoke slowly. "The Archie burst was well above him, Captain. Easily out of lethal range. The way the wing folded in; the shell must have gone through the main spar. I had a good look at the airplane as it rolled over. The fuselage and tail were intact. The cockpit, too."

"And?"

"He was alive and unhurt all the way down. If he'd had a parachute—"

"The RFC doesn't use parachutes, Pete. You know that."

"I know Roger would be alive if the commanding general wasn't a complete—"

"That's enough, Lieutenant." Fleming sat up and cut him off. "You're welcome to your opinions about senior officers. But you'll keep them to yourself. Period. We're officers in the Royal Flying Corps, and we obey orders. It can't be any other way."

Fleming was right, of course. Like it or not, he was going to have to move on. He nodded at Hugh Fleming, whom he had always liked and respected. "Understood, Captain."

Fleming sat back and sipped his beer again. Softened his tone. "Like yourself, I read history. Isandlwana. I'm guessing you know the story?"

Pete knew it. South Africa. Anglo-Zulu war. 1879. "Not as popular with our historians as Rorke's Drift. But yes, I know the story."

"Likely the worst defeat in the history of the British Army. Overconfidence, bordering on arrogance. Poor decisions made in a critical situation. But our soldiers obeyed orders. They fought. They died. That's the same British Army you and I are part of, Pete. It hasn't changed. It can't."

Despite his black mood, Pete's historian wheels were turning. "Isandlwana was only a few years after Little Bighorn in the United States. Splitting one's forces in the presence of a powerful and mobile enemy. How many times must that lesson be learned?"

"I don't know, Pete. I'm only a one-handed recording officer."

"As you say, Captain, our greatest military defeat. Although I wonder if the Somme will replace it for that dubious honor when our government owns up to what really happened, and when the historians have had their say."

"Could be. The lives lost at Isandlwana might make page three in this war." Fleming stood up, leaving his glass over half full. "I'll write a letter to his wife. Let me know if you want to add a note. And by the way, good work today. Sounds like you saved Duncan's backside. His airplane looked like Swiss Cheese—the fellows will be patching all night."

Pete nodded. He'd brought his wingman home and almost got killed doing it. Roger was just bloody bad luck. He looked around the bar after Fleming had gone. His three fellow A-Flighters were still there. He didn't feel much like talking, but being alone would be worse. He picked up his glass and went to join them.

Hugh Fleming read the combat reports again and decided against having Pete do his over. Although not his usual detailed sequence of events, it was good enough. He'd never seen Pete like this—like he was about to explode. Fleming gave a little shake of his head as he picked up his pen. Another letter to write, and this time it was Roger. He put his pen down and looked out his little window.

The parachute issue was difficult; there were legitimate questions of weight and practicality. But why the constant emphasis on the offensive? Why suffer these enormous losses with the Americans on the way? Did they need to win before Russia dropped out? Obviously, fighting a major European war went beyond the battlefield. International alliances, domestic and dominion politics, needs of the military versus industry. Issues that went to the War Cabinet itself. Meaning to some extent, just like Pete and himself, Generals Henderson and Trenchard obeyed orders. And agree with them or not, those two were nobody's fools.

He let out a sigh, put the combat reports in his outbox and took the top piece of paper from his inbox.

*Submit a detailed accounting of all bedding related materials on hand (cots, sheets, blankets, pillows) cross-referenced with the approved levels per officer and ranker as stipulated in regulation…and include an explanation…*

# Horizontal Relaxation

*Hazebrouck, Northern France*

Blake got behind the wheel of the tender; announced they'd been working far too hard and it was time for some relaxation. Harry was in full agreement. He'd been in 6 Squadron over two months and didn't have a scratch on him, but at least twice Hun bullets had passed within inches of him. He looked down at the O wing on his chest: Second Lieutenant Harry Booth, RFC observer. He couldn't wait for his mom to see him in uniform.

He'd enjoyed their little artillery field trip, despite everyone and everything being coated with a film of mud. The Battery B commander welcomed them to his command post, complete with a kitchen and dinner table, cots in a back room, and an RFC wireless operator. All under twelve feet of sandbags and dirt.

The major gave them a rundown on operations as they had tea and biscuits. A pair of rats eyed them from a dark corner. "Can't get rid of those bastards," said the major, nodding toward their audience. "We tried locking a big cat in here one night. The rats ate him. Maybe I'll get a pack of nasty terriers in here. Or close it off and gas the lot of them."

When they finished their tea, the major had a corporal walk them down to the gun pits. He was the chatty type, with a West Country accent. "Be careful to stay on the boards, gents. We've lost horses in the mud. A bloke or two, I suppose. I guess some farmer will plow 'em up someday. Maybe use 'em for fertilizer. Hope the Hun will leave us alone today. It can get ugly around here when he starts shooting. They told me one of the chaps got both legs and an arm blown off the other day. Lying right here. They said he was trying to push up on his one arm, but that it sank in the mud. He kept asking for help. Glad I missed that one. I was back with the ammo fellows that day. Course that ain't the safest place in the world, neither. The Huns know our route. Drop a few now and again."

The corporal took a few breaths, but he wasn't done. "We don't like them Hun spotters flying about here. Appreciate it when you RFC fellows shoot them down. Great sport—better than football. One crashed in that field right out in front there a few days back, and some of the chaps ran over for souvenirs. German stuff is best—it goes quick. A couple of the fellows stayed too long and the Hun artillery got 'em. I looked later that night. The pieces were 'ardly big enough to bury. Glad I'm not on that duty. But at least we're not like them Froggies. Heard they take their dead ones and use 'em for sandbags. Think about looking at your mate's rotted face while you eat your blood sausage."

The wind shifted as Harry took in that last comment, and a rotten stench hit him. Like feces mixed with sewer water, but worse. "What's that smell?" he coughed out, holding his nose.

The corporal sniffed the air. "Oh, that's the horses. Over there—you can see part of one looking at us. The burial chaps aren't so particular about the horses. Only pick up the big pieces."

Harry was focused on the slippery boards under his muddy boots and didn't look where the corporal pointed. They kept walking, and he started up again. "One of your chaps crashed here last week. Right in that field.

The pilot looked to be hurt bad and the observer bloke was trying to pull him out. Bunch of Aussies ran over. They were passing through. Rough lot, them. The observer saw 'em coming and waved—suppose he thought they were coming to help. They all tore souvenirs from the airplane and ran off. I bet your observer fellow was a mite put out.

"Anyhows, an officer showed up and made 'em go back and help. But we don't like you fellows crashing here. Brings the Hun artillery. But it was raining hard that day and I suppose the Hun couldn't see. Your chaps came around that night and took the airplane away. The pieces of it, that was."

The corporal paused. He wasn't done, but his tone had changed when he spoke again. "Back in England, people told me war was about heroes and glory and such." He looked across the pockmarked mud landscape and frowned. Wiped his runny nose with the back of his hand. "If there're heroes or glory around this place, I'd hate to see what hell looks like." Harry was beginning to enjoy the corporal's less-than-cheery stories, but the guns started firing and the corporal gave up trying to talk. A second lieutenant greeted them at the gun pits.

"Lieutenant Jeremy Spencer, gentlemen," he shouted between the booms, adding, "One- Ninetieth Royal Field Artillery Brigade, Battery B," as if they didn't know. He motioned toward his two guns. "Quick-Firing eighteen-pounders. We can fire over fifteen rounds a minute if need be. But we have to stockpile a lot of shells ahead of time to keep that up. Makes the chaps nervous. We've had some problems with the recoil springs and the oil dampening. But it's a great weapon."

Harry swore his internal organs bounced each time the guns fired. Fortunately, they didn't stay long, but on the way back to the tender a rat startled him and he stepped off the boards. Sank in the mud to his knee and had to sit down on the filthy boards to extricate himself, much to the amusement of all. He cleaned up as best he could and sat in the middle seat with Thomas and one of the B-Flight observers, Louis. Once they got moving, Louis asked Thomas how he ended up in the RFC.

## HORIZONTAL RELAXATION

"I'd finished OTC at Winchester College. Volunteered in '14, and they made me a supply officer. Bored me to death. I put in for flight training, and the doctor tells me I can't see well enough. Observer corps, he says. I was tempted to ask how one can observe with poor eyesight, but all I said was, 'yes sir,' and here I am. To be honest, I'm not sure I'd do it over again. Supply isn't looking so bad now."

Harry knew he'd get the same question. How much of the story did he want to tell?

"Harry, take these bolts down to Murray's for me, please. Then you can go home."

Harry glanced at his uncle. Short and stout, with short white hair. Decent sort, if a little humorless. Maybe thirty-plus years in a fabric shop did that to people.

"Will do." Harry checked the time: five minutes to six. He wrapped the fabric bolts carefully to protect them from the Liverpool winter weather. The City of Grime, he had christened it. Grabbed his coat and scarf and wrapped up. "Good night, Uncle."

"Good night, Harry. See you at nine."

Harry pushed the door open and stepped into the cold. The wind had died down and the gray air wafted about, covering everyone and everything with a thin layer of black soot. He walked the four blocks to Murray's, treading carefully on the slush and the filthy snow. It'd be easy to slip and crack an elbow or his head. Or worse, get the fabric dirty. He arrived at the familiar yellow and black sign: "Murray's Expert Tailoring." Not just any tailor shop, Murray's. Expert. And his uncle's best friend.

Harry pushed the door open. Murray and his younger sister were standing at the counter, looking at some dark green fabric. "Evening, Harry." Henry Murray was even shorter than Harry's uncle, with the same stout build. "Put them on the back bench, please."

"I think it will be perfect," Murray's sister was saying as Harry came out of the back room. "It will set off the yellow of the curtains."

"Good. Let me close up, and I'll carry it home for you."

"I'll be happy to do that, sir," said Harry. "Mrs. Crawford's house is on my way home."

Charlene Crawford looked at him. Nodded to her brother. "Thank you, Harry." She gave a little toss of her brownish-blonde hair. She'd been in his uncle's store a few times. She always stood close and put her hand on his arm when she asked him a question. Murray wrapped the fabric in heavy paper—it was a slipcover for a chair. They bundled up and Harry held the door for her. Fifteen minutes later they arrived at her house. Cold; their boots wet with dirty snow.

"Put it in the living room, Harry, and light the lamps, please. I'll make tea."

Harry wiped his feet and remembered just in time to help her out of her coat. He set the slipcover in the living room, lit the two gas lamps and sat down in the kitchen. The house was quiet. "Are your children at home, ma'am?"

"They'll be home next week for the holidays," she said over her shoulder as she lit the small gas stove. Not needing to know more, he leaned back and looked at her. She was a little taller than her brother. Not thin, but not fat. Maybe forty years old? "And you can call me Charlene. There are no uncles or brothers around." She put the water on the stove, turned and leaned against the counter. The streetlights were lit, and it was starting to snow. "You'd think after all these years I'd hate snow, but I still like it."

She brushed her hand across her ample breasts, still looking out the window. Once, twice, three times. Brushing away some invisible dust. But if the gesture was intended to entice, it did so, and carnal thoughts began circulating in his nineteen-year-old brain. He looked at her dress, how it curved around her breasts. Down to where it formed a little V between her thighs. She filled the teapot with boiling water and set the tea basket in it. Poured some clear liquid into one of the oversized teacups. Gin, maybe? "Milk or sugar, Harry?"

"No, thank you, ma'am. Charlene."

They drank their tea. She asked him about work. He didn't like it. Boring.

She asked about his plans for the future. He didn't have any, other than not to work in a fabric store his whole life.

"I'm glad you're home helping your uncle. Not off fighting this crazy war. All those boys being killed. Why is it our fight?"

He opted to be safe with his response, his knowledge of international politics being effectively zero. "I don't know, Charlene. War is crazy."

She refilled their cups and gave hers another shot. Leaned toward him and held his arm. "They say it should end soon. You won't have to go."

He was intensely aware of her hand on his arm and the proximity of her breasts, and searched for something to say. It wouldn't do to ask about her children again. He asked about her brother's store—she worked there a few days a week. He asked about the slipcover.

"Let me show you." She put the tea away and showed him the living room. It was dim, almost dark, despite the two little yellow pools of light cast by the lamps. She talked about the colors, her hand resting on his shoulder. That she would get a new rug when she could afford it. Perhaps a dark yellow. It was colder there than in the kitchen, and she asked him to put some coal on the fire. When he turned around, she wasn't there.

"Charlene?"

"Come on up, Harry," she called. "You can help me."

He went up the stairs, heart pounding. Was this going to happen? He peeked into the little bedroom. She had lit the lamp and was putting a chair next to the curtain.

"Don't let me fall, Harry."

She climbed onto the chair and fiddled with the curtain. He stood next to her, hands on her hips. Moved his fingers the tiniest bit. The friction of the wool as it moved across her skin was electric. She took her time. Adjusted and readjusted. Each time she shifted her weight, little bolts of excitement shot from his fingertips to his loins. He edged closer, almost close enough to kiss her hip through her dress. Finally, she stepped down;

landed on his foot and lost her balance. He caught her and pulled her to him. Kissed her lips, her face, her neck. Ran his hands over her breasts and pushed on the fabric of her dress between her thighs. His fingers went to the buttons of her dress. They were stiff and didn't want to go through the little holes.

There. He got the first one undone. The second one.

He struggled with the third one, and she put her hands over his.

"I'll do it. You might rip it."

She walked to the bed, undoing the buttons. The dress came off, followed by the white dress thing underneath, and he stared at her white drawers and brassiere—they were thin enough to see through. She pulled back the covers and got in, covering herself below the waist. Rolled onto her side and drew the back of her hand across her brassiere and down to her hips. "If you promise to be careful, I'll let you take the rest off."

He was undressed and in bed in less than thirty seconds. Got her bra and drawers off, and about two minutes later they were finished. He rolled onto his side, his heart pounding. He'd done it. He'd really done it, and it was as good as everyone said. Charlene was talking to him—something about not being in a hurry. He half listened, needing to rest a bit, feeling proud of himself. A few minutes later he pulled her to him and rolled on top of her.

"Nice and easy, Harry. Not too hard. Yes, that's better. Like that."

He forced himself to slow down—he was getting the idea as she coached him. He'd just finished when a door banged downstairs.

"Charlene, are you all right?"

She sat up and pushed him out of the bed. "It's my brother. Get dressed."

"Is Harry up there with you?"

Hell, he'd left his coat in the kitchen—not that there was anywhere to hide. He was pulling on his trousers when Murray walked in. Charlene had stayed in bed, the covers pulled up to her neck. Murray glared at Harry. At his sister. At Harry again. "Get out."

## HORIZONTAL RELAXATION

Harry grabbed the rest of his clothes and scurried down the stairs. He stopped in the kitchen long enough to finish dressing and ran out the door.

Murray, Harry, and his uncle were standing in the back of the shop. The "Sorry, We're Closed" sign was hanging on the door. "She had a couple of drinks. Said he seduced her."

"Bloody hell—" began Harry.

"Shut up," his uncle almost yelled.

"Her husband is in India," said Murray. "He's been away for years, but they're still married. Adultery. Rape maybe."

"Rape? There was nothing—"

"Be quiet, Harry." His uncle again, more subdued this time.

Murray looked at Harry, more sad than angry. "There's no excuse for this. All young men have urges. You have to control them. She could be your mother." Murray turned to his friend. "If this gets out, the neighbors will talk. We'll lose customers. Her husband will find out sooner or later. He might not care. Or he might." Harry's uncle looked at him.

"What would your mother think about this? She worked her whole life to bring you up proper, and this is her thanks."

Harry didn't say anything. But when he'd watched Charlene take her dress off, nothing was going to stop him. Please, God. That they don't tell his mom.

"I spent six years in the army," said Murray. "Local regiment, then the Highland Light in South Africa. Boys go in, men come out. Might be just the thing. Of course, there's a chance he gets killed, with the war going on and all. But he'd have served his country. Made his mother proud. And conscription has passed now. They'll find him soon enough anyway."

*The army? Get killed?* He needed to get out of the shop. But the bloody army? In the middle of a bloody war? His friend Billy Simpson knew people—he already had his exemption lined up and said he could manage one for Harry. Of course, friends or not, Billy didn't do anything without expecting something back.

His uncle was looking out the little window into the back alley. He spoke slowly. "He might even manage a commission. He's plenty smart enough, if he'd ever put his mind to anything." He turned back to Harry. "That's it, young man. The British Army. Or you and I have a talk with your mother."

They got into Hazebrouck and Blake spent the next ten minutes driving about.

"Never been to Margarite's before, chaps. Only heard stories."

"Right. And I'm the Cardinal of York. Where'd I put me robe?" said Tyler, the other B-Flight observer. Louis looked at Harry and Thomas.

"You two ever been to a place like this before?"

Harry shook his head. "Nor I," said Thomas.

"It's a nice place. All the girls speak some English. If you decide to partake, I think it's twenty-five francs to go upstairs, and giving a tip is good style if you like her. Maybe another five francs. But please, don't even think about falling in love with one of these girls."

They pulled up to a dimly lit establishment, with a blue light on each side of the "Welcome to Margarite's Place" sign. Apparently, Ms. Margarite catered to the English-speaking world. A large doorman was standing outside.

"I thought they used red lights for this," Harry said to Louis.

"Blue for an officers' establishment. We can't be running into the rankers here. Would be bad for discipline."

"Here we are, gents," said Blake. "Understand I'm only here to make sure you fellows stay out of trouble."

Harry's initial impression was favorable. Electric lights. Dim, but bright enough to see the goings-on. Thick red carpet. Someone was playing the piano. British Army types occupied two tables, and a couple of blokes were sitting at the bar. Lots of girls. The five of them sat down at a table, and Harry's roving eyes stopped on a blonde seated at the bar. She was on the tall side. White blouse over a black brassiere. Short black skirt slit almost to her waist. Black fishnet stockings and standard-issue black high heels. She looked back at him and smiled.

The age-fortyish and reasonably well-kept hostess welcomed them. Silver-blonde hair flowed onto a dark-green dress, and she was wearing a pearl necklace that even Harry could tell was fake.

"Good evening. My English gentlemen are always welcome. We are not busy tonight. Lots of nice girls. All clean. You gentlemen have some drinks, talk to my girls. We have nice rooms upstairs."

Blake ordered five whiskies. Sat back and scanned the scenery. His initial reconnaissance complete, he looked around the table. At Harry. "You're smiling, Harry. Don't know that I've seen that before. Anything strike your fancy?"

"They all do."

Tyler chuckled. "You're young, Harry, but you might want to limit yourself a bit."

"Something tells me Harry will be the first to fall tonight, gents," said Blake. "Any takers?" There was a general shaking of heads around the table.

"That reminds me of something Oscar Wilde said," remarked Louis. "That he could resist anything except temptation." Harry had no idea who Oscar Wilde was, and no one followed up on Louis's missive. Harry pushed his chair back, crossed his legs and sipped his whisky. Excused himself to go to the loo a few minutes later, and the black-skirted blonde intercepted him on his way back.

"My name is Suzette," she said in practiced English and proffered her cheek for a kiss.

As he kissed her, she pressed against him and said something in French that he didn't understand. She motioned upstairs—which he understood but wasn't ready for. They stood there looking at each other. He wasn't familiar with proper brothel protocol. Did one treat prostitutes like other girls—or could he just walk away?

After a few more seconds of mutual staring, he took her hand and led her to the table. A dark-skinned girl was sitting on Tyler's lap, and Blake had a well-built brunette next to him. Louis and Thomas were holding off.

Harry held a chair for Suzette, and they sat down. Twenty-three to twenty-five, he guessed. Reasonably pretty face. Small breasts. He'd enjoyed Charlene Crawford's big baps, but something might be said…

Louis looked at him. "She'll expect you to buy her a drink. It's more expensive than our club, but you can manage it."

"You're not going to partake?" asked Harry.

"Maybe later."

Harry looked across at Blake. The brunette was sliding onto his lap. "Nice choice, Harry," said Blake. "She'll take your mind off the war." Harry motioned to a waiter, and Suzette ordered a glass of wine. She took a few sips, moved closer to Harry and kissed him on the neck. Put her hand on his thigh, and prostitute or not, his John Thomas let him know that he was ready for action.

Harry was quiet as they motored back to the aerodrome. *Let's face it, Harry, having sex with prostitutes wasn't something to make mum and uncle proud.* But the image of Suzette stretched out on the bed…long blonde hair and fair skin, set off by black lace drawers and brassiere. That was the prettiest picture he'd seen in a long time. Maybe ever. The sex had been good but anticlimactic. It was the picture of her lying on the bed that was going to stick with him.

"All good, Harry?" Louis asked.

"All good. Just relaxing."

"Do me a favor and don't fall in love with her."

"Fair enough." He didn't think he would, but he was already thinking about another visit. "What did you think, Thomas?" asked Harry.

"I enjoyed it," he said half-heartedly. "But I stayed downstairs. Christian. It isn't something one switches off and on."

Harry turned back to Louis. "How was your girl?"

Louis had paired up with a little brunette later in the evening. "She was nice. She speaks good English. I bought her a drink, and we chatted. She's from Serbia, and her parents are still there. She's worried to death about them, of course. I gave her a nice tip but stayed downstairs."

Harry gave an invisible shrug. Closed his eyes and went back to his vision of Suzette lying on the bed in her black undies. If he was supposed to be feeling guilty, he'd worry about it later.

# A Story to Tell

*66 Squadron RFC, Sopwith Scout Fighter Aircraft*
*Liettres Aerodrome, Northern France*

Pete was sitting on the edge of his bed, rubbing the sleep out of his eyes. His little window looked east, and the sky was turning from black to gray. The sun was insisting on rising yet again, to burn away the morning haze. To shine its light into the dark trenches; onto the freshly killed bodies of men and horses. The fellows would have been working through the night. The ones who were still breathing would be thinking about breakfast. About sleep. That they'd lived through another night. There were footsteps on the walk outside, followed by two gentle knocks on his door.

"Four o'clock, Lieutenant," said a quiet voice. Cockney accent.

Pete stood up and opened his door a few inches. "Thanks, Nate. I'm up." The first week Pete had been in the farmhouse, one of the orderlies had been a little enthusiastic when knocking him up. Pete's landlord had shown up in ill humor and armed with his twelve-bore, and the word had gone out.

Twenty minutes later he was eating a boiled egg and drinking coffee in the Mess. Traded sleepy nods with a group of B-Flight pilots at the next table. John Wilcox and Billy Duncan came in, the latter with dark shadows under his eyes. Like Pete, John went with coffee and a boiled egg. Billy sat down, staring into space.

"You okay, Billy?" asked Pete.

Billy shrugged without looking at him. "Can I get you a coffee?"

Billy gave a single shake of the head. Newly appointed A-Flight commander, Jimmy Musgrave, came in. As usual for the early go, Jimmy was unshaven and in pajamas. Pete wasn't quite ready for OTC inspection, but he was shaved and in uniform. Perhaps it was silly, but if he was going to be killed, he wanted to look like a British officer when they pulled him out of the wreckage. Jimmy grabbed a coffee and sat down, with only a brief glance at his three pilots. Read from the ops order. "Offensive patrol. Ten airplanes. Comines, Menin, G-Velt. B-Flight will lead. Maybe Archie won't be awake yet."

Jimmy sipped his coffee, crossed his legs and burped. Despite the moderate range, Pete caught a whiff of reprocessed beer. "V formation. Billy, you're on my right. Pete, you and John on my left. Flare gun signals are July standard. Any questions?"

Pete shook his head. "All good."

"You chaps follow us, Jimmy," said Rory Campbell, B-Flight commander. "A mile back and two thousand feet above, if you can. Ops order says ten thousand feet. I don't know that's going to happen."

Jimmy gave Rory a thumbs-up and turned to his three pilots. "The loo for me. Suit up in ten minutes."

Thirty minutes later, four A-Flight airplanes were skimming below the clouds at 4000 feet. A mile ahead were four B-Flight airplanes. They'd lost one due to no engine start, and a second had turned back after takeoff with a mechanical or gun problem. The forward visibility was maybe three miles in the haze, and it would go lower when the sun got up. Here and there low fog blotted out the ground.

# CHANGES WROUGHT

Pete made a quick, left and back to neutral, motion with the column. Moved a few feet wider on Jimmy; swung back parallel. Checked on John as the rotary hummed and the moisture streamed off the wings of the Pup. Scanned the sky around them, sector by sector. It was automatic now, and even easier when he wasn't responsible for flight navigation. His eyes snapped shut—one of the B-Flight pilots out front had fired a white flare. Jammed Vickers or a bum engine. The four B-Flight airplanes swung into a 180-degree turn. Jimmy pressed ahead, and as they passed abeam three of the four airplanes turned to slot in behind them. Pete frowned under his scarf. It was Rory who had dropped out, so Jimmy was in charge.

They went through a rain shower, and Pete pulled his scarf tighter as the water worked its way down his back. Wiped his goggles clean enough to see the river to his right and, a couple of minutes later, the Menin Road to his left. Beyond that, there wasn't much to see. The occasional town. Mud. Some patches of green here and there as they flew further east. Through another drenching rain shower. He thought about Roger, and put it out of his mind. Jimmy turned north, descending to stay below the clouds, and Pete shook his head. The ceiling was down to 3000 feet and the entire mission was worse than pointless. Any enemy airplane they found could easily escape into the clouds. For the same reason, their own spotters wouldn't need watching over. This would be nothing more than live target practice for Archie whenever he finished his coffee and started shooting. They did a few north-south circuits and drew some rifle fire. At least someone else was awake.

Jimmy, likely getting bored, turned them east again. Pete's unease grew as each mile clicked by. They had plenty of fuel to get home, but they were way out of their patrol area and flying deeper into the German side every minute. Risk versus reward, and this wasn't adding up. Some more flashes from the ground, and the first stream of tracers as a machine gun joined in. All it would take was a single bullet in the wrong place and his war would be over. Or his life. On this miserable wet morning in Flanders, courtesy of their new flight commander. Or maybe he'd land back at Liettres without a hole in the airplane, and enjoy a nice, hot breakfast. Chance—fascinating subject. Funny the Romans had no understanding of probability theory, as much as they'd liked to gamble. Basic combinational probability wasn't… Jimmy was pointing to the right, and Pete stared for three long seconds before swinging away from him. As he and John separated, he spied an open area in front of them. He rested his eyes for a couple of seconds; opened them and focused…a row of large tents and two parked airplanes. He blew out his breath. Were they really going to attack a heavily defended German aerodrome in a bunch of Sopwith Pups? Without a bomb in the group?

They were in the bar and Pete had chased the others away. He chose his words carefully. "We were way out of our patrol area this morning, Jimmy. Captain." It was going to take a while for him to get used to calling Jimmy, "Captain Musgrave." If he ever did.

"So? Take the offensive against the Hun, Pete. Every chance we get. That comes right from the top. I didn't make it up."

"It wasn't worth the risk. Not with a bunch of single-gunned Pups. Scheduled aerodrome attacks always use bombs. Billy Duncan's dead, along with the B-Flight chap. So we could shoot a few holes in some hangars and a couple of old recce airplanes."

Jimmy snorted. "I like you, Pete. Always have. But this is war and A-Flight is going to kill the enemy." Jimmy finished his beer and stood up. "That Canadian bloke who replaced Roger is going to hospital, so two new ones will be in tomorrow or next. You'll do most of the checkout flights."

Jimmy went to the bar, and Pete moved to a table by a window. God, he hated this place. Attack a German aerodrome with a bunch of slow and under-gunned Sopwith Pups. Two dead pilots—to accomplish almost nothing. But no doubt a resounding success in the insane logic of the Royal Flying Corps.

*Going above and beyond their assigned mission, in the most adverse of weather conditions, our pilots fearlessly attacked a well-defended German aerodrome, inflicting serious damage on enemy airplanes and facilities, and disrupting his air operations. Our losses were light…*

He let out a long breath and drummed his fingers on the table…but perhaps he was missing the higher logic. They needed to replace the Pups anyway—new airplanes were finally on the way. Then have the chaps fly suicide missions and save the bother of flying the Pups back to England. Inspired. Colonel Jimmy Musgrave. No, General Musgrave. General in chief—pilot manning and aerodrome attacks.

Pete drummed his fingers on the table again. Then just his index finger. He looked down at the dark-brown tabletop. There were some burns on the edges, where cigarettes had been set too long. Another burn mark in the middle of the table. A butt fallen from its ashtray and forgotten? Some faint blotches of darker brown. Whisky? Beer? Vomit? A fifty-year-old bloodstain? Perhaps someone had his throat slit while sitting at this very table? *Most sorry, monsieur, but that's what you get for cheating at cards.* Or perhaps a cuckolded husband taking vengeance on his wife's lover? *I understand your pain, monsieur, but at least you shan't be lonely. Madame will be joining you soon.*

He leaned forward and studied the blotches more closely. Traced the outline with his finger. Had some renegade Prussian soldiers held a barmaid down while they raped her—the sweat from her naked skin pushing its way into the porous wood as she struggled? The deep gouge on the edge? The table hitting the floor as she slid off and ran away, once they'd finished with her?

That said, as a fledging historian he needed to avoid bias. Was he being unfair to the Prussians, assuming they were the culprits? Historians seemed to agree that at least a few of Napoleon's soldiers were not above rape and pillage. Was the table that old? There might be a date stamp on it somewhere. He could tip it over and look.

Rumor was contact patrols for the Pups during the next big attack, as the SE5s and the Camels took over the fighter role. Fly over the line and look for panel signals or flares marking the position of the forwardmost troops. Except there wouldn't be any panel signals or flares, because the infantry chaps weren't about to get killed running about spreading panels or shooting off flares, telling the enemy where they were. The only way to find them was to get down to fifty feet and look. Brown uniforms—good, keep going. Green-gray uniforms—bad, turn around. If the machine guns didn't get you first, and if you can even tell the difference, because everyone and everything is covered in mud. Mark the forward troop positions on a map; fly back to division or corps and drop it. Repeat the above process until shot down and killed.

He lit a cigarette and tossed the burning match onto the table. Set the cigarette on the edge, put his fists down and his chin on his fists. Watched the match burn down, then out. The little blue-gray smoke trail curled up. He flicked the match with his finger and looked at the little burn mark. Felt it. Still warm. His contribution to the table's character. He straightened up and looked over to the bar. The old heads, somber. The newer chaps louder, their arms around each other now and again. Hands flying about—refighting air combats with alcohol-reinforced vigor. The occasional song or argument.

The bartender set up another row of whisky glasses and filled them. Alcohol—one constant of existence in the Royal Flying Corps. Along with cigarettes and castor oil. Diarrhea. Dead pilots and new pilots. Drawn from Britain's inexhaustible supply of young men.

He pushed his cigarette to the middle of the table. Flicked the end of it and watched it make little red circles as it spun to the floor. Like an airplane going down in flames. He ran his eyes across the tabletop again. There was a tiny, sharp gouge he hadn't noticed before; the wood was gray where the point had chipped the finish away. Someone had stabbed his knife into the table years before. Had the knife passed through a hand on its downward plunge? More cheating at cards? If he had a microscope, could he see tiny bits of blood and flesh in the hole? Or had the evidence long since been washed away?

A whisky glass appeared in front of him. A second glass opposite him.

He looked at the two whiskies. At John Wilcox.

"I didn't think you were a whisky drinker, John." His voice came out husky.

"I'm not." John sat down and took a sip of his whisky. "Shame. I wasn't close to Billy, but he was a good chap."

Pete was looking at the whisky glass in front of him and didn't say anything.

"The farmhouse this morning," said John. "I thought you'd gone crazy. But I figured it out once I saw the staff car. It had to be their jasta building. I picked a different window and put thirty rounds through it. We sure woke somebody up."

Pete had stayed outside the perimeter of the aerodrome during their attack, keeping away from the Hun machine guns. He'd seen the car and two motorcycles outside the farmhouse, and put fifty rounds through two different windows. He let out a sigh and looked out the window. The haze had burned off and the sun was touching the trees. It would be a nice summer evening if the war would go away.

"I talked with Jimmy. It didn't do any good, of course." He turned from the window and picked up his glass. Swirled it around. Set it down and watched the brown liquid come to a stop.

He lit a match and held it inside the glass until the whisky caught. The blue flame wavered, and the glass discolored.

"I've learned a lot since I've been in France," said Pete, watching the little blue flame. "Ways to shift the odds, to stay alive. But ultimately, we're playing pilot roulette. You play roulette long enough, your number comes up and you lose. There's even a nice maths formula for how long it should take. Roger's dead. My little brother. Now Billy. A month from now, you or I will be rotting in the mud. Maybe both of us."

Pete made a circling motion with his finger on the table. "Every time we get in the cockpit, the wheel spins."

He made a smaller circle. Smaller still.

"The little ball goes around and around. Slows down." He lifted his finger and tapped the table twice.

"And drops into one of the slots. Someone's number came up. Tell the War Office we need another telegram."

John leaned over and blew out the still burning whisky. "New airplanes are on the way, Pete. More Yanks every day. It will get better."

"Good RFC-approved answer. I'll tell Trenchard to make you a general next time I see him."

It was John's turn to look out the window. "At Sandhurst, you get this picture of charging up a hill. Routing the enemy and planting the regimental flag. It's not like that here. But we have to do our duty, Pete. Same as all the other chaps. It's what we signed on for." John took one more sip of his whisky and stood up.

"Good Christ, Pete, get some rest. You look like hell."

# The Lady in Black

*Southwest London*
*August 1917*

Mark Newin went down the steps of Bushy House, the home of the National Physical Laboratory, and wandered around the grounds for a few minutes. He needed a break from the endless technical reports. He sat on a bench next to a chap he vaguely recognized; the gent nodded and went back to his book. Mark closed his eyes and smelled the wet bark of the trees. It had rained early that morning. A bird chirped; the hooves of the horses clapped on Queen's Road behind him. The occasional motorcar or lorry. Someone honked their horn. Technology was changing London. Changing the world. The wind picked up and the leaves tumbled against his black shoes, which, for once, were polished to a nice shine.

He and Rachel had gone out to dinner Saturday night. It had been their first real date, and it had gone well, up to a point. She'd invited him to come inside, and he followed her down the dim hallway to her flat. Stood behind her while she opened her purse and rummaged around for the key.

He looked at her back and her long hair in the light cast by the one small electric bulb. He thought of a different world—a world in which Mark Newin puts his arms around her as she fumbles with her purse. She puts the key in the lock; stops as he kisses her neck. She turns around, still in his arms, and their eyes meet. She tilts her head back, licks her lips, and—

*Click.* The lock turned. Metallic, harsh, in the quiet hallway. She pushed the door open and flipped on the lights. Excused herself.

He closed the door gently. For some reason, he didn't want it to click again. He sat on the sofa; got up and peeked out the window. Closed the blackout curtains carefully and pulled at the corners. Made one more adjustment. They didn't need the police knocking on the door.

He looked at the pictures on a side table, including one of her and her late husband. Tall thin chap. Older than Rachel. But if she was ready to move on, wouldn't she have put that picture away? There was another of her parents and the two girls, when Charlotte was a baby. A large green vase sat in a corner, mounted on a wooden base with leaves carved into it. Not something one would find in his flat—it was too nice. In the adjacent corner, a hideous ceramic elephant with painted toenails and jeweled eyes looked up at him. They'd lived in the East for a time and must have brought some junk back with them. Everyone who went there did. Maybe this stuff looked good in India.

She made tea and sat next to him on the sofa. She'd taken her shoes off. They'd chatted a bit, and in the excitement of being alone with her, he'd forgotten he was bumbling Mark Newin. He'd picked up her hand, lifted it toward his lips, and froze. Looked at the beautiful object in his hands: the long fingers, the well-trimmed nails painted a discreet pink. It was beautiful, but at that moment had struck him as some sort of laboratory specimen, requiring careful handling. A few eternal seconds went by—Mark holding her hand out in front of him and Rachel looking at him.

Finally deciding he couldn't sit there all night holding her hand, he lowered it gently and set it on the sofa, as if it were fine china. He tried to edge away from her without moving his lower body, which only resulted in an awkward tilt away from her. In another few seconds he would have fallen onto the floor. She'd made light of it, and had even given him a hug and a kiss when he ducked out ten minutes later.

He let out a sigh. Another chapter in the *Inept and Unhappy Life of Mark Newin*.

The kiss had been on his cheek, but still, it qualified as their first kiss. He'd held the embrace an extra second, his hand on her back, feeling the push of her small breasts against his chest. Was there a chance?

A pigeon was looking up at him; Mark returned his gaze. *Sorry mate, no peanuts. I'll try to remember tomorrow.* The pigeon gave up and moved on. There was talk of a wind tunnel for the Lab. The Sopwith Triplane study relied on America's MIT wind tunnel data. Where was the payback for the inefficiency of the middle wing—for the extra weight and drag? He'd concluded there wasn't any payback, but there were rumors the Germans were building their own triplane. That was hardly something they'd do without thinking it through. What was he missing? Was there something hidden in the relationship between the stagger and the intervals? The shape of the airfoils? Should the middle airfoil be different?

His eyes went to a couple on the sidewalk. The man was in uniform, but it was the woman he was looking at. Rachel. She was holding on to the bloke's arm, her head tilted toward him. Smiling at something he was saying. Her head wasn't quite resting on his shoulder, but close. Oh no, she was looking his way. Her head straightened up; she'd seen him. The soldier was looking now, and they turned toward him. He should have gotten up and walked away the instant he'd seen her. He blanked his face and stood up as they approached.

"Hello, Mark. Enjoying the weather?"

"I am." He paused, tempted not to say anything else. "I needed a break from the office."

"Mark, this is Major Ronald Guthrie. An old and very dear friend."

The major put out his hand. Firm military-style handshake. The major was a well-built type with an impressive mustache. Mark couldn't grow one even if he wanted to. "You're the physicist." Deep voice. "Good to meet you. Important work you civilians do here. We can't win this war without good equipment."

The tone was gruff but neutral, and Mark couldn't tell if there was a put-down of civilians in there or not. Probably so. He made an effort to be civil. "Are you home on leave, Major?"

"No. Ordnance Branch. Here in London." The major turned to Rachel. "You'll be seeing more of me. Schedule permitting, of course. There's a war on."

Rachel gave him a little smile before turning to Mark. "Ronald was one of my late husband's dearest friends." She tugged on his arm; she hadn't let it go. "I need to get back to my desk. I'll see you inside, Mark."

He replied with a nod and mechanically expressed his pleasure at meeting Ronald, who didn't bother to acknowledge. He sat down and watched them walk to the front door. Ronald gave Rachel a hug and left without looking in Mark's direction. *You let yourself dream a little, didn't you, Mark? Don't you remember that day at the university?* He'd been sitting on his favorite bench, reading. The girls had been chatting and laughing as they walked by, oblivious to his presence. One of them was likening his personality to that of a shoe. Mark Newin—the inanimate object.

"Quitting time, Mark." Professor Stanton was standing in the doorway.

Mark looked up from a graph of trajectory data for a British 13-pound 9 CWT anti-aircraft gun. "Let me put this away, and I'll be ready."

The professor's flat was near his and they walked home together a couple of times a week. He suspected it was his boss's way of chasing him out of the office. As usual, neither of them said much during the walk home. Mark looked at the words on the storefronts without attaching any meaning to them.

*Wheels of All Sizes*

*Brass Beds—Royal Bargains*

*Life Assurance—A Safe Investment for your Children*

"Pardon me, ma'am." He'd almost bumped into a lady.

She didn't move, and he looked at her. She was about thirty years old, dressed in black, without any make-up. She was looking at him and not smiling.

"I have something for you."

She wasn't speaking loudly, but her voice was harsh. Maybe from smoking.

"On behalf of our soldiers serving their country."

She held out her hand to him. There was something small and white in it. Puzzled, he looked at her face. At her hand again. He accepted it—could hardly be dangerous. It was a white feather.

Professor Stanton spoke, angry. Mark looked up. He'd never seen the professor angry before. "Miss, Mark is a physicist working at the National Physical Laboratory in direct support of the British Army, the Royal Flying Corps, and the Naval Air Service. He has an approved exemption from military service."

The woman turned her gaze from Mark to the professor. The movement was mechanical; reminding Mark of one of those little birds that pop out from a clock and turn their head side to side. "I'm sure our soldiers fighting and dying in France are proud of him."

"Let's go, Mark." The professor pulled him around the woman, and they started walking. "This woman understands nothing of the war effort. Of what we do at the Lab." He looked at the little white thing in Mark's hand. "Throw it away, Mark. It means nothing."

Mark put the little feather in his pocket.

They arrived at the professor's street, and he put his hand on Mark's shoulder. "Forget about what happened, Mark. The RFC and the Royal Navy fly better airplanes because of what we do at the Lab. We save British lives every day."

"I know, professor. Thank you."

# THE LADY IN BLACK

Mark stayed on the corner for a couple of minutes after his boss left, watching the people go by. Turned and walked back to the Lab, taking a different route to avoid the lady in black. It was only six o'clock and Charles always worked late.

"Forget about it, Mark." His brother's voice came across the line. Tired. "Throw it away."

"But why a feather? What does it mean?"

He heard Charles sigh. "They're suffragettes, Mark. They do this to get attention. Stir things up."

"What does women voting have to do with me? And a white feather?"

"I can see you don't read the papers much." Another sigh came across the line. "It's a cowardice feather, Mark. I think the idea came from a novel. They see a man of service age in civilian clothes and assume he's shirking military service. The idea is to shame the supposed coward into doing his duty. The whole thing's a farce. It's about publicity for their cause. We don't have many people who can do what you do. Throw it away and go back to work. The woman's an idiot."

"Thanks, Charles."

Mark hung up the phone and walked down the quiet hall. Went outside and sat on his bench; the sun wasn't down yet. Mark had always preferred the dark. In the dark, the Mark Newins of the world and the handsome football types were more equal. At least he understood now. Charles and the professor were right, of course. What he did was important, and there weren't many people who could do it. But three brothers and two cousins and thousands of others had gone to war while Mark Newin stayed home. He thought about Rachel. About the invisible disdain on the major's face.

The whistle blows and Private Mark Newin climbs out of the trench. Charges forward, bayonet fixed. An artillery shell bursts to his right, knocking one mate down. To his left, the Hun machine-gun fire cuts down two more. A bullet slices through his side, he staggers and drops to a knee. Gasps for air...pushes himself onto his feet and keeps going forward. The barbed wire tears at his hands and face, but he fights his way through and jumps into the first German trench. Fires from the hip, bringing a Hun down. Lunges forward with his rifle, just in time to knock aside the plunging bayonet of another, saving his best friend's life.

And that was about as unlikely a scene as he could possibly conjure up. Twenty-eight-year-old, overweight and out-of-shape Mark Newin, who had never fired a gun in his life—the war hero. If he put this in ledger form, it wouldn't be a close call. He could do far more good at the Lab than he could trying to play army. But there'd be that one nagging footnote on the "Stay at the Lab" side of the Mark Newin ledger. Had he stayed at the Lab because he was afraid?

Ian Crosse glanced at the water temperature gauge: the Hispano was running hot. He nudged the radiator shutters toward open. After eight months in the Pup, he wasn't used to having a real engine in front of him. He scanned the sky around them. Good visibility with some scattered clouds; the late afternoon sun low in the western sky. Checked on his wingman—no problem there. That arsehole Davidson had been in France for three months and despite having the brains of a brick, he knew how to maintain position. Those beautiful words floated across his mind again: *Captain* Ian Crosse. *Flight Commander* Ian Crosse. Now *he* would pick their battles, and his wingmen would watch after *his* backside. Yes, having an uncle in Parliament had its advantages. Not that he was undeserving, of course.

He glanced down at the airspeed indicator: 9000 feet and they were doing almost 125. He smiled under his scarf—those derelicts back at Sixty-Six were welcome to those Pups. Not only was she fast, the SE5 was an excellent climber and diver. If need be, he could get out of trouble quick enough. To celebrate his promotion, he'd gone into Bethune the other night. He'd found a nice, off the beaten path establishment, and had impressed himself by passing on several high-class, and clearly airworthy, French prostitutes. *Ian Crosse, maturing with responsibility. Minister Crosse, Bristol South. Fighter Pilot. War Hero. The new face of the Liberal Party.*

They passed Arras and swung into their patrol area. Made a few orbits. Not much going on down there. All the action was up in Flanders—Haig had finally launched "The Big One." Or the latest Big One. Well, good luck fellows. How best to set up the Parliament run? Finding a wife would be child's play…RFC pilot. Distinguished-looking silver hair and muscular build. But go with the money, or a connection to the working class? There should be less risk in going with the money. Maybe find one that liked kids. She could stay in Bristol with the urchins and leave him a free hand in London. Looks wouldn't matter so much—turn off the lights and do his duty. He'd have the mistress for real sex when the mood struck, although he'd have to manage that carefully. Couldn't have the young lady getting ideas about her station. But there'd be no getting around spending time in Bristol. He'd need those dirty factory workers and shopkeepers to keep him in office. Chat them up now and again. Make them think they mattered.

His uncle could work the British and Colonial angle. As a test pilot, people would look up to him. Sir Robert's unmarried daughter…was she a possibility? That would be perfect: money, political connections around Bristol, and a job at B&C. Would his uncle come through with the birthday party invite? The RFC didn't normally cut their pilots loose to go to parties, but there had to be at least fifty pilots going back and forth across the Channel every day, and he'd mentioned General Henderson owing him a favor. Maybe they could call it a fact-finding mission: how best to integrate the Bristol Fighter with existing RFC assets blah blah… Well, if it happened, maybe he'd have someone do a little digging on Miss Judith Cawthorne. He absently scanned the sky as he turned it over. Still nothing going on out there.

The mistress? Maybe a tall Russian? Eighteen years old, long blonde hair and blue eyes. After all, ministers of the crown didn't travel in steerage. And if she didn't speak English, she couldn't make trouble. But it wouldn't do to get her pregnant. Could he have her sterilized? But that would mean doctors, interpreters, complications. It might be simpler to find a French girl living in London. The French understood these arrangements.

The sun glinted off something above and to his right. Mildly annoyed at the interruption, he blinked twice and focused on it. A single airplane headed west. He squinted…was it light colored? He throttled up and eased the SE5 into a climb as the intruder disappeared behind some clouds. Crosse studied him when he came into view again. It was light colored, which meant French or German. And if this fellow was German, he'd be a two-seater. A single-seat fighter wouldn't be out there alone, headed west. He slid in behind their visitor and turned to follow. Rested his eyes and scanned the sky before coming back to their friend. Made out the Iron Crosses. A Hun two-seater, and he looked to be alone. Bad luck for him.

He moved Davidson fifty yards behind him as they ran the German down, so both airplanes would be shielded by the Hun's tail. He sorted through his options as they closed the gap. He could go with the (late) Albert Ball Special: angle the overwing Lewis up forty-five degrees, stabilize below the Hun and blast him. Or he could make the traditional nose-on attack using both guns. He decided on the more familiar option and eased the SE5's nose up.

He studied the Hun again as they ran him down. The lower wings were rounded off and smaller than the upper wings. Unusual. Crosse didn't waste time studying drawings of enemy airplanes, but he'd seen this somewhere…early model Rumpler, maybe? He held his nose in front of the German, the airspeed bleeding down to eighty mph. Leaned forward and looked through the Aldis sight—the Hun's wingspan filled about three quarters of the outer circle. Call it medium to long range, which was close enough for a straight and level target.

He eased the column forward and set the aiming dot one ship-length in front of the German's nose. Pushed both triggers for three seconds, enjoying the combined thumping of the Vickers and the Lewis. The rattling of the ammo drum above him; the Vickers belt in front of him. The tracers streaking through the blue sky and disappearing into the Hun. As he let off the triggers he snapped the SE5 onto her back and pulled down and away. He saw no need to give the observer a shot at him.

When he rolled upright, the Hun was in a descending right turn, finally awake to the danger. Davidson was attacking from below and inside the turn. Both the SE5 and the Hun observer were firing—Davidson's faster airplane closing the gap. Crosse pulled his SE5 into a climb, staying between the German and home while keeping his distance. This was the kind of game he liked: two SE5s against a Hun two-seater, on the British side with nowhere to hide. Nor did it matter if this fellow was a Rumpler or an LVG or an XYZ. No two-seater was going to outrun a 200-horsepower SE5.

"He fired one burst from long range and ducked out. But watch. He'll take half the kill."

Crosse was having a beer with one of the other flight commanders and heard Davidson's Scottish accent clear across the room. He raised his voice loud enough to be heard above the chatter.

"Lieutenant Davidson. I saw him. I tracked him. I fired first and put twenty rounds through the forward fuselage. Likely the pilot was half dead before you ever fired a shot."

"Ballocks."

"A succinct rejoinder, Lieutenant, if perhaps lacking in substance. If you'd like to make a formal complaint, we can speak with the major. I believe he's in his office."

Davidson turned to his mates, still muttering. Crosse shrugged and went back to his beer. As far as he was concerned, lieutenants needed to do what they were told and stop thinking they knew anything.

# Pete Catches a Break

*66 Squadron RFC, Sopwith Scout Fighter Aircraft*
*Liettres Aerodrome, Northern France*

"You wanted to see me, sir?" Pete asked Major Stockard. It was his day off and he'd spent most of it in his room with stomach pains, until one of the orderlies had retrieved him.

"Yes. Have a seat, Lieutenant."

Pete sat down and nodded hello to Hugh Fleming, who was sitting in the other chair. The major was holding some official looking document. His fingers were stained from smoking. Other documents were scattered around his desk and overflowing from his inbox. And, of course, the wilderness of papers was paired with the ubiquitous, RFC-approved dirty ashtray.

"Congratulations," said the major. "You've been awarded the Military Cross."

Pete managed a smile. He supposed his mother would be proud of him.

"I know it isn't much. But Britain and the RFC appreciate what you do."

"Thank you, sir." He waited to see if there was anything else. If there wasn't, he'd go lie down again. It turned out there was.

"I think Captain Fleming has a job for you. One you might like. That's all, gentlemen."

Pete followed Hugh Fleming to the office and waited while Fleming found what he was looking for. "They put B1741 back together, and Wing wants it at St. Omer. Fly it over there tomorrow and spend the night. I'm not sure what you'll bring back. There might be a Camel we can borrow, or you may get a nice lorry ride home. Call me Friday morning and I'll let you know."

"Will do, sir. Thank you."

"If you get in a Camel, be careful. They've already crashed a few of them. I'd hate to see you get killed on a simple depot run."

"I appreciate that, sir."

Pete went outside and sat on one of the benches. It'd be dusk soon. He loved that time of day. Peaceful—airplanes and the war aside. St. Omer was a popular trip. It was a way squadron commanders could give their chaps a break, and it was understood pilots often had some mechanical problem that delayed their return for a day or two. It wasn't his style to game the system, but…

He was in the Mess at eight the next morning. Said hello to a pair of B-Flight pilots; sat one table over and picked up the menu. The AM2 came to take his order. "The early fellows said the blood sausage is right good this morning, Lieutenant."

Pete managed not to grimace. He was still getting twinges from his stomach. "I think I'll pass on the blood sausage, airman. Let's go with tea and dry toast."

"Tea and dry toast it is, Lieutenant. That's all me great auntie ate for breakfast, and she's going strong at eighty-three."

"I don't know if I can match great auntie, but let's give it a shot." He ate a leisurely, if sparse, breakfast. Read yesterday's newspaper. It was amazing how many words they could put on a piece of paper without saying anything of substance. Modern journalism.

After breakfast he went back to his room. Did some reading and took a nap. Packed his kit and told his landlady that he wouldn't be home that night. She didn't appear interested in his schedule. He walked down to the squadron building and went to the orderly room; parked himself in front of the situation map. The army was attacking along the entire front. The fellows grinding through the mud and the wire. Through the machine guns and shrapnel shells of the artillery. Clearing out the Huns, yard by yard. He let out a long sigh and went outside. Wandered down to the rigging shop and waved good morning to Paul Fletcher.

"Morning, Lieutenant. What brings you down here?"

"I need to take 1741 to depot, Paul. But first, some good news. We won the Military Cross."

Fletcher raised his eyebrows. "You mean *you* won it, sir. Congratulations."

"No, I mean *we* won it. I couldn't have done it without you and your mates. But more importantly, the flow of cakes from Devon seems to have dried up. I'll see if I can't get things moving again. Chocolate?"

"We won't complain about any cake, Lieutenant. But chocolate is tops for me."

"Good enough. I'll write to my mum as soon as I get back."

Pete had the mechanics walk him through what they'd done. Not that he didn't trust them; rather, it was another chance to learn something. Like most girls, the Pup liked to keep her secrets.

"She came down in a plowed field, sir," A-Flight's lead rigger explained to him. "You know how that is. Broke the undercarriage and the propeller. Bit of wing damage. But she's all good now, sir."

"I'm counting on that, Sergeant."

"She won't let you down, sir. Shame we don't fly two-seaters. I'd sneak on board and go with you."

Pete smiled at that last bit. The ground fellows didn't run the dangers the pilots did but were mostly stuck around the aerodrome. He stowed his bag carefully; he didn't need it hanging up on a control wire. Checked the ignition off, fuel and oil tanks full. Vickers loaded with 250 rounds. Once in the seat, he took extra time checking the flight controls. All the surfaces responded normally to his inputs.

"Switch off."

The mechanics turned the prop and sprayed fuel into the cylinders. "Ready now, sir."

Pete turned the main fuel valve on and pumped up the fuel pressure. And always the last step, flipped on the ignition.

"Switch on."

The mechanic threw the prop and the Le Rhône gave a little snort. Same on the second try. And the third. This wasn't unusual when the airplane had been sitting a few days.

"Switch off, sir."

The chaps were used to this. They shot a little more fuel into the cylinders and the Le Rhône fired up on the next spin. He let her warm up for thirty seconds, did the full power check and headed to the end of the field. As always, idle power was more than the Pup needed for taxi, and he used the blip switch to keep his speed down.

The takeoff was uneventful. He made a quick check of the flight controls as she climbed—all normal. He leveled at 4000 feet and set the throttle and petrol for seventy-five miles per hour. There was no need to hurry, not going to depot. He had to hold a little forward pressure on the column; B1741 was even more tail-heavy than his B5305. There was good visibility and only scattered clouds…it would be a nice day for some sightseeing. He flew southwest toward Abbeville, enjoying the scenery as he got farther away from the war. The occasional village. Farms. Green fields instead of mud. The Germans would have swept through there in '14 on their run toward Paris, but he didn't see anything that looked like a battlefield.

The channel came into view on his right…that soothing presence of the sea. He passed west of the city and turned southeast to follow the muddy and meandering Somme toward the battlefields of last year. He swung south of Amiens; it was clear enough to see the outline of Paris to his right. Beyond Amiens, he'd follow the Ancre up to Albert. To Mametz, where his cousins Martin and Ritchie were buried.

He was looking at Paris and thinking about swimming in the river and climbing on the rocks with his cousins when an odd fluttering came from in front of him. He snapped his eyes forward, and cringed as a metallic chopping and grinding replaced the fluttering. The engine cowling was flapping about and the airplane was yawing to the right. He controlled the yaw with left rudder and throttled the engine back. There was an unusual vibration in his flying boot as he pressed on the rudder bar.

It was unlikely anyone was shooting at him, but he checked the sky behind him to be sure. Scanned the ground for flashes—some Allied troops took anything that flew as fair game. Nothing. He checked the airplane for bird remains and didn't see any—the cowling had just let go. The speed was back to sixty and he let her descend, keeping the wings level and holding a little left rudder pressure. He inspected the Pup. A piece of cowling had torn a chunk out of the forward right upright, kept going and ripped into the horizontal tail. The Pup was flyable, but the cowling was still moving around. If pieces of it kept flying off and hitting things, this could get serious. And was the Le Rhône down on power?

He shook his head. It wasn't worth it. St. Omer could wait. He closed the throttle and petrol lever, and the Le Rhône shut down. He could restart it quick enough if need be.

He let the airspeed roll back to fifty, the wind past his face lessening, and pushed the nose down. There were plenty of fields around to choose from, but he needed one that wasn't plowed and fairly level. A large green field to his right might do the trick, and he swung over to take a closer look. It was fenced in with some trees and a small barn in a corner, but was reasonably level and he'd have plenty of room to work with.

He swung east of the field to land into the wind and made some S turns to work his way down. Frowned as he approached the edge of the field—he was too high. He fed in left rudder and held the wings level with aileron; the Pup nosed sideways and descended faster with the increased drag. He spotted some horses off to his right; they must have been under the trees. Well, they should know enough to stay out of the way. At thirty feet he took the cross controls out and switched off the ignition, chuckling as the horses scattered.

*Nose coming up at five feet...hold her off, Pete...touchdown.*

It wasn't a bad three-point landing, but the ground wasn't as level as he'd thought. The Pup hit a bump and the right wing came up. He went hard right with the column, but she was slow to react and the left wingtip caught the grass. The Pup kicked up dirt and grass as she slewed sideways, the undercarriage flexing under the side load as the wheels chattered across the ground. He cringed, waiting for the snap as the wheel struts gave way...but the undercarriage held and she skidded to a stop. He pushed his goggles up and sniffed the air; he didn't smell fuel. Heard a noise to his right. Four horses were glaring at him, one of them snorting in displeasure. Well, they'd get over it. He double-checked the switches off, climbed out, and dusted off. All in a day's work in the Royal Flying Corps.

First things first, he took his leather jacket off. Collected his things from the Pup and set them on his jacket. Had a long drink of water. An old Frenchman was shaking his fist and shouting at him from the fence—the gist of the message was that he should have landed somewhere else. Pete gave him a friendly wave and turned back to his Pup. The single screw that held the cowling in place had backed out, and as the cowling came loose the spinning rotary had chewed into it. Of course the cowling was done for, but more importantly the rotary had a bent rod and some rocker damage. There were a couple of nasty scratches on the copper intake tubes, but he didn't see any punctures.

He unloaded the Vickers and worked his way around the airplane. Besides damage to the right inboard strut and the fabric of the horizontal tail, the upper support wire to the tail was broken. Despite his bouncy arrival both the undercarriage and the propeller were intact, but the left lower wingtip and aileron were damaged. He slid under the front end of the Pup and inspected the engine area: no fuel or oil was leaking. At least, no more than normal.

His inspection complete, he stood up and looked around. There was a large house at the top of the hill, and he smiled as he remembered Gaspard's story about château breakdowns. He spied two chairs under the trees. Picked up his water bottle, walked over and sat down. He wasn't going to hurry. If the RFC had to do without him for a few days, so be it. He sipped his water and watched the horses, which were keeping their distance. That was fine with him. He'd never been comfortable around horses.

There was activity in front of the house. The old Frenchman must have given the alarm. Two men in uniform came down the hill. They unlatched the gate and came across the field toward him. The first was short and thin, maybe thirty years old. The second man was heftier, in his fifties. Both were wearing a brown military uniform he didn't recognize. The younger man was an officer, the older man an NCO. The officer said something to the NCO as they approached, and it took Pete a few seconds to process what he'd heard. They were speaking Russian, and the man had said something about not hitting the horses.

Pete stood up. "Good afternoon, gentlemen," Pete said in his basic Russian. "I am sorry for arriving like this."

The two men looked at each other. After a few seconds, the officer replied. "You speak Russian, Lieutenant."

"I speak a little Russian," Pete replied slowly. Mark and Charles were old enough to have missed out, but Pete and Phillip had been subjected to three years of tutoring at the insistence of his mother. The officer was considerate enough to speak slowly.

"Are you injured, Lieutenant?"

Pete shook his head, and the officer continued. "I am Captain Mikhail Rudnev, in the service of General Leonid Shuvalov. The sergeant will stay with your airplane. Will you accompany me to the house, Lieutenant?"

"Of course, sir. Let me get my things."

As they walked up the hill, Pete mused on running across Russian military personnel in France. He wasn't particularly surprised. It would be an easy train ride into Paris from there, and there had to be military and diplomatic coordination going on between the two governments. There were lots of moving parts in those days, surrounding the enigma known as Russia.

Pete eyed the large, two-story house. A pair of youths were cleaning windows. Red, white, and yellow flowers welcomed him from well-kept beds. There was a smaller house off to the right, presumably the servants' quarters, and two good-sized barns. A French servant opened the front door for them. He was about fifty years old, dressed in black and white.

Pete brushed himself off again and followed Captain Rudnev through a large foyer and into a sitting room. "There is a washroom if you wish to clean up, Lieutenant," said the captain, motioning toward a closed door. "If you will excuse me."

Pete washed his hands and face. Used his trousers to dry off, rather than ruin the clean white towel. Went back to the sitting room, where the same servant was waiting with a lemonade. "Merci." Pete sat down and sipped the wonderful lemonade. Looked around. Electric lighting. Nice, if somewhat dark furnishings. A pair of French armchairs that had to be a hundred years old. Fortunately, he hadn't plopped down into one of those in his dirty uniform. He felt a twinge of sleepiness by the time the captain came back. "The general will see you now, Lieutenant."

They went through another sitting room into a large room which appeared to be both office and library. A stoutly built man with short white hair was sitting at a desk, wearing a brown military uniform without insignia. Sixty-five years old, Pete guessed. An almost full bookcase covered one of the long walls of the room, and there were two tournament-size chess sets. One was a Staunton, the other had thin red-and-white pieces carved from stone. The butt of a cigar sat in a large glass ashtray on the desk and there was a faint trace of smoke in the air.

"Please sit down, Lieutenant." The voice and tone were gruff, but not unfriendly. "I am General Leonid Shuvalov. Captain Rudnev tells me you speak Russian."

Pete was confused whether to salute or not. He decided against it as the general was not in a proper uniform. He sat down. The captain remained standing. "I speak a little Russian, General, and some French. Although I shall have to ask you to speak slowly, if you don't mind."

"We shall continue in Russian," said the general, not appearing to notice Pete's request. "I do not speak English, although my wife does. You are not injured, Lieutenant?"

Pete shook his head. "No, General."

"I presume you need to inform your unit of your whereabouts?"

"Yes, sir."

"We have a phone here. Captain Rudnev can assist you. We shall move your airplane for safekeeping. My barns are large enough. Nor am I sure my horses appreciate the company of your airplane. Are the wheels intact?"

"They are, General. Nor is it leaking fuel or oil."

"Excellent. I'll have them pull it up." The general leaned back and pulled on a small rope. "You'll want to accompany them?"

"If you please, General."

The same servant appeared. The general gave him some rapid-fire instructions in French and turned back to Pete. "They'll be ready in a few minutes. André will show you to your room when you're finished. Dinner will be at nine. I'm sure my wife will be happy to meet a young English flier."

## PETE CATCHES A BREAK

"I'm sure it will be my pleasure, General. Nine o'clock it is." Pete only paused for another second before standing up. Generals normally didn't pass the time of day with lieutenants.

"I noticed you were looking at my chess sets, Lieutenant."

Pete paused. "I was. They're beautiful quality." Pete motioned toward the red-and-white set. "It's a Calvert, isn't it?"

"Very good, Lieutenant. It is a Calvert. Made in London, around 1830. You must play."

Pete bent down and admired the detailed carving of the pieces. "I used to play quite a bit, General. I'm afraid I don't have the energy for it these days." He straightened up and looked at the far more familiar, light-and-dark-brown wooden set. Staunton. Beautiful in its simplicity. Its functionality. How many hundreds of hours had he spent poring over those pieces—to one win away from reaching the Group of Twelve in the 1912 British Chess Championship.

"We shall play tonight. You will have several hours to rest this afternoon."

Pete knew better than to object. "Would you mind if I borrow a book, General?" Pete asked, motioning toward the bookcase.

The general had already returned to his correspondence. "Consider yourself at home here, Lieutenant," he said without looking up.

Pete looked over the books. All of Tolstoy's works were present, including a well-worn *Anna Karenina*. He'd already washed his hands, but wiped them on a clean spot on his shirt anyway. Opened Volume 1, and as he'd suspected, it was a first edition. He opted for *Resurrection*. Tolstoy's Russian would be well above his level, but such things had never stopped him before. He turned to Captain Rudnev. "If you will accompany me, Lieutenant, I will have the call put through."

A few minutes later, Pete was giving Hugh Fleming a rundown of his situation.

"Russians?"

Pete smiled at the surprise in his voice. "Yes, sir. A general and his wife." Pete stopped there. He doubted Captain Rudnev spoke English well, but there was no need to risk saying the wrong thing.

"Where did you say this place was?"

"Six or eight miles south of Amiens, sir. The South Essertaux Château." He sensed Fleming looking at the map next to his desk.

"Did you make a wrong turn somewhere, Pete? Or are there gale-force winds out of the north today that I'm not aware of?"

"No to both, sir. I was doing a little sightseeing, and was about to turn north when the cowling let go."

"We had one of those last month. Sounds like we need another screw or two on there." Fleming paused for a moment. "Aileron and rigging damage. The cowling. What about the engine?"

"One bent rod. Some rocker damage."

"Propeller? Undercarriage?"

"Both look good, sir."

"I'll talk to the major. I imagine we'll leave you there and send a crew out in the morning. If they can fix it, can you fly it out of there?"

"I think so, sir. If we don't get too much rain."

"Good. Call me back tomorrow afternoon. I don't know that I can get a line to you."

"Will do, sir." Pete rang off.

They went outside. Four Frenchmen were waiting with a horse and cart. Once they got down to the field, the Frenchmen dug the fence posts out and secured ropes from the undercarriage to the cart. They pulled the Pup up the hill without incident, untied the ropes and pushed her into a barn. Pete found some boards to chock the wheels in place and walked around the airplane once more. Looking her over, moving the flight controls. The Pup was a bit battered but seemed content in her new home.

André was waiting for him at the front door, and led him upstairs to a guest room with a small balcony and a bathroom next door. Someone had put a plate of fruit and cheese on the side table, along with a pitcher of

# PETE CATCHES A BREAK

water and a small bottle of wine. Two Russian uniforms without insignia were on the bed. One looked to be for everyday use; the second was more formal, with a tie. "If you put your clothes in the bag and leave them in the hallway, Lieutenant, I will have them washed and pressed. Is there anything else you need?"

"No, thank you."

"If you need anything, or if the clothes do not fit, ring the bell and someone will come."

Pete went onto the balcony after André left. Below him was a large patio with tables and chairs, and a small lake with shade trees. Impressive, and likely more expensive than what could be managed on the salary of a Russian general, however much that might be. Well, it wasn't his concern how they acquired their château—he'd already given up thinking of it as a house. He went back inside and looked in the mirror. He was still grimy despite the washup downstairs. If they rated engines on the amount of muck they threw off, the Le Rhône would win hands down.

He drew a hot bath, stripped off his clothes and put them in the bag. Took his time in the bath. Dried off and put on the everyday Russian uniform; lay down on the bed. After lying there for twenty minutes, surprised he didn't fall asleep, he picked up his book and went out back. Found a chair in the shade of an oak tree and started working his way through *Resurrection*. As he'd suspected, it was tough going.

"Bon après-midi." He greeted the old French gardener, who had set to work on the shrubs.

"Bon après-midi, Lieutenant."

He managed a short nap in the afternoon and took another bath to be one hundred percent sure he didn't smell like castor oil when he met the general's wife. Dressed and ready, he inspected himself in the mirror. The dress uniform was only a little too large. He made one last adjustment to the tie and looked at the clock. It was fifteen minutes to nine. He'd wait ten more minutes before going downstairs. Not that he was hungry. He'd been reading in one of the sitting rooms around five o'clock and they'd brought him tea and biscuits—presumably an English-based adjustment to their normal meal schedule.

"My dear, allow me to present Lieutenant Peter Newlynn of the British Air Service. Lieutenant, my wife, the lady Anya Nikolaevna Shuvalova."

"Welcome to our home, Lieutenant." The general's wife greeted him in Russian. Her voice had a tiny scratch in it, as if her vocal cords had been damaged years before. She gave him a practiced smile and extended her hand. Pete bowed and brushed her hand with his lips. Looked at her as he straightened up. She was tall and on the thin side. Fair skin. Long dark-red hair and blue eyes. Pointy, attractive features. She was wearing a blue dress with black lace trim and a white pearl necklace. He guessed she was a year or two older than himself.

"Thank you, Madame. It is a pleasure to be here and make your acquaintance. And that of your husband." He'd reviewed his Russian greetings earlier in the afternoon, and didn't correct the general on his last name.

"I hope your room is comfortable, Lieutenant," said the general.

"Very comfortable, General."

"And you were able to communicate with your unit?"

"Yes, sir. They will send a crew tomorrow, although it will take a day or two to fix the airplane. If more convenient, I can remove myself to the town. I do not wish to be an imposition on you or your wife."

"Nonsense, Lieutenant. My wife and I would take it very much amiss if you did not stay with us. Also, you and I have a game later."

"Yes, General. I'm looking forward to it." Which wasn't quite true, but he was rested enough to deal with a game of chess. The general's wife looked at him with a friendly expression.

"You must certainly stay with us, Lieutenant. My husband has claimed you to play chess, and so it shall be. Also, a friend of mine is visiting tomorrow, and she will wish to meet you."

"Come, dear, let us have dinner," said the general, and motioned for Pete to follow his wife.

As Pete was closer to her, he held her chair out. He glanced at her shoes as she sat down. Well-polished black high heels, with white stockings showing underneath the crisscrossing straps. A tidbit his stepfather had passed along: women with class pay attention to their shoes. Not that it mattered that night.

"Thank you, Lieutenant" she said, sitting upright on the front half of her chair.

Pete waited for the general to sit before sitting down. He glanced at the general's wife again and reminded himself to watch his manners, and his posture. He'd worried they might sit at some enormous table and have to shout, but this looked like a table for eight. The dining room itself was large; no doubt they had more tables when needed.

As he'd expected, dinner was a drawn-out affair. The general didn't say much, tending to his appetite. His wife ate sparingly and kept up the conversation with Pete, who replied between small bites. He was careful not to overeat; his stepfather had counseled the boys that social lunches and dinners were not for eating. She asked about his home, his family, how he became a pilot. He kept his answers friendly but short, having to mentally go back and forth between English and Russian each time.

"How is it you speak Russian, Lieutenant?"

"My father died when I was young, Madame. My stepfather is half Russian, and my mother engaged a tutor for us. I have to admit neither my brother Phillip nor I was terribly interested at the time."

"Call me Anya, please, and I shall call you Peter. If you don't mind?"

"Of course not, Anya." Pete wasn't comfortable calling her by her first name. But she had asked, and the general didn't look concerned.

"I'd rather not hear stories of people being killed, Peter. But can you give me an impression, an idea, of what it's like to be a pilot at the front?"

Pete thought carefully before answering. He was speaking with a Russian lady at the dinner table. "Some days it's the greatest feeling in the world, Anya. When a mission goes well. Or on a day off and the chaps are relaxing by the river. Other days it's frustrating. Some of the orders we get from headquarters don't make sense…and the Germans have better equipment than we do. But the pilots know that we're in France to support the army. Ultimately, it will be the armies—Russian, French, British, and eventually the Americans—who will win this war for us."

The general gave a little snort. "I wouldn't count too much on the Russian Army, Peter."

"My husband fought the Germans in 1914, but is no longer on active duty," said Anya. "I don't believe he misses it."

The general nodded agreement without looking up from his roast beef.

After dinner, they retired to one of the sitting rooms. The general poured vodka for himself and Pete, and a glass of wine for his wife. "Dear, perhaps Peter is wondering why we're here in France," said Anya.

"Of course, my dear." The general didn't seem upset at his wife's prodding him to speak about their situation. They appeared to have a polite marriage.

"After the defeat at Tannenberg, I was removed from active duty and made an adviser to our ambassador to France. My family lived here when I was young, and I speak the language. As the problems within Russia became more serious, and Anya and I being fond of horses, we purchased this château. We also keep a small apartment in Paris as I travel there for my government work."

The mention of Tannenberg caught Pete's ear. "Were you at Tannenberg, General?"

"I was." The general's face was blank.

"I've read everything I could find, but it's all very muddled. Would you mind telling me about it? Without giving away any secrets, of course."

The general looked at Pete for a couple of seconds—perhaps deciding how much he wanted to say. "I commanded an infantry division in the Second Army. Almost everything that could go wrong, did go wrong.

Besides being a fool, the front commander was too far removed to know what was happening. Even if we had executed well, the plan was flawed. First and Second Armies were too widely separated to support each other. Not in the face of German rail mobility." The general paused to sip his vodka.

"The army commanders didn't know where their corps were, the corps commanders didn't know where their divisions were, and no one had any idea where the Germans were."

The general let out a sigh, and his tone was more resigned when he resumed. "I knew it would be a disaster days before the Germans struck. Their reconnaissance airplanes were overhead—they knew where we were. Headquarters transmitted some of our orders in the clear. It is likely the Germans were listening in. Other times, we received coded messages and my radio teams couldn't decode them." The general finished his vodka and poured another.

"In the larger sense, there were many reasons for what happened. Tension between the war ministry and the general staff. The tsar, and even the tsarina, were making command appointments. General Rennenkampf, in command of the First Army, was a fair soldier. General Samsonov, Second Army, was more the plain, old soldier type. But they hated each other and the plan required close cooperation between them. Nor did our seniority system help. My corps commander had no field experience. Not one day, in a thirty-five-year career." The general shook his head. "No field experience. Fighting a modern war against the German Army."

"Your soldiers paid a terrible price. But if the newspapers were correct, your offensive took some pressure off France. That the Germans shifted several divisions to the East."

"That is true, Peter. And there was enormous pressure to attack. But throwing the armies forward before they were ready was foolish. If we had waited a few weeks, organized the troops better and rethought the plan, it might have turned out differently. But that is not the Russian way."

Pete looked from the general to the floor. The British press often characterized Russian generals as overbearing, arrogant, drunken fools. This man was strong willed and drank vodka, but he was no fool.

"Might you return to active duty someday, General?"

The general shook his head. "Many officers fell out of favor after Tannenberg, including myself. It is unlikely we will return to Russia."

Pete waited, but the general left it there, and Anya spoke. "As he says, my husband works for our government. But who or what the Russian government is these days, that is a little difficult to say. What do you think of the Bolsheviks, Peter?"

"I hate them," came out before he could stop himself.

"Pardon me. I did not intend to speak so harshly." He looked from Anya to the general, but no offense had been taken.

"Please continue, Peter. You are among friends here," said Anya. He was watching her as she spoke, the yellow white of the light bulbs highlighting her red hair. He changed his mind. This woman wasn't attractive—she was beautiful. Stunningly so. He forced his eyes away from her. "Very well. The Bolsheviks say they're all about helping the common man. But what I see is a hunger for power, and a willingness to use terror to get it." The general nodded.

"If the Bolsheviks take over, it will be anarchy." He finished his vodka and set the glass down on the wood table with a little *thunk* sound. "The tsar shouldn't have taken command of the army. He has no knowledge of military affairs. Perhaps someone with more strength of character could have done it, by appealing to the soldiers. But Tsar Nicholas wasn't that person. When he left Petrograd the tsarina and the monk stepped in, and events spun out of control."

The general had moved to the window. He spoke without turning around. "Their Soviet Order Number One undermined the authority of the officers. Soldiers refusing to obey orders after eight hours on duty. The Provisional Government is caught between the socialist parties on the left and Kornilov and the industrialists on the right. Most of the soldiers

## PETE CATCHES A BREAK

simply want an end to the fighting, and the Bolsheviks are the one party that promises that. Along with land reform—the great desire of the peasant class. And no doubt the Germans are watching closely. The rumor is they helped Lenin return to Russia. If they obtain a separate peace in the east, they can concentrate all their power for an offensive in the west. It would be their best chance yet to win the war." The general turned around. "Come, Peter. Enough talk. Let us play."

Anya stood up. "I shall leave you gentlemen to it. Good night, dear. Good night, Peter."

Both men said good night. The general drew the white pieces. "Ninety minutes each, Peter?"

"That's fine, General."

The general opened with Ruy Lopez—one of the oldest and most famous chess openings. Pete went with the exchange variation and the first six moves ran according to theory—to a position he'd seen many times before. Pete slowly gained the upper hand, arriving at the endgame up a knight and two pawns and over thirty minutes ahead on time. The general studied the board for another few minutes before turning the clock off.

"I think we can stop here, Peter." The tone was the slightest bit icy. "Very well played. Of course, I shall insist upon a rematch."

"Well played on your side as well, General. And I will be happy to play again, subject to my RFC duties. But not tonight, please."

"No, not tonight, Peter. I think we both can use some rest." The general motioned to the door. "After you," he said politely.

Pete didn't sleep well and was up early the next morning. He shaved and put on the everyday Russian uniform. Went downstairs quietly, found yesterday's paper and sat on the patio. One of the maids brought him a cup of coffee. "Merci."

She smiled at him and gave a little curtsy. She had a pretty but worn face and was missing a front tooth. He sat back with his coffee and enjoyed the quiet of a summer morning away from the war. Finished his coffee and the non-news of the newspaper; set it aside and walked down to the pasture.

The sun was up, shining off the wet green of the grass. Wisps of fog shrouded the ground here and there. There was a ragged brown tear in the grass from where the Pup's wheels had skidded sideways. It was quiet; the horses weren't out yet. The only noise was the faint chirping of a bird from somewhere in the trees.

He walked into town and found a little café. Ordered breakfast and read *Le Matin*. There were a couple of stories reprinted from the *Times*. The navy shot down a Gotha returning from a raid. The bombers had only made it as far as Southend, where they bombed a bunch of civilians. Again. There was a row in the War Cabinet—the one Labour member resigned when the rest of the cabinet wouldn't go along with his proposal for an international conference on the war. Whatever.

He walked back to the château and worked his way through Tolstoy for a couple of hours before needing a break. He lay down, and a knocking at the door woke him. He sat up and straightened his hair. Had a crazy thought it was Anya at his door. "Come in."

André appeared in the doorway. "Good morning, Lieutenant. I have brought you some breakfast, and the lady Anya asks if you would join her for lunch on the patio at one o'clock." André pursed his lips at Pete's appearance. "She will have company, Lieutenant. You may wish to clean up. I have your uniform here, and I believe it would be suitable for lunch."

Pete thanked him and ate some toast and fruit. Took a leisurely bath. Dressed carefully and read more Tolstoy, this time without falling asleep. At one o'clock, he went downstairs and found Anya and a small, silver-haired lady on the patio. "Good afternoon, Peter. May I present the Countess Natalia Miklailova Dumina."

"Good afternoon, Countess." Pete brushed the small, soft hand with his lips. "It is a pleasure to meet you." He turned to the general's wife.

"I hope you slept well, Madame."

She was wearing a silver dress with a black silk scarf. He preferred the dark blue, but she was one of those women who would look good in almost anything. "I did, thank you. And please call me Anya."

"Yes. Anya." He was still struggling with that. "And I apologize for missing breakfast. I was up early and had walked into town."

"Not a concern, Peter. We don't do a formal breakfast here, as Leonid and I keep different schedules."

"You and the general played chess last night, Peter?" the countess asked.

"We did. I'm afraid I was a disrespectful guest, and won." Anya looked at him, eyes slightly wide.

"You won, Peter?"

"I did, yes." Pete didn't know what the issue was. He'd won lots of chess games.

The ladies looked at each other. "How did he take that?" asked the countess.

Anya shook her head. "I don't know. I don't see him at night. He prefers his French lover. I'm told she's only twenty, with lovely long blonde hair."

At that last bit, Pete took a few moments to admire the garden. The countess nodded. "Yes, men are like that. Not all men, of course," she added, looking at Pete, who was finishing up his study of the foliage.

"No, my dear. Peter strikes me as a proper English gentleman."

"Though I imagine it was hard on your husband. He fancies himself quite the expert, doesn't he? Along with food and the army, he seems fascinated with chess."

"He spoke politics quite reasonably last night. As I told you, Peter shares our dislike of the Reds." The countess looked at Pete again. Sizing him up?

"As to how Leonid took it…well, since Peter is here with us, Leonid didn't have him shot. And someone would have told me if Leonid had died of a heart attack during the night. Apparently, he has weathered the storm."

"We have a rematch set for tonight. But the RFC will expect me to return to duty as soon as my airplane is fixed."

Anya smiled, looking beautiful as the dappled sunlight shone on her fair skin and red hair. "Leonid has quite a bit of influence around here, Peter. I wouldn't count on your airplane being fixed too quickly."

Two footmen in black and white brought lunch. First, a thick Russian black bread with butter, which he loved. Followed by beef and vegetables, which he ate reluctantly, already full on the bread. All served on ornate but worn china. Both women ate sparingly, making small talk about Paris. The countess looked at him when they finished eating, and he guessed the small talk was over.

"Peter, no one knows how the struggle at home will turn out. If the Provisional Government can hang on—"

She was speaking quickly and Pete struggled to understand. He looked to Anya for help.

"My dear Natalia. We are all impressed with how well Peter speaks Russian. But please try to speak a little more slowly. I doubt he speaks Russian frequently these days."

"Of course, my dear. My apologies, Peter. Would you prefer we speak French?"

"No apology necessary, Countess. And thank you, but I prefer we continue in Russian."

"Civil war is coming to Russia, Peter." She was speaking slowly, and he nodded he understood. "The Reds are powerful and will stop at nothing to take over. The Allies will not want a Russia controlled by the Reds. Would they fight with us to stop that?"

Pete looked from the countess's earnest face to the trees. Would the Allies intervene in a Russian civil war? Foreign military incursions into Russia often didn't turn out well. The difficulties were well documented. The general joined them, and after an exchange of greetings Pete did his best to answer. "Assume the Allies defeat Germany and there is open war in Russia. Would the Allies intervene against the Reds? Our Unionist Party would be in favor. The Liberal Party, perhaps not. Labour, no. France is weary of war. America…I don't think President Wilson would be in favor. And he has the American Congress to answer to."

The general was watching him, but didn't say anything. Pete moved from international politics to more familiar ground. "Intervention would not be easy. Russia is a large country and a long way from Britain and America. The terrain is rugged, and there is extreme weather in both summer and winter. Could the Allies intervene with enough force to make a difference, and sustain that force for the time necessary? Years, presumably. Would our leaders be willing to pay the political price of more war?"

"As you say, there would be difficulties," said the countess. "But we will have to fight the Reds and Allied help could make the difference." She looked to the general.

"You are both correct. As Peter says, meaningful Allied assistance would be difficult. But the Reds are powerful and ruthless. It will not be easy to defeat them."

The four of them were silent for a few moments, and once again, Pete was struck by the quiet beauty of the château. "You are a lieutenant now, Peter?" the countess asked.

"That is correct."

"If the war were to last two more years, what rank should you attain?"

"Most likely major. Squadron commander. Assuming I stay alive, of course. Pilot losses are high."

"Someone like yourself could be valuable to our side. It would be good to keep you alive. And, of course, we are most fond of you."

"I appreciate that, Countess." Pete kept the skepticism out of his voice. Surely these people wouldn't bother about a lieutenant, on the very unlikely chance their influence extended to RFC personnel decisions. Nor would he want them to.

"There are several French squadrons operating in Russia now," said the general, "and some of our pilots are being trained in Britain. These efforts are made in the fight against Germany; however the framework could prove useful. Of course, the Reds will be thinking the same thing."

Captain Rudnev arrived and whispered something to the general. "Some British personnel are in the town, asking for the château." Pete started to get up, but the general motioned for him to sit. "Let us have another glass of wine in the company of these lovely ladies, Peter. If your people don't find us, we shall go and find them."

"What do you think?" Pete asked. Paul Fletcher and two other A-Flight mechanics had finished looking over the Pup.

"The cowling and the tail won't be difficult, sir. We'll tape up the strut. But the wingtip damage and the aileron will be a lot of work. No chance we'll finish today."

Pete turned to A-Flight's engine mechanic. "Tom?"

"I need to replace two rockers, sir. The bent rod. Four or five hours, I'd say."

Pete explained to Captain Rudnev that the crew would finish sometime tomorrow.

"Very well, Lieutenant. I will speak with the general. There are rooms in the servants' quarters. They are not as nice as your room, but perhaps nicer than what these gentlemen have at the unit."

Pete turned back to Paul Fletcher. "They take good care of their guests here, Paul. You chaps work until dinner. After that, you're due some rest."

Pete watched as they went to work. He always learned something from watching the chaps, but that said, they didn't need an officer looking over their shoulders. "I'll leave you fellows to it. Knock on the front door if you need me."

"Sounds good, sir," said Paul Fletcher from under the wing.

Pete retrieved his book and made himself comfortable in one of the sitting rooms. An hour later, he was back in the barn. Fletcher and another mechanic had the aileron off and were working on the wingtip, and Tom had engine parts scattered around the nose of the Pup. Knowing he couldn't keep bothering them, he went back to the house and read for most of the afternoon. Worn out by Tolstoy, he took a long nap, followed by an English-style tea in one of the sitting rooms.

"Your maintenance gentlemen did not wish to stop working, Lieutenant," André told him. "I had their tea served in the barn. I hope that is acceptable?"

"Perfectly acceptable, André. Thank you."

He finished his tea and stared at the book on the side table. Decided he needed some fresh air and went outside. The sun was low in the western sky, without a breath of wind. He walked down to the pasture and sat under the trees. The sun lit the bright green leaves, but on the shadowy side they were almost black. A pair of squirrels darted about the branches above him. A horse walked on the grass. One could forget Europe was at war.

He spied a horse and rider; it was easy enough to recognize Anya with her long red hair. She waved to him as she reined in, and exchanged a few words with a boy who must have been in the barn. She pointed at the horse's left foreleg as she stroked his muzzle with her long fingers. The boy squatted down and looked at the leg before leading the horse into the barn. Pete stood up as she walked toward him.

"Do you like sitting under trees, Peter?" she asked in Russian-accented English.

"I do, Anya. Especially at this time of day."

"Then let us sit. We have a few minutes before dinner." She sat in the other chair and shook out her long hair.

"You must enjoy riding. You looked comfortable."

"I love horses. So does Leonid. It is one interest we share."

"What else do you like to do?" he asked, not wanting the conversation to move to the general's other interests. Young blonde Frenchwomen, for example.

"I work in the garden. With my flowers. I read. Paris is interesting. Leonid goes there for his government work. I don't go so much anymore. It's quiet here, but it's home."

"Did you meet the countess in Russia?"

"Only once or twice. Our families are acquainted, in the south. I was good friends with two of her cousins, and Natalia and I became the best of friends here in France. As you know, she is most concerned about our Mother Russia."

He looked for something innocuous to say, to stay away from politics but keep the conversation going. To sit with her as the sun went down. "Did you buy the horses with the château?"

"Three of them, yes. The black mare showed up one morning a few months back. The doctor took a piece of metal out of her hip. She's better now, but we don't ride her." Anya shook her hair again and brushed it back with her hands. One of those simple and lovely motions women make. "You're not married, Peter?"

He didn't flinch at the change of subject. "No."

"Do you have a woman you are planning to marry? Or am I being too personal?"

He didn't see any harm in playing along. "There's a French girl I care for," he said slowly. "Am I planning to marry her? I wouldn't go that far. And I should call her a woman, not a girl. She's twenty-four and has two children."

"I was nineteen when I married Leonid. My father arranged it. We met once before we were engaged. It didn't work out as planned. As you can see, no children."

He considered making a veiled compliment—that she was still young. Decided against it. She was looking at the horses and he studied her in the fading light. A beautiful woman to be sure, but more than that. Was it the way she carried herself? Proud. Yet reserved. What was behind that beauty? Behind that Russian dignity? Boredom? Emptiness, if not outright sadness? Had this woman ever made love, as opposed to having her body used for sex? He'd guess that she hadn't, not that it was any of his business.

She gave him a side look. "A woman always knows when a man is thinking something, Peter."

She'd caught him off guard, but he recovered quickly.

"I know what your husband said last night, but would you like to return to Russia someday? If the Reds don't take over?"

She looked at him with eyebrows raised, seeming to know that wasn't what he'd been thinking. She shook her head. "Not with Leonid. But he's almost forty years older than I. After that…return to Russia? I have family there, but I don't think so. Although I would not stay here. It would be too lonely."

"Paris?"

She frowned. "I would tire of the opera and society. I much prefer horses. I have cousins in England, somewhere west of London. I would enjoy living there."

"My home is west of London, although I imagine farther west than your cousins."

"Then we may be neighbors someday. Come, Peter, let us return to the house. We mustn't be late for dinner."

He stood up and put out his hand, and wasn't surprised by the strength of her grasp. As he followed her through the gate, he couldn't stop his eyes from going to her small hips.

Anya and the general had insisted on lunch before he left, and he'd been happy to comply. After all, he was only going to depot, then back to the war. After a leisurely lunch, the mechanics pushed the Pup down to a second, less bumpy, pasture. He shook hands with Anya and the general, both of whom insisted, for the second time, that he return to visit. He promised he would try.

The Le Rhône was reluctant to start, but Fletcher and the chaps were used to that. They turned the propeller a few times and shot fuel into the cylinders until she cooperated. The smell of castor oil hit him as she fired up—he hadn't missed that. Preflight checks done, goggles down. He gave one last wave and pushed the throttle to three-quarters. The Le Rhône coughed at the extra air as he brought the petrol lever forward to 40 percent. The engine caught and roared, and the Pup started forward. He tweaked the petrol lever back as the Pup gathered speed, bouncing across the uneven ground, and eased the column forward to bring the tail up as the airplane came alive. She was light on her wheels…gave one last little skip…and lifted off.

As she rose he nudged the mixture forward, listening to the hum of the rotary. Banked left as the Pup climbed and held her in the turn. Came back right…and steadied up. The Pup was responding normally, and the cowling was rock steady with three new screws holding it in place. At 500 feet he turned back toward the house, taking care not to fly over the horses. Lowered the nose to build airspeed, pulled up and did two small barrel rolls followed by a goodbye wing rock.

He turned the Pup north. Climbed to 5000 feet and set the throttle and mixture for a comfortable cruise. Automatically scanned the vacant sky as he weaved around the occasional cloud. There'd been more discussion of Russia's future last night. At the first break in the conversation Pete had asked about the horses, and the general had talked for a good ten minutes. Not that Pete was interested in horses, but he'd had enough of Russian politics.

They'd played chess after dinner and Pete won again, running through the combinations more quickly than the night before. The general was polite enough, but it was clear he didn't enjoy losing. Pete gave an invisible shrug. He liked the general, but if you don't want to lose, don't play.

# The RE8

*6 Squadron RFC, RE8 Reconnaissance Aircraft*
*Abeele Aerodrome, Western Belgium*

"You ready, Harry?" asked Norman from the next table. Harry was finishing up lunch with Thomas and Ethan—their two wonderful days of heavy rain and low clouds were over. He and his roommates had relaxed by playing cards, engaging in mindless chatter, and (other than Thomas) drinking whisky. The weather outside wasn't great, but it wasn't bad enough to ground them.

Captain Harvey and their intel officer were waiting in the orderly room. "C-Flight's switched over, Norm," said Harvey. "It's the RE8 today."

Norman didn't seem excited, but to Harry, this was excellent news. The RE8 was faster and sturdier than the BE2, and he'd be in the backseat. Where he belonged.

"Have you flown it before, Norman?" he asked.

"No. But all airplanes fly the same. Up, down, left, right. Push the throttle forward to take off. Pull it back to land."

Harry shrugged. If Norman wasn't worried, neither was he.

## CHANGES WROUGHT

Lieutenant Brooke spread a familiar map out in front of them. "Standard trench bombardment, fellows. Your target is the Hun's reserve defensive line—the back side of the ridge, running from Zandvoorde up to G-Velt. Your battery position is…right here. Battery C of the One-Ninetieth. Six eighteen-pounders. Check-in and targeting procedures are laid out in the ops order. They're all standard—I imagine you fellows have seen them before. The battery commander told us overcast skies with a ceiling of about fifteen hundred feet and fair visibility. Any questions for me?"

Norman shook his head. "Done it before once or twice." He looked at Captain Harvey. "No escort today, Captain?"

"None dedicated, but Fifty-Six will be sweeping the area. They're supposed to be at medium altitude. Doesn't sound like that's going to happen."

"They have the SE5 now, don't they?" asked Norman. The RO nodded.

"I'd be willing to transfer to the SE5, sir. You know, for the good of the service."

That brought a smile from the normally dour Captain Tom Harvey. "That's great, Norm. I'll run down and tell the major. I imagine he'll put a call in to General Trenchard straight away."

Harry stared at them. Levity from these two? Loosening up? Cracking up?

Ten minutes later, he was admiring their RE8. For starters, she had a real engine: a 140 horsepower RAF V-12. She should do at least a hundred miles per hour—which meant getting across the line quicker. A forward-firing Vickers along with his Lewis gun, not that they'd be doing much dogfighting. At least he hoped not. He climbed into the rear seat and looked around his new home. A rack with five of the new double-stacked ammo drums. Almost five hundred rounds. He'd have to be careful about overheating the barrel, but he wouldn't need to worry about running out of ammo. Excellent field of fire. But like most two-seaters, firing forward or dead astern would be out of the question.

# THE RE8

Engine start and taxi-out were uneventful, other than Harry appreciating the extra five feet of space from the engine. Norman leveled them at 2000 feet, skimming the bottom of a solid cloud deck. Harry peeked at the airspeed indicator as the moist air rushed past him. Smiled under his scarf: 105 miles per hour. He tapped Norman on the shoulder and pointed to the Lewis gun; fired a five-round burst. The low clouds would mean fewer options for the Hun fighters, and if he and Norman got into trouble they could disappear into the clouds quick enough. Even better, Archie struggled with airplanes at low altitude. The only problem was they'd be within range of the German machine guns. Well, couldn't have everything one's way.

They motored along below the clouds, with no sign of the sun. Some familiar rubble came into view left of the nose, shrouded in a smokey haze: Wipers. He spotted six single-seaters south of them, headed east. SE5s. They came abeam the lake and Norman circled. It began to rain. Harry leaned outboard and checked the altimeter: the ceiling was down to 1300 feet. Norman's head went down for the check-in—what a relief not to have to deal with the wireless. They made three circles as his scarf soaked up rainwater. He was more than willing to go home, and snorted as they got the "Being Received" signal from the ground. *Too bad.*

They turned east, leaving the artillery behind. Ahead of them, the forward British trenches formed dark lines in the mud. Farther on, the dead gray strip that marked no-man's-land. A strip which, according to the intel fellows, had agonized its way a thousand or so yards east over the last two weeks. The chaps were pushing forward—the big attack (another big attack?) had finally come. And just in time for the rain. He shook his head as he scanned below them. If there was anything in the world as ugly as the forward area in Flanders, he hadn't seen it. Made the Liverpool docks on a rainy day look downright cheery. Norman eased them up into the clouds and they droned through the gray for a few minutes before descending. Norman studied the ground below…and banked hard right. Harry put a hand against the railing to steady himself and looked down as they turned…a few isolated trees shorn of their leaves. Other trees lying on the ground, an occasional branch pointed skyward. Like little toy soldiers tossed about by a child. *Kneeling rifleman, over there, you're dead. Officer with a pistol in one hand and waving with the other, right here. You're dead, too.* He went back to his defensive scan, still marveling at how much he could see from the rear cockpit. A couple of flashes came from the ground. Rifle fire. A machine gun joined in, the tracers passing off to their right, and Norman swung the RE8 left. Six shells exploded into the mud below them as the battery opened fire. Norman hadn't bothered with ranging shots today; maybe he had a date and was in a hurry to get back. If so, that was fine with Harry. Six more explosions followed a few seconds later. Six more. Harry stared at the impacts—at the clouds of smoke and dirt. At a tree trunk cartwheeling through the air. The RE8 wobbled from the shock waves, and he smiled grimly. All that from one little six-gun battery of eighteen-pounders, and there were hundreds of RFA batteries in Flanders.

Norman pulled them back into the clouds and got on the wireless, likely switching to another target. With nothing else to do, Harry inspected the airplane. There were three holes in the right wing, about halfway out. *Tisk, tisk.* Some nice ladies had done all that work, and the Huns had ruined their new fabric.

They slid out of the clouds and another stream of tracers reached toward them. *All right you bastards, two can play this game.* He swung the Lewis around, set his sight level with the flashes and adjusted back to allow for the speed of the RE8. Let go a three-second burst, kicking up mud short and left, but close enough to make the Huns stop shooting. *Weren't expecting that, were you, fellows?*

He saw something moving under the netting, reset his aim and fired again. Saw two little sparks as bullets hit metal. Maybe that'd be one less machine gun to deal with. As he finished that thought a stream of tracers passed by them. Close. Closer, and he instinctively leaned away as he swung the Lewis around.

# THE RE8

*Thud, thud, thud.* He winced as the RE8 absorbed bullets, sounding like someone was hammering on plywood, and a split second later the floor underneath his feet exploded in a shower of splinters. Something stabbed into his right leg—he gritted his teeth as pain shot through him. Eyes wide and watering. With one hand squeezing the Lewis, he grabbed the railing with the other and twisted around to look forward. Cringed as more bullets ricocheted off the engine, and Norman's head jerked back.

The RE8 rolled slowly right, its nose falling toward the ground. She went steeper into the dive, still rolling. Almost onto her back. The rush of the air got louder as she accelerated downward.

Harry stared at the mud rising toward him. *No, he agonized, No! I'm not ready!*

He yelled at Norman. Nothing. He looked past him; he could see it clearly now. The sucking mud, the bits of trash and broken metal, flanked by shell holes and busted up barbed wire. His grave.

He yelled at Norman again. Lunged forward, grabbed him on the shoulder and pulled. Norman's head came back and lolled to the side, and Harry's heart sank. He tried to ask forgiveness and gave up after a few words. Watched with sick despair as the mud rose toward them. His arms went to the railings. Pushing. Trying somehow to stay away from the rising mud. And then, the most beautiful thing he'd ever seen—the RE8 was rolling upright. He bit his lip and tried praying again. The nose tracked up and the mad descent slowed. He looked at Norman; he was sitting almost straight up in his seat. The airplane pulled through the horizon and into a climb, bottoming out low enough for him to see the dirty faces of the Huns. To see their scruffy beards as they blasted away with their rifles and machine guns.

An incredible wave of relief washed over him. They were alive, and he forced himself to breathe through the throbbing and searing of his leg. He pressed gently with both hands to slow the bleeding. Was he bleeding to death? If he was, he didn't want to face up to it yet, and looked at the ground as the RE8 rose. They were paralleling a large road, which faded into the haze, then disappeared as they went into the clouds. He'd seen that road before. But where?

They came out of the clouds a few seconds later, nose low and in a left bank. Was Norman flying the RE8, or was it flying him? Well, he'd worry about that later. The airplane settled down and he studied the road again… It was the Menin Road; he recognized it from the photoshoot. But something wasn't right. He leaned forward and looked left, then right, careful not to move his leg. Forced his brain to process what his eyes were seeing, which looked nothing like the frontline area. A couple of seconds later it clicked. They were headed east.

He grabbed Norman on the shoulder, but gently this time. "Turn, Norman! We need to turn around."

Nothing. He made a sweeping motion with his arm. "We're going the wrong way! We're headed east!"

Norman didn't move, but a few seconds later the RE8 banked left. The nose dropped as she turned and the airplane descended, but Harry didn't say anything. Altitude didn't matter much right then, as long as they didn't hit the ground. Once they got turned around, he pointed straight ahead and pumped his arm twice.

"Roll out, Norman! Roll out. We're headed west."

The RE8 was bobbing up and down, wandering left and right like a drunken sailor, but they were headed in the general direction of home. He took a deep breath; noticed his gloves were sticky with blood. He held them against his leg again. Coughed twice. Black smoke was streaming past his face, covering his goggles with a sooty film.

He leaned outboard and looked at the engine: smoke was pouring out the side. The Huns had holed the exhaust manifold, or maybe a cylinder wall, the way it was running. He tried to spit the taste out, but it stuck to his mouth and tongue. A stream of tracers went by his head, the last few bullets punching through the tail section. The bastards didn't want to leave them alone.

# THE RE8

He let go of his leg, swung the Lewis around and fired a long burst. Reset his aim and fired again. Kept at it until the Lewis quit. Deciding he wasn't up to changing the ammo drum, he looked around the cockpit. At least three bullets had come through the floor—bloody good shooting by some Hun down there. And now the part he'd been dreading. Sick to his stomach, he pulled at the torn fabric and looked at his leg. Would the blood be bright red, pulsing from the torn artery? No, thank God. There was lots of blood, but it was a reassuring, dull red.

They disappeared into the clouds again and came out about a minute later, in a shallow dive and banked left. He went to grab Norman when the RE8 steadied up. Harry focused on his breathing for a few seconds, holding pressure on his leg as he studied the ground in front of them. They were descending and heading southwest, and that was good enough for now. But they needed to get on the ground. Bailleul would be closest. He grabbed his map and held it against his leg; red blotches appeared as blood soaked into the paper. He eyeballed the distance to Bailleul...maybe twelve air miles. Could Norman make it that far?

They weaved and wobbled toward home as tracers streamed past, punching more holes in the airplane. They were almost over the line when the RE8 shook from more impacts. That horrible scraping of metal smashing against metal; bullets ricocheting past him. He hunkered down for a couple of seconds, but he hadn't been hit. Turned forward and got a blast of fuel vapor. Norman looked frozen in his seat. Harry unbuckled and leaned forward. Fuel was spraying from under the instrument panel. He pushed Norman's hand off the throttle and closed it. Stretched his arm out, wincing as his leg screamed, and switched off the ignition. He looked for a main fuel shutoff and couldn't find it. Norman didn't move, but their eyes met.

Harry pointed right of the nose. "The field, Norman. Put it in the field. You can do it."

He sat back and tried another prayer. Got an answer as the airplane banked right. Maybe his mum had a point about that church-going stuff.

They'd crossed over no-man's-land, tracers still zipping past them. The engine was quiet and the trail of black smoke was dissipating.

Four hundred feet. Something kicked his boot and rattled his seat.

Three hundred feet. More tracers. Closer, and something pushed against his glove. He lifted it up and looked at the railing. A bullet had cut a groove in the wood, sliding under his glove.

Two hundred feet. The horrible tracers had finally stopped.

It was quiet. The only noise was the chugging of the propeller as it turned with the wind. He took a close look at the field for the first time. Mud and shell holes, of course. What else?

One hundred feet.

Fifty feet. The waterlogged shell holes were flicking past, like in the cinema. He leaned around Norman and looked at the airspeed indicator: eighty-five. If they hit the mud at eighty-five miles per hour, they were dead.

Thirty feet.

Twenty feet. He watched the shell holes race by, eyes wide. Leaned forward and gave Norman the palms-up signal. To raise the airplane's nose.

"We're too fast, Norman! We need to slow down!"

Ten feet. He tried the palms-up signal again. Leaned closer to Norman and shouted in his ear. "We need to slow down, Norman!" The mud and shell holes raced by faster. He sat back and braced himself... and... *Yes!* The RE8's nose was rising, the deadly rush of air beginning to slacken. Norman raised the nose further to hold them level, and they must have flown like that for fifteen seconds, although it seemed like an eternity.

The airplane began to rise. Harry looked down and guessed twenty feet. Twenty-five feet.

The RE8's nose was high in the air. Too high. It was almost like he was lying down, looking up at the sky. The wind noise died and the airplane gave a little shudder. Shuddered harder as she lost flying airspeed, like a horse had kicked her. The right wing dropped and the nose pitched down. Harry braced himself with his arms and left leg as the mud rushed at him.

The nose and right wing plowed into the mud and his face bounced off the forward panel. The airplane paused there in a two-point stance, as if mulling things over, before falling slowly forward. He was sliding out of his wet seat…and stopped. The weight of the broken RE8 had pinned him to the muck of Flanders.

He pried his face out of the mud and wiped his eyes. He'd lost his goggles somewhere. Blinked and tried to focus. There was about six inches of space between his cockpit railing and the mud. He tilted his head and listened…there were some faint booms of artillery in the distance. Otherwise, it was quiet.

Well, they couldn't just sit there in the middle of a mud field trapped in an RE8. He pushed with his legs and gasped at the pain that shot up from his right leg. Took a deep breath, grabbed the railing, and pulled with both arms while pushing with his left leg. He made a few inches of headway and had to stop.

*Okay, Harry, we can't stay here.* Another push and pull, and another few inches of progress through the sticky mud. Another deep breath, and on the third try, he made it out. Pulled himself onto a knee and looked around, his heart pounding. The visibility had been rotten all day, but right there it had to be at least five miles, and a Hun observation balloon was visible below the clouds. *What was it that West Country corporal had said?* "We don't like you chaps crashing nearby. Brings the Hun artillery."

He looked toward the nearest British trenches, but no one was rushing to their rescue. Looked at the Hun balloon again. Maybe if he gave them a friendly wave? Surrendered? He crawled to the forward cockpit and looked at Norman. His eyes were alert and he was breathing, but he didn't give any sign of trying to get out of there. There was space between the railing and the mud; he should be able to pull him out. He fumbled with Norman's safety belt and got it undone. Grabbed hold of him as the first shell hit, which answered the question if a beat-up RE8 was worth shooting at.

The shell landed a few hundred yards short, but was big enough and close enough to rattle the airplane. Likely a seventy-seven. But whatever it was, they needed to get the hell out of there. He pulled and grunted; his knees slid out from under him and he ended up on his back. Sat up and braced his left leg against the airplane. Took a deep breath and pulled Norman tight to him. Leaned back and pushed with his left leg. As he fell back, Norman slid out of the cockpit, squishing through the mud. He got the two of them onto their knees, his heart pounding. Got them upright, leaning against each other.

They started forward, but he stepped on the edge of a shell hole with his third step. The mud gave way and he slid down into the dark water. His feet crunched against something, which yielded its space reluctantly. He held his head out of the scummy water, his arms braced against Norman. If he slid in too, they'd never get out.

He jerked around as something moved in the water behind him. Two empty eye sockets were staring at him. The green skin was pulled tight across the skull like wet paper and the blackened teeth were locked in a wide grin, as if enjoying Harry's predicament. Harry kicked at his new mate, who regarded him for a few more seconds, unmoved. The teeth slowly sank into the water, followed by the eye sockets. Harry turned back to Norman, shaking his head. *Would love to stay and chat, mate, but we need to run along.*

Another *boom* shook the ground; he clawed at the edge of the hole as chunks of mud plopped into the water around him. Got one knee under him, then the other. Pushed and pulled, digging his fingers through the mud. Again. Digging two little trenches with his hands as he squirmed forward. He cried out as a jagged piece of metal dug into his knee on the next push. Gritted his teeth and kept at it. Digging with his hands, pushing with his left leg, and finally pulled himself into the scum of watery mud on the edge of the hole.

He gasped for air as his body told him to wait. To rest. But there wasn't time. He got his arms around Norman, pulled in his breath, and stood the two of them up. Norman still hadn't said a word since they'd been hit, but his muscles were working. Harry reached a wet foot out and took a step. He planted his foot and water squished out of his boot. Pause. Step. Again. Not too close to the holes this time.

Better now. Norman was bent over and wobbling, and the mud under Harry's boots pulled at every step. But they were moving and he'd spotted some sandbags about fifty yards away. Time was up and he pulled Norman down into a small indentation in the mud, on their hands and knees. He didn't want to fight his way out of another shell hole. Norman moaned; his eyes closed.

*Boom!* Harry was pulling Norman up as the mud rained down on them. They were moving faster now, zigzagging around the shell holes. With twenty yards to go his internal clock told him time was up. He kept going.

*Boom! Boom! Boom!*

Hell—the Huns were firing for effect. The shock waves and flying dirt pounded his back.

*BOOM!* Something lifted him off his feet and slammed him into the mud. He slowly raised his head. There was no noise, except for the roaring of the ocean in his ears. He absently brushed dirt off his face; spat out mud and blood. He must have bitten his tongue. *Where was he?... Hun artillery. Norman.* He rubbed his eyes and blinked. Norman was lying in front of him, and a dirty face was peeking through a hole in the sandbags. He pulled one knee under him and, ignoring the pain from his leg, the second knee. Pushed Norman with all his strength. He slid backward and Norman didn't move. *Damn it!* Pushing wasn't going to work. He'd need to pull him. He crawled past Norman, and jerked back as something metal dug into his face. Blinked twice and got his eyes to focus. Barbed wire. How in hell was he going to…

More *booms*, the shock waves pounding up at him through the ground. But the *booms* were farther away, and dark shapes were moving about in the haze. The wire moved away from his face, and arms lifted him up.

"Come along, sir," he heard from somewhere. "We have to hurry."

The doctor looked down at him. "Twenty-six."

Harry thought for a moment. "Stitches?"

The doctor nodded. "I pulled bits of your trousers out of the wound. Along with the splinters. But we got it all cleaned out and your private parts are fine. You should be able to go home tomorrow."

The doctor had a Yank accent. Curious. "Home to England, Doctor?"

The doctor smiled, which only accentuated the exhaustion on his face. "I'm afraid not, Lieutenant. Home to your squadron. Although you won't be flying for a few days."

Harry thought back to the flight. The bullets smashing up through the floor. The blood. The horrible struggle through the mud. "Lieutenant Frazier? The pilot I came in with?"

"We sent him on to hospital. He has rib and head injuries. They're serious, but he has a good chance to pull through."

"Thank you, Doctor."

When the doctor left, Harry carefully raised onto his elbow and looked around. He was in some sort of medical facility and vaguely remembered being carried there through a maze of trenches, followed by an ambulance ride. There were about fifty cots, almost all of them occupied. Some orderlies, plus a couple of nurses, although they didn't look to be in the young and pretty category. Too bad. They had a transfusion going into his arm and had bandaged his leg. But it wasn't hurting. They must have given him Novocain.

He lay back and let out a sigh. Beat to hell by Hun machine guns and artillery, and still not hurt bad enough to get back to England. Or even to a proper hospital. He glanced around the room again without moving his head. If he stayed quiet, maybe they'd forget about him.

# Point-Blank Range

*66 Squadron RFC, Sopwith Scout Fighter Aircraft*
*Liettres Aerodrome, Northern France*

Pete wandered down the dim hallway, feeling completely wiped out. He'd just finished his eighth flight in three days. Three days—three wingmen. One dead, a second in hospital with a shattered hip, and a third either dead or a POW. It was almost nine o'clock, but there was a light on in the squadron office. He poked his head in—Hugh Fleming was working on a report of some kind. Pete sat down and closed his eyes for a few seconds. Opened them and motioned to Fleming's desk. "Evening, Captain. The life of an RO?"

"Yes. But unlike the other war, the paperwork war never goes quiet." Fleming looked up from his report, then down to his desk.

"I got a call from the RO at Eleven Squadron, Pete." The tone was flat.

It took Pete a few seconds to process: 11 Squadron. Bristol Fighters. *Oh God. Mark Henderson.*

"Aerodrome attack."

He waited, that familiar sick feeling in his stomach.

"The pilots reported heavy machine-gun fire. Mark crashed on the aerodrome."

He tried to speak. Cleared his throat and got the words out on the second try. "Any chance he survived?"

"Not much. Sounds like they went in at high speed."

Pete looked across the room. Out the dirty window. Mark. One of the good ones. Another widow at home. Another boy growing up without his father.

"Sorry, Pete. He was a good man. You're due leave next month. Stick with us."

Small nod. The death of a friend. He'd been down this road before. It wasn't getting any easier.

The Pup was spiraling down and he writhed in the cockpit, trying to get out. Everything was moving slowly. The air was thick, like syrup. The Black Albatros was behind him, following him down. Checkerboard below: light and dark green. The war was over and the farmers had replanted the fields? The black rook bumped him and the Pup slewed sideways. Roger was there, talking with someone at the bar. Wilcox? He saw the short sword. Sharpened for battle, but the nicks were there. The plunge into his stomach. The wine breath of the Roman soldier, his short black beard, the crush of his shield against Pete's chest. The blade twisted, grinding against a rib—

He jerked awake, his heart pounding. Looked around. He was in his room in the farmhouse. Sat up and took a couple of deep breaths. His undershirt was soaked. It was that same dream again. He looked at the clock: 10:45. It was the same as always—the bad ones came early in the night. Maybe he'd start keeping a bottle of whisky in his room. Some of the chaps did that. Whatever it takes to get through the day. Through the night.

A-Flight had the nine o'clock go, but he was up at six. Thinking about Russians. About Roger and Mark Henderson. His little brother. It'd been brutal writing the letter to his mom. He'd kept it short. What else could he do?

He'd managed some breakfast and was sitting in the orderly room. Eyed the ops order on the table in front of him. Should he tear it into little pieces? Everyone turning to look at the sound of paper tearing. Dead silence in the room as they looked at him. At the pieces of paper in front of him. Confused. Unbelieving. But what could they do—make him a Sopwith Pup pilot in Flanders?

His eyes went to the duty sergeant behind the counter. He was on the phone, coordinating takeoff times with 9th Wing.

Hugh Fleming and their intel officer were poring over the mission folders, sorting out some detail.

Charles and Uncle Charlie would be at their desks in London, grinding through the endless staff work.

Somewhere down the flight-line a Hispano V-8 started up. A second Hispano. The 56 Squadron chaps were heading out.

His talk with Arthur about a soldier's duty.

He let out a sigh and picked up the ops order. Northern Ypres sector. Twenty-five minutes going up, a little longer coming home. At least it was a defensive patrol—indicating one person at Wing might have a small understanding of fighter operations. He'd doubted that more than once over the last few months.

They leveled at 15,000 feet. He set the throttle and mixture; squirmed in his seat. It was still summertime but they'd gone through some showers on the way up and his scarf was soaked. Aided by the eighty-mile-per-hour wind swirling around the cockpit, the water was working its way down his torso. But on the bright side, his backside was content in the Pup's comfy new wicker seat. *My arse thanks you, General T. I take it back. You are good for something, after all.*

He checked on his wingmen: Drew Harris on his left, and the new bloke on his right. Arthur Burke, Royal Irish Constabulary. Proud Unionist. If Pete had been A-Flight commander, they would have chatted about leaving divisive political issues at home. Since he wasn't, such things were Jimmy's to deal with. Or not.

The railroad track in front of them curved from east to northeast to southeast. A town sat one mile north of the northernmost point of the track, and there was an aerodrome east of the town. Bailleul. Over the last couple of months, he'd had plenty of chances to get familiar with the charming Flanders countryside. One might even say more chances than he'd cared for. They were less than ten miles from the line. Hun fighters could show up anytime, although they mostly stayed east of the line these days. Why go to the enemy when he comes to you? What else did he need to worry about? This was Arthur's third combat patrol. He'd taken off with two wingmen— it would be better if he landed with two. He picked up Messines to his right and turned to follow the road up to Ypres. Friendly territory now—Plummer had done it right back in June. Good man. As for this latest offensive…well, maybe Haig would get it right for once.

Ypres. Hollow shells of buildings. Piles of rubble. Smoke and dust. In other words, the same as always. He turned the three Pups into their patrol area and fired another burst from the Vickers. Artillery was pounding the German side, like every other day in Flanders. Judging by the size of the explosions, it looked like the heavy stuff was joining in the fun.

He studied the ridgeline to his right. Pilckem Ridge. Westhoek. And a little farther up the road, the fellows had pushed the Germans out of Langemarck. Just names to the people back home reading the newspapers. But for each of those names there had to be thousands of soldiers buried in the mud below him. Thousands more back in hospital, missing some body parts. All for some worthless mud. And no way was Haig done. Hell, he was just getting going. And he wouldn't stop as long as the Huns held the northern half of the ridge, anchoring the defense of their U-boat bases. Or until he ran out of men.

*Haig?* Pete drummed the fingers of his left hand on the throttle lever. Maybe he could find his staff car down there, on the off chance the general ever came near the front line. *Excuse me, the field marshal. Military decorum at all times, Pete.* The Pups weren't carrying twenty-pounders, but he might be able to get him with the Vickers if he got in close enough. It would be his contribution to the war effort. They wouldn't hang him—firing squad for soldiers. Although they could call him a German spy, who would stop them? But didn't they shoot spies, too? He wouldn't be popular with the British press, but history is a fickle mistress and Pete Newin's stock might go up as the war moved further back in time. Not that he'd be around to see it. Should he go all in and get Trenchard while he was at it? Boom Trenchard wouldn't be afraid to be up near the front line. Hell, he says so himself: offensive spirit conquers all. Élan, British style… That's it. That's what the RFC was lacking: élan. He'd write a letter to the general suggesting, hell no, demanding, that RFC pilots wear red trousers and tasseled silver and gold helmets. À la the French cavalry, 1914. Dispense with the Vickers and arm the airplanes with lances. Have a bugler sound takeoff—racing alongside the airplanes on horseback. Squadron commanders to carry swords and execute suspected miscreants.

His eyes stopped on some dark spots low to his right…brown. British. Six bombers headed home. He looked above them and farther back and found the escorts: Nieuports. Not too many of those little fellows around anymore. Might be 40 Squadron—they were up here somewhere. He swung the three Pups back to the south and picked up a pair of RE8s low and to his right, headed east. Shift change for the artillery spotters. The RE8s crossed the line and a single shell burst in front of them. A second burst, followed by four more a few seconds later. Archie didn't like reconnaissance airplanes; Pete had learned that back in his Strutter days. He resumed his scan and immediately spotted four more airplanes to his left and well below. Fighters, headed west. More Pups. Must be 54 Squadron. Funny they were down so low. He checked his two wingmen in place before scanning the airspace behind them: all clear. The Pups were almost directly below them now, except…they weren't Pups. The outline was similar, but the wingtips were more rounded at the front, the horizontal tail smaller. *Well, what do you know? Sopwith Camels on the continent. It was about goddamn time.*

He turned the three Pups back north. Checked the time: forty minutes to go. Squirmed in the wicker seat and shifted his torso. His scarf had dried out, but the temperature had to be around freezing. Scan again. Nothing. Back to the south. Some British airplanes going back and forth below them. Turn back north. More nothing. The Black Albatros. He'd done some digging through the German papers. Hauptmann Otto Lutz, Jasta 37. A picture of the bastard standing in front of a dark Albatros. He got his eighteenth kill in Flanders on the twelfth of June: a British reconnaissance airplane. The dates matched up. It was him. Murderer. He'd find the hauptmann one of these days and punch twenty or thirty .303 round through his Albatros. With luck, he'd burn on the way down. Or machine-gun him while he floated down in his parachute. Or even better, run him over with the propeller and watch pieces of him spin around and around. The spray of the blood and chunks of flesh mixing with the castor oil spun off the engine. Coating the fabric of the Pup—a red stucco to brighten up its lackluster brown-green. Something was moving left of the nose, well below them. He narrowed his eyes and focused…a pair of two-seaters, headed west. They were light gray or silver. German. And with his height advantage, there was no way they could run away from him.

He searched the sky above and behind them, but the Huns looked to be alone. He held his heading for a couple of minutes before swinging behind them. In the sun. Studied them again. The leader was on the left, nearer to him. *How did he want to handle this?* He pointed at Harris with his left arm and swept it across the cockpit, pointing up and right. Harris immediately pulled up and rolled right. Pete froze, eyes wide. If Harris rolled as he pulled, good chance he'd rip Pete's upper wing off as he crossed. But Drew Harris had turned into a competent pilot, if a bit reckless, and he stabilized one hundred yards on Burke's right. Pete pointed at Burke and dipped his left wing. Burke obediently, and less flamboyantly, crossed under to his left side. He pushed Burke out to one hundred yards and grabbed a drink of water. Checked behind them once more. He was ready.

He pushed the Pup's nose over, aiming for the leader. It wouldn't be a perfect shot, he was offset left, but if he moved directly behind the Hun he'd come out of the sun. Steeper into the dive now and he closed the throttle and petrol. He pointed for Harris to separate farther right—to go after the wingman. The only noise was the faint hum of the wind through the wires and the chugging of the windmilling propeller. He eased back on the column to break the descent as he approached the German's altitude; pushed the throttle to two thirds and the petrol to one third, and the Le Rhône fired up. He leveled her off and set the bead just in front of the Hun's nose, with the sun at his back he could see the pilot and observer clearly. The Hun's wingspan extended beyond the diameter of his iron sight. Range: about seventy-five yards. He'd moved out of the sun, but the German hadn't reacted. Pete held his breath as he steadied the airplane, saw the sun glint off goggles as the observer turned his head. He pushed the trigger and the Vickers thumped in response. His tracers reached out and tore into the German's left wing as the Hun observer opened fire.

He shook his head. *Wake the hell up, Pete.* He made a quick adjustment to the right and was ready to fire again as the Hun rolled into him—rolling past ninety degrees of bank and pulling into a dive. Pete flicked the Pup up and right toward the Hun's tail; came back hard left to follow the German down. The Pup was nimbler than the two-seater and he pulled lead to set up his shot as the German came around the turn. Two ship-lengths lead… the Pup was racing downhill now. *Steady, Pete…* he pushed the trigger as his eyes went wide—the German was huge, almost blotting out the ground. He sucked in his breath; let off the trigger and pulled hard on the column. The Hun was somewhere just in front of and below him, and he prayed he didn't feel the impact. Feel the shattering of the fuselage as the airplanes collided and broke apart. He sensed the groan from the Pup's spars as the wings bent under the load…and breathed again as the Pup rose and he spotted the two-seater. But the Vickers had jammed—he'd only gotten out two rounds. He clawed at the charging handle as he rolled over the Hun, his heart pounding from the near midair collision. The handle wouldn't budge. He grabbed the hammer as he sliced toward the German and whacked the charging handle. Whacked it a second time, and it came down. He cycled it once and pressed the trigger. *Pop, pop, pop.* He was back in business, and took a few seconds to check behind the Pup. Burke had dropped back about a hundred yards, and the sky behind them was clear of other airplanes.

Pete moved inside the Hun's turning circle to close the gap as the observer tracked him with his gun. He glanced to his left. Harris was firing at the wingman, who had turned to stay close to his leader. Pete was still inside the turn and closing… Hell—he'd misjudged it and was too far forward on the Hun's wing-line. He pulled up and right as the observer opened fire from long range. Dropped back down behind the Hun. Better now. He was almost dead astern. He closed in again, darting back and forth as the German turned. Hiding behind their tail. At 150 yards he set his lead and fired a long burst. The bullets looked to be on target and he pulled off to reposition.

Out of range and above the German, he took a few seconds to regroup. Burke was safely out of his way and Harris was still wrapped up with the Hun wingman. He scanned the sky for unwanted visitors again—one couldn't be too careful. It was still all clear, and he turned back to his quarry. The German had turned east and was running for home, but he'd need at least five minutes to get across the line, and he didn't have them.

Pete rolled the Pup onto her back and pulled into a dive, planning another attack from below. The Pup accelerated and he was in long range as he dove past the two-seater, but the observer didn't fire. He came back with the column and pulled the Pup into a climb, working his way back to the Hun's altitude. He looked more closely…the observer was slumped over. Must have gotten him with that last burst. He allowed himself a closed-lips smile. He was already in range and the German was an early model Albatros two-seater, slower than his Pup.

# POINT-BLANK RANGE

One hundred and twenty-five yards, and the observer still hadn't moved. The Hun turned hard left and Pete angled to cut him off. He still had speed from the dive and was closing steadily.

One hundred yards. The Hun was descending, wings level. The pilot must have pushed over on the column. Pete did the same, moving a little closer. The German made a quick right turn—rolled out and swung back left. The observer's head flopped from one side of the cockpit to the other, bouncing off the railing. The Hun was trying to work his way east, but Pete was almost directly behind him.

Seventy-five yards. The German swung left, rolling into a dive. Pete stuck with him, staying on the inside of the turn. The hum from the Le Rhône had gone out of tune with the altitude changes. He moved his left hand inboard from the throttle. Found the petrol lever and nudged it forward.

Fifty yards. The Albatros went up and right and Pete followed—at the high airspeed the Pup was reacting instantly to his inputs on the column and the rudder bar. He kept working the angles, moving closer.

Forty yards. The Hun leveled off. Made a quick left turn and rolled out. The pilot was looking back at Pete and the nose of the Albatros came up—that natural tendency for pilots to ease back on the column when looking behind them. The Albatros slowed and the Pup moved closer.

Thirty yards. Point-blank range.

The pilot's face rose into his gunsight. It was pasty white under the goggles, the mustache small and black. Pete pushed the trigger button and the tracers punched into the Hun's cockpit. The pilot's head snapped back and the Albatros reared up into a crazy barrel roll. Its nose plunged as it rolled onto its back.

It rolled a second time, its nose dropping even lower.

The Albatros was spiraling down now, leaving a trail of corkscrewing black smoke. Most likely oil smoke from the engine, but it didn't matter.

The Hun was dead.

Pete had seen the blood splatter across the dirty white scarf.

## CHANGES WROUGHT

Two of the fellows helped Harry climb down from the cockpit, so he didn't jolt his sore leg. The fitter was bent down near the tail, his head tilted. Along with some torn fabric, the almost brand-new RE8 had a splinter sticking out sideways. The corporal looked at Harry. "The longeron's broken, Lieutenant. Looks like a chunk of shrapnel tore through here."

Harry nodded, but he couldn't give a rat's arse about the airplane. He ran his hand over the six-inch cut on his leather jacket, courtesy of Archie. His shirt was wet underneath. Well, he'd worry about it later. Maybe he'd collapse from loss of blood, and they'd have to take him to hospital. He was pissed off at the RFC and the world, and didn't bother to get cleaned up. He ran into Captain Harvey on his way to the bar.

"Afternoon, sir. Any more news on Norman?" Harvey gave Harry his standard, "why are you bothering me," look.

"Last I heard, a few more days in hospital. Then home to England."

*England. Lucky sot.* Harry turned back toward the bar. Captain Harvey wasn't one for small talk with observers. "Lieutenant?"

Harry stopped and turned around. *What now?*

"I spoke with the company commander of the chaps who brought you and Norman in. They watched you all the way from the airplane. Nice work."

Harvey turned away, and Harry stared at his back. A kind word from Captain Sourpuss? What was this place coming to?

He found Ethan sitting by himself in the bar, drinking whisky. Harry ordered a whisky and sat down with his friend, who had black circles under his eyes that Harry hadn't seen before.

"You look like hell. Same as I feel."

Ethan's eyes swiveled toward Harry. "George is dead."

Harry only looked at him.

"We'd just finished up with the last target. They were there, then just some wreckage was falling through the air. Could have been Archie, but

289

they'd stopped shooting a few minutes before. I bet one of our batteries fired when they shouldn't have, and they caught one in midair."

Harry looked at the floor. God, he hated this war.

"He got a letter from a friend last week. His wife's been having a visitor at night. That the whole street knew about it. You've seen her picture. Pretty. George was tough on the outside, but it was tearing him up. He asked for a few days leave. Not possible, of course. Needs of the RFC."

Ethan stood up, knocking his empty glass over. Wobbled his way to the bar and paused there, one hand on the counter. Pushed off and went out the door, still wobbling. Harry drank his whisky, looking at nothing. The brown liquid was tasteless. Three young observers came in; they'd been around a week or two. Ordered whiskies. Talked the loud talk that comes with having survived their first few missions.

Not wanting to listen, Harry went outside. Sat on a bench and lit a cigarette; he'd started smoking a few weeks back. There had to be a way out. They used rat poison in the Mess. That would put him in hospital. But how much to take? He couldn't very well ask someone. And even if it worked, he'd have to live with it for the rest of his life—that he'd taken the coward's way out. But did he care about that? He'd already done more than thousands of chaps back in England, with their nice little exemptions. Working in the factories with the ladies.

"Mind if I sit with you, Lieutenant? It's a nice afternoon out here."

Harry looked up. Flight Sergeant…Timmons. Senior NCO in charge of squadron maintenance. Or something like that. "Sure, Sergeant. Have a seat."

Harry offered him a cigarette and they smoked for a couple of minutes, neither of them saying anything. Timmons blew a smoke ring, then a second one through the first. Gave Harry a side glance. "How go things, Lieutenant?"

Harry snorted. "Fine. Other than a friend being killed while his wife sleeps around back home. That we have junk to fly against the Hun Albatrosses. Do you know they call the RE8 the 'Harry Tate?'"

"Heard it once or twice. After the comedian?"

"Yep. 'Cause it's a joke. But I'm serving king and country, so all must be well."

Timmons took a long puff and blew it out. "How old are you, Lieutenant?"

"Twenty. Feels like a hundred."

"I joined up at nineteen. They sent me to South Africa to fight the Zulu. Twenty-Fourth Foot. Have you heard of it?"

Harry shook his head.

"It was a long time ago. We were in the center column." Timmons was speaking slowly, pausing between sentences. "Bright red wool tunics in the African sun." He gave a little shake of the head. "It was slow going. Teams of oxen pulling the wagons. Not much for roads. We crossed the Buffalo River and set up camp." There was a long pause. Long enough that Harry looked at him to see if he was finished. Timmons was looking out across the aerodrome.

"The hill looks like the sphinx from Egypt. Spooky-looking thing. Our scouts found the Zulu, and most of Second Battalion moved out. Lord Chelmsford left five companies of the First, plus one of ours, to guard the camp. Six companies of regular British infantry armed with the new Martini-Henry Mark II. Accurate to eight hundred yards. Against a bunch of natives armed with spears and a few outdated rifles.

"The next day the Zulu went around us and wiped the camp out. To the last man. We made it back after dark. You couldn't see much. Just as well. We spent the night with the bodies and moved out before first light. My cousin was in First Battalion. Like an older brother to me, he was."

Harry looked at Timmons. The eyes were old. Worn. They were quiet for another minute, smoking their cigarettes.

"I'll never forget that night, Lieutenant. Longest of my life. The smell of the blood. Waiting for first light. Every little noise sounding like the Zulu coming back. Not one soldier slept a wink."

Timmons took a last drag on his cigarette and ground it out. Looked at Harry again. "That American general had it right, Lieutenant. War isn't fun. It isn't glamorous. It's hell. You gents come back to clean sheets. To a hot meal on white linen. But it's still hell."

Timmons stood up. Harry flicked his cigarette into the grass and watched him go. If that was supposed to be some sort of cheer-up talk, it wasn't like the ones the generals gave.

Rachel's eyes widened. "Say that again."

"I've been accepted into the army," said Mark. He was both pleased and disconcerted at the shock on her face, but he knew better than to smile. "I'll leave for training next week."

There was a long pause.

"You're joking?"

"No, Rachel, I'm not joking."

She looked at him. At the ground in front of the bench. She slid her foot forward and back in the grass. "What…what about your heart?"

"The doctor listened to it twice. He didn't say anything."

"This is for real? You're leaving the National Physical Laboratory to join the army? To go to war?"

"Yes."

She looked at him again. Confused. "Why would you do this, Mark? You're…you're needed here."

What should he say? It wasn't as if he could tell her the real reason. "It's difficult, Rachel. All I can say is…it's something I had to do."

"That's no answer, Mark." There was an edge to her voice that he hadn't heard before. "You'll be going to officer training?"

"No." He tried to smile as he thought back. His performance in the Officer Training Corps had matched his performance in sports: bottom of the class. "At least to start, I'll be Private Mark Newin. Although my uncle thinks they may grab me for officer training—"

"I can't believe you did this, Mark." She had tears in her eyes, and he tensed up. He didn't handle displays of emotion well. Her foot went back and forth in the grass again, harder. Getting her black pumps dirty. "I care for you, and I know you care for me."

"You have Ronald," he tried.

"Ronald? Ronald is an old friend. You and I—" She picked up her purse and set it on her lap. Put it back on the bench.

"When you told me you needed to talk to me, that it was important, I thought you were going to talk about marriage. I thought about what to say to put you off. That neither of us are ready for that."

The edge in her voice was more pronounced, and the fellow on the next bench looked up from his book. She picked up her purse again and stood up.

"Instead, I hear Mark Newin, the brilliant physicist doing critical wartime work, wants to run off to war and be a hero. Or get killed."

She turned and stalked toward the front door. He watched her leave, biting his lip. He hadn't expected the conversation to go well, and it hadn't. But she had said they weren't ready for marriage? Which meant he could have proposed marriage to Rachel and gotten something other than a flat-out rejection. So there was a chance—a chance that someday she'd agree to be Mrs. Mark Newin. To wake up in the morning next to her. To look at her pretty face as she slept. To kiss her. And instead, he was going off to fight in the deadliest war in the history of mankind.

# Lutz

*66 Squadron RFC, Sopwith Scout Fighter Aircraft*
*Liettres Aerodrome, Northern France*

Late afternoon, northeast of Ypres. XIX Corps sector. The third day in a row of photo-recce escort. The two RE8s were running northeast along the Z-Beke to Passchendaele highway, but at least the RE8 didn't toddle along like a BE2. The highway was deserted—the Huns didn't dare move in daylight anymore. Some desultory black bursts below them, near the RE8s. About one every forty-five seconds. Archie was breaking in some new gunners, or saving his ammo. Or maybe the Huns just didn't give a damn. Some general from Brigade had visited the Mess last night. Pete didn't bother with names anymore, or who commanded what. He didn't care.

Major Stockard had glared at them as he'd requested their full attention, well aware that 66 Squadron's Mess had come up short more than once on military courtesy. Pete and Rory Campbell, their irrepressible B-Flight commander, were ensconced in the back row and exchanged bored, "here it comes again," looks. The general stood up, his midsection straining the buttons of his tunic, and started off with the standard visiting general line.

"You fellows are fine chaps—"

A whisper came from next to Pete. "Should I tell him he has potato in his mustache? Bit disconcerting for us fine chaps who are trying to pay attention."

Pete blinked. The general did appear to have a bit of baked potato in his mustache. He gave Rory a side glance and shook his head.

"How much General Haig, General Trenchard, and all of Great Britain appreciate what you fellows do. Day in and day out."

Another whisper. "Then have all of bloody Great Britain come here and do it. Hell, I'd even settle for half."

"We know losses are high, and it's terrible when we lose good men—"

"But it's all right to lose the not-so-good ones. I wonder how high losses are at Brigade."

Pete suppressed a giggle and gave Rory his best stern look—to minimal effect.

"The RFC leadership understands what you're going through—"

"What's he know about the RFC? Even if he could squeeze into a cockpit, the airplane wouldn't get off the ground. Maybe he's in charge of taxi procedures. Or balloons."

Pete couldn't suppress a giggle at that one.

"British industry is turning out excellent fighter airplanes. The Camel, the SE5, and the Bristol outmatch anything—"

"He forgot something. Most of us fine chaps will be dead before Sixty-Six switches over."

"We're at a critical point—"

"Hell, we've been at a critical point ever since I came across. You're a smart bloke, Newin. Can every point be critical? That sounds like a maths thing."

"Shhh. Be quiet."

"One more big push and we can break through. Roll through the Huns and end the war."

"And he can be a major general. What's he done to deserve that—besides eat?"

Pete couldn't help responding. "Maybe he fought early in the war. At Mons. Or maybe against the Boers."

"Christ, he looks like he fought in the Crimea."

Pete stifled a laugh, and looked at the floor as Hugh Fleming turned and glared at them.

He ran through his defensive scan again: only those same two Huns up there. The rest of the sky was empty. Good visibility for a change. No rain, no haze. Billowy white clouds towered over the British side, their tops far above where the Pups could fly. Their sculpted edges were a beautiful golden orange. What might Dante Alighieri, recast as a Sopwith Pup pilot, have to say about towering cumulus? "Abandon all hope, ye pilots who enter there?" Well, that might be an exaggeration, but fortunately, he hadn't yet tested the Pup's severe weather penetration ability. If it existed. To the east, the sky was clear. Higher ground over there. Drier. Less fuel for nature's weather-making machinery.

The two Huns had moved closer. Halberstadts. He checked Burke on his left, Wilcox and Harris on his right. His conscious self thus occupied; his subconscious attended to its duties. The buzz of the Le Rhône. The faint hum of the wind as the Pup pushed the air aside and bent it to her purpose. The air pushing back, finding the dead areas. Under the Vickers, around the cowling. Anywhere to grab hold and slow the Pup's progress through the air. The nonstop struggle amalgamated into the force on the control column, the vibration in the rudder bar, the wind on his face. His subconscious gave him a green light—all was normal for medium altitude cruise.

He crossed behind the RE8s as they overflew Passchendaele and turned north. The Germans were well spread out this far behind the line. There were spots the terrain didn't look natural. Concrete pillboxes covered in dirt? Something moving across the blue sky caught his eye. An airplane, left of the nose and headed east. Two airplanes. Brown? He rested his eyes for a couple of seconds. No, they were a dull red, or orange. A pair of Albatrosses going home. He shrugged. If they didn't bother the RE8s, they weren't his concern.

He went back to his scan…something was out of place low and to his left. He cocked his head as he studied it: a pencil-thin gray line. He followed the line to its source: it was an airplane, trailing smoke. He started as if he'd touched a live wire. Body tensed. Eyes narrowed. Two Albatros single-seaters. The nearer one with a black fuselage, black-and-white striped tail, and a silver spinner. Standard mottled camouflage on the wing and a familiar white symbol behind the cockpit. It was *him*.

He drew in a long breath and let it out, fighting the urge to plunge into the attack. *Think, Pete.* Burke was on his left, John Wilcox and Drew Harris on his right. *How best to handle this?* He'd much prefer to keep John or Drew with him, but there wasn't time.

He looked across at Wilcox and rocked his wings. Pointed to the new arrivals. John looked for a few seconds and returned the wing rock. He had them in sight. Pete pointed to himself, to Burke, to low and left. Pointed at John and made a sweeping motion: low and to the right, coming around to the left. To handle the wingman. He sensed the questioning look under John's goggles, and ignored it. The RE8s would have to look out for themselves. He'd come up with something for the court of inquiry if they didn't make it home. Or maybe he'd just tell them to bugger off.

He got a reluctant thumbs-up from John and swung hard left to get behind Lutz. To get between him and the sun. Rolled out and grabbed a drink of water as he watched the spacing develop. The gray smoke from Lutz's airplane had to be oil smoke from his Mercedes. *Bad luck, Otto.* Approaching a mile from the German, he rolled right and pulled the Pup into a dive. Stared at his enemy as he rolled back wings level, letting the airspeed build. He'd never been so ready to kill. The Hun wingman was on the far side. Another V-Strutter; dark green with a white nose and the same black-and-white tail. He was behind their wing-line and faster as he traded off altitude, and he'd have the angle to cut them off. He nudged the petrol lever forward for the lower altitude and took a couple of seconds to listen to the buzz of the Le Rhône. All good. It was time. He rolled right and pulled the Pup into a sweeping descending turn. The wind swept past his face as she accelerated, reacting more quickly to his control inputs.

Approaching long gun range…and the German rolled and pulled into him.

*Damn!* He had way too much closure. He snapped the Pup left and pulled up. A lump stuck in his throat—was he going to overshoot and end up in front of the German? The Pup passed overtop the Albatros and Lutz reacted instantly, coming back left, pulling into him. Pete rolled back right and the two airplanes were cockpit to cockpit as they pulled toward each other, each standing on its wingtip. They crossed, Pete slightly above and behind the German. Unload, reverse, pull back left. Cross again. Start the roll back to the right as they crossed—coordinate the aileron input with the rudder. Every tenth of a second counted.

He was about a ship-length back and still above the Albatros. They crossed again. Reverse. Cross again. He could see it now. They were in a level crisscross and the Pup was gaining the advantage. Lutz's engine must be down on power. Otherwise, an Albatros could easily handle a Pup down this low. Two more crosses, and on the next one Pete lowered his nose and got off a short burst. He got a few bullets home, but the maneuver cost him his nose-tail advantage. He'd tried it too soon. *Patience, Pete. We got this bastard. Take your time.*

He snuck a quick look behind him on the next cross: Burke was tagging along a couple of hundred yards back. *That's fine. Just stay the hell out of the way.* They crossed again, and Pete had the beginnings of a smile. But he had to get the timing right—reversing direction just before they crossed. Improving his position a little bit each time. He worked his way to three ship-lengths back. They approached the cross… *and…now!* Roll and pull with the German. Trigger down…and he punched some bullets through the right wing inboard. *Plenty more where those came from, Hauptmann.* But Christ, what he wouldn't give for a second Vickers. Pull toward the bastard's tail. Reverse. Repeat. They were back into it. Was the trail of smoke from the Albatros a little darker? A little thicker? *Be a shame if your Mercedes quits, Otto. But no quarter today.* He was winning, but Lutz was dragging him east. And down—they were no more than 1000 feet, both airplanes bleeding energy with each pull. Roll back, pull, cross again. Reverse. But Lutz hadn't reversed. Instead he'd kept his turn going and rolled out southeast. He was running for it, and likely he was still faster than the Pup.

Pete pulled in behind him. He had one good shot—he had to make it count. He set the bead just in front of the nose of the Albatros, steadied… and jumped as an invisible fist smashed into his instrument panel. Another fist smashed the panel a half second later. Something sliced through his side as splinters bounced off his goggles and cut into his neck. Grunting in pain, his eyes watering, he pushed against the railing with his left hand and forced his head around: Albatros. Left of his tail, 125 yards, slightly high. Setting up to shoot again. Pete rolled hard left; past ninety degrees and into a dive, and the Pup shook as the speed built. By diving he was giving the German more turning room, but it would take a steep dive at low altitude for the Hun to get his guns on him. The German followed him down for a few seconds…thought better of it and pulled off, turning to get behind the Pup. It was an orange V-Strutter, and it must have come from the other flight of two. He'd thought they were too far away.

He pulled the airplane out of the dive and rolled out northwest. Managed a couple of deep breaths, holding his left side. He smelled fuel and the Pup was shaking: there had to be propeller or engine damage. The clouds were his only chance, about eight miles away. He twisted around to look behind him again, grunting at the stab of pain from his side. The Albatros was closing in.

He waited a couple of seconds…and went up and right. But not too hard—he needed to conserve energy, down low with a damaged airplane.

The Hun moved inside his turn, already in range. Pete leveled the wings and pulled for three seconds; but the Pup was sluggish, slow to respond to his inputs on the column. There might be damage to the flight controls as well. The German reacted quickly, following him up, almost directly behind him. Pete went forward with the column, floating up against his belt as the Pup nosed over. He bit his lip: the airspeed was down to fifty. Tracers passed just to his right, tearing into his lower wing. More damage he didn't need.

He braced himself with his left hand against the railing, teeth clenched and half-twisted around to keep the Hun in sight. He went left with the column and the Pup didn't respond. He went almost full rudder and aileron, and she slowly rolled left. He got her past ninety degrees of bank and pulled her into a dive. *Easy, Pete.* Too hard of a pull and she'd snap into a spin, and he didn't have the altitude for that, even if she stayed in one piece. But he needed airspeed. He was just wallowing around the sky, and the Hun's nose was tracking in front of him, setting up to shoot again. *Keep her nose down, Pete. Right rudder, hold the bank with aileron. Slip the airplane. But just a little—too low and slow for much of that.* He heard the rattle of the Hun's Spandaus, the tracers passing two feet above his head. He rolled right, eased her around the turn for a few seconds, and rolled out. Took another deep breath, wincing at the jolt from his side.

He'd made it halfway to the clouds. But he was down to 500 feet and sixty miles per hour, and the Hun was coming again. He counted off three long seconds, faked further right and came back left. Anything to change the flight-path while working toward the clouds. The German was shooting again, the twin Spandaus flashing, and Pete watched with eyes wide as bullet holes marched up the fuselage. One after the other, like a spoiled child poking holes in a papier-mâché airplane. But the holes slid off the side of the fuselage three feet short of the cockpit.

He rolled right, past ninety degrees of bank, back into a dive. Dished her out at 300 feet. Waited a few seconds and came back left. The Le Rhône was misfiring now—the Pup was about worn out. But not much more than a mile to go. To that beautiful, towering cloud. Fake left, roll and pull right. Once again, the *tap tapping* of bullets punching through fabric, the Pup flinching as a bullet broke a wooden frame member somewhere behind him.

It was darker now and the first few raindrops hit his goggles. He was coming under the cloud. A little left turn; pause; come back right. He needed almost full deflection of the column and the rudder bar to make the girl respond. Looked behind him, trying not to twist his torso. The Albatros was still there, no more than seventy-five yards back. The rain was heavier, the visibility coming down. Control column forward, and he floated up against his belt as tracers shredded the upper wing a foot above his head. He held the column steady for three eternal seconds. Teeth clenched, and he realized later he'd tried to protect the back of his head with his left hand—as he'd waited for a bullet to slam into his head. He eased the control column back…he'd timed it right. The Albatros stopped shooting as the Pup's nose came up, and she began to rise toward the safety of the gray.

There was no sensation of speed. It was as if they were hanging on a string, suspended in the gray. The rain was pounding on the wings, on his leather helmet. He wiped his goggles and peeked at the airspeed. Forty-five. He nudged the nose down. He had to keep flying airspeed…and finally… finally, the cloud swallowed the Pup. Left aileron and rudder, and ever so slowly, the little girl responded. Arrows shot past on his right—shock waves from the Hun's bullets passing through the moisture. The Pup jumped, but not from the bullets. She'd hit the first air pocket. The cloud tossed him left, right, and back left. He held the control column neutral and braced his left arm against the railing, to keep his torso from moving. But he wasn't the pilot anymore. He was only a passenger along for the ride as a giant hand lifted the Pup up.

Further up. Everything was black and purple as the rain pounded harder, drenching the cockpit as the altimeter wound itself up like a runaway clock. The hair on his body stood up, the air charged with electricity. A little river of water ran past his boots.

*Think, Pete.* This could kill him as easily as Hun bullets. The Pup was shoved to the right and he bounced off the cockpit railing, jolting his side. The altimeter had paused at 2800 feet, and he felt light in the seat. Was she standing on a wingtip? The static electricity was stronger, crawling over his body. Over the metal in the cockpit. But the air was strangely calm, and he heard the engine. It was still running. He closed the throttle and petrol and she went quiet. The altimeter began to unwind: 2750, 2700, 2600. Was she spiraling right? On her right wingtip? He pulled left and back for two seconds, but not too hard, and brought the column back to neutral. Grunted as something shoved the Pup down and left, then jerked them back to the right. Like the ocean tossing a small boat about. His stomach came up as the airplane dropped. 2000 feet. 1700. Did he feel a left turning motion? Column right, wait two seconds, back to neutral. 1600, 1500, 1400. He rolled left for two seconds and came back to neutral: 1300, 1200. She was still going down. How was that possible? Banked left, or right? He came halfway back with the column and started counting to three. The cloud gave them one last shove, and they were out.

He blinked twice, and his eyes slowly focused. He was looking at the ground, through light rain. More detail came into view as he stared. The Pup was nose low and in a steep right bank. He rolled wings level and gently pulled the nose to the horizon. Took a few breaths, trying to ease his pounding heart. Trying to make his brain work. He looked around as best he could without straining his left side or his neck. There was no sign of the Hun.

There was a canal in front of him, and a battered city to his left. He looked at it stupidly. Ypres, of course. He wanted to shake his head, to clear the fog. He didn't dare. He needed to get on the ground, and Liettres was too far away. There were two aerodromes at Pop, due west from Ypres. He turned toward the sun. He didn't bother inspecting the Pup—knew without looking that she'd been shot and battered almost to pieces. He put his gloved hand against his throbbing neck. It was wet and sticky, and there was something stuck in it. The size of a fat cigarette.

The visibility was down. Thick haze or fog—unusual for that time of day. The Pup was bobbing up and down, wandering left and right as he followed the highway. There was the town, but he was almost level with the tops of the buildings? *Oh hell, the engine wasn't running.* He pushed the throttle and petrol forward—the Le Rhône fired up and immediately began misfiring. The Pup leveled off, hanging on her nose, her misfiring engine shaking the airframe. He gritted his teeth as the vibration rattled his side. Forced himself to breathe as the Pup wobbled forward. There. Just left of the nose. Hangars. Airplanes. The landing ground.

He swung right to get some spacing. The Pup was trying to climb as the engine wound up. He pushed the column forward and came back on the throttle. Left aileron to get her lined up. *Turn, Pete. More. Use the rudder. Get her around. Down. Too high, Pete. Push her down. Back on the power. To the right. Back to the right. Watch the airplanes. Stay with her, Pete. Stay with her…* He pulled the throttle back as the Pup's undercarriage slammed into the ground; grunted out loud as the wings flexed down and back up in a triumph of Sopwith engineering. The Pup came airborne and he went neutral with the column; he was too tired to do any more than that. She hit again. Smacked one wingtip, then the other, and her tail came around. They were on the ground, sliding backward, but she was slowing down. Slower still. Through the haze he saw shadows grabbing hold of her wings. Bringing her to a stop.

The shadows came closer. Voices. Through the haze, an arm reached in front of him and switched off the ignition.

He slid his fingers along the fabric. Clean sheets. Shifted his head. Pillow. Blinked his eyes open. Wood ceiling. The smell of alcohol. Hospital. He glanced at the window without moving his head. Early morning, maybe. Flexed his fingers and checked himself over with his hands. There were bandages on his torso and neck. He thought back…a ride in an ambulance tender. Orderlies undressing him. A doctor pulling a bloody splinter out of his neck and tossing it into a pan—making a funny little, *thud*, sound. Blood. Bandages. Someone talking about infection. Being too warm. Too hot. Juliette—had she been there? A little girl with blonde hair? He closed his eyes. Too much effort.

He was awake again. Looked around the room without moving. The landing. More like a crash. Big bounce and a ground loop. B5305's goodbye salute to the war. They'd cut the fabric away and slid him out; propped him up against the wheel of the Pup. He'd smelled fuel. It must have been a pinhole; otherwise, he wouldn't have made it. He'd tried counting the bullet holes in the wing. Had given up. The smell of castor oil. Heat waves coming off the engine. A transfusion, still sitting by the Pup. Someone pushing on his neck. Those horrible minutes in the storm cloud. The burnt-orange Albatros—twin Spandaus flashing. Lutz. Damn it. He'd had the bastard, and he slipped away. A young orderly was looking down at him.

"How do you feel, Lieutenant?"

*How did he feel? Good question.* "Weak. Where am I?" His throat was dry and scratchy.

"Base Hospital Nine, sir. Calais. Second CCS bandaged you up and sent you on to us. You look better today."

Pete raised an eyebrow. *Whatever you say.*

"If you're wondering, sir, you've been here four days now."

Pete eyed him. *He'd been there four days?*

"You lost a lot of blood. The wound on your neck got infected, and you had a high fever. They were worried about pneumonia. That might have done you in, sir. Let me take your temperature." The orderly put a thermometer in his mouth and felt his wrist. "Good. Fever's almost gone, Lieutenant. Pulse is normal. I'll tell the doctor you're awake."

*Four days? Calais? Juliette couldn't have been there. He must have been dreaming.* He closed his eyes.

Some idiot was shaking him. "Try to eat some soup, sir. It's not bad." It was the same orderly again. "Let me prop you up."

He took a spoonful of soup. Chicken noodle. Salty, but wonderful. He had a few more spoonfuls, and his mind began to clear. The orderly was still there, looking at his chart. "My left side. Do you know if they took a bullet out? Or a splinter?"

"It was a bullet, sir. Clipped the rib but went on through. The splinter in your neck was the nasty one. It was in deep, and the doctor had to do a lot of cutting."

Pete finished his soup and waited for the doctor. He was restless and there wasn't much to look at. Wooden walls that had been painted light green a few years back. A little window. Two other beds, both occupied. A stand with a bedpan. A sink with a stack of white hand towels.

The doctor showed up along with a nurse and the same orderly. Looked at his chart and felt his cheek and wrist. "Good. Another day or two, Lieutenant, and you should be able to go home." Pete started to make his case to go home right then, but the doctor shook his head and moved on. He sighed and lay back. Slept on and off through the day, then the night. Four days. Five now. When was the last time he'd seen Juliette? Three weeks, maybe? More? They'd been flying nonstop as the army chaps bashed away at the Germans. He looked around, still restless. The chap in the first bed was covered in bandages, facing the ceiling. The fellow in the middle bed had bandages around his nose and mouth. He was awake and looking at Pete.

"Afternoon. Or morning," said Pete.

"Morning, I think." Raspy whisper. He pointed to his mouth. "Gas."

Pete frowned. One good thing about the RFC, they didn't deal with gas. God, what an invention. He ate a proper breakfast and drank some heavenly coffee. Made his case to the orderly to go home. Made it to the senior orderly, who said he would speak with the doctor. About an hour later a different doctor came in. Young, Irish type.

"You think you're ready to go home, Lieutenant?"

"I am, Doctor. I'm a little weak, but I don't need to take up one of your beds."

The doctor looked at his chart. Felt his wrist and cheek. "Walk to the door and back for me."

Pete did so. Slowly, but without weaving. "Stand on one leg, then the other."

Pete complied, careful not to lose his balance. "Stretch out your arms for me."

It hurt a little, but he managed. The doctor frowned. Drummed his fingers on the chart. "I'd rather keep you one more day, Lieutenant. But you're right, we need the bed." He turned to the orderly. "Set up an ambulance for him. We don't need him bouncing about in the back of some lorry."

"Thank you, Doctor."

Now, where was his uniform? He'd need to shave. His leave was almost due. England. Devon. Away from the war.

He'd walked into town. The weather was nice and he didn't want to risk crashing his bike. Felt his heart beating as he stopped in front of the café. The long walk. The anticipation. He saw her through the window, taking someone's order. That same faint smell of rotting trash. He went up the three wooden steps, the last one giving its familiar little *creak*.

The front door opened, and he stood aside to let the person pass. Arthur. Pete smiled and put his hand out. Arthur shook it, his face blank. "Can you stay for a coffee, Arthur? It's been a while."

Arthur was looking at the bandage around his neck. "Are you hurt, Peter?"

"A little. They got me in the side, too. But better now."

Arthur was looking at him, expressionless. Something was wrong.

"Peter, I need to tell you something."

Pete put his hand on the railing to steady himself, to take some weight off his left side. Looked at his friend.

"Hugo's grandson Leo is home on leave. He's an airplane mechanic. Leo went to school with Juliette when they were children." Arthur was pausing after each sentence, as if choosing his words carefully. But it sounded like the boys were okay. That terrible thought had already passed through his mind.

"Leo has been in love with Juliette his whole life, Peter. He asked her… he asked her to marry him, and she said yes. They will marry tomorrow."

Pete stared at Arthur, processing what he'd heard. He looked at the dirt and the grass. At the dirty wooden steps. At Arthur again. He nodded and managed a smile.

"She cares for you very much, Peter. We both do. We'd seen you two or three times a week, then nothing for almost a month."

It was his fault. Roger. Phillip. Lutz. This last big offensive. The fellows on the ground dying by the thousands every day. New pilots needing their hands held. Needing to be taught east from west. The café and Juliette had been another world. He took an invisible deep breath—information received and processed. He waved his hand that he understood. That there was no problem. "I understand, Arthur. I'm happy for her. And for Leo."

"Will you go inside, Peter? I know she would like to speak with you. To know you're all right."

It would be easy to run off and sulk, but that wouldn't do. "Yes, of course. I need to wish her and Leo all the best. I'll write to you sometime, if you don't mind."

"We're friends, Peter," Arthur said simply. "That will never change."

Pete gave Arthur a gentle hug. Took a few seconds to compose himself, and opened the door.

# England

*The RFC Club.*
*13 Bruton Street, London*

It was just as he'd been told. Pilots, alcohol, cigarettes. Music from a scratchy gramophone. And women. Lots of women. He zigzagged toward the bar where several air-to-air combats were in progress—the British right hand maneuvering for the kill on the German left hand. Cheers as another barroom kill was consummated. One British hand overshot its target and knocked over a full mug of beer, the foam splattering across the counter. The bartender righted the mug with one hand as he poured whisky with the other. Pete squeezed in and ordered a beer. The wall behind the bar was adorned with a large Iron Cross on a square white background—according to the note, from a Fokker Eindecker in September of fifteen. Back in the early days. A blue-and-white vertical tail, complete with two bullet holes, likely from a Halberstadt. Other miscellaneous airplane parts of German origin. Refreshment in hand, he navigated the tumult toward an unoccupied column that should be a good vantage point. Halfway across, a light-colored silhouette closed rapidly on his right.

He took evasive action, but he'd left it too late and mid-aired with a girl with long blonde hair who was only a couple of inches shorter than he was.

"Cuse me," she said with a little laugh, holding on to him as her drink spilled onto his trousers.

He glanced down: white top over a black skirt. Style points for clothes. Back to her face. She was cute, with an upturned nose. "If youuuuu ask me to dance, I'll say yes." She wobbled a bit as she smiled. Nice teeth along with breath that smelled of whisky.

"Not now, sweetie. I'll look for you later." He set her up straight and nudged her toward the bar, while keeping his hands near her shoulders. Tracked her through two zigzags, but she steadied up once she'd regained her forward momentum, and he was able to break off.

He leaned against the wooden column, keeping the pressure off his side. Sipped his beer. They'd said the splinter in his neck was the bad one, but it was the cracked rib that periodically reminded him he'd been in the fight of his life. Had Lutz seen the other Albatrosses? Was that why he broke off when he did? Probably so. Not an easy thing to do—look around in the middle of a tight turning fight, but the German had managed it. He lit a cigarette, his first of the day. Sipped his beer and surveyed the battlefield. In his front right quarter, a pilot was gyrating drunkenly on the dance floor, linked to a young lady in temporary endearment. Or perhaps for stability considerations. A couple went out the door with arms locked, and several other courtships appeared well underway.

"Pete! Pete!"

He looked toward the shouts and spotted a familiar face under a waving hand. Reggie Dixon. One of his buddies from training. Hearty handshake and Pete squeezed in, making the sixth at a table for four. Four pilots (three of them drunk or well on the way) and two girls.

"Bloody good to see you, Pete. Bloody good. Long time. And both of us still alive."

Reggie was his normal reserved self, although he'd added a few pounds since Pete had last seen him. The other two pilots ignored Pete, fixated on their targets. "On leave?" Pete asked over the din.

"Absolutely not. I'm far too valuable for that. Training Brigade. Teaching the new chaps the tricks. Word is they'll give me a squadron before long. Or maybe it was a brigade. I can't remember. We'll get you transferred. Fly together, like the old days. Are you still flying the Pup?"

"Afraid so."

"I'll kick Trenchard's butt about that when I see him. Get it taken care of." Reggie sat back with his beer and scanned the female terrain at the bar.

The pilot next to Pete headed to the dance floor with his friend, and the remaining girl had slid onto her pilot friend's lap. Based on the kisses being given and received, Pete estimated less than one more drink to consummation.

"How's the training world these days?" Pete asked.

"Dangerous. These little British Huns kill as many of us as the real Huns do."

Pete smiled. "Huns" was instructor pilot speak for student pilots.

"About the only days we don't lose an airplane or a pilot is when the weather's down. They've got a proper training program now, and we fly with the little Huns until they know what they're doing. That's the idea, anyway. Not like the good old days. Do a couple of circuits and get out before he kills you."

Pete nodded. But proper training program or not, he'd be more than happy to be an instructor back home. His eyes went to the dance floor, and he grimaced as he watched his former tablemate in action. There was some vague resemblance to the Argentine Tango, but per- formed by two people who were drunk, sexually aroused, and incapable of dancing.

"We even take them up and get them in a spin. On purpose. To show them how to get out of it. If someone had suggested that back in '15, we would have shot them."

# CHANGES WROUGHT

They were quiet for a few moments, looking at the girls at the bar. Pete absently, his friend more intently. "You hurt?" Reggie had noticed the bandage around his neck.

"Splinter. Albatros up in Flanders. Better now."

"Another reason for you to come home. It's too dangerous over there."

Pete sipped his beer and watched his friend's face. Reggie was still scanning the terrain, his eyes stopping on each female. Looking for any weak points in the defenses; checking if any (competing) friendlies were in the area. Categorizing and moving on to the next target.

"Remember Bobby Watts?" Reggie was looking at him again.

Pete struggled to place the name. "At Filton with us? Accountant type—North London?"

"That's him."

"What's up? You two getting married?"

"Funny chap. We were in the same flight at Nineteen. He force-landed on the Hun side last month. Out of the war."

Pete waited. There had to be more to the story.

"We'd been trench strafing for a couple of weeks. Twice a day. Strap on four twenty-pounders. Drop them on the Hun, then strafe the trenches. Easy range of their machine guns. I don't care if you're the ghost of Albert Ball or the bloody Blue Baron. The bullets get you, or they don't. We were losing someone almost every day. I knew the stress was getting to him. Bobby was always strung tight, and he looked like hell. But it was getting to all of us. You know the signs. Fights in the bar. Blokes getting sick."

Pete knew the signs. He'd seen them lots of times.

"Turns out Watts had been talking about landing on the Hun side. That the army was in some plot with the big industrialists. British and German both. That his mate had seen a copy of the agreement. The war's not to end until 1925. Meanwhile, all of us peons keep getting killed while the bigwigs get richer."

Pete gave a little shrug. The army was willing to accept casualties, no doubt about that. But some sort of industrial secret plot with the Germans was more than a little far-fetched.

"Were you there that day?"

"No. But the flight leader saw it. He wasn't burning or spinning. Just went into a field."

"He might have been wounded. Fuel leak. Anything."

"Could be. Not very reassuring, though. Chaps start thinking like that."

Pete started to tell him about the French mutinies, and stopped after the first few words. Reggie wasn't listening. Pete followed his friend's eyes to a tall redhead at the bar. Thought of Anya.

"I saw that redhead here last week, and a damn Aussie beat me to her. Great to see you, Pete. We'll talk again soon."

Pete sat back and watched Reggie roll in on the redhead. Sipped his beer with the trace of a smile. He was at home there. The uniforms. The pilot wings. England. Nor would anyone mistake him for a newbie, not with a Military Cross and the bandages. Not that he cared. He knew who he was. Finally.

*Juliette. She couldn't even wait three weeks. That's love for you.* He scanned the female terrain again. Brunette near the bar. Dark skin, big chest. India, maybe. Talking to the blonde he'd mid-aired with, who was looking at him and smiling. Maybe in RFC Club terms, they were already old friends.

Another brunette, fair skin, wearing a black skirt with a slit on the side showing some calf. That was always a nice touch. He caught a flash of yellow at the far end of the bar. Tall and dark, the yellow dress setting off her dark skin nicely. West Indies, maybe. She turned and leaned her back against the bar. "Well-built" was an understatement, and she was looking at him. Christ, she'd be an experience. Likely he'd bust some stitches.

A pilot rolled in on her and she responded with a smile. Glanced at Pete again as she listened to the newcomer, who set his drink on the bar and immediately knocked it over as he reached up to touch her shoulder. He'd never understood how chaps could enjoy being drunk. Losing control and feeling like hell the next day. He finished his beer and let out a sigh. Maybe he should just go back to the hotel. Scanned the room again and came back to Yellow Dress. The pilot's attack appeared to be faltering. Good chance he could roll in and seize the initiative. But there'd be a risk of fisticuffs, which he had no interest in.

He looked away and picked her up coming out of the loo. Shoulder-length brownish-blonde hair. Short. Tanned skin. Pretty face. With only a little imagination… He stood and set up a front-quarter intercept. Made a small course correction as they closed, and a final check of the target as she came into range. Her gait was steady, her eyes alert.

Smile and extend right hand to complete the intercept.

"Dance?"

Ragtime was playing. He could lead any woman alive through one-step, even with a cracked rib. Walk and move the hips a little. Anything more than that was a throw-in. She stopped. Her eyes went from his face to the bandage around his neck. To his rank, his wings, his Military Cross. Back to his face. All in about two seconds.

"Love to." Nice smile.

They sat down three dances later. He'd always enjoyed dancing. In particular, the graceful beauty of the waltz, but that wasn't something one danced in a bar. She asked for white wine and sat close to him. Answered when he asked her name (Susan) and bypassed further small talk. "What airplane do you fly?"

He told her.

"Tell me about shooting down a German."

He half smiled. She knew what a Sopwith Pup was. But telling war stories to women in a bar wasn't his style. Trivialize death. Like it was some sort of football match.

She squeezed his hand. "Tell me. They killed my little brother last year. Tell me how you killed one of them."

He looked down at her, and her blue eyes bore into him. She had pretty eyes, but there was a toughness behind them. This girl wasn't the Victorian, "Lovely Madame, would you care for another scone with your tea, Madame?" sort. She wanted to hear it, but not because it was barroom fun talk. It was coming from somewhere deeper.

He decided on the Albatros two-seater near Ypres. Took his time and let the story build. The cold. Seeing the British airplanes. The smell of the castor oil. Firing the Vickers to keep it warm. Spotting the enemy; moving his wingmen around to set up the attack. Susan hung on every word; nudged closer. The initial attacks, using his hands as the airplanes. The Vickers jamming. Hitting the observer. Following the Hun through each turn. Through the pushover. Working the angles and closing to point-blank range. The final detail of the Albatros's nose coming up as the pilot looked back at him. The white face rising into his gunsight. The hammering of the Vickers, the blood splattering across the dirty white scarf. The Albatros corkscrewing toward the ground, trailing smoke.

She took a few breaths. Looked around the room. At him.

Never in his life had he seen a woman so captivated.

"In the old days, knights carried a lady's token into battle."

He smiled at that. He'd known pilots who wore a lady's stocking over their head, the leg wrapped around their neck. Ostensibly for the cold.

"If we're talking undergarments, Your Ladyship, count me in."

She set her glass down and looked up at him. Slid onto his lap and put her arms around his neck.

"Such things can be arranged, good sir knight. Such things can be arranged."

"Colonel. Uncle." Pete shook hands with Lieutenant Colonel Charles (Charlie) Wallace, his mom's younger brother. He'd always liked Uncle Charlie, who didn't make life any harder than it needed to be. Pete sat down and looked around the small, windowless office. Papers and folders on the desk and (of course) a map of northern France and Belgium on the wall. A picture of his wife and the three children—their little girl the only one left.

"I'm sorry about Martin and Ritchie."

His uncle nodded, looking at the photo. "I got a nice letter from the regimental commander a few weeks later. It happened on the first of July. Near Mametz."

*July first, 1916. The Somme. That name again.*

"Machine-gun fire crossing no-man's-land. They brought the bodies back that night. He said there's a lovely little cemetery there for the Devons. I promised their mother we'd visit after the war. She needs to see it. We both do." His uncle's eyes were wet, and the two of them were quiet for a moment. "Sorry, Pete."

Pete waved it away. "So this is what the Imperial General Staff looks like. It's not quite as glamorous as I was expecting."

"If you're looking for glamor, Lieutenant, you're in the wrong place. It's work, work, and more work here. I haven't had a day off in three months, nor do I want one. Tedious. Or it would be, if one forgot people live or die based on the decisions made here. How long are you home for?"

"I'll spend eight or ten days in Devon. See Mark tonight and take the midnight train home. It seems Mark has a lady friend, and I'm being introduced to a younger sister. I tried to see Charles, but he's in France on some sort of temporary duty."

"Nephew Mark has a lady friend. Well, that should be good for him." His uncle's expression changed. Serious. "It will be good for your mother to see you. She's struggling."

"Phillip was her baby. I was there when the Huns got him." His uncle sat up.

"Tell me."

Pete told the story. "I spoke with the stretcher-bearers back in the trenches. Phillip was halfway out of the cockpit when they found him. He must have been trying to climb down when the Hun strafed them."

His uncle looked at Pete. At his desk.

"I went over to Wing and found an article in the Berlin daily. Hauptmann Otto Lutz of Jasta Thirty-Seven shot down a British reconnaissance airplane on June twelfth. I spoke with the intel chaps there, and they verified the black-and-white striped tailed airplanes belong to Jasta Thirty-Seven. And Phillip was the only recce airplane lost in Flanders that day."

"Fair enough, Pete. It sounds like this Hauptmann Lutz was the pilot who killed Phillip. Where are you going with this?"

"I ran into him last week. It was tough, but I had him. Another Albatros jumped me. That's when I got hurt. But I'm going to get that Hun—even if I have to find him after the war and put a bullet through his face."

"You will do no such thing, Lieutenant."

"He murdered Phillip."

"I understand your feelings, Pete. But Phillip came down on the British side. He was still a combatant. We're British officers at war. You'll have to let it go."

Pete dropped it. He asked about his aunt and his cousin Sarah. "She must be sixteen now?"

"Seventeen. She's doing well. She's strong, you know that. But she was hurt badly, and it isn't something one gets over easily, strong or not."

"She'll be a handful for some young man a few years down the road."

"Oh yes. She's a budding suffragette, and she's already written to the nursing service. If the war runs long enough, she'll be off to France. There'll be no stopping her. She's talking about being in Parliament someday."

Pete smiled. He adored his younger cousin. "That sounds like Sarah." His eyes went to the map on the wall. "How goes the war on your end?"

His uncle looked from the map to the doorway. Kept his voice down. "I suppose if this were football, we're one-one at the seventy-five-minute point, but with a deeper bench than the other side. It's no secret we can't break through. That, and the Germans have gotten smarter. They don't try to hold onto their first defensive line anymore. Instead, they let us wear ourselves out, then counterattack in force. Casualties are enormous. Our artillery has gotten more powerful and more accurate, but their infantry can ride out almost anything. And there's no good way to communicate with the lead units once the attack gets underway."

"Tanks? To break through?"

"Maybe. But we need better reliability. Terrain that will support their weight." His uncle pushed his chair back and crossed his legs. Looked at the map again.

"On paper, we win the war. Our blockade. A war-weary Germany and the internal pressures tearing at Austria-Hungary. The enormous potential of America. But the reality is more difficult. The pressures on the home front are severe, and the Americans won't be ready for serious combat operations for another year. With Russia likely to drop out, it still could go either way."

"If it makes you feel better, Uncle, the RFC is going full bore. Maybe even trying to do too much, but they don't ask me what I think."

"Nor is my opinion earnestly sought after, nephew. A colonel on the staff is like a second lieutenant anywhere else." His uncle lowered his voice another notch. He was almost whispering. "It seems clear enough there is disagreement between Generals Robertson and Haig on one hand, and Lloyd George on the other, as to how best prosecute the war. Major disagreement."

"That wouldn't surprise me. I haven't seen any sign our generals feel the human cost of what they're doing. Whether Lloyd George does…feels that cost…or is simply thinking about the next election, I have no idea." Pete drummed his fingers on his leg. "But I suppose in fairness to Generals Robertson and Haig, they have a job to do, and people are going to die."

His uncle didn't respond, perhaps becoming uneasy discussing the senior leadership with a junior officer. Pete checked his watch.

"Lunchtime, Uncle. Myles will be wondering where we are."

It was four blocks to his uncle's favorite restaurant. Pete looked at the storefronts as they walked. At the people on the street, mostly women and old men. At the sandbagged entrances to the tube stations. Here and there boys were selling bags of peanuts. Newspapers. They stopped in front of a bombed-out building one block from the restaurant. The rubble had been pushed into piles while they searched for survivors, but hadn't been cleared away. His uncle looked at the rubble. At Pete.

"One of the Gotha raids back in June. Eight people were killed here. More wounded. Apparently, some of them had come outside to watch the show." His uncle shook his head. "Most people understand the danger. But to others, it's like the cinema. I suppose sooner or later, they'll learn. There's talk of leaving it as is. As a memorial to the civilians killed by the bombings."

Pete stared at the wreckage. Broken bricks, twisted metal framing. Half of a ceramic sink, trailing its plumbing lines. Britain must never forget this war and the changes it wrought. The English Channel and the Royal Navy—the impenetrable barrier of the British Isles for 500 years. But not anymore. Aviation was only fourteen years old, and the rubble in front of him was proof of its reach.

Pete's stepfather was waiting for them at the restaurant. He was a little chap. Silver hair and mustache. Good talker. Pete scanned the limited menu and went with curried vegetables and rice. Soda water to drink. He'd drunk three beers last night, exceeding his limit.

"What goes on in your world, Myles?"

"Lots. I'm headed to Petrograd next week. Working with the Provisional Government. It's no secret what His Majesty's government is worried about."

They were worried about Russia making a separate peace, which would free up German troops for an offensive in the west. It didn't take a field marshal to understand the dynamic facing the Germans. Attack in the west before the Americans arrived in strength, or lose the war to the growing power of the Allies.

"I dropped into a French château last month. The cowling came off and ripped up the airplane. A retired Russian general lives there with his wife. He's some sort of government adviser now. Interesting fellow. Fought at Tannenberg. Good chess player."

His stepfather's expression had changed when he heard the word "Russian."

"I've met some generals over the years. What's his name?"

"Leonid Shuvalov."

"I've heard the name. Corps commander at Tannenberg?"

Pete shook his head. "Division."

"Major general. We don't see them much in Petrograd. What did he have to say?"

"That the Provisional Government is struggling and there's lots of unrest. That if the Reds take over, they'll make peace with Germany. That they're all about class struggle and not countries fighting each other."

His stepfather looked unconvinced. "Possible. Not certain. No Russian government would want to make significant territorial concessions to Germany. They might not survive the aftermath. What else did he say?"

The question came across a little too direct for Pete. His stepfather was British foreign service, but they'd never been close. "That was about it. We played chess twice. Talked about horses." Pete turned the conversation back to the family, and the small talk continued through lunch.

Mark opened the door to his tiny flat. Pete smiled and gave his brother a hug. Looked past Mark. Magazines, books, and clothes were strewn about. "You didn't have to clean up so nice on my account, Mark."

"Funny chap. Like always." Mark nodded toward his neck. "How are you feeling?"

"Better now. Just a little stiff."

"Good to see you again. To know that you're okay."

"I appreciate that. How's life at the Lab?"

"It's fine, but a career change is in the making. We can talk about it later. But first, I have something that might interest you."

Mark cleared the little table and spread out the blueprints of an airplane. Pete recognized the silhouette: the Sopwith Camel. "It has roughly the same wing area as the Pup," said Mark. "Shorter fuselage and smaller horizontal tail area. Empty, she's about one hundred and seventy pounds heavier than the Pup. About half of that is due to the bigger engine."

Pete bent over the table. "What engine?"

"The Clerget one-thirty for the Ruston-built ones. Sopwith got the second order, and I've heard both the Clerget one-forty and the Le Rhône one-ten mentioned. I don't know if they've decided yet. There's been some griping about the one-thirty—that power drops off above ten thousand feet or so. They're not sure why."

Pete studied the drawings. The engine, dual Vickers plus two ammo belts, and the pilot were all bunched together. "I bet she turns like a crazy woman, but will slip and skid all over the place if you're not careful. Is she stable in pitch?"

"Not by much."

"Why'd they put the fuel tank behind the pilot?"

"We asked. We didn't get an answer. Sopwith doesn't answer to the Lab."

Pete's mouth went side to side as he tried to recall his basic aerodynamics. "The fuel tank is well behind the center of gravity, isn't it?"

"Yes."

"Meaning the handling will change as the fuel burns off."

Mark nodded. "The center of gravity will move forward as the fuel burns off. Increased stability, reduced maneuverability."

"Gyroscopic effect will be larger than on the Pup," mused Pete. "Need to be careful with right turns down low in this little fellow. Hold some left rudder and back stick to keep the nose up."

"Very good, brother. We'll make an engineer out of you yet."

"No thanks. War has made me mentally lazy…once a pilot gets comfortable flying her, she should be a good dogfighter. And if you need to duck out in a hurry and have the altitude—put her in a tight right spiral. No Hun is going to stay with you."

Pete continued studying the diagrams, comparing them to the airplane he knew best.

"Tail-heavy like the Pup?"

"I'm told she's worse. The upper wing cut-out mitigates that and improves visibility, although the cut-out seems small to me."

"How big is it?"

"Eighteen by eight."

"It is small. The SE5 has an elevator trim wheel, doesn't it? To relieve the pressure on the control column?"

"Yes."

He looked the question at his brother, and Mark shrugged. "As I said, Sopwith doesn't answer to the Lab."

Pete drummed his fingers on the table. How would the Camel react to control inputs? It would depend on airspeed, of course. And the gyroscopic effect would be greater at high power settings.

"I bet she's a tiger at low altitude. But you put a new pilot in her... He pulls the nose up—it's too high. He overdoes the correction and hits the ground. Or he makes a hard right turn at low altitude. The nose comes down, maybe he's distracted for a second. Boom. I don't suppose they're going to build dual-control trainers?"

"I know it's been mentioned, but there isn't much room to work with. I suppose if they went with a smaller fuel tank, they might be able to squeeze in a second seat."

"The dual Vickers. Right and left feed?"

Mark shook his head. "Right only."

"It's going to be tough to clear a jam on the starboard gun. Can't be that difficult for Vickers to come up with a left-hand feed three-oh-three."

"One wouldn't think so."

"You're not helping much, Mark."

"I'm a little cog in a big wheel, Pete."

Pete moved some books off a chair and sat down. "I need to tell you about Phillip. He was your brother, too."

Mark listened without interrupting, and his eyes were wet when Pete finished. He looked at the floor.

"If you can get this Hun, Pete, I'm all for it. Phillip was a good kid. But Uncle Charlie is right. War is no place for personal vendettas." Mark wiped his eyes and checked the time. "We need to go. We don't want to keep the ladies waiting."

It was after eleven when Pete walked out of Bishop's Road station. It had rained earlier, and the moisture hung thick in the night air. At Paddington he bought a ticket to Exeter, mildly amused at the extreme courtesy he was receiving at each step of his little journey. British officer; wartime; a bandage around his neck. He'd have to find a lift down to Holcombe in the morning, but that wouldn't be a problem. People would be asking him how they could help.

The platform wasn't crowded. An older couple spoke with him for a few minutes. Next up was a young lady, maybe eighteen years old. Plain looking with straight, shoulder-length black hair. She wasn't afraid to talk to him but was in obvious awe of his uniform and wounded neck. The train was a few minutes late, but soon enough he settled into a window seat. Struggled with the dirty window, got it open a few inches and relaxed into his seat. He was looking forward to seeing his mom, although it wouldn't be easy. He wouldn't tell her about Phillip's death. No point in going there. He'd give Phillip's silver cross to Alice.

The girl from the platform sat across from him, one seat over. Crossed her legs and hitched up her dress enough to give him a nice ankle shot. She paired that with a smile, which may have been a, "you know, Lieutenant, I'm of age," sort of smile. He smiled back at her and looked out his window.

It had been good to see Mark. He'd always been the bumbling-scientist type, but he seemed more at ease. It was tough to judge the relationship with Rachel. It was her, not Mark, who had broken the news that Mark was joining the army. She'd said it with a certain coolness and hadn't looked at his brother when she did. But not even the army was dense enough to send him to the trenches; he was too valuable where he was. They'd give him a uniform and he'd analyze airplanes in some office in London.

Charlotte…she was gorgeous. He could picture her on a magazine cover. But she came across as shallow, not that Pete Newin was Mister Sophisticate. She'd talked about killing Germans. The cinema. Parties. Mark and Rachel had tried to pin him down for another dinner on his way back through, and he'd put them off.

The RFC Club. He had to admit he'd enjoyed it. Talking with Reggie. Watching his friend in action.

Susan. He'd ring her up for a proper lunch on his way back. He'd closed the door to his hotel room and rather than kiss her, he'd pulled her dress off, followed by her chemise. Gently pushed her onto the bed and pulled her drawers down to her ankles. She'd kicked them off and lay back, naked except for stockings, heels, and brassiere. She bent her knees and looked at him. Estimated time from hotel room entry to female entry: 120 seconds.

Afterward, they talked. Comfortable. Which surprised him as he thought about it now, as neither of them had put clothes on or pulled the sheet up. He talked about the war, but without the details. About life at the squadron. She traced the wounds under his bandages. Kissed them.

Later he made love to her, as opposed to banging an alternate Juliette as hard as he could, but he suspected she'd enjoyed their first round more. Lunch should tell him if there was a connection—a connection beyond the bedroom.

He'd been home five days. Mum, Deb and the girls. Phillip's Alice. Tears. Food. Too much food. He'd missed Emily. She was off managing a theater group in Birmingham. Both moms had pushed him to visit her. He said he'd try. That afternoon, he'd begged off and walked down to the sea.

# ENGLAND

He watched a big wave gather itself. It rolled in, reared up, and dashed against the rocks. Foam and spray. It receded, to regroup for another attempt.

It was windy and he felt the spray up there on the rocks. Tasted the salt. He crouched down and put one hand on the ground. The grass was wet, the rocks slippery. At least the war couldn't ruin this. Devon was still Devon.

He looked across the blue-gray water to the horizon. The water that would carry him back to France. Back to the war. Perhaps to Germany one day. Or even to Russia.

But first, he'd go to Yorkshire.

Cheryl had written back. Thanking him, telling him he didn't need to come.

But he would go. For Roger.

For his friend.

# Glossary

**Acceptance Park**—An RFC facility that accepted newly constructed airplanes from the manufacturer.

**Aileron**—The movable control surfaces on the outer wing(s) area. Used to roll the airplane.

**Aldis**—A British gunsight that improved on the earlier ring and bead sight.

**AM1**—Air mechanic 1st class. Enlisted rank below corporal.

**AM2**—Air mechanic 2nd class. Enlisted rank below AM1.

**ANZAC**—Australian and New Zealand Army Corps.

**Archie**—British slang for anti-aircraft artillery.

**Asquith, Henry**—British Liberal Party MP. Prime Minister from 1908 to 1916.

**Battery**—An artillery unit commanded by a major. A British battery consisted of six guns divided into three two-gun sections, most typically eighteen-pounders.

**Baps**—Slang for a woman's breasts.

**B&C**—The British and Colonial Aeroplane Company. Sometimes referred to as "British" or "Bristol."

# GLOSSARY

**Bead**—Along with the ring, one of the two primary components of a basic World War One airplane gunsight. The pilot would line the bead up with the center of the ring to ensure he was looking down the axis of the gun. The bead would be placed on or in front of the target, depending on the amount of deflection required.

**BEF**—The British Expeditionary Force.

**Bessonneau**—A large wood-framed canvas hangar used by the RFC.

**Big Ack**—Armstrong Whitworth FK8. A British two-seat reconnaissance airplane.

**Blip switch**—A switch on the control column used to cut ignition to the cylinders. Used to momentarily reduce power on a rotary engine.

**Bob**—Slang for a shilling (one-twentieth of a pound sterling).

**Brigade (RFC)**—An organizational unit of the Royal Flying Corps. Each RFC brigade contained two RFC airplane wings and a balloon wing.

**Brigade (RFA)**—The Royal Field Artillery was also organized into brigades. An RFA brigade contained four batteries and an ammunition column.

**Bristol**—Shortened form of "British and Colonial Aeroplane Company." Also, a city in southwest England.

**CCS**—Casualty Clearing Station. The intermediate point in the casualty evacuation system, typically located several miles behind the front line. Serious cases would be transferred from the CCS to a permanent base hospital.

**Chocks**—Wooden blocks placed against the wheels of an airplane to keep it in place when parked.

**Churchill, Winston**—Liberal Party MP. Commander, 6th Battalion, Royal Scots Fusiliers, Belgium, 1916. Appointed Minister of Munitions in July 1917.

**Coalition**—The coalition government led by Prime Minister David Lloyd George (Liberal Party) from December 1916 to after the end of the war. Lloyd George relied heavily on Unionist (Conservative) support to remain in power.

**CO**—Commanding Officer (in *Changes Wrought*, this usually refers to a squadron commander).

**Critical area**—The area of an airplane consisting of the pilot, fuel tank, and (normally) the engine.

**Deflection**—The amount of lead required for an air-to-air or a ground-to-air gunshot.

**Distinguished Service Order (DSO)**—A British medal for meritorious service. In the hierarchy, the DSO sat above the Military Cross but below the Victoria Cross.

**Easter Rising**—An armed insurrection by Irish Nationalists in April 1916 in support of Irish independence.

**Élan**—Vigorous offensive spirit. Accepted French military doctrine in 1914.

**Elevator**—The moveable part of the horizontal tail surface. Use to raise and lower the nose of the airplane.

**EO**—Equipment Officer. The chief technical officer of an RFC squadron.

**George, David Lloyd**—British Liberal Party MP. Prime Minister from 1916 to 1922.

**Gotha**—A German twin-engine long-range bomber.

**GHQ**—General Headquarters of the British Army.

**Haig, Douglas**—Field marshal and commander of the British Expeditionary Force.

**Henderson, David**—Director general of military aeronautics in London.

**Hindenburg, Paul**—Field marshal and chief of the German General Staff.

**Home Rule**—The issue of self-government for Ireland. Home Rule became law in 1914 but was suspended for the duration of the war.

**ILP**—The Independent Labour Party. A socialist offshoot of the Labour Party.

# GLOSSARY

**IPP**—The Irish Parliamentary Party. The IPP was committed to obtaining Irish Home Rule via the parliamentary process. They were eventually supplanted by the more force-oriented Sinn Féin.

**Intel**—Slang for "intelligence officer" or "Intelligence Department."

**Jasta**—The German equivalent of a British squadron, although smaller. A jasta would typically have six to twelve operational airplanes, although the number could vary significantly based on circumstances.

**John Thomas / Johnny**—Slang for penis.

**Kitchener, Horatio Herbert**—Earl, field marshal, appointed Secretary of State for War in 1914. Drowned on June 5, 1916, when the cruiser HMS Hampshire struck a mine and sank off the Orkney Islands.

**Lansdowne Letter**—An open letter written by a former cabinet member and published in the *Daily Telegraph* in November 1917. In a nutshell, the letter asked if an armistice could be negotiated, as opposed to fighting to the bitter end. Public reaction was negative—the letter was seen as undermining the war effort.

**Le Rhône**—A French nine-cylinder rotary engine.

**Lewis gun**—The standard British machine gun used by the observer. On some airplanes (e.g., SE5) a Lewis gun was mounted to fire forward above the propeller arc. Rounds were carried in a drum which could be changed in flight.

**Limber**—A two-wheeled vehicle drawn by horses or a tender. Used to carry artillery shells when the guns were moved.

**Loo**—Bathroom.

**Longeron**—Main internal supports of an airplane fuselage, running lengthwise.

**Lorry**—Truck.

**Ludendorff, Erich**—Chief of staff to Field Marshal Hindenburg, although in practice Ludendorff was effectively a "Co-chief of the General Staff" along with Hindenburg.

**Luftstreitkrafte**—The German Air Force.

**Messines**—A city in Flanders about five miles south of Ypres. The site of a successful British attack in June 1917.

**Mixture lever / control**—The fine fuel control of a rotary engine. Used in conjunction with the throttle. Also called the petrol lever / control.

**MP**—Member of Parliament.

**Nationalist**—The movement for Irish self-rule or for an independent Ireland. The Nationalist movement drew most of its support from southern (predominantly Catholic) Ireland.

**Northcliffe**—Alfred Harmsworth, 1st Viscount Northcliffe. Owner of the *Daily Mail* and the *Daily Mirror*. Northcliffe was easily the most influential British newspaperman during World War One.

**OOC**—Out-of-Control. Meaning an enemy airplane was driven out of the fight.

**Ops**—Pilot slang for "operations" or "squadron operations."

**Orderly Room**—The nerve center of an RFC squadron. Contained the readiness board, phones, maps, and mission planning folders. Chairs and tables for the pilots.

**OTC**—Officer Training Corps. The military training portion of a public school / university curriculum. Similar to ROTC in the United States.

**P-Dale**—British slang for "Passchendaele," a city in Flanders northeast of Ypres. Also a name for the Third Battle of Ypres (autumn, 1917).

**Petrol lever / control**—The fine fuel control of a rotary engine. Used in conjunction with the throttle. Also called the mixture lever / control.

**Plummer, Herbert**—General and commander of the British Second Army.

**PM**—Prime minister.

**Pop**—British slang for "Poperinghe." A town in Belgium eight miles west of Ypres. Also, the site of an important British aerodrome

# GLOSSARY

**Pusher / pusher prop**—An airplane in which the pilot sits in front of the engine and the propeller pushes (as opposed to pulls) the airplane through the air.

**Ranker**—Enlisted personnel or a noncommissioned officer.

**Recce**—Slang for reconnaissance.

**RFA**—Royal Field Artillery.

**RFC**—Royal Flying Corps. The forerunner of Britain's Royal Air Force.

**Ring**—Along with the bead, one of the two primary components of a basic World War One airplane gunsight. The pilot would line the bead up with the center of the ring to ensure he was looking down the axis of the gun. The bead would be placed on or in front of the target, depending on the amount of deflection required. Target size relative to the ring would assist the pilot in judging the range.

**RNAS**—Royal Naval Air Service.

**RO**—Recording officer. Second-in-command of an RFC squadron. Called the adjutant in peacetime.

**Robertson, William**—Field marshal. Chief of the Imperial General Staff 1916–1918.

**Rotary (engine)**—An engine in which the cylinders project outward from a central shaft. The cylinder assembly is fixed to and rotates with the propeller when the engine is running, creating an undesirable gyroscopic effect.

**Rudder**—The moveable part of the vertical tail surface. Used for directional control during takeoff and landing, and to assist the ailerons in rolling the airplane.

**Spandau**—The standard German eight-millimeter air-to-air machine gun. Capable of being synchronized to fire through the propeller arc.

**Spar**—The main internal support of an airplane wing. Most World War One fighter airplanes had two spars in each wing, although some Nieuports and Albatrosses only had one in the lower wing.

**Strutter**—Slang for Sopwith 1 1/2 Strutter. A British two-seat reconnaissance airplane and light bomber.

**Tate**—Short for "Harry Tate," a British comedian. Also, a non-complimentary term for the RE8.

**Tender**—A large car with room for approximately ten people.

**Trenchard, Hugh**—Major general and commander of the Royal Flying Corps in France. Occasionally (and unofficially) referred to as "Boom" or "General T."

**Ulster Volunteers**—A militia formed in Northern Ireland in 1912 to oppose Home Rule for Ireland.

**Unionist**—The movement to oppose Irish self-rule and remain part of the United Kingdom. Also, a name for Britain's Conservative Party during the World War One era.

**Unload**—To reduce the drag on an airplane by moving the control column forward. This allows the airplane to accelerate more quickly, understanding at some point it will begin to descend.

**Vickers .303**—Standard British air-to-air machine gun. Capable of being synchronized to fire through the propeller arc.

**V-Strutter**—Albatros D3 or D5. Called this because of the V shape of the wing struts (due to the single spar structure of the lower wing).

**Wing**—An organizational unit of the Royal Flying Corps. Each RFC wing contained approximately five RFC squadrons.

**Wipers**—British slang for "Ypres," a city in Flanders.

**Y-Chat**—British slang for "Wytschaete," a city in Flanders located between Ypres and Messines.

# Author's Notes

Book 1 of *Changes Wrought* opens on the Western Front of World War One in May of 1917. The events in the book center around three major land battles and two Royal Flying Corps squadrons:

- The Battle of Arras/Chemin des Dames: April–May 1917
- The Battle of Messines: June 1917
- The Battle of Third Ypres (Passchendaele): August–November 1917
- RFC 66 Squadron: Sopwith Pups (Pete Newin)
- RFC 6 Squadron: BE2s / RE8s (Harry Booth)

It's difficult for those of us used to modern aircraft, with their triple redundant computerized flight control systems, satellite navigation, and automatic pressurization, to appreciate how little World War One pilots had to work with. Not much more than airspeed, altitude, and tachometer for instrumentation. Wood and fabric construction with the pilot fully exposed to the elements. For example, the Sopwith Pup flown by Pete Newin could reach 18,000 feet, and often higher, depending on conditions. The temperature at that altitude could be below zero Fahrenheit, plus the wind chill generated by the speed of the aircraft.

In terms of design survivability, the A-10 attack aircraft that I flew in the 1980s had a gyro-stabilized ejection seat and fire-resistant, self-sealing fuel tanks that were well separated from the pilot's titanium "bathtub." World War One aircraft had unprotected metal fuel tanks placed close to the pilot. In the German LVG two-seater, which was considered a relatively good combat aircraft at the time, the pilot literally sat on the fifty-two-gallon brass fuel tank.

World War One combat aircraft may be roughly divided into four categories:

- Single-seat fighters:
    - British: Sopwith Pup, Sopwith Camel, SE5
    - German: Albatros D2 and D3, Halberstadt D2 and D3
- Two-seat reconnaissance aircraft:
    - British: BE2, RE8
    - German: Albatros C3, DFW C5, LVG C5
- Two-seat bombers:
    - British: DH4, DH9
- Heavy bombers:
    - British: Handley Page Type O
    - German: Gotha

World War One single-seat combat aircraft were called scouts. Fighter aircraft had two seats, with the observer armed with a machine gun (e.g., the Bristol Fighter). In *Changes Wrought*, I refer to scout aircraft as fighters and most two-seaters as reconnaissance aircraft, as I believe this will be less confusing. German aircraft were normally designated C.II., D.III., etc. To

# AUTHOR'S NOTES

remain consistent with the British nomenclature, I refer to these aircraft as C2 and D3.

*British Military Organization:*

The British Expeditionary Force (BEF) was made up of several armies. For example, the attack on Messines Ridge in June of 1917 was entrusted to the British Second Army under General Sir Hubert Plummer. The Second Army was organized as follows:

- IX Corps:
    - 11th, 16th, 19th, 36th Divisions
- X Corps:
    - 23rd, 24th, 41st, 47th Divisions
- II ANZAC Corps:
    - 25th, 3rd Australian, 4th Australian, New Zealand Divisions

Each infantry division, in turn, was typically made up of three brigades plus support units. For example:

- 41st Division, X Corps:
    - 122nd, 123rd, 124th Brigades
    - 19th Battalion Middlesex Regiment Pioneers

In the same vein, brigades were comprised of smaller units, and so on, all the way down to platoons of about fifty men commanded by a second lieutenant.

*The Royal Field Artillery:*

The basic combat unit of the RFA was the battery. An RFA battery was a major's command and was comprised of about two hundred men and six guns, most typically eighteen-pounders. An RFA brigade was comprised of four batteries and was commanded by a lieutenant colonel. Four RFA brigades, along with an ammunition column and several other units, were assigned to support each infantry division.

*The Royal Flying Corps:*

With one exception, the Royal Flying Corps (RFC) in France was organized into brigades. Each RFC brigade was, in turn, divided into two wings: an army wing and a corps wing. An army wing primarily contained fighter aircraft (e.g., Sopwith Camels). A corps wing contained two-seat reconnaissance-type aircraft (e.g., RE8s). For example, RFC 1st Brigade was assigned to support the BEF 3rd Army during the attack on Cambrai:

- RFC 1st Brigade (November 1917):
    - 1st (Corps) Wing: Four squadrons flying RE8 and Armstrong Whitworth FK8 reconnaissance aircraft.
    - 10th (Army) Wing: Four squadrons flying Sopwith Camels, SE5s, and DH4s.
    - 1st Balloon Wing: Observation balloons.

The one exception to this brigade / army wing / corps wing structure was RFC 9th Wing. The 9th Wing was under the direct control of the Commanding General RFC in France, Major General Hugh Trenchard.

An RFC squadron normally contained eighteen aircraft divided into three flights of six, plus a headquarters flight (supply, administration, etc.).

The Royal Flying Corps was part of the British Army during 1917. The Royal Air Force came into existence in April of 1918.

The main characters in the book are intended to be entirely fictional. High-level referenced historical figures (e.g., David Lloyd George) are included in the glossary.

While a modern author enjoys the perspective of history, nothing can match what was written by the men who were there. For further

## AUTHOR'S NOTES

reading, I highly recommend the books by Victor Yeates, Cecil Lewis, and Arthur Lee.

I've kept the dialogue as realistic as possible. Some of the words used may be offensive by today's standards, especially to readers of German descent. I apologize in advance to any of my readers who may be offended.

I'd like to thank those very knowledgeable folks at the Great War Aviation Society (United Kingdom) and at Over the Front (USA) for their support. Also thanks to my editor, Ms. Manda Waller for her hard work, and to my artist, Mr. Jim Laurier for his beautiful cover artwork.

Finally, and most importantly, special thanks to my wonderful wife, Ruth Margarita, for her love and support throughout this process.

*Michael James MacMurdy*

## About the Author

Michael J. MacMurdy is a former USAF and airline pilot. Michael lives in Frederick County, Virginia, with his wife, Ruth Margarita. While in the USAF, Michael flew T-37s at Vance Air Force Base, Oklahoma, and A-10 Warthogs at RAF Bentwaters, United Kingdom. After his USAF service, he flew for a major US airline.

www.ingramcontent.com/pod-product-compliance
Ingram Content Group UK Ltd.
Pitfield, Milton Keynes, MK11 3LW, UK
UKHW040651210725
6985UKWH00038B/247